OVER THE HORIZON

DOYLE SINCLAIR

Barcentor Books

This is a work of fiction. Although historical figures are portrayed, the incidents, actions, and dialogue presented herein are the product of the author's imagination and are not meant to be construed as a part of the historical record.

ISBN – 978-0615752082

First edition – first printing Dec. 2012

Fiction - Adventure - horror - romance - women pilots - Pacific islands - historical fiction - Survival - Coconut crabs - rats - cannibalism - rape - search and rescue

This book is dedicated to –

This book is dedicated to my brother Larry, who is a fearless world-traveler and adventurer. If anyone could survive 'Rat Island' it would be him.

Also, thanks to several friends and beta-readers who have offered encouragement and advice throughout the years. My first beta-reader, Marie B., Bob Walker, Marshall A., Walt Eddy, and others.

Also by DOYLE SINCLAIR

Blue-Eyed Son – 2009 - available now on Amazon.com in print and on Kindle

Red Door - paranormal mystery - coming in spring 2013

Tales from the Left Eye - a collection of short stories- summer of 2013

The 3rd Derivative - psychological thriller - fall of 2013

Deliver Unto Me the Innocents - mainstream urban thriller - fall of 2013

Nestor's Loop - sci-fi mindbender - Spring of 2014

All titles published by Barcentor Books

Over the Horizon

By – Doyle W. Sinclair

●●●

We sailed for parts unknown to man,
where ships come home to die
No lofty peak, nor fortress bold,
could match our captain's eye
Upon the seventh seasick day
we made our port of call
A sand so white, and sea so blue,
no mortal place at all

Now many moons and many Junes
have passed since we made land
A salty dog, this seaman's log:
your witness my own hand . . .

Salty Dog – by Procol Harum

CHAPTER 1

July 2, 1937 – somewhere over the Pacific Ocean

"Brace yourself Noonan, we're going in!"

"Amelia! For God's sake pull the nose up! We're going in too steep! We need elevation!"

"I'm doing everything I can. The stick is dead, we're going down."

"Turn the nose around, we can make it to that beach, there's enough room to set it down."

Amelia grabbed the radio handset and frantically pushed the button. She wanted to make one more broadcast before it was too late.

"Itasca! *We must be on you, but cannot see you — our fuel is running low. Have been unable to reach you by radio. We are flying at 1,000 feet.*"

Amelia dropped the radio handset and pulled the yoke as hard as she could and they leveled out. She scanned the vast table of blue beneath her. Ocean as far as the eye can see. Except for one small comma of land ahead. A particularly small island. Noonan scurried forward and peered over her shoulder.

"Come on Amelia, we can land it. Turn it parallel to the island, come on, we can make that beach."

"How big is the island? You get a good look at it? Is it on your charts?" Amelia yelled over her shoulder at him. She hadn't given it too good of a look as she was focused on the instruments in front of her. Noonan retreated back to his little table further back in the fuselage where he had his charts and navigational plotting instruments laid out.

"Not on any charts, but from what I saw, it looks to be about three or four miles in length," Noonan yelled up to her, "maybe a mile or two across.

Horizontal to us now, so you better swing about and then come parallel so we can try for the beach."

The Lockheed Model 10 Electra was Lockheed's first all-metal and twin-engine design, and relatively new, having been introduced only three years earlier. She knew that the maximum safe water depth for landing the Electra was six inches, but they were not going to be able to make it that close to the beach.

The engine sputtered, their fuel completely spent now and the propellers ceased turning. For a moment their world was silent. To Amelia, the sensation of being airborne with no thrust was like being on the beginning of the drop of a roller coaster after just having rolled over the topmost curve, and they dropped silently towards the surface of the ocean. With no thrust to propel them, gravity began pulling the nose of the airplane dropped towards the waves. Amelia's stomach lurched as she realized they were dropping; the end of their flight being forced upon them, not by actions, but by some sort of capricious unsmiling fate.

She heard Noonan retching in the back of the fuselage at his navigation station.

The plane dropped and then skipped off the ocean like a flat rock skipping the surface, the jolt of the underbelly of the plane making contact with the water threw Amelia forward against her seat restraints and she saw the waves rushing up towards them. They were airborne again, but she knew it was only for a few moments.

She heard Noonan struggling with the door latch and knew he must be getting it open so that they could escape quickly when they hit the water. A sickly sweet stench reached her and she realized where she'd smelled that odor before. Then she remembered; her father, from years ago when he'd been such a drunk. His once handsome face, had become sloppy and slurry from drinking. Amelia could still remember that stinking sweet smell and she wrinkled her nose at the recurrence of the odor.

"Noonan, have you been drinking *hooch?*"

"Don't you worry about it, Amelia, just fly the damn plane."

"But you're soused!

"That's a bunch of malarkey, you just worry about getting us down without killing us! Get us onto the beach!"

Amelia was stunned, but there was no time to think about his unprofessionalism and his moral improprieties now. She had to focus on what was about to happen.

Skipping again on the surface of the water, they lifted for a moment, floating; airborne again, and Amelia thought that they might make it all the way in up to the beach. She knew that directly beneath the waves under them was coral, and as soon as the tires hit it they'd be shredded, but if they made it far enough up the beach they'd be okay, as long as they didn't come in too fast and go into the tree-line of the jungle beyond the beach. If they hit the trees, they'd be killed for sure. Sinking in the water would probably kill them too, Amelia was no swimmer.

Coming down heavily, the plane shuddered and then the nose of the Electra dipped into the waves, its flying days forever ended. Amelia's neck wrenched violently and she heard a metallic snap as her seat restraint came loose and she was thrown against the dashboard.

The noise in the cabin was deafening as the cargo crashed boxes full of supplies, crashed forward into the cockpit. She heard a garbled scream from Noonan, "Dammit, Amelia!"

She pulled herself back into a sitting position, and almost immediately there was a screeching sound of scraping metal as the underbelly of the fuselage dug into the coral. She saw a flash of sunlight as Noonan wrenched the fuselage door open, probably to make it easier to exit the plane once it settled on the water.

She was thrown violently forward again and smashed into the windshield above the instrument panel. Her head swam with dizziness and she lost consciousness.

CHAPTER 2

Coming to, Amelia gagged, and spit out sand and water from her mouth. She felt the scraping of hot wet sand on her cheek and she gasped. She gasped another lungful of air and then retched out another mouthful of sea water onto the beach. She was aware of pain, she felt as if she'd been kicked in the stomach over and over. She knew she'd be bruised, but at least her arms and legs felt intact.

She lay with her head down with the grainy sand digging into her cheek, but she didn't care; her only thought being sleep. Though the sun beat mercilessly down on them, her fatigue was overwhelming and she wanted nothing more to do but give in to it, but knew she shouldn't. Her eyes were closed but she could tell it was dark. Raising her head up from the sand and opening her eyes she saw the beach, and further out, the ocean and the endless water stretching from left to right on their horizon. The sunlight sparkled off a sliver of the Electra's fuselage out in the waves, a place where no plane should ever be. One propeller tip stuck up out of the water. The beach they were on was wide; an expanse of bright white sand and there was no sound other than the seagulls chirping as they floated overhead, and the surf ebbing in and out; on the far horizon, an enormous bank of billowing black clouds. They seemed to be building higher and higher with every passing moment. They were dark purple, almost black, and seemed angry. Lightning flashed with the cloud-bank causing it to throb with light. She wished for rain, for cool raindrops on her skin, but the clouds seemed too far away, and there was no breeze to drive them here.

The waves rushed in up the beach and slowed, depositing a sand dollar a few inches from her face. She could see the green foamy edge of the water as it stopped, and then it receded back. She wanted nothing more than to close her eyes and give in to the warm sand and the delicious pull of her sleepy fatigue. Instead, she struggled up into a sitting position and reached over and shook Noonan's leg.

"Wake up Noonan, come on, we're alive."

Noonan flipped over on his side and raised his head to look out to sea.

Amelia pointed, "The Electra. It's there."

He sat up.

"Yes, Amelia. I see it. It's in the water and completely useless to us. Why didn't you do as I asked? You could have come parallel to the beach and set it down right here."

"There's no way it could have been done, Noonan, we were dead-stick. I couldn't have brought it around. No one could have done that. We're lucky we made it in as close as we did. What island do you think this is? You were the last one to see the maps."

"Probably Nikumaroro, Gardner Island; which is bad news for us."

"If we're on Nikumaroro, then we're saved, right? The Itasca should be just over the horizon. A day or two away from here, at best, right?"

Noonan shook his head, looked around wearily, and rubbed his face with his hands, and turned back to face her.

"I could have done it, landed us, right here on this beach! You stupid woman, do you realize what you've done with that contemptible bit of flying? You've killed us, sure as hell."

Amelia stared, flabbergasted by his hostile tone.

"You could have done it? Not while you were coming off a bender and still sauced on whatever it was you were drinking. Noonan, it smelled like a gin mill back there. You should be ashamed. Go ahead, Noonan tell the truth and shame the devil, you were soused weren't you?

"You're crazy, Amelia."

"And you're a drunkard."

Noonan glared at her. "Yeah, and you're the bee's knee's aren't you? The great Amelia Earhart. Yeah you're a real rip-snorter, you are. Couldn't even get us to the beach!"

"We should look for the airstrip; there must be a shack there with maps, maybe a radio. Maybe there's some canned food or something, some sort of shelter. There must be something here that we can use as sanctuary until the rescuers arrive."

Noonan shook his head, "No, Amelia, this is not Howland Island. I know it isn't. I had a good look at this island when we were coming in. First of all, there's no airstrip. Plus, Howland has very little trees and vegetation, whereas the interior of *this* island is jungle."

"But, can you be sure we're not on Howland?"

"It's not Howland, Amelia. Believe me. If this was Howland, I'd be slap-happy with joy, because that would be the first place they'd look. You've stranded us, Amelia. You've pretty much killed us, sure as hell."

"Now look here Noonan, I won't have that kind of talk. Your disparaging tone will not be tolerated. I, *we*, did the best we could!"

Noonan stared at her with hatred in his eyes, "Amelia, if we're not off this wretched island in seventy-two hours, I swear to God I might just kill you for having done this."

Amelia's mouth dropped open, "Noonan, you can't possibly blame me for this, why, *you're* the navigator! And you were *drunk*!"

Noonan sneered at her, "If you were half the pilot you think you are, we wouldn't be here, and the Electra, wouldn't be out there in the fucking water!" he jabbed with his finger towards the plane.

"Noonan, you've gone batty. And furthermore, I demand that you cease that guttersnipe talk, *immediately*."

Amelia wanted to stand, but her fatigue was so great that she didn't attempt it. The blazing sun overhead seemed to sap her energy. There seemed to be a small rocky outcropping at the south end of the island. She could see the jumble of brownish rocks at the end of the beach, and she could see and hear the waves crashing on them. She could feel the sunburn on the back of her neck and on her forehead. They'd need to get out of the sun and into shade; otherwise they'd be in pain in a few hours. Her skin was unused to being out in the sun for any prolonged amount of time, and the sun here was brutal. The small whisper of breeze that there was only seemed to be blowing hot air at them. It was stifling.

Noonan lay back down and too tired to move away from the beach, Amelia did the same; facing the waves coming in and she watched as the foamy green bubbles at the edge of the water approached her face, slowed and then receded. For the time being, it seemed as if their lives had come to a standstill. The whole world out there was still turning, and here, they were marooned, in a place where time had learned how to stop.

A tiny sand crab skittered away from them and it was then that Amelia first noticed the heat. The air was deathly still, the heat oppressive and stifling, as if they were in an oven. Looking down at her body she saw a smudge of blood on her wet jeans, even though she couldn't feel any pain, but realized she could be in shock. She remembered that she and Noonan had talked, but had that been mere minutes earlier, or hours ago? She was confused.

She sat up and put her hand on Noonan's ankle and shook him, "Noonan?"

"Uhn."

She realized that they needed to take stock of themselves and what possessions they had. They hadn't even discussed whether or not they had injuries, and they hadn't looked around for anything useful from the plane. They'd simply squabbled and then they'd both gone to sleep. She hadn't moved off this spot on the beach and there was no telling how many hours had passed by since they'd come ashore.

"Noonan, are you okay? Are you hurt anywhere? Broken bones or anything?"

He grunted something unintelligible.

"Noonan, are you okay? We need to get out of this sun. If we don't we'll regret it later."

She saw his shoulder move in answer; a barely perceptible shrug. She heard a grunt, or a moan. Was he hurt, or crying?

"Noonan, answer me!"

He turned to face her, his face a grim mask of anger,

"I hope you're satisfied, you stupid bitch. You've killed us! *I* should have landed us, because you botched it. But then you're well known for bad landings. You ditched us in the drink, and now we're dead."

He shook his head and muttered something, obviously livid at their circumstances. Amelia was shocked by his cursing and his blaming her for what had happened. She had no idea why he might think she was known for bad landings.

She'd heard rumors that he had a mean mouth, but up until now he'd kept his remarks to himself. He'd made some biting remarks about her to his friends, and she'd put it down as jealousy. He never knew that his words had been repeated verbatim back to her, by men who would jump at the chance to fly with her. Even though he was a pilot for Pan Am, she felt that commercial pilots were nothing more than bus drivers. There were dark rumors that he was a lush, but she hadn't known him long enough to see much drinking, so she'd never given voice to her suspicions. Amelia remembered her father often saying, *"Don't bandy rumors about, Amelia, always give a person the chance to prove what they are, and once they do, hold them to it."*

She knew that Noonan perceived her as some sort of land-lubber who just happened to have some skill at flying. She'd heard the disdain in the tone of his voice when they talked about flying. He'd obviously come on this trip to further his own ambitions, and it galled him especially deep to have to sit back seat to a woman. But it wasn't her fault that he'd fallen short of his own career expectations. The fact of the matter was that she was the pilot, he was the navigator, not even know as her co-pilot, which was another galling aspect that he must be chaffing about. Too bad though because first and last, those are the terms of their agreement. He'd signed on for it, and there was no turning back now. In effect, she was the boss on this trip. She knew he would never obey her commands to the letter, but she needed to let him know that she was in charge. It would be a difficult thing to do too, because she had heard many of his boasts and knew him to have an exceedingly high opinion of himself.

Of course, another question now was, had the trip ended with their crash landing and subsequent marooning on the island? Or, as Noonan had suggested, had all law, had all rules themselves been thrown out the window, since they were no longer a part of 'civilization?'

And whereas she was famous, Noonan was a footnote to her derring-do. There were hundreds of available co-pilots, and most of the navigators who had confided his rude comments about her were doing so, hoping that she'd grow tired of his attitude and place them next to her in the cockpit. Of course, his seafaring days made him more expert in the ways of the sea, but on this island, whatever knowledge he may have accrued regarding anything land-wise that could help them, seems to have vanished. On the island, they were both relegated to land-lubber status, and the only criterion that separated them was whether one saw things as positive or futile. She wanted rely upon hope and he seemed content to sneer at the world and everything in it.

She'd accepted him for this trip only because it was her opinion that one co-pilot was just as good as the next. She would just as soon have found another woman to navigate for her, but knew her sponsors would never go for it.

Noonan was civil enough and competent mechanically, and while she'd never actually seen him drunk, she had found that he was prone to dark moods. He was in fact, a very good navigator. But now it seemed that this wreck had tossed them out of the sky along with all pretenses towards common civility as well. She was about to make a remark that Harry

Manning, her first choice as navigator, wouldn't have gotten them lost in the first place, but she bit her tongue, telling herself that she wouldn't sink to his level.

Now, he was acting petulant and rude, lashing out at her, placing all of the blame upon her for their predicament. He glared murderously at her; his face was already tomato-red from the sun, his eyes dilated and wild, his hair matted to his skull. Amelia could only imagine what she must look like to him. She could feel the burn in her face, the back of her neck, and her ears from having been exposed for god-knows how many hours here on the beach in the direct sun.

Staring at him, she decided right then that she would nip this in the bud before the rescue crews arrived. He obviously felt that her flying skills had somehow gotten them into this fix. It shouldn't be too hard to put him in his correct place though, seeing as she held the purse-strings to the rest of his career. One press conference from her with a less than glowing report regarding his competency, and he would be hard pressed to find any company or pilot who would allow him to sit in the cockpit as navigator. Imagine, being the man that caused the famous Amelia Earhart to crash on the world record flight! He needed her much more than she needed him, but there was no point in arguing over and over about their crash landing. It was done and they couldn't change what had happened. He seemed intent though, upon picking at that wound.

"I did . . . *we* . . . did the best we could, Noonan," she turned her head towards the surf and looked at the Electra. The only thing visible was the top of the fuselage and the bent propeller tip. The rest of the plane was below the water, except for the very end of one wing where a few inches of wingtip poked above the waves. Past that was nothing more than ocean stretching across the horizon line. Her heart skipped a beat, "as soon as the rescue crews arrive, we'll see where it all went wrong."

"It don't matter nohow where it went wrong, because there won't be a rescue. You've killed us."

"Look around you, Noonan, we're *alive*. The rescue will come soon enough. We just can't afford to slacken our efforts to be seen. We'll make a signal fire. A sign on the beach for planes to see when they do a flyover."

Noonan raised his head, "I've already had a look around. There's no rescue, Amelia. This island is deserted. You've killed us sure as hell."

"Noonan, you need to leave off that common language. Get your wits about you. And by the way, must I remind you that if we are lost, you share some of the blame, since you were our navigator? So, why would you want to be such a naysayer? All we have to do is look for something to eat, papayas, bananas, coconuts, and the like . . ."

He glared at her, "There's *nothing* here."

"You've already explored the island?"

"One simple turn was all you had to do. Turn and land us on the beach. There's plenty of room here," he swept his arm towards the beach; "we'd have landed safely. But no, you had to hot dog it. Were you hoping for an exciting chapter for your next book, Amelia is that it?"

"That's enough of that Noonan! Have you forgotten that we ran out of fuel? How could I have taken a turn and made an approach? We were falling like a rock, the fuel was gone. You can't second-guess that! It was dead-stick all the way in."

"All I know is that you killed us, *sure as hell*."

"Well, I insist that you belay that type of talk. Of course we'll get rescued. We just need to be positive and wait it out. It should only be a few hours, or a day or two at the most. How much looking around did you do?"

"I walked the perimeter of the island."

"There are no natives?"

"This place is uninhabited, leastways as far as I could see it is. It probably always has been, and from the looks of our situation, it probably will remain unchanged. As soon as we're gone, it will revert to what it always has been. A small unknown, uninhabitable island unfit for anything except birds, snakes, and a few rats."

Amelia frowned and looked out to sea. She kept expecting to see a ship coming over the horizon; it was just a matter of time.

"The beach around the entire island is anywhere from one hundred feet to fifty or a hundred yards wide, beyond that is two or three hundred yards of jungle. There is a small lagoon with a narrow entrance through the rim, which opens into the ocean at high tide."

"So it's obviously not fresh-water."

"No. The highest elevation on the island looks to be about ten feet, not including the height one could access by climbing the numerous coconut trees. Lots of shore-birds, lizards and rats, and judging from some hoof prints I saw; there are a couple of small pigs."

He crawled to his knees then stood up with his back to her and slapped his hands together, brushing the sand from them. He began walking away, going towards the tree line filled with coconut trees and palms and beyond that, the jungle.

He yelled over his shoulder to her as he plodded away, "Stay away from me, Amelia. Stay away from me or I'll kill you!"

Amelia shrank back at his words, as if he were walking towards her, instead of away. Her face colored and she watched numbly as he walked away. Her body began to feel shaky the way she always felt in hostile, or confrontational situations.

"Noonan!"

He ignored her and kept walking.

"Get back here, Noonan, we need to make a plan."

He stopped and turned towards her, his face twisted in anger, "I'm no longer taking orders from the famous goddamn *Amelia Earhart*. I gave you the layout of the island. I didn't have to do that."

"Why would you talk to me this way Noonan? Why air your grievances to me. We're all in the same boat here, as it were."

"No, *you* put us here with your sorry flying skills. As far as having aired my grievances, I'll do so as I see fit, but for now let's just say that *an empty stomach makes a fierce dog* huh? Now, leave me alone or you'll be on your own." He turned and kept walking.

Amelia's face reddened at the blasphemy, and she got to her feet and stared after Noonan as he walked off the beach and into the jungle, disappearing into the thick foliage. He'd always looked sickly and too skinny and she'd always thought he was unhealthy. Now she thought he appeared mad, as if he was not right in the brain.

She looked around and realized that she was completely alone. She glanced at the sky, hoping to see some clouds that would provide a respite from the unbearable heat, but the sky was empty, save the fierce yellow sun. The wind was just a whisper every now and then, a slight cooling across the sweat of her forehead. The jungle had bird sounds and mysterious rustlings of vermin, or something larger moving around, either that or her imagination was teasing her. Still though, she wanted to be further out on the beach and away from the forbidding darkness of the jungle. Moving further out onto the beach though, meant getting fried by the sun.

●●●

She wondered if he'd simply gone into the jungle to relieve himself out of her sight, or if he was searching for inhabitants of the island, or maybe scouting for possible food sources. Surely he hadn't truly intended to just walk away and leave her there on her own? Should she have followed him?

Looking inward to the jungle, Amelia realized that food would be the least of their problems. It was a decent sized island, about four miles in length and a couple miles across, and the lush jungle should offer many food sources, not to mention the fact that they could find crabs, fish and fruits of all varieties. She decided also that shelter shouldn't be too much of a problem for them. They'd simply get under the trees where it was cooler, and wait for the rescue. The biggest problem she could imagine was in finding drinkable water. She was determined that she would get through this. Not that she was brave or heroic; it's just that she was stubborn. She'd come to realize that courage was not necessarily bravery; it was just a stubbornness, a stubborn inability to give in, a willingness to keep trying.

Sitting with her back against a tree trunk, Amelia tilted her head back and looked up. Like all of the coconut trees that bordered the jungle and the beach the trees ranged from fifty or sixty feet in height, and a few must have been close to a hundred feet. Many had clusters of green coconuts up near the tops of the trees. The palm fronds at the tops of the trees waved in the breeze. For some reason though, the breeze that moved the palm fronds wasn't available at ground level.

The area she was sitting at the edge of the jungle facing out to the beach was a horseshoe-shaped indention. It provided shade, and because it fronted the beach it offered a view towards the Electra and also, the direction from where any rescuers would be seen. Any sea borne breeze would also cool them here, whereas, it wouldn't if they went any further into the jungle it wouldn't be able to reach them. Amelia realized that this spot would be a perfect place to make their camp. The tress provided shade, and it looked out towards the beach, and the sea. To the left of her viewpoint she could see the wing of the Electra, jutting up out of the waves. The horseshoe-shaped clearing was about thirty feet across, and a coconut tree on the far side grew out at an almost forty-five degree angle from where the trunk met the ground. One could climb it and at mid-point, be almost directly over the center of the clearing at about eight feet off the ground. The tree trunk bent upwards at that point, rising up forty or so feet higher at the top. Amelia noticed that many of the coconut trees on the island grew at crazy angles like this one, and yet many grew straight up. Most of them had to be a hundred feet tall. There was a jungle of other foliage around them, beach mahogany, oil nut trees, Pacific Island Silver Grass, and several dozen others no doubt, that Amelia had no idea what names they went by. She'd heard that there was some sort of breadfruit trees in the Pacific islands, but she had no clue what they looked like, or whether or not the fruit was edible. Even if it were, she had no idea what months the fruit was likely to be found. She doubted that they'd be here long enough to find out anyway.

Behind her in the jungle, she could hear birds squawking and chattering, and some sort of clicking sounds and hissing. Just glancing back into the direction of the jungle she could see it was teeming with movement, small animals making the bushes and leaves move as they scurried to and fro, no doubt.

The island was probably home to all sorts of native wildlife, and it shouldn't be too difficult to catch enough food for sustenance until their rescue ships arrived for them.

She also decided that it was nigh time to get busy. They'd need to make a signal fire, and maybe even make a sign in the sand on the beach. The rescue operations would be unable to miss the plane too, as it would be highly visible when flying over.

She decided to get busy and use the beach to her advantage. She stepped off a hundred and twenty feet, and then used her hands and feet to dig out the letters, H E L P and then she went into the jungle to get armful and armful of coconut tree branches and she filled in the letters. That would be a good start for a signal if there was a flyover, which there probably would be in the next twenty four hours. Their approximate position was known, and since they hadn't been checking in, and obviously they were long overdue at Howland Island, so someone would be out and looking for them.

As she worked on the sign, she thought about how to deal with Noonan. She would simply reassert her position as leader of this expedition, and Noonan would just have to buck up until they were rescued. He was probably in shock anyway. A clear thinking man does not simply wander off alone in an unknown environment.

Amelia started walking towards the tree-line to try to catch up with Noonan. When she stepped into the jungle, she was shocked that it wasn't much cooler under the jungle canopy. Not only was it almost as hot in the shade as it was on the beach, the air felt thicker, and it was harder to breathe. She was clammy all over, and already in dire need of water.

Lying on the beach, she'd been soaked by the ocean, and in the few minutes since, had dried off, and now was soaked again by sweat. It was amazing just how unbearable the heat was. Even in the shade it was sucking her dry. She was already feeling light-headed and groggy, which she knew was a sure sign of heat-exhaustion.

The racket from the birds in the jungle was incredible. Everywhere she looked there was movement, birds fluttering from tree to tree, lizards sunning on tree trunks in the slices of light that filtered down through the foliage, and rats; thousands, if not millions of them. They swarmed in and out of the brush as she walked by. Many ran straight past her, and didn't bother giving her a wide berth. She felt their furry bodies brushing her ankles as she walked. They didn't stop and bite, so she tried to ignore them, even though she shuddered and wanted to vomit. The bushes in the jungle actually vibrated with swarming rats. She wished she had her shoes. She'd left them back on the beach.

She kept her eyes forward, hoping to get a glimpse of Noonan, getting even angrier with him for having simply walked away from her. It was a deplorable way to act in these circumstances. The way to survive was to stick together, make a plan and conserve energy. Build a shelter, find water and food. Even though they were just a few hours, or a day or two away from rescue, his actions were simply unconscionable.

She saw movement ahead and realized that if there were inhabitants on the island, they'd have shelter and water.

"Noonan! Is that you? Come forth and reveal yourself, I know you're out there. It's pointless to pretend."

He ignored her.

She walked out of the jungle and into a clearing, and saw water and realized that this was the small lagoon that Noonan had told her about. It was good to be able to get the lay of the land, see exactly what the island held in store for them.

"It's not drinkable, if that's what you're thinking."

Amelia gasped at the sound of his voice and turned back around to see him sitting a few feet away stretched out in a pose of languor.

"Why did you leave me back there? We need to stick together and make a plan. Build a shelter that we can use until the rescue. We need to make a fire, signal the rescue ships with smoke."

Noonan laughed, "There's not going to be a rescue, Amelia. We were off course when we went down, which means they won't be looking for us in this area. This is where we'll die. Does it matter a whit if we're together when we die?"

"Noonan, I beg of you, please stop talking like that, as it's very disheartening."

"What does it matter? What does anything matter anymore?"

"Noonan, the misery you're complaining about . . . that's just the cost of living. We must conquer our fears and misgivings about the hand we've been dealt. There's no time to bellyache about our lot in life; we need to do something to improve it."

"The end is going to be soon, Amelia. There's no fresh water and with this heat we'll be lucky to make it three days. But for the time being, these little crabs are delicious."

Amelia's eyes widened when she realized that he was chewing, and had something in his hand. He cupped his hand like he was holding a handful of peanuts, tilted his head back, and dropped whatever was in his hand into his mouth and began eating.

"Where, how'd you get them?"

He chewed until he could swallow, and then waved his hand towards the beach, "They're everywhere, just catch and eat them. Of course, they might be better if I cooked them."

"I take it you're not sharing?"

"You're on your own," He laughed and shook his head, "You got us here, and we're going to die soon, so it's your fault anyway. I'll be goddamned if I'm going to feed the person who's responsible for my death."

Amelia was horrified at both his attitude and blasphemy. "You've gone off the deep-end Noonan. You must have hit your head too hard on something in the crash, because it's just a matter of time before we're rescued!"

"You're certifiable, Amelia. Look around you. You landed us in fucking hell. We'll never leave this island. Not alive."

"Noonan, could you please act civilized and leave off that whore-house language?"

"Civilized? What's the point in acting civilized if there's no civilization? What are you anyway, some sort of bluenose?"

"At least I'm not the stinkard that you are. And there's no point in us falling back into animal behavior simply because we're stranded for a while. Civilization may not be here, Noonan," she waved her hand out to signify the island, 'but it's right there," she pointed towards the ocean, "just over the horizon, and it falls upon us to heed the restrictions and conventions that society deems important and just, because we will be judged by our actions here, once we're back there. You just mark my words, Noonan; we mustn't become like vermin, just because we've seen them in our front yard. It's uncivilized, it's ungodly."

Noonan scoffed and shook his head at her, "Your problem is that you can't deal with what is in front of you, and that's why you're always trying to hark back to *civilization*."

Amelia hmmphed and turned to look towards the water line of the beach. She saw four or five of the little crabs. She ran towards them and tried to grab one, but they skittered away. She looked back at Noonan and saw him laughing.

"You'll starve quick using that technique."

"Okay, tell me how it's done."

He shook his head at her.

"Like I said, Amelia, you're on your own. Maybe you can use your fame to make them give up."

Amelia was shocked by his cold-bloodedness. Apparently this attitude was something that he intended to keep up. She knew though, that once their rescue was underway, he'd revert back to his old self. There'd be apologies and guilt. Maybe he *had* been knocked senseless by the crash. He had a bloody forehead and scratches on his arms. Her whole body felt bruised, and she had a few small cuts, but it was mostly superficial. Still though, they'd need to keep their cuts clean, and find a way to bandage them.

The problem was that she just wasn't agile enough to trap the tiny crabs.

"Noonan, you need to consider what you're doing."

"What are you suggesting?"

"We need to work together if we're going to survive-" she held her arms out to signify the island, "to survive until the rescue. What's it going to look like for you, after we get back to the States and the story gets out that you treated me so poorly? You'll be a laughing-stock. You'll be reviled if it gets out that you would leave a woman all alone in a survival situation."

"But you're not *a woman*, you're a hero, you're the one and only *Amelia Earhart*," he laughed ruefully, "my question to you is what will they think *of you* for crashing us here? Or what will they think of *you* for *needing a man*?"

"That's ridiculous, Noonan. Common courtesy dictates that you treat a woman with respect."

"We are going to fucking *die* on this island, Amelia. You should prepare *yourself*. It's going to be soon, too. Probably within the next thirty-six hours. There's *no water*. Hell, we may not even see the sun rise again."

"We don't know that yet. We haven't searched the entire island yet. For all we know there are natives here."

"No, Amelia, this island is uninhabited. There's nothing here but us, some birds and rats."

"Think how this will look, Noonan, you refusing to even help me catch a crab to eat. Once we're rescued, do you want the world to know how you're acting? That you were unwilling to help your fellow castaway? You'll be crucified in the papers."

Noonan laughed, "It's as if you actually *believe* all the claptrap that's written about you, Amelia. It's all a bunch of hero-worship and hogwash. You can't live forever. No matter how famous you are, you're going to die. We'll never even *see* another paper."

"You believe what you want, Noonan. I believe in hope, and in the human spirit."

"Well, don't take any wooden nickels, sweetheart."

"I believe can survive here, on my own if I have to, can you?"

"But you also believe that you can fly."

"I can fly-" Amelia stammered, trying to think of something to say.

"You'll end up a footnote in American history. You'll be forgotten long before the next generation learns to fly. In fact, if you're so worried about what the papers will say about *us*, consider this . . . they might very well portray *you* as the cause of our deaths. The hot-dog pilot who killed herself and her co-pilot because she was blinded by her own press clippings. They'll say that the great Amelia Earhart perished in what was basically a publicity stunt designed only to help her sell her next book. What a folly. Pathetic is what it is."

"Noonan, you know that's not true! Why can't you think positively about this, this *setback*, and realize that we *will* be rescued?"

Noonan snorted, "Setback?" He stood up and threw his hands out, "look around you Amelia! You call this a *setback?*" He shook his head slowly, "the fact that you casually refer to this as a *setback* tells me just how much you really *have* fallen for your own press clippings. This-" he spread his arms out, "this is more than a setback," he paused, "this is the absolute fucking *end* of the line."

"I've had enough of that *disgusting* language Noonan, and I demand that you leave it off immediately. Consider it a simple courtesy. You want to talk like that to your drunken sailor friends, fine, but I won't listen to it. In fact, I deplore it."

"You deplore it? Well, aren't you the countess?"

He turned and began walking away again, this time parallel to the beach. Amelia followed him silently. At one point, he turned in mid-stride and they began walking back the way they'd just come. When they reached the original point where they'd come out of the jungle and reached the lagoon Noonan angrily pulled his shirt off and dipped it into the water at the shoreline of the lagoon. She could hear him muttering to himself, as he spread the shirt out with his hands. Suddenly, he stopped and threw the shirt forward, where it landed on a group of about five or six of the tiny crabs. He knelt and gathered the shirt up and turned it over and picked the crabs out of the wet folds and kept them trapped in his cupped hands. It was a simple idea for catching the little creatures.

She was doubly surprised when he turned and gave her the handful of little creatures.

He spoke gruffly, "I was lying when I said they were delicious. They taste like hell. But an empty stomach never breeds fine thoughts."

He motioned for her hands and he turned his over hers, and cautioned her, "Don't let them crawl out, they're deceptively fast."

"Do I crush them in my hands to kill them before I eat them?"

He laughed and shook his head, "Don't even worry about that. Just tilt your head back, drop them in, and start chewing. You get hungry enough and you'll get the hang of it."

Amelia felt her stomach growl in the anticipation of food and she tilted her head back, brought her hand up to her mouth and dropped three of them in. They looked like small crayfish. No shell, white, and almost clear, they were about as big as her thumb. Inside her mouth they began crawling, and it felt to Amelia as if they were trying to attach to the insides of her cheeks, and tongue. She gagged.

She nodded, closed her eyes, and tilted her head back and started chewing the moment they were in her mouth. When she'd finished them, a slimy, pasty after-taste lingered in her mouth and she wished they had clean drinking water. She remembered that there were several packs of Beech Nut chewing gun in the plane; a gift from one of the sponsors of her trip. They were meant to give them something to do to stay awake on the long flight. Of course, the plane along with everything else was under water and ruined.

"But that's it. No more from me," he scowled at her, "You fend for yourself from here on out. You're on your own now."

He turned and started walking, his skinny frame moving along in a straight line, as if he knew exactly where he was headed. Amelia followed along, simply because she had no idea of what else to do. She was stunned speechless by his vicious attitude. He was actually willing to let her die? Surely he was still in shock and not thinking clearly.

Of course, their situation was not nearly as dire as he proclaimed. They needed only to find some form of drinkable water, then sit back and wait for the rescue. They'd probably be back to civilization before she had to cut her nails again.

•••

She followed him until they came out from under the jungle canopy at the beach and she saw that the sun was dropping quickly towards the horizon.

"Just another couple of hours of daylight," Amelia remarked, pointing to the sun.

Noonan just glared at her.

For a moment, back in the jungle, she'd considered stopping, just to see how long it would take before he'd realize that she was no longer trudging along behind him and turn to come back for her. Then she realized that he probably wouldn't even care, and she had no intention of being left alone in the jungle with millions of rats.

There were millions of them too. Of that there was no doubt. They were scurrying everywhere. In some places, there were so many underfoot, that she couldn't avoid stepping on them. Several times they'd clawed her ankles as she stepped on them, and they scurried across the top of her feet as they ran across the ground in front of them as they trudged through the jungle. It was all Amelia could do to keep herself from screaming when this happened.

Running from them would be pointless; they were everywhere, except for the beach. If there were any humans on this island, other than castaways such as themselves, they were certainly outnumbered by the rats.

Broiling hot or not, it was a relief to see the wide expanse of white sand again, and not a rat in sight.

Amelia decided to sleep on the beach to stay as far away from the rats as possible. Stopping at the water's edge, Amelia allowed the surf to roll in and cover her feet up to her ankles. The sea-water was cooler than the air, and she had to fight every instinct she had, not to drink it. She knew that it would be filling and it would cool her down, but she knew that it was not a smart thing to do.

Noonan had kept walking when she'd stopped in the surf, and he was waist deep now, walking out on the sand bar to look at the plane. She called out to him,

"Noonan, shall I come out with you to inspect the wreck?"

He gave a dismissive wave of his hand over his shoulder, and a grunt.

She watched as he went out until he was chest deep in the surf, and then he swam the last few yards to the wingtip and stopped. Amelia could barely swim, and certainly not for distance. She looked around fearfully, hoping that there were no sharks in the area. Noonan, for his part seemed unconcerned. He was holding himself onto the submerged wing, and staring at something under the water on the fuselage of the plane.

"What is it, Noonan?" She cupped her hands around her mouth and yelled out to him, "What do you see?"

He ignored her and she snorted angrily and waded out deeper into the surf. Maybe he hadn't heard her over the sound of the ocean waves constantly breaking.

"Noonan, have you found something?" she yelled and as soon as the words came out of her mouth she realized how ridiculous the question was. What was there to be found anyway? They knew why they'd wrecked. Nothing that he could find out there would have surprised her anyway. Nothing of value could come from the plane at this point. Every instrument was water-damaged at this point. There might be materials aboard that they could use for survival, but that was almost a moot point anyway, since their rescue would probably be within the next forty-eight hours anyway. It would certainly come about before their conditions became dire in any way. She did realize though that they'd need something to cover up with, as her skin was already becoming red from the sun. She'd be blistered soon if she didn't get back into the shade. The shade had its drawbacks though, namely, the rats.

Noonan was pointedly ignoring her.

Amelia considered wading out further, where she could talk to Noonan without having to shout over the sound of the surf, but she realized that it was a waste of time if he wasn't going to talk to answer.

She stopped and was up to her waist in the surf. With one hand on her hip, one hand on her brow to block the sun, she scowled at him. He was standing on the wing next to the fuselage, bent over and peering at something below the water line. Whatever it was, it had his total interest.

"Noonan? What is it? What are you looking at?"

He ignored her.

"Noonan, answer me!"

Instead of answering her, he leaned forward and flipped off the wing he was standing on and went under the water. Amelia frowned. Obviously there was something under the water, or on the underside of the fuselage that he wanted to take a better look at. She waited for him to surface, and wished that she felt more comfortable in the water. She glanced around nervously keeping an eye out for the sinister fin of any sharks that might be in the area. She turned back to face the wreck and began wondering just how long Noonan could hold his breath under water, and she saw two ominous fins slicing through the water in between her and the Electra.

Noonan came up from his dive and clambered back up onto the submerged wing of the Electra and shouted.

"I got it!"

She stood and watched as he came running up from out of the surf holding a piece of metal in his hands.

"Did you see that?" she pointed out at the water.

"See what?"

"Sharks!"

Noonan looked around, but the ominous fins had dipped below the surface.

He shrugged, "I don't see them, but we should be okay, just stay out of the water and don't panic."

"I did *not* panic."

Noonan looked off into the distance, and raised his arm and used his sleeve to wipe his face, "Okay, it's just that you're a woman, you told me that you can't swim very well."

"Noonan, I may be a woman, but that doesn't mean I automatically lose my nerve every time something happens that I'm not prepared for. I'm telling you, there were two sharks."

He looked at the beach and seemed to study it for a moment, and then held out the metal in his hand, "this is a piece of the underside engine cowling. You can really see where that coral scratched it up," he turned it over and ran his fingers along the scratched grooves from where the coral had gouged it, "it will make a good bowl to boil water in for drinking. I can use it to cook with too."

"*You* can?"

He nodded, "I'll try, why?"

"Noonan, I can help too."

"Look, Amelia, it's all fine and dandy that, back there in the civilized world," he pointed with his hand out towards the ocean, "you were famous because, *as a woman* you did some things that were mostly men's jobs, but out here your fame is not going to do you any favors. So, why don't you just let me, *the man*, do what *men* do best, and take care of things. Tell you what, when I catch dinner, I'll let *you* cook it, how about that?"

"Noonan, don't talk to me like I'm some ditzy flapper straight out of some speakeasy club. I'm an accomplished woman in case you've forgotten."

"Sure, you accomplished a lot too, stranding us here."

"But you act as if you're the only one with skills that can be of use here. I can help you know, it will take both of us to weather this out until the rescuers arrive."

"Sure, Amelia, you keep believing that, meanwhile, I have work to do, and as the only man around, I am in charge."

Amelia stared blankly at him, seething because he had dismissed her so quickly.

"First thing is to get a fire started."

"Wait a minute, Noonan."

"What?"

"What says that you're to be in charge? I didn't hear the king name you as Viceroy of this island."

"Don't be silly woman. I'm in charge because; well, because it's only natural. I'm the man."

Amelia started to say something, but stopped herself. She was far too angry to speak.

"Now, it won't be a problem if I find some flint type rocks, and I can get something steel from the plane. I should be able to provide fire in no time at all. We'll cook up some crab."

"Noonan, you listen to me now. I don't intend to be-"

He looked up from the metal 'bowl' and his face twisted into a mask of anger, "That's what I'm *not* doing anymore, Amelia, *listening to you.* You're the one who got us into this mess. Maybe if you'd been more like 'Lucky Lindy' and less a 'Lady Lindy' we wouldn't be in this shithole right now."

He waded ashore then turned and began walking away, his metal 'bowl' under his arm.

Amelia's mouth dropped open and she blurted out, "and maybe, if you hadn't been stinking *drunk* we might not have gotten off course!"

Noonan turned and took a step back towards her, and his eyebrows went up and his face reddened. For a moment, Amelia feared that he might actually strike her. Instead, he wheeled around and stormed off into the jungle like a child who doesn't want to share his toys. This time she didn't follow. If he was captain of the island, she'd mutiny. With their positions here not being so clear-cut though, there was no authority to question. Noonan's greatest flaw was that he thought he thought he had no weakness, and in his folly, he self-deceived himself. Amelia wondered if she was weakened by her own feelings of strength and absence of fear. Could r own Achilles heel be her positive attitude?

She walked to the edge of the jungle and sat down in the shade of a coconut tree with her back against the trunk and stared out at the ocean.

For several hours she stared at the horizon, wanting to see a ship breaking the monotonous line between sea and sky, but nothing appeared. The fluffy white clouds floated past overhead, and every now and then the breeze rustled the leaves overhead, but nothing appeared on the horizon. Once or twice she felt her eyelids closing and she must have dozed, because once when she woke up she noticed that the sun had slid across the sky and the shadows were changing direction on the sand in front of her.

She could see now that the tide was coming in. She scanned the horizon again, looking for a rescue ship and upon seeing nothing, her stomach lurched violently and she jumped to her feet and ran forward a few steps and looked up and down the beach in both directions thinking that she must have gotten turned around. The Electra was gone!

She cupped her hands around her mouth and yelled out, "Noonan! Get back here and hurry up!"

She stared out at the ocean, towards the spot where the Electra had been. She kept her eyes glued to the spot, willing it to appear.

When Noonan came out of the jungle she pointed out towards the spot where the Electra had been an hour earlier.

"Noonan, it's gone, the Electra!"

He placed his hands on his hips and walked forward a few feet and scanned the horizon left and right and then back.

"It's just high tide, that's all. The plane can't be *gone*, Amelia."

After a few minutes they sat at the edge of the jungle and the beach, and looked out towards the ocean just fifty yards away.

"Okay, maybe you're right, so where did you go?"

"I was looking for sticks in the jungle."

"Sticks, what do we need sticks for, Noonan?"

"You mean what do *I* want with sticks?"

"Noonan, we're in this together. There's no need for us to fight."

"*I'm* going to build a fire, and then find some water so *I* don't die of dehydration. I don't know what *you're* going to do."

"Noonan, we should work together to make this ordeal as easy as possible for both of us. There's no point in both of us getting dehydrated."

"Get your own water, Amelia," Noonan said as he stood up and began walking away, "you're not getting any of mine."

Amelia noticed that he was still carrying the metal 'bowl' that he'd torn off the underside of the plane.

"Noonan, that's deplorable! You'd actually let me die of thirst?"

"Yes, Amelia, I will, because *you* killed *me* by landing us here the way you did. In fact, I hope you die soon too. I might last a few days longer because of it."

Amelia was about to ask him how he would benefit from her death, but then it dawned on her what he was saying. Her mouth dropped open, but she was too shocked to speak.

She watched as he sat down fifty yards further down the beach and spread out his materials on the sand in between his legs; a flat rock, several sticks and handful of dried moss and leaves. He was obviously going to try to get a fire started. She wanted so badly to say something pithy to him, especially after all the barbs he'd thrown at her. Maybe say something like; *hey Noonan, looks like you're really putting on the Ritz over there*. But, she just didn't have it in her to get into a spitting match with him.

Amelia reached up and wiped sweat off her face with her forearm. The sand scratched her face, and the sweat she wiped away was instantly replaced with more sweat. It was literally pouring out of every pore in her body. She knew that they were in a dangerous situation now. They needed water, badly.

Amelia turned and looked back into the jungle. She saw a flash of color as a bird flew through the upper reaches of the branched canopy of the jungle. The underbrush rustled and several rats jumped out of a bush and scurried by. They were almost two feet in length. Amelia shuddered.

She turned back to watch as Noonan got his rig set up and began rubbing the sticks together. He managed to get a wisp of smoke, and he immediately dropped the sticks and blew on the kindling and moss from where the tendrils of smoke had drifted out. He got nothing in reward for his efforts.

Amelia lay back on the sand, exhausted. The heat, along with a lack of food and water had completely robbed her energy reserves. She wondered why there weren't rescue planes circling overhead yet, or a freighter offshore, sending in a rescue craft. Something was wrong. Could they have flown that far off-course, or was the rescue just slowed down by some unknown contingency?

Noonan had said that he'd explored, and that had been before their little trek through the jungle to the lagoon and back.

She stood up and walked to where Noonan was still hunched over his rig, a stick in between his hands. He rubbed his hands against each other briskly and the stick smoked against the stone again, and he tried once again blowing on the tinder to coax it to flame, but got nothing.

"Noonan, you're doing it wrong."

His head jerked up at the sound of her voice. He scowled, "You're all wet. What would you know about survival? You're just a woman." He bent back over his task and kept rubbing his hands together. Amelia could hear him huffing and knew he would soon be unable to continue his attempts much longer.

"Oh for Gosh sakes, Noonan."

"What?"

"You can't really believe that just because I'm a woman I can't be of any help out here, do you?"

"Women are not meant for this," he spread his arms out to indicate the island, "it takes a man to deal with the outdoors, despite what you think."

Amelia shook her head. She watched him struggling with the fire-making attempt.

"You'll never get enough friction like that, Noonan. You need some string to make a . . . a doohickey. I forgot what it's called. Oh! It's called a *hand bow*. That's what you need. When I went camping with some of the girls in the Ninety-Nines club, we all learned how to make fire this way. I've *done it* before, several times in fact."

He ignored her and bent down even closer to his hands, blowing on the moss and leaves when a wisp of smoke drifted up.

Noonan fell forward as Amelia heard one of his sticks snap.

"God-dammit!" he yelled and flung the broken stick away from him.

"Noonan, do you mind not cursing? We can at least act civilized even though we may not-"

"Go to hell, you stupid bitch!" he screamed at her as he picked up his flat rock and threw it at her.

She jerked her head to the side as the rock whizzed past her. She whimpered and glared at Noonan.

"Noonan, do you have to be such a ruffian? There's no reason to get physical."

"Stay away from me, Amelia! I don't want you anywhere near me," he stood up and walked away. Amelia could see him leaning down, looking into the edge of the brush in the jungle, hoping probably to rebuild his fire kit.

"What's wrong with you Noonan?" she called out to him, but he ignored her, "It's a simple thing to make fire, we just need to work together on it! Don't you want to be rescued? I can make fire, which we need so that the rescue ships can see us. We don't want them to accidently pass us by in the middle of the night. We can make torches too."

He turned to face her.

"I don't need you, Amelia, in fact, I consider you a liability out here. There's nothing to gain for me to be tied to an apron-string out here."

Amelia opened her mouth to speak but he continued, his voice rising in anger, "Women know nothing about the outdoors, hunting, fishing and survival, and besides that, I despise you. Always have, always will. But I'll be rid of you soon enough anyway. You obviously don't realize it, but we're both going to die soon. There will be no rescue. My only hope is that I'm alive to see your death."

"Noonan, we're in this together. I don't understand why you're being so hateful, and morbid. And truthfully, you're being stupid because we have a better chance of survival together, not alone."

"Amelia, we have *no* chance of survival. No more than a few days anyway. That's it. There will be no rescue, and our 'survival' for as long as it will last, is going to be brutal. So, I'd just as soon not have to look at you; until your last day, that is."

"Oh, for Gosh sakes, Noonan, that's a horrible way to act. We crashed here together, and no matter whose fault it was, we still need each other until we're rescued. Why can't we be civil about it?"

"*Civilization* is gone, Amelia. This is all there is" he spread his arms out towards the beach, "and because this place is uninhabited, it's each man for himself."

"Why? Why not try to help each other?"

"Because Amelia, everything I do to help you, every drink of *water* I provide for you, every *animal* I catch and allow *you* to *eat,* means *less* for me. That's why. I don't intend to die *one* fucking *moment* before I'm supposed to. I want to hang on to each day, each hour, each minute, hell, each second before I die."

"Noonan, can't you talk without the guttersnipe language? What is wrong with you? Just because we're away from other people-"

"What the fuck does it matter, Amelia? There's no one else around to *disapprove* of my language. If *you* don't like it, then get the hell away from me!"

"Two heads are better than one, Noonan. If we could just work together to find water, and make ourselves comfortable, then we can just wait out this . . . this *delay* that's occurring in our rescue. This will all be over with in twenty-four to thirty-six hours, at most. Can't we just manage to get along-?"

Noonan exploded, "There's not going to be a rescue Amelia! It's *not* going to happen. We're *dead*. We just haven't actually died yet, that's all."

"I refuse to believe that, Noonan. We're alive and our rescuers are somewhere just over the horizon. We're in bad shape, but it's not dire, not by a long stretch."

"That's bullshit, Amelia. You seem to really believe that you are the heroic 'Lady Lindy' or the 'famed aviatrix' or whatever other ridiculous appellation the press has dreamed up for you. You sincerely believe that this world wouldn't *dare* let you die, because you're so famous, or because you've got so many great things ahead of you to do." He shook his head at her.

Amelia stared back at him, trying to think of a way to convince him to stop being so obstinate, and help her help them to get along and survive this mess until the rescuers arrive.

"What you need to do, Amelia," he shook his head slowly side to side, "is . . . you need to stop thinking like a 'famous' person and start thinking like a flesh and blood mortal. Think like a woman, if that's what you are, hell; try to think like a man, if you can. The world doesn't owe you the luxury of survival just because you've become famous. On this island you're nobody. It's not pilot and navigator out here. It's survival of the fittest, *not* survival of the most famous. On this island we're not *famous person* and *regular guy*. It's not even man and woman. It's down to two life forms and a harsh environment that will kill them at its earliest possible opportunity with no regrets."

"What does that mean, Noonan? Of course I'm a woman!"

He looked her up and down as if seeing her for the first time. He shook his head side to side.

"You may have the biological parts needed to claim womanhood," he said slowly, "but you're far from being a woman per se. I suppose that it's all those years of flying planes, and trying to act like one of the boys," he chuckled, "and even dressing up in men's clothes," he paused, "and I'll give it to you, yeah, you did some things, flew a plane and maybe even went camping, but the end result is that you've pretty much turned yourself into a man now. Not even a real man, just a woman *acting* like one. The end result is that you're far from anything most men would take interest in."

"That's a crude thing to say!"

"Now I know why sailors consider a woman aboard to be a jinx. You sure are. You are the biggest jinx of all time."

"Noonan, you're repugnant. I'll leave you to your fire-making attempts, even though you'll never get a flame the way you're doing it. Go ahead, go for broke, and see who gets fire first!"

Amelia's cheeks had burned in embarrassment at his blatant dismissal of her as a woman, and worse, as jinx. Not that she cared what he thought, for he was a heel, but that he'd said it as if it was a commonly held sentiment.

She turned and walked away, mad as a wet hen, as the fading light of the day slowly dissipated, continuing down the beach until she was a hundred yards away from him and began gathering rocks, sticks and moss for her own fire making supplies. Reaching for a stick, she saw that her hand was shaking in anger.

Amelia filled her pockets with small sticks for kindling and stripped bark from trees, then found some clumps of dried moss on the tree-line of the beach for tender. She looked out towards the ocean where she'd last seen the Electra. Far off, on the lower edge of the horizon, she could see a thin line of darkness; a tropical depression that was likely bearing rain. It was just a purplish slice that separated water and sky. Within that small slice she saw flashes. Lightning. Hopefully the squall would come their way. She could only imagine what a fresh cooling rain would make her feel like at this point.

After a few minutes of watching the flashes of lightning it disappeared and Amelia was unsure if it had ever really even existed. Had her mind conjured it up, or had the rain been there, and the winds pushed the squall away, rather than towards them? Their sky over the island was ever unchanging. Puffy white clouds, no air movement to speak of, and nothing else, other than the constant white flecks of the sea-birds that flitted about going overhead to visit the jungle deeper inland, or heading away from them further out to sea, never to be seen again. Where did they go, she wondered. Was there another island near this one; one with better food for the birds, one with more birds but fewer rats, snakes, and lizards? Did they fly constantly when out over the ocean, or could they land upon the surface of the water and float, rest their wings until ready to fly again? For all the kinship they shared, their ability to fly, they were mysterious creatures to Amelia. She should ask Noonan. He seemed to know about those things. She would surely get an answer if she asked Noonan, but she wasn't certain that his answer would be correct, though he'd definitely insist that it was. In the end, she decided, some mysteries were meant to be enjoyably unknowable. Let the mysteries of the birds be one of those.

She thought that Noonan was wrong regarding the Electra. The hide tide had not covered the plane; it was simply gone. Maybe it had sunk into the sea-bed and was still there, just below the surface. To think about it being gone, their last link with their past and civilization itself scared her.

She took stock of her belongings, which amounted to what she was wearing, and two shirts and another pair of her pants that had washed ashore. The contents of her pockets consisted of a nail clipper, a soggy pocket-bible, and an opened pack of the Beech-Nut chewing gum. It was ruined, having been in the water, but she didn't throw it away yet. She hoped that it would be okay once it dried out sufficiently. She had no make-up, no comb or brush. That she carried no feminine articles or make-up of any sort just made her think of Noonan's remarks from earlier. Deep down though, she knew that there was some truth to what he'd said. She'd always been tomboyish, and since she'd matured, she'd spent as much time as she could spend doing the one thing she enjoyed, flying.

Now, with her skin breaking out in blisters from the sun, stringy matted hair, and her cracked and broken lips, her emaciated look from having no food in days and her general appearance, she knew that she probably looked more dead than alive. Not that she cared for how she looked in Noonan's eyes, but she cared enough about her appearance to want to be seen as a woman. Of course, Noonan was nothing to look at either, what with his hollowed out cheeks, his gaunt frame and his face already peeling from the sunburn, and those wild crazy eyes.

Noonan's assessment of her wasn't the first time she had been accused of being un-ladylike. She knew that there had been rumors for years about her. Her marriage to GP, George Putnam, had been a marriage of convenience for each of them. For her, it was a sigh of relief that she could skip all the dating rituals and awkwardness. Some of the things that had been whispered about had gotten back to her, and just remembering them now caused her face to burn in shame. There were bizarre rumors that she had consorted sexually with women. One rumor had speculated that she was actually a man. These bothered her, and shamed her to a point of distraction. When GP had come along, with dollar signs in his eyes, she'd felt put-upon and in a state of vulnerability that was foreign to her. But after weighing the pros and cons of what it would mean to accept his proposal, namely that it would allow her to publicly scoff at the rumors, and spend more time flying, she'd accepted. His sixth proposal though, humbly and artfully phrased as it had been, allowed her to realize that for once in her life, she had some power in the bargain. Before her yes, she'd extracted several promises from him. He was to maintain a public stance that their relationship was completely normal in every way. Their sex life was fulfilling and he was satisfied in every way. As for their private matters of the heart, she released him from any bounds of forced intimacy, for marriages sake, and told him that if he was ever in the mood for more than she cared to contribute, he was allowed to discreetly, seek affections elsewhere. Though she never stated it outright, she was more in favor of his doing so.

No forced sex, and hopefully their marriage would quiet the whispered public rumors about her; this was the essence of their bargain. For his part in this, she agreed to allow him to control her business affairs. This was something they could both live with and when they married, and GP seemed to be ethical in his upholding the bargain they'd made, and Amelia had felt a huge weight lifted from her shoulders. Now that the ugliness of the spotlight of fame shone less harshly upon her, she could focus her time and attention upon flying. This made her happy in ways she couldn't even begin to describe.

The awkward specter that sex represented to her had come to a head years earlier, and it seemed too big a mountain to climb successfully until GP had come along with the perfect solution.

The awkwardness of sex had first confronted her years earlier when she'd had her first experience and it had not gone well. Amelia had always been self-conscious about her gangly looks, and she knew that she lacked the social graces that the more feminine girls had so easily acquired. Plainly put, she was not ready for sex, and had only agreed to it just to get it over with. It never occurred to her that it might be an ongoing problem.

The boy had been too eager, too fumbling, too forceful, and he had physically looked similar to Amelia's father. They had the same nose and eyes, and the idea of doing what they were doing made Amelia feel extremely uncomfortable when kissing him. When the boy felt that their petting session was ready to escalate beyond kissing, Amelia had begun to sweat furiously. She was grimly determined though, to get her first sexual experience behind her though, so she closed her eyes and allowed things to continue. She tried to shut out the image in her mind, of his face, which had become that of her father. The boy grunted and squirmed on top of her and she was unable to keep her eyes closed. At one point she felt as if she was going to vomit, and wondered if this was what losing one's virginity was like for every girl. Maybe what she was experiencing was normal. Was it supposed to be pleasurable? If so, was it supposed to be so for both the man and the woman, or just for the man?

When he'd thrust himself deep into the area between her legs, the pain has caused her to cry out. At first it had been a yelp of surprise, at the pain, but then she'd called out "No! Dad . . ." and this had caused the boy to stop, mid-thrust, and his eyes went wide as he looked into her face. She could smell the beer on his breath, see the sweat on his brow, and the look in his eyes was one of revulsion. "You sure are weird, Meely," using the nickname that her father and others used for her. Then he continued thrusting in and out until she'd felt the stickiness on her. She'd scrunched her eyes tight and had wrapped her arms around him and held him tight, not in a loving gesture, but one designed to help her avoid seeing his face until their session was finished.

Afterwards she realized that the stickiness was hers and his; her blood, his seed.

Since that one disastrous coupling, Amelia had felt queasy and awkward during sexual encounters. She relied on her trick of wrapping her arms around her partner and holding him close to avoid the face, and this seemed to have the desired effect in that it blotted out their face to her, so she was spared that particular torment, and it fooled her lover into thinking that she was holding on tightly in some sort of sexual or romantic enrichment. She'd also learned to squeeze her thighs together tightly, as if she was using her womanly regions to squeeze and choke the intruder. This caused the man to finish his thrusting much faster and then it was just the matter of receiving his seed. Usually, as fast as possible afterwards, she would get up and go to the bathroom and cleanse herself of all traces of her lover's stickiness, as the wetness in her made her feel dirty and ashamed. Since her first 'encounter' she had been unable to be around her father for very long with being uncomfortable. This made her feel guilty but she had no way of knowing how to rid herself of the feeling. When her parents divorced, she'd been secretly thrilled. She hoped to never feel guilty again just from looking in a man's face.

While searching wood and kindling and materials for tender she saw a man-made object under the brush. She leaned down and saw that it was her shoes! She pulled them out of the underbrush and squealing with delight she sat and laced the shoes up. It wasn't until she was almost through lacing up the left shoe that she realized that she had found something very important. She immediately unlaced the shoe and pulled the entire shoestring free of the eyelets. Now she could make a hand-bow and get a fire started. She unlaced the other shoe and then bit and chewed the shoestring until it was broken and she had two identical length pieces, then she re-laced both shoes with the two shortened shoestrings.

The light of the day was almost gone now, and she concentrated on what she knew about making a fire. She went back to her area, where she intended to make her permanent camp, and set up her fire-making rig.

Her 'camp' area was a semi-circle of large light-reddish rocks that were pitted and rough and was set back about twenty yards from the beach at the highest point from where the surf washed in at high tide. The rocks were buried into the sand protruding up about two to three feet in height, and they curved to form a natural wall so that Amelia could lean back against her 'rock couch' and look seaward. Looking west (to her right) along the beach, the wing of the Electra jutted up from the surf on the left (seaward) and further down across the beach to the right, almost a full mile away, she could the indented area of the jungle where their original camp was. Now it was Noonan's camp. She'd estimated that his camp was a mile from hers, which meant that the island was about two miles in length.

The only man-made item in sight other than the downed Electra was a shirt that hung from the upper branches of a coconut palm. She'd climbed the tree trunk on the second day to hang the distress flag. It had been hung there to alert rescuers that the island was not as barren as it might seem at first glance. No longer white, now it was washed out and faded and barely visible against the tree-line, as if the island itself wanted to keep their presence a secret. Now the pathetic 'flag' barely moved in the slight breeze and was hard to see from a mile away. From a vantage point offshore of two or three miles out, it would be practically invisible. Looking upon that flag was meant to provide them with hope, but it caused a deep despair within Amelia. She took her eyes away from the flag to stop the tears before they started.

If she sat with her back against the rocks, to her left, the island curved back to the east, and it was here that the rocky area met the sea, and formed a shallow pool. This was the farthest and Eastern-most edge of the island. The water here was just a two of three feet in depth, but she had already seen the two sharks visiting the pool area. Almost as if to remind her that they had more access to the sea that she would ever have.

On her immediate left, jutting forward from her rock-couch was a flat surface which she intended to use for eating, and maybe for building a cooking fire upon it. Heat the surface up and then plop down a fish or whatever meat she could find, and use the hot surface as a grill of sorts.

When she'd finished the hand-bow she set up her kindling and other materials on the flat rock. She looked around for any signs of Noonan, but could see nothing. It was completely dark now, the final rays of light had leached out of the sky a few minutes ago, and the only light was the soft light from the moon and stars above, and the whiteness of the sand on the beach. The surf rolled in from the sea, causing the white foamy edge of the water to advance and recede, and the volume of night sounds coming from the jungle behind her increased with the darkness, the ever-present birds, and what she assumed were monkeys even though she'd not seen any yet, and other assorted sounds. Other than these sounds she was utterly and completely alone. If she put her hands over her ears and closed her eyes she would for all intents and purposes, completely alone on the planet. For that matter, she wouldn't even need to close her eyes;

just wait a few moments for the moon to slide silently behind a cloud, cover her ears and she could convince herself that she'd become the new Eve, all alone on earth.

Turning her thoughts away from the maudlin, she considered fire-making. It would be much easier to make the fire with Noonan's help, but she dismissed the idea of heading into the jungle to look for him. Just one glance into the underbrush belied the presence of the rats, and that stopped her cold. Luckily the rats favored the cover of the jungle and she intended to give them a wide berth from now on.

She could walk the beach looking for Noonan, but the island was several miles around, according to what she'd seen before they'd gone down. The island was a three or four mile comma-shaped circumference, with an edge of a hundred yards of beach all the way around. It was maybe a mile and a half across at the thickest part of the island. Not much of an island.

She wondered if Noonan was still trying his own attempts to make fire. Unless he got lucky he wouldn't get one going, because he was doing it all wrong.

Amelia knew that a fire would help in many ways, but it was still a miserable island. It was difficult to sleep, what with all the fearsome noises coming from the jungle on one side, and the eerie silence of the ocean on the other side. Worse that the heat though, and the noises, almost as bad as the lack of water and food, was the sand. It was extremely fine-grained, like ground glass and it got everywhere. It rubbed one like sandpaper in every crevice and crack the human body had. It was in between her butt cheeks, in between her legs (in *that* area, which made the simple act of walking an excruciating experience), it was in the corners of her eyes and mouth, in her nose, in her scalp, on her elbows, and in between her toes. It was a constant source of irritation and it was impossible to rid oneself of it. Sleeping on the beach was like sleeping on sandpaper. But it was either sleep on the sand or take chances in the jungle with the rats. It simply *was* the island. The worst part was that she constantly had a dry mouth, and the sand-granules were always on the back of her throat or stuck to the roof of her mouth. She'd noticed Noonan being aggravated by it too, he was always spitting, as if he'd just tasted something disagreeable, and she knew that he was dealing with the same nasty taste in his mouth from the sand as she was.

•••

Noonan kicked a rat off of his foot as he watched through the brush. Amelia was making some sort of doohickey with string and a stick. He had been following her hither and thither, watching from a position just inside the tree-line of the jungle. The rats swarmed all around him. There must be millions of them. If you stood still long enough they'd try and climb up your legs under the pants, so he'd tucked the pants cuffs into his socks. Every now and then, one would fall from the branches over his head and land on his back or shoulders. He never imagined these small islands being so overrun with rats. He'd thought he'd heard monkeys howling too, but hadn't seen one yet. There were birds, of course, colorful parrots and other species, and lizards too. He had to assume that there were snakes, but he hadn't run across any so far.

Standing completely still, barely even breathing, seemed to cause the rats to lose interest, so he willed himself to become a statue as he watched Amelia trying to get fire by rubbing sticks together. She was doing it all wrong of course. They may teach survival courses in Boy Scouts and Girl Scouts, and they might use some fancy string bow to turn the sticks, but he didn't believe that it would work. All it took was good old-fashioned elbow grease. He gave Amelia ten minutes before she would get frustrated and give up. He knew, because he had tried for hours to make fire, but in the end, all his efforts were in vain.

He lifted his 'bowl' up and took a deep swallow of the water that he'd filled it with. He felt so much better since he'd filled up with water. He had been pretty dehydrated, and now he felt cooled and refreshed. The water tasted horrible, but there's no doubt his body needed it. Something dropped from the branches overhead and landed on the back of his neck. He reached back quickly to grab the rat but it dropped below the collar of his shirt and was trapped in between his bare back and the fabric of the shirt. He reached around to grab it, but it was frantically trying to escape. He thrashed around and got a hand on it, but it wiggled loose. He could feel its tiny feet on his bare back, and the tail swishing furiously across his skin. Then he pushed himself and fell backwards against the trunk of the coconut tree behind him. He heard and felt the squish as the rat was trapped and crushed. A thick flood of blood and guts dripped down the small of his back. He reached back and pulled the rat carcass out.

He heard a pop, a crackle, and he turned his focus back towards Amelia. He could see her face as she bent over to blow on a flame. She quickly fed kindling to it and within seconds her face was lit by a small fire. Noonan was stunned by the sight of the flames.

He reached back and wiped the rat guts off the small of his back. When he pulled his hand out he could see the oily black and red mixture of blood and guts smeared across his fingertips. He pulled his fingers forward and held them under his nose and sniffed the guts. They were a rank, oily smell. He stuck the tip of his tongue out, thinking maybe he'd check the taste, just a scotch, no more than a spoonful, but pulled back and decided it was foolish. There had to be better ways to eat on this island. Eating rats was simply uncivilized no matter where you happened to be, and no matter what the circumstances were.

●●●

CHAPTER 3

Amelia was comforted by the fire. The warmth obviously wasn't needed, but the light it offered gave her a sense of security as well as accomplishment. Her stomach growled, reminding her of her hunger, and she immediately began thinking about the crabs. She would need a way to cook them. Maybe Noonan's bowl would work at a way to cook them. She hoped they tasted better cooked than they had raw. Now they'd be able to boil any water they could found to make it drinkable. They could scoop up fifty or a hundred of the tiny crabs and boil them!

Off in the distance, over the darkness of the sea, she could see lightning again. She didn't even bother wishing that the rain would come their way. It was a wasted exercise. The rains would get here only if and when the winds pushed them here. Until that time, the lightning was just another reminder of something else that had been subtracted from their lives.

•••

Noonan walked away thinking that Amelia had gotten very lucky in her attempts to make fire. He could have made fire; it's just that the energy necessary to get the sticks moving with sufficient speed had made him dizzy. Plus, he was exhausted from their ordeal. She had simply gotten lucky. He marched stolidly along, determined that he would duplicate her feat.

Searching for kindling and dried moss and other forms of tender was difficult in the dark. Several times as he was reaching for a suitable stick, rats had jumped out and swarmed his hand. He wondered how it was that rats could get to such a desolate place as this island. It just didn't seem possible, it seemed against nature.

One ran up his shirt sleeve, up his bare arm, and came out from under his shirt at the back of his neck. Surprised by the attack Noonan had twisted violently and reached quickly around grabbed the vermin and threw it savagely against a tree trunk. The carcass fell a few feet away and the other rats swarmed it and began a feeding frenzy.

Watching the rodents feasting upon their fallen comrade, Noonan decided there must be millions of rats on this island. He decided that this island should be renamed 'Rat Island.'

When he'd reached for the rat, his hand had brushed against his ribs. He absently ran his hand up and down his chest and stomach. He'd always been thin, but healthy. Now though, his ribs stood out from his chest. His stomach was caved in as if someone was pushing an invisible ball against his stomach. His belly-button was about to be pressing against his backbone. His hand ran up and down, and his ribs were easily, individually felt by his fingertips. He needed food, badly. Being weak with hunger was one thing. He could deal with that. The fear that flashed wildly through his mind when he contemplated the idea that he might not eat again, that was a dizzying thought that made him frantic.

Nevertheless, he decided that eating rat would be a last and desperate choice, and the rat would definitely need to be cooked. He'd rather starve to death, and he would, if it came to eating raw rat.

He wandered through the jungle, hoping to get lucky and find something edible, or to find something man-made, something useful that previous visitors to the island had left behind. In his mind he ran through a long list of items that would be useful to stumble across and as he was fantasizing he saw a glint of white out of the corner of his eye. He turned to see what it was, and could see, forty yards away down the jungle trail, buried in the earth was something white. He ran towards it, and he looked around quickly, making sure that Amelia wasn't following him; he dropped to his knees to dig the object out of the ground. When he pried it out if the earth he gasped in surprise, it was a human skull! At least it looked human, it could be an ape or chimpanzee skull for all her knew, but it certainly looked human. Maybe this island wasn't too far off the shipping lanes after all.

He tried to imagine if there was a practical use for the skull, and couldn't think of one. He was about to toss it away when he realized that he did have a use for it. He unzipped his pants down and, setting the skull carefully on the ground, he peed into it. When he was done, he zipped up, and looking around quickly, he determined that he wasn't being spied upon. He picked up the skull and brought it to his lips and drank his pee. When he had a mouthful, he realized how badly it tasted and he spit it out. It was rancid and foul. Now he had a foul taste in his mouth and a useless skull. Angrily, he tossed the skull back into the jungle, and spit, hoping to get the offending taste out of his mouth. He decided that the skull was unlucky.

He walked away in a sullen mood glancing out towards the ocean where he saw a small dot of light on what must be the horizon. Because it was dark, he could delineate no discernible line that signified the separation between ocean and sky. He watched as it traveled across the horizon and then made a turn, there was no doubt that the light was man-made. A flicker of dual lights crisscrossed each other, and Noonan knew that these were powerful searchlights, obviously searching the surface of the water, looking for survivors. There was little doubt that this was a search party vessel, looking for them.

He turned and walked away, muttering to himself, wondering what he'd do if he couldn't get a fire started.

•••

Amelia scooped out a shallow depression in the sand to create a bed and fed her fire with branches until it was blazing. She immediately noticed one very welcome benefit that the fire produced, that it kept the rats at bay. The light and heat from the fire illuminated a circle about twelve feet around her, and the rats seemed unwilling to come any closer. It was as if an invisible barrier had been drawn around her. This development cheered her almost as much as any food would have. The problem of drinkable water though, loomed large in her mind.

Curling up, her arms crossed across her chest, she dropped her chin down and allowed her fatigue to pull her into a deep sleep.

•••

Noonan refilled his bowl with water after drinking his fill, and headed back towards Amelia and the fire. The sky over the ocean was dark; the white foamy edges of the incoming waves as they rolled up the beach being the only visible sign that anything existed beyond the beach. The beach itself was dark, with no moonlight to illuminate it the sand appeared muted and lifeless. Noonan noticed that there seemed to be hundreds of black rocks strewn across the beach, and he couldn't remember having seen them during the daylight. He didn't trust his memory though, since he'd only been on the island one day. The rocks appeared to be moving too, but Noonan knew that was impossible, and decided that it was some sort of optical illusion.

He snuck in close to the campfire and saw that Amelia was asleep. She'd scooped out a hammock-like depression in the sand, and was laying in it. Noonan wondered if this was something else that she'd been taught by someone on her 'camp-outs' with her girls group.

He carefully placed the water bowl next to him, and then lay down next to the fire. He grinned when he looked back towards the tree-line and saw that the rats were unwilling to come any closer to the fire than the edge of the circle of light and heat that the fire produced around them. Maybe the depression in the sand allowed her to sleep near the fire and still avoid some of the heat. He scooped out his own depression and lay down in it.

He laid his head down using a large piece of driftwood as a pillow. He was just drifting off to sleep when he heard a snort from Amelia who'd just woken.

•••

Amelia woke with a start. Some outside noise had intruded into her dreams and brought her back to consciousness. She sat up and looked around, thinking that the rats had come for her. Then she saw Noonan sleeping across from her on the opposite side of the fire.

He must have just lain down because he wasn't asleep yet. He looked at her defiantly.

"What are you doing here, Noonan?" as soon as the words left her mouth, she realized just how accusing she sounded.

"I'm sleeping, just as you are."

"This is *my* campsite, Noonan," she said, "*my* fire, not yours. You walked away, saying you don't need me; that I, a woman, would only get in your way."

"We can share the fire Amelia. It's not like it's hurting you to let me sit over here."

Amelia stared at him for a moment, wondering if she should send him on his way. Could she even do that? If he physically wanted to overpower her, he could. She also wondered if she had it in her to be cruel enough to send him away. It was her belief that as survivors, they should work together as a team, and help each other until the rescuers arrived. That was their best chance of making it through this accident in the best shape.

Still though, he had told her in no uncertain terms that he felt that she was a liability.

"This is my campsite, Noonan; you should go and make your own."

"Amelia, you aren't God. You don't *own* fire. It's a natural resource. You can easily share it."

"Well, I own *this* fire. You want fire, go make your own. I'm just playing by your rules, Noonan. You know what they say, 'What's good for the goose is good for the gander."

"Are you saying that you will not share your campsite and your fire with me?" Noonan asked incredulously, "Are you really saying that you think that you can survive on your own, without me?"

"Yes, of course I am. I don't know why that gets your dander up, especially after the way you've acted towards me."

"You better think about this Amelia."

"Yesterday you were completely scornful of me, and you avowed that you'd watch me die, Noonan. Now you've taken a turn of face and you are begging to share with me?"

Noonan's face dropped when she said the word begging, and she knew that his temper was about to flare. Maybe she should reconsider. See if he would be amenable to starting over, as partners, just to survive until the rescuers arrived, which would be soon.

As she debated with herself what to do, she noticed something odd about Noonan. He looked different than he had several hours ago. Then she gasped with the understanding of what it was. He'd found water. He looked refreshed, as if he'd been hydrated. Then, as if to prove her assumption, she noticed the 'bowl' next to him.

"What's that, Noonan?" she asked, pointing at the bowl.

"It's water."

"You found water?"

"Yes, I did. And a lot of it too," he smiled slyly, "you have no idea how good it feels to get your fill."

Amelia's eyes widened. Almost unconsciously, she licked her lips, which were already cracked and broken and bleeding. Her stomach rumbled. The idea of getting her fill of water suddenly became her only thought.

"How much do you have there?" she nodded at the jagged steel bowl.

"Plenty to get you more than filled up, a gallon or so," he said as he reached down and picked up the crude bowl and held it up to his face. He couldn't see her now, the bowl blocking his face from hers, "unless I decide to drink it all there's plenty for you too," he tilted the bowl up and opened his mouth and poured some into his mouth, and he allowed a generous splash of it to run down his face and onto his shirt front and the ground in front of him.

"Don't waste it, Noonan!" Amelia gasped as she sat up to her knees. She looked at the precious water that had soaked the sand next to him. She noticed that the surface of the water was covered in the green bubbles that she'd seen in the ocean surf. Maybe he'd gotten it there, and then had boiled it to purify it. Or maybe he'd found a water source inland, and it too had the green bubbles that were in the surf. Maybe it was some sort of moss.

"Waste it? Well, it's mine, Amelia, and I'll do what I want with it."

"Don't be wasteful, Noonan. Let's make a bargain."

Noonan lowered the bowl and set it on the sand next to him. "What kind of deal do you have in mind, Amelia?"

"You can stay here, and use my fire," she hesitated, and looked again at the bowl. She sensed that Noonan might try to trick her, but she couldn't sense how he could do it. The water was right there, she'd seen him drink it. She needed it, more than anything. At this point that water was life, more so than her fire.

"That's the bargain, Noo- Noonan. You share my fire, we use it to cook, and keep those stinking rats at bay, and I get some of your water."

Noonan pretended to think it over, "Sounds like a fair bargain, Amelia," he grinned, "I certainly wouldn't want to leave you high and dry."

"Great, I just want a drink, right now-" she started to get up, but Noonan spoke and stopped her in her tracks.

"-but, I want," he paused.

"What?"

He grinned, "I want the fire-making materials. Your little bow-thing, and the rocks, the sticks, and whatever kindling you have left, all of it, Amelia. I don't trust you any longer, so I want the whole kit and caboodle, *everything*."

"Noonan it surely wounds me to hear you speak like that."

Amelia looked back and her tiny stash of belongings. The sticks, the shoe-string, the flat rock and a small handful of kindling that she'd laid out for when the fire needed to be rebuilt. To give up her materials would be foolish, but it she died of thirst, all the fire-making materials in the world wouldn't be of any use to her.

She sighed, "Okay, it's a deal, but I get my share of water now. Shall we swap now?"

"Even Steven," he nodded and held his hand out for the fire-making kit.

Amelia gathered up her fire-kit and walked around the fire towards Noonan. She held it out to him, but pulled back just before he got it into his hand.

"but-" she said, and he glanced up at her, anger in his face.

"You are going to go back on your word? A deal's a deal, Amelia."

"-just one stipulation, Fre- *Noonan*."

Their eyes locked and Amelia tried to see into his head, to see if she could see into the corners where duplicity lurked. She could make nothing out for his eyes were like shutters on a house. You knew they covered windows, but that knowledge wouldn't allow you to see inside if they were closed.

"What Amelia?"

"I want to see the source of the water."

Noonan smiled and then nodded, "No problem, A E."

Amelia grimaced. Very few people called her 'A E', just G P and some friends. Noonan may be her navigator, but he was no good friend. She knew, upon hearing his greasy rendition of her nickname that they would never, ever, be friends after their rescue. Once they left this island she never wanted to see him again.

She handed over the fire kit which he immediately tucked down into the front of his own shirt.

"Give it up, Noonan," she snapped her fingers in front of him, "give me the water bowl," the words coming out a little angrier than she intended.

He smiled and Amelia instantly sensed something was wrong, and she immediately feared that he would be the one to *renig* on their deal. Instead, he simply stood and walked towards the fire. He sat down and looked around him. Amelia knelt down on her knees and picked up the bowl. The water in it sloshed and Amelia realized that there was probably a half-gallon of water in the bowl. She leaned forward and tilted the bowl towards her mouth and then took a deep swallow, the cool water ran down the sides of her mouth and onto her shirt.

As soon as the water went down her throat she began choking, coughing and spitting the water out. She set the bowl onto the sand in front of her and turned,

"Noonan, this is seawater!" she glared at him.

Noonan grinned, "Yes, it is."

"That's ridiculous. That's not what-"

"I drank my fill, and nothing has happened to me, I haven't dropped dead yet."

Amelia's mouth dropped open, "Noonan! How could you? You know it's wrong. The last thing we're supposed to do is drink sea-water. It won't help us. In fact, it will kill us eventually. I can't believe you've done this. How much did you drink anyway?"

"I drank my fill Amelia that's how much, and I'm none the worse the wear for it."

"But Noonan, you'll get sick, and I probably will too. What you've done to us is simply . . . unconscionable."

"Nonsense, Amelia. It's just to help us get by until we find a water source."

Amelia sat down and stared at him. Had he lost his mind?

"That was not our bargain, Noonan. I want my fire kit back."

"That's baloney. We traded fair and square."

"You cheated me, Noonan. You said that you found a water source and that you'd share it with me."

"No, Amelia, I didn't skin you. I told you I found a water source, and I did. The water source is," he waved his hand towards the ocean, "right there."

"That is not right and you know it Noonan. I meant a source of fresh-water. The fat's in the fire when we stoop to drinking sea-water."

"It's not the beginning of trouble to slake our thirst, Amelia. Besides you didn't say that my water source had to be fresh water."

"Noonan, you rooked me and you know it. You know very well what I meant and yet you shystered me into thinking you'd found a real source of fresh-water. You didn't *find* the ocean any more than I *found* the sky. Your part in our deal was conceived in duplicity from the very start."

Amelia wanted to scream at him. What had happened to the mild-mannered man that she'd come to know over the past few weeks and months? Since the crash he'd changed. If she had just met him she'd say that he was mentally unbalanced.

She tried to think in terms of their situation here. Their priority was to find food and water for survival. Survival would be easier if they worked together, especially if their rescue was delayed a few days, as it appeared to have been, for some unknown reasons. Amelia felt sure they'd spend less than three days on this island, and a week tops if something had gone wrong with rescue ships, or some sort of a hang-up in their being spotted and tracked.

It seemed paramount to her that she should convince Noonan that they needed to work together, rather than fight, during their short stay on the island. It just made good sense to act as a team, just as they did when flying, rather than being at loggerheads with each other. Amelia had always prided herself at being level-headed. She never gave in to emotion, and never flew off the handle if she got upset. Her cool head was what was needed in circumstances such as these. She may not be a leader, but she was intelligent, and always made the correct decisions, even in times of crisis.

"Noonan, we need to work together to make it through this situation, as a team. We can't keep fighting like cats and dogs like this."

"Why, Amelia?"

"Why? Because it just makes *sense*, that's why. Two heads are better than one."

"But *you* have nothing that *I* need Amelia. In fact, you need me more than I need you. As a team, you weaken me, whereas, in a team, I strengthen you."

Amelia blinked, completely at a loss for words.

"That's just a ridiculous statement. I made fire. What have you done?"

"I saved our lives. I found water."

"You *found* water?" she laughed, "You did no such thing. You don't *find* the ocean, you can't miss it."

"Did you not just drink water for the first time since we crashed?"

"Not fresh water. Noonan, if anything, you have decreased our chances of survival. If our rescue wasn't on its way here this very moment, I'd go so far as to say that you have actually endangered our lives. As it is we will probably get sick from the sea-water we drank."

"That's hooey. There's nothing wrong with that water. Beats drinking our piss like we've been doing."

"It goes against all medical opinion *and facts* and you call that *nonsense?*"

"I think it's just medical *theory* that sea-water is bad for you."

Amelia shook her head, "Noonan, you can try to defy medical knowledge if it suits you, but as for me, I'll not be drinking any more sea-water. Furthermore, based upon the deceit on your part in our bargain, I'll ask you to hand over my fire kit. It was gained by your own treachery and dishonorable intent and I'll not allow it to stand. I'll share it if you want to work together as a team, otherwise, that fire kit constitutes the fruits of my labors, and you have come by it dishonestly, you . . . boondoggled me out of it by outright fraud."

"It's survival of the fittest Amelia. So you can go to hell for all I care," Noonan said as he rubbed his hands in front of the fire as if warming them, despite the fact that sweat ran down his forehead in rivulets.

Amelia was again shocked by Noonan's behavior, and wondered if perhaps his head had been damaged in the crash. She knew that sometimes a person could receive a blow to the head, and they were forever changed. When she saw his grin though, she realized that his words and actions were deliberate.

Amelia sighed and looked down at her shoes. She still had an entire shoelace, plus a half. That alone made her decision, and she knew what she must do. She stood. She picked up the bowl of sea-water and walked back towards Noonan and the fire.

"In that case, *Noonan,* I'll be returning your water to you, even if you won't return my fire kit to me," Amelia held the bowl up and poured it out over the fire, the water and fire meeting with hissing, sputtering noises and the smoke floating up into her face.

Noonan yelped, "What the hell!" and jumped up to push Amelia back, but it was too late. He grabbed the bowl from her hands, its final drops of water trickling through his fingers, and Amelia turned and walked away, wishing she'd had the gumption to snatch the hand-bow away out of his hand.

•••

Noonan watched as the darkness came in over the beach and his eyes went wide when he saw the rats coming out from the underbrush and threateningly towards him. The light began to disperse, and Noonan felt sweat break out on his forehead. He backed away from the tree-line and closer to the beach behind him.

Backing slowly away from the edge of the jungle, he felt the warm white sand crunching under his feet. The fire had hissed out only moments ago, and already the jungle tree-line was swarming in blackness. Black dots moving on a blacker background, the thousands of rats filling the void where once had been light. His eyes were unable to see the individual rats, and the effect of the black swarming mass of the vermin against the black night caused him to feel dizzy. The jungle floor where the mass of rats was swarming seemed to grow outward onto the white sand, pushing him further backwards towards the waterline of the waves upon the beach. There was no reason to dilly-dally, so he turned and walked faster, making it to the waterline, where the wet sand was a different color than the dry beach. He looked to his left as he walked towards the water, trying to make out the dark silhouette of Amelia as she walked down the beach away from him, but he saw nothing but the white sand of the beach, the inky blue water to the right, and the black density of the jungle on the left. He shuddered as he considered what would happen if he fell asleep near the jungle where the rats could swarm over him. It was unimaginable.

When he felt the cool wet sand underfoot, he turned to contemplate the jungle. He knew that he must sleep, and he couldn't sleep on the wet sand, but he didn't want to get too close to the jungle and the rats, so he decided to make camp about twenty yards away from the jungle tree-line, which put him about another fifty yards away from the high tide line on the beach. He walked out into the surf up to his knees and dipped his bowl into the surf, and then he tilted the bowl up to his mouth and drank enough to fill his stomach. He didn't know why he bothered with the bowl anyway, all he had to do was walk into the waves and drink, but it seemed like a good idea to have water with him wherever he went, just in case. He looked seaward and saw nothing but the blackness of the ocean. There was no moonlight. The edges of the incoming waves were tinged in white foam. He watched as the waves rolled in, then receded back to where they'd come from. He turned back towards the island and was walking back up the beach when the meteorite flashed across the sky, and brilliant fiery ball driving across the sky above the trees, travelling from his right to his left. It blazed across the sky and then fizzled out on the horizon in a fiery burst, as if it had exploded onto the ocean's surface. He wondered if it was a harbinger of some sort, foretelling dire circumstances ahead, or perhaps great luck, untold wealth. Noonan closed his eyes, and the fiery meteor light trail was still there, burned into the back of his eyelids. He kept his eyes closed until the image dissipated and then continued walking up the beach.

He walked back up the beach to an area that he thought was far enough out that the rats wouldn't attack him, and he sat down, spread his legs and pulled out the fire kit that he'd finagled out of Amelia. He wondered if he could use the bowl as some sort of frying pan, once he got a fire started, and then wondered what he could find to cook and eat. He began rubbing the sticks together, this time using the hand-bow, but he was unable to get the right rhythm that would produce flame, or even a spark.

The thought flitted through his mind that the rat population was a plentiful source of meat, and he thought about finding a stick to club them with. The hot bowl would fry up the rat meat rather nicely once he had enough of it. Of course, he'd have to rig up some sort of handle so that he could manipulate it over the fire. Then, realizing he was thinking about eating rat, he shuddered. He was starving, but he didn't think he'd ever be hungry enough to eat rat.

•••

Amelia flung the rats off of the stick and threw the stick itself further out onto the beach. She kept repeating the process until she had a good sized pile of wood. It was far enough out on the beach that the rats didn't go to it, and one or two of the pieces were small enough that she could splinter them into small enough pieces to make a new fire kit. The remainder would be for the fire. Once she had the wood, she skirted along the very edge of the jungle and gathered enough dried moss and kindling pieces to ensure that she had enough starter materials. Then she sat down, spread her legs, and arranged her materials in front of her. Unlacing her shoe she measured off enough length to make her hand-bow and then using her teeth, chewed through the shoe string until she bit it in half. She re-laced her shoe with the leftover shoelace, and then set to work making a new hand-bow. It was a difficult task because she had nothing more than moon light to work with. Plus, she was sweating profusely and her weakened state was slowing her down. She knew that she should try to get along with Noonan. That bowl was valuable as a tool. Boiling sea-water in it, until they found a supply of drinkable water made that bowl a life-saver. Until she convinced him to share with her, and help *them* survive, she was going to be forced to continue drinking her own urine. That wouldn't last much longer anyway. She was producing less and less urine to drink. Not to mention that it couldn't be healthy having urine as one's only source of water. Not only that, but it was difficult to drink her own urine. Since she had nothing to collect it in, her only way of managing the feat was to pull her pants down, or off, and then spread her legs and cup her hands underneath her. Then she had to pee, which was a difficult task in that position, and then she had to keep her hands together until she finished. Then she had to slowly, carefully bring her hands up to her mouth and drink, praying that she didn't spill the precious liquid. All in all, it was a very difficult maneuver, and made unnecessarily more difficult to perform when she was afraid that Noonan would catch her with her pants down. But, it was her only way to get water, unless she happened to come across a coconut that had been split open with a few ounces of juice left inside. Those were very rare treats though.

After finishing the hand-bow, she went looking for a piece of sea-shell or rock that would serve as a base. Once she found what she needed, she sat back down, arranged the materials, and set the kindling next to the base. She huffed out several breaths, and then began rubbing. After a few minutes she had a spark, but she was unable to get the soft kindling next to it in time for it to catch. She re-arranged her kindling until it was actually underneath her stick and tried again. Within minutes she had a small fire and she fed it with larger and larger pieces until it was crackling nicely. She sat back and took a deep breath and relaxed, satisfied that she had overcome the obstacle that Noonan had created for her. As long and she had shoelaces, she had fire. She thought she could make it without the shoelaces, using vines from the jungle, but knew that it would be much more difficult to manage. She also knew that some of the many types of palm trees on the island had thin fibrous strings that she might be able to adapt, but keeping the shoestrings was a priority. Of course, it was all a moot point, since they would probably be rescued tomorrow or the next day anyway.

Several times during her efforts, she'd heard noises coming from the jungle. She knew there were rats and birds, but whatever other jungle life there was, she had no clue. Several times while trying to light the fire she'd had the feeling that Noonan was watching her.

She was almost certain that he was out there. She could feel his eyes watching her from the cover of the jungle a few yards away. It's a wonder that she couldn't smell him. His stink of shit, piss and vague odors of some unknown sort was palpable, and figured hers was too, but thankfully she hadn't smelled any rank odor emanating from herself. The thought that he might be lurking a few yards aways set her on edge. It terrified her that he might try to harm her, or steal her fire-kit again. She dared not sleep either, because he was almost certainly lurking nearby in the darkness. Was he planning to pounce upon her as soon as her eyes closed, or was he just seething in his strangely misplaced anger, his new hatred at her success in making fire? She didn't want to have to regret choosing him as her navigator, but so far, he was making it easy to do so.

•••

Noonan had no intention of going near the jungle tree-line in the dark. The rats would surely swarm him. His throat tightened up at the very thought of being swarmed by them. He shuddered.

He stayed at the line where the surf met the beach and walked from one end of the beach to the other. He stopped where the beach gave way to a shallow crossing. It was low tide and the channel that led into the interior lagoon of the island was probably no more than knee deep. He would have gone across, but he saw two shark fins and lost his enthusiasm for further exploration. He turned back and made his way back down the beach, never once spying Amelia. He guessed that she was unable to get a fire started, just as he had been.

He dug a shallow indentation into the sand in the shape of his body. He lay down in it and almost immediately fell asleep.

•••

Amelia kept the fire roaring, and woke up several times during the night to pull more kindling into it. The fire seemed to keep the rats at bay, though it was fiercely hot. She lay on her side with her back to the fire facing the beach. She slept fitfully, and every time she woke she looked fearfully behind her to see if the rats were advancing upon the camp. An hour or so before sunrise she woke up and couldn't sleep anymore, and decided to have a look around.

She walked up and down the beach, looking for anything useful that would allow them to be more comfortable until the rescue. Glancing out towards the water she scanned the horizon and her heart began pounding. A rescue ship!

Screaming at the top of her lungs for Noonan, she ran to the surf and ran forward until she was knee deep in the oncoming waves. She put her hand across her brow to block out unnecessary light. She leaned forward and took a few more steps into the crashing surf. Her whole body leaned forward, as if by doing so she could close the distance between herself and the ship.

Her eyes were not deceiving her either, as it was definitely a ship, crawling slowly across the horizon on the thin line edge that marked where the ocean met the sky. It was travelling from left to right, and it seemed like a decent-sized ship too. Something large, either a Navy ship, or perhaps something that G P had hired to do searches. Whatever it was, it was not small. There was no doubt in her mind that the ship was a search and rescue ship, looking for them. She turned her head again and cried out to Noonan.

"Noonan! Get down here, quick, it's the rescue ship!"

She swiveled her head back around quickly, so as not to lose her sight-place of where the ship was on the horizon, and she realized then that she was making a horrible mistake. Instead of watching the rescue ship steaming across the horizon, she needed to be sending it a signal. What was needed was fire and smoke.

She backed out of the waves and back up onto the beach without once turning around. She was afraid to take her eyes off the ship. As if, by blinking, or by turning her head away from it, it might vanish, or simply cease to exist. Then she realized how foolish that thought was, it wasn't a mirage, the ship was real.

Finally, she tore herself away from the scene and ran as fast as she could to the fire and threw herself down in front of it. There were embers still glowing and she grabbed a palm frond, leaned down, her cheek almost on the sand, and began blowing and fanning them. When a puff of flame rose up, she scrabbled backwards and grabbed handfuls of wood chips and bark that lay scattered about and began throwing them into the fire. As soon as the fire was roaring, she ran towards the jungle and began loading up with everything she could find that would burn and produce smoke. Hands trembling she fed the fire until thick black smoke was billowing into the sky.

Heart hammering, her hands trembling, she allowed herself the luxury of running out to the beach where she scanned the horizon line for the ship. She could still see a speck on the far right side of the horizon. Then she blinked, and the ship must have slid over the edge of the world for all she knew, because one minute it was there, and the next it wasn't. It was gone. She felt tears rolling down her face.

She startled when she heard the voice behind her.

"What are you screaming about Amelia?"

She spun around.

"Noonan! A rescue ship, out there! I've been watching them. I made a signal fire. But now they're gone," she explained.

Noonan said nothing, just stared at her.

"Noonan, did you hear me? I just saw a rescue ship! Right out there," she pointed towards the ocean.

"So what," Noonan said blandly. He didn't even glance at the direction she pointed. Instead, he turned to walk away.

Amelia was stunned. She stepped towards him and grabbed him by the arm and spun him around to face her.

"So what? Is that all you can say, *so what?*"

Noonan simply stared at her and said nothing.

"Noonan, don't you understand? We're rescued! We've been spotted, aren't you happy?"

Noonan harrumphed, "No, Amelia, we're not rescued. Take a look out there," he said as he grabbed her by the arms and spun her around, "where are they? Huh? They didn't see us."

"Noonan, how can you say that? They might have seen my signal fire smoke."

"No, Amelia, they didn't," he pointed to the horizon again, "They didn't see us, or your stupid smoke because if they did, they'd be heading in here right now. Instead, they've moved on, most likely to start searching another grid."

Amelia looked to the horizon again. The ship was still gone. It seemed that Noonan was probably right. Her heart sank.

"But..."

"No butts, Amelia. Besides, that ship, out there on the horizon, was probably fifteen miles away, maybe even twenty or more. I think the curvature of the earth is sixteen miles from one point to the horizon over a flat surface. So, even if you did see them, there's no way they could have seen us. It's impossible."

He shook his head slowly, as if he couldn't believe he had to explain something so basic to a pilot.

"It's not impossible, Noonan," she argued, "Nothing's impossible."

He guffawed, "Amelia, you remember how long it took us to see this tiny little island from the air? Up there," he pointed a finger straight up, "that's the best vantage point there is. And *we* didn't see this tiny little sliver of land, which is damn near four miles long, until we were right on top of it."

"Still, they could have seen the smoke..."

"Not even possible at that distance. Forget it, Amelia; don't waste your time and energy getting your hopes up."

"Noonan, why must you be such a naysayer, a cynic and constantly deride our chances of rescue. Don't you even *want* to be rescued?"

"Of course I do."

Amelia turned away from him and crossed her arms across her chest and stared out at the ocean.

Noonan continued, "But I also know the reality of our situation. If we went crazy every time we saw a ship steaming across the ocean twenty miles out, we'd drive ourselves insane rather quickly. This is why I said nothing the other night-"

Amelia whirled around, her eyes fiery with indignation, "What? You mean to tell me that you saw another rescue ship, maybe *that same one*, and you decided to say *nothing* about it?"

"What's the point Amelia?"

"What's the point? The point, Noonan, is *rescue*; getting off this God-forsaken island and back to civilization, to our families!"

Noonan shook his head, "You're not thinking clearly, Amelia."

Seething, Amelia turned her back to him again and began using her eyes to re-scan the surface of the ocean, from left to right, hoping to catch another glimpse of the rescue ship.

"You're deluding yourself, Amelia. The so-called *rescue*, is centered on the area where our last known radio call emanated from. That's where they're assuming, *wrongly*, that we went down. Meanwhile, we're fifty or sixty, or a hundred miles further away. So, Amelia, your *rescue*, is doomed from the start."

Amelia ignored him, but wanted to go slap his face, knock some sense into him. She sat down, drew her legs up, and rested her elbows on her knees and kept her eyes on the water and the sky overhead. She wanted to be ready when they returned.

●●●

CHAPTER 4

The next two days were miserable.

At some point Amelia realized that she had somehow turned her right ankle, and it was swelling and turning bluish. It was now causing her to pull up instead of putting weight on it. She limped over to the edge of the beach and sat down at the waters edge. The incoming waves rolled in towards her, the edge of the waves foamy with the green bubbles. She wanted to go out into the incoming rollers and let the cool waves wash over her, but one glance offshore showed the duo of sharks patrolling the surf, horizontal to the beach. Back and forth they swam, in what must be less than three feet of water. Amelia had no interest whatsoever in testing them to see how close in to shore they were willing to swim. Instead she sat at the water's edge, where the incoming waves washed ashore up to her legs, and she allowed the foamy edge of the surf to wash up over her feet. The edges of the surf, with the algae colored bubbles foamed over her legs, the waves receding back into the larger surf, leaving behind the green bubbles on her ankle. The bubbles dissipated into the air when the water receded, leaving her ankle feeling warm. The water itself was cool, but the green foamy bubbles somehow felt warm on the ankle. Amelia lay back and left her legs soaking in the incoming surf. She must have slept for a few minutes because when she came awake, the tide had receded enough that the water was no longer coming in enough to cover her feet and ankles.

She got to her feet and began walking back to her camp. As she walked she realized that she was no longer limping. She stopped and looked down at the ankle. It was no longer swollen or discolored. She slowly put her full weight on the foot. No pain whatsoever. She decided that maybe she had over overestimated how badly it had been hurt. It looked and felt perfectly fine now.

The heat was so intense that Amelia felt as if someone had thrown a hot blanket over her and she was slowly suffocating. The lack of food had created in both of them, a lassitude that negated the will to move about. The less energy expelled the better. Every movement came at a high-cost, through pain, general discomfort, or the knowledge that every unnecessary movement put them into energy debit. Food was energy, and food was so scarce that one needed to carefully plan every move so that when food was obtainable, the energy needed to procure it was available. Their food to energy to food circle was rapidly getting smaller and smaller. If something regarding their food supply didn't happen soon, they would be relegated to digging in the sand where they lay for insects.

Noonan had wandered off and Amelia had no idea where he was, probably trying to find a shady spot to sleep where he wasn't pestered by the rats.

Amelia hadn't been bothered too much by the rats, but then, she had no idea how close they were creeping up to her as she slept. She shuddered at the thought. She finally slept, but at one point during the night she was awakened in a cold sweat by a scream from the jungle. She'd sat up and swiveled around towards the sound, and it came again. The scream sounded like a man screaming in pain and, heart hammering in her chest she'd jumped to her feet and cupped her hands around her mouth and yelled out for Noonan.

The only answer to her call-out had been the usual noises from the jungle, which were disquieting enough for her. The hissing noises of the rats, the click-click-clicking of the crabs claws, and something large rustling around in the brush just a few yards away, just out of sight in the inky blackness of the jungle. The sounds were unnerving and every time she closed her eyes to sleep the noises would fade, lulling her to sleep, and then some sound would bring out of a dead sleep fully awake, shaking with fright and instantly she'd be jerking around towards the sound to see what it was that was sneaking up on her. No sooner than she'd jerk around at the sounds that the rats would scurry back into the foliage, but she could swear that she could make out their beady red eyes in the void of the jungle. It seemed to her that they were there, peeking out at her, waiting; biding their time until she was relaxed, asleep and vulnerable so they could launch their attack. It was unnerving and deeply unsettling to her psyche, and it said more about her physically exhausted state that she actually did, finally drift off to sleep.

CHAPTER 5

Noonan was sleeping deeply when a noise awakened him. He jerked awake, startled, his mind had already accepted the idea that foreign noises on this island would be man-made.

The sound rang in his ears and he tried to identify it, but he had no source by which to name it. A completely unfamiliar sound that one had never been confronted with was rare. The old saying about the tree in the forest, if one cared to analyze it, simply meant that every sound heard by man could be identified, simply because most all sounds are familiar. He sat up and looked around. It was still dark, and he turned and peered into the darkness that was the jungle. He decided that it must have been Amelia doing something that had caused the sound.

He looked back out towards the sea, and he ruminated over the mystery of the Electra. One moment it was there, and then it had simply disappeared. When Amelia had told him that it was gone he figured that she was turned around, but he could see that she was correct; the plane had disappeared. Noonan had waded out from the beach and was stunned to see nothing there, where hours earlier, an airplane had sat on the coral in the water. He was convinced that it had simply fallen off the back of the coral ledge and dropped into the deeper water. Tomorrow morning he'd swim out further and dive down to see if he could spot it. If it wasn't too deep, maybe he'd be able to salvage some useful items from the interior.

He jerked his head around at the sound and then got to his feet. There it was again, that same sound. Almost like a bat hitting a ball. It was a hollow 'plonk' sound. His eyes picked out the tiniest bit of movement in the shadows where the beach met the jungle.

It wasn't Amelia. Whatever was moving was too small. If it had been her he would have known it immediately. Whatever this was it was small, maybe an animal. Maybe one of the pigs whose tracks he'd seen. Now that would be some good eating, roasted pork. Almost as if on cue, his stomach rumbled. Then the noise repeated itself and he saw the movement again, *plonk,* and then something small moved out from under a coconut tree at the edge of the jungle.

Whatever it was that had moved now became still. Noonan locked his eyes upon the small shadow and he walked towards it. He expected it to run, because it was almost undoubtedly some small animal, but whatever it was didn't move. Noonan hoped it was edible, because if it was injured, it would be more easily caught.

Keeping his eyes locked on it he approached the tree-line. When he was within fifteen feet he stopped. His eyes must have been playing tricks on him, because there was nothing here but a green coconut at the base of the tree. He squatted down and looked around.

The *plonk* sound had been the coconut hitting the trunk of the tree as it fell. The movement he'd seen had been the coconut falling and rolling. Noonan sighed. This was disappointing. He had already allowed his imagination to conjure up a meaty feast. He knew that these coconuts were almost impossible to open without a knife, a machete, or something very sharp or heavy enough to smash them with.

He heard a rustling in the jungle as was about to stand up when a coconut smashed into his shoulder and the side of his head. The blow stunned him and he jumped up and looked up to the leaves above him. There was some sort of movement up there. Probably just a breeze making the fronds move a little. Then he just about jumped out of his skin as he heard a voice behind him.

"What the heck is that?"

He spun around, heart pumping wildly, and stepped back from the voice. Amelia. He slumped, and noticed that his hands were shaking.

"God dammit, Amelia, you scared the hell out of me. Why are you sneaking up behind me like that?"

"Noonan, I will ask you once again, could you please not use such foul language?"

He ignored her.

She pointed her finger at a spot halfway up the long-curved trunk of the coconut tree.

"What the heck is . . . that hideous *thing*, Noonan?"

Noonan sight-followed the direction she pointed and then his eyes went wide when he saw it.

"Oh my, that's a doozy!" Noonan said. Out of the corner of his eye he saw Amelia back up a few steps. Whether she did so out of fear or in order to see it more clearly he didn't know.

"What is it, Noonan?"

"That, Amelia is a *Palm Thief*, also known as a *Robber Crab*, or *Coconut Crab*."

"That's a crab? I've never seen a crab that large before. I didn't know they got so large. That must be what, a foot and a half across?"

"More like two and a half, almost three. That's a small one. I've heard that some get as big as six to six and a half feet across. They are strange creatures too. They have ten legs, you know."

Amelia shuddered, "And apparently, they climb trees."

Noonan nodded, "Yes, they climb coconut trees and cut down the hanging coconuts. The coconuts can burst open if they hit on something hard or sharp down below. If they don't crack open from the fall, these crabs have sharp enough pinchers that they can cut them open. That's how they eat the coconuts. They've been known to drop out of the trees onto people below. At least that's what Peterson, the pilot who told me about them, says. All this time I thought he was just bullshitting me about these things. He was a dipsomaniac, never went anywhere without his flask of whiskey, but he lived on an island for over two years."

Amelia's eyes got wide and she quickly stepped out from under the tree. So, with snakes and rats to watch out for, now she was apparently going to have to watch the trees overhead to make sure that these ugly creatures didn't fall on her head. Could this island get any more miserable? She shivered just thinking about one of the nasty creatures falling onto her head, or back or shoulders.

"Well Noonan, since you're the resident crab expert on this island . . . are they edible like other crabs?"

Noonan shook his head, "I've heard it both ways; that they're a delicacy, but he also said that once in a blue moon they're highly poisonous. Peterson also said that these crabs, once they became adults, couldn't live in sea-water. It kills them rather quickly."

"That's hard to fathom. They're crabs, which come from the sea, but once they're grown the sea-water will kill them?"

"That's what he said, and he seemed to know an awful lot about them too. Until I saw this one," he pointed up the tree, "I would have sworn the guy was pulling my leg about them. But the thing that interests me most is that they are a delicacy-"

"Or they are highly poisonous."

"Believe what you want to believe, I say we cook one up and see for ourselves."

"We better not chance it. We don't want to get poisoned. Besides, the rescuers should be here soon."

He gave her an incredulous look, "You can act like a high-brow connoisseur and starve if you want Amelia, but I'm going to have a go at it and eat some crab!"

"But Noonan, if you get sick, there'll be nothing that I can do to help!"

He shook his head at her, "Doesn't matter, we're going to die here anyway. Besides, I'm betting that they're not poisonous."

"And that's based on what?"

"It's a hunch, and I say we get on with it. Dinner awaits," he grinned at her.

Amelia wondered if he was crazy or just careless. He was gaunt enough from their forced starvation that she wondered if she wouldn't do the same. She was only in marginally better condition that he was. His eyes still had that crazy gleam and the hair on one side of his head appeared to have been chopped short.

"Noonan, have you found some scissors?"

"Scissors?"

"Yes. It looks like you've given yourself a partial haircut, there." She said as she reached up and touched the side of her own head, to show him where she was referring to on his hair.

He reached up and touched the side of his head just over his ear. With his fingers he tested the length of the hair. He shook his head,

"No, I didn't. I think the rats chewed it while I'm asleep."

Amelia groaned and she went weak in her knees at the thought of rats chewing on her hair while she slept. She knew it was probable though. They were so fatigued, their bodies so depleted of energy that when they did manage to sleep, it was as if they were dead. For all she knew, the rats crawled all over her while she slept too. She shuddered again, just at the thought. There were so many indignities that they suffered here on Nikumaroro; or Rat Island as they taken to calling it; you'd think that sleep would at least give them a chance for respite, even an unconscious relief, but she knew that it wasn't so. Noonan was always harping on the grand idea of 'survival of the fittest' and the rats seemed to rule the island, therefore they must be the fittest. There was literally nothing they could do to keep the rats away, other than what they were already doing. So Amelia tried her best to not think about, or at least not to dwell upon the daily indignities that they were forced to suffer during their stay on the island.

"Well, what about it Amelia? You going to join me for a crab dinner?"

"So, you're willing to bet your life *on a hunch?*"

"Why shouldn't I? Every move we make on this rat-infested island can wind up killing us, so why not follow a hunch? At any rate, we'll find out in a wink, because I'm having crab for dinner."

"Why chance it?"

"Ah, but the question is, why not chance it?"

"Because I'm not a gambler, that's why."

"Suit yourself," Noonan laughed at her and then jumped onto the trunk of the tree, "help me out here, and get me hoisted up here so I can have a look, this should be short and sweet. I'll get mister crab down, you just watch." he held his arm out for her to grab and help lift him up onto the tree trunk.

Like many coconut trees the trunk was curved and didn't grow straight up, but at a low angle to the ground before going straight up. Noonan straddled his legs across the truck and then began scooting himself up the truck until it was vertical enough that he had to hold on just to keep his perch. He was not a good climber and Amelia saw him look down at the ground twice with a grimace on his face.

"Worried about falling, Noonan?"

"Nah," he shook his head, "this is in the bag."

Amelia could tell by the look on his face that he was lying and that he *was* worried about falling. She noticed the same black and green fungus that was growing on his hands; just like hers. He had some of the fungus on his elbows. She didn't want to look at her own elbows. She couldn't make out his fingernails, but she knew his were probably like hers, with the black-green fungus growing under the nails, and the nails themselves turning yellowish.

Earlier that day Amelia had looked over her body. In a short period of time, she'd become roughened by the island. She picked at the peeling skin on her leg. She had an ugly rash on one wrist, and there were bloody scrapes and black bruises all up and down her body. In between her toes an island fungus of some sort was green and black and spreading all over her feet. Her heels felt soft and squishy and it hurt when she got to her feet every morning. After walking around for a while though, that feeling went away.

Her hair was getting longer now, and that bothered her, because she'd always kept it short. She knew that short hair was un-ladylike, but that had never bothered her. If some of those people back in 'civilization' could see her now, they'd be horrified. Even the hair on her legs was getting longer. It looked terrible, but she knew that her face must be a mess too. She could feel the constant heat on her face, on her cheeks and forehead. She knew that she was peeling all over, and her face must look like a tomato. But it was all nothing that a week back in civilization wouldn't cure. She longed for that time.

He stopped a few feet from the huge crab and lay flat against the trunk and reached a hand up towards the back legs of the crab above him.

Amelia called up to him, "How will you kill it?"

"Hopefully the fall will kill it, although Peterson said he'd seen them drop from twenty feet and it didn't hurt them."

"That doesn't sound promising."

"If the fall doesn't kill it, I'll just bash it with a stick, or slam it against a tree trunk."

Amelia watched as Noonan grabbed one of the hind legs and start pulling against the crab to try and dislodge it off the tree. The crab wrapped its front legs around the tree trunk and held on.

Noonan continued talking to Amelia as he pulled.

"Peterson said he'd seen these things dragging small carcasses off into the jungle. He said they can easily move a something that weighs close to a hundred pounds. I didn't believe him," he grunted with his effort at pulling on the crab's hind legs, "but seeing the size of this bastard, now I damn sure believe him."

"Noonan; *enough* with the profanities, please."

Suddenly the crab came loose and dropped and the absence of weight to pull upon caused Noonan's weight to shift and he almost fell off the trunk with the crab. He wrapped both arms around the trunk and hung there, suspended, his legs waving in the air over Amelia's head.

Amelia gasped and yelled out, "Hang on, for God's sake Noonan!"

Noonan laughed and swung his legs up and wrapped them around the trunk and righted himself.

He collapsed against the trunk and looked down, "That was a close one!"

Amelia rolled her eyes, "Thank goodness you didn't fall and break your arm, or a leg, or God forbid, your neck!"

"Hey! How's the crab?"

Amelia walked over to where it lay. It was upside down on the ground and its legs waved feebly in the air.

"You've either stunned it and it's slowly coming to, or it's dying. Its legs are still moving, so it's hard to tell, and don't ask me to get any closer to it."

"It can't hurt you, Amelia. It's a crab! You can outrun it by taking two steps."

"I don't care. I'm not getting anywhere near that nasty-looking thing."

Noonan peered out towards the beach. It was too dense in the jungle to see anything. He could hear the surf rolling up on the beach.

"This would be a great lookout too. I can crawl up here and see miles out to sea, although there's nothing out there for us to see."

"Other than the rescue ship, you mean? It's out there somewhere, Noonan, just over the horizon. I know it is. We've seen them, and I know they're still searching. I haven't given up, even if you have."

Noonan slid backwards now, coming down from the tree in reverse, "I'd rather be on the lookout for some storm clouds, to bring some rain and relief from the heat for a few hours, but to answer you . . . no, Amelia. I still maintain there won't be a rescue. We are stuck here forever. Well, until we die that is."

Amelia glared at him, wondering what it would hurt him just to have a positive thought towards their rescue. He couldn't possibly really think that they wouldn't be rescued.

Once on the ground, Noonan stood over the crab and inspected it. The creature was in the process of trying to right itself.

"That's amazing. A fall from twenty feet and it's barely stunned."

"Once you kill it are you going to eat it raw?"

"No, I'll strip the meat out of it, get a stick and hold it over the fire. Or, we'll toss it into the bowl and use that as a make-shift frying pan."

"So, you've got a fire ready to go then?"

"No, Amelia, obviously I *don't* have a fire going yet. And you know it," his voice took on an edge of anger at being reminded that she'd done something he was unable to do, "I was thinking maybe that we could *share* it. I'll give you some crab if we can use your fire to cook it."

"Earlier, Noonan, you wanted nothing to do with me, you gave me the boot, and now you're ready to share again."

Noonan glared at her. He looked around, trying his best not to explode in anger. He took a deep breath.

"Look Amelia, I know you're hungry. I am too. Let's just cook this thing and eat, okay?"

"But Noonan, I refuse to eat that, that *thing*. You yourself admitted that it may very well be poisonous." She wondered if she should volunteer that she had a nifty cooking pan. If she did they'd be able to cook the crab in her pan, or in his bowl, and boil water in the other. She was about to say something about it, when she stopped and said nothing. If he found out about her sauce pan, he may very well steal it from her. She definitely wouldn't put it past him. She could eat now, and have her own water later. She'd been able to keep the pan hidden this long, and to give it up now could very well mean death. Better safe than sorry.

"It's also supposed to be a *delicacy*," he raised his eyebrows at her.

"Every food I've ever tasted that was recommended as a *delicacy* was just horrible. Take caviar for instance, it was just awful-tasting. What if this is the same way?"

"Food is food Amelia. We need it for fuel, for energy, for nutrition if nothing else. Now come on, let's not be at loggerheads over this, and let's go and have us a square meal."

"But Noonan, I'm not going to eat something that could be poisonous."

Noonan was getting exasperated.

"Okay, here's a deal," he stood before her, and opened his arms, "we use your fire, and I'll cook the crab. I'll eat first, I'll be the guinea pig, and you don't eat until you see if I get sick from it."

"That could be twenty-four hours or even longer, Noonan."

"Not really, Amelia. We'll know in a few hours if this will make me sick. And I have my mom's delicate stomach, so it should be faster than that."

Amelia considered it. Food of any sort sounded good. Her mouth was already dry and she'd never gotten the bad taste of the tiny crabs out of her mouth, and the sea-water had just made things worse.

Her stomach growled, and the thought of waiting hours filled her with misery. She was hungry, and she wanted food *now*, she smiled, "Okay, let's try it."

Noonan grinned and picked up the huge crab. He had to lift his arms up over his head just to get the creature off the ground. As soon as he did, its legs and pinchers began reaching for him. He arched back, holding his arms out further and bending over, and even that was almost ineffective against the long legs of the creature and it almost got him. When its arms relaxed more and it drooped down, Noonan took a few steps backwards, and then pulled his arms back, then he stepped into a swing and hurled the creature against the tree trunk. It hit with a wet smack and Noonan let go of the back legs. The crab lay in a heap at the trunk of the coconut tree. Its legs undulated weekly.

"I'll be damned. That was a hard smack and it's still not dead!" He looked at Amelia in amazement.

"Maybe this is not such a good idea, Noonan. Can't we just make do with the smaller ones?"

"Those tiny things are foul. Between those little ones are barely as big as a fingernail clipping, and these monsters are a more usable size. There has to be a couple of pounds of good meat on this thing. We'll cook it up, break off a piece and eat hardy tonight. Stand back now; another strong smack should peg it out once and for all."

He bent over to pick it up and this time he grabbed three legs on each side, making sure not to get near the pinchers. This allowed him to fold the crab in half in length, and that allowed him to swing harder with a longer arc of swing. This time when the crab slapped against the tree trunk the body broke away from the legs. Noonan laughed and gathered up the biggest pieces, including the clawed legs.

"Okay, Amelia," he held the crab up grandly, "our repast awaits; so let's get cooking."

•••

An hour later they had two fires going. One was for boiling water in their bowl. Noonan dug a small depression into the sand and they set the bowl, filled with seawater into it and then built the fire under it. Amelia had insisted on boiling the seawater before she drank anymore and Noonan had agreed.

Noonan gutted the crab, which eventually yielded two large chunks of meat weighing close to two pounds apiece. Amelia scrounged around and found two sticks that they fashioned into small spears. Sliding the meat down the stick, they held the sticks over the flames.

Amelia complained that her arm was getting tired of holding the stick out over the fire.

"I've got an idea," Noonan said as he walked around the fire to her side, "here, hold mine and I'll rig something up." He stuck the end of the stick into the ground and moved the meat-laden end over the fire.

"It's just like a rod-holder on a fishing boat."

He took his stick did the same, and they watched silently as their dinners cooked.

After a few minutes, the crab meat was sizzling and popping and turning milky-white.

•••

Amelia watched as the crab meat cooked. The smell was making her stomach rumble. She knew that she wouldn't have been able to wait for hours for Noonan to eat his and then determine if the meat was a delicacy or poison. She doubted that she'd even be able to wait a few minutes.

Her mouth was actually watering and it made her jaw hurt. They would definitely have to allow the water to cool though.

She watched Noonan closely. It was possible that his odd behavior was due to a bump on the head during the crash, but it was also possible that she was simply seeing his true identity. She had never known a man to be so misogynistic and found it very difficult to deal with. Most of the men she'd known had been helpful to her in all of her pursuits, and some had been downright obsequious. It mattered not to her, except for the fact that here, stranded on an island, his attitude towards her could be a very deadly thing. They needed to work together until they were rescued, which would probably come tomorrow.

They also needed to keep the fire burning brightly so that it could be seen during the night.

"Noonan, we should build up that fire after we take the bowl of water out of it and make sure we keep it going all night long. Would you rather take the early shift or the later one?"

"The early shift, for what purpose, Amelia?"

"To tend the fire during the night, so the rescuers-"

Noonan laughed, "Amelia, I keep telling you, there isn't going to be any rescue. We're *never* going to be found. I'm not staying up all night watching the fire for a rescue. I have no problem keeping a small fire going to keep the rats away, but I'm certainly not worried about a rescue. Again, I'm *telling* you . . . there will *not* be a rescue. We're going to die on this island. You need to get used to the idea."

Amelia stared at him and wondered how he could just give up so easily.

"They will be here tomorrow Noonan, you just watch and see. Keeping the fire going all night may just help them see us. That's why there's no allowance for either of us to shirk our duties," Amelia said with as much finality and conviction as she could muster.

Ignoring her, Noonan pulled his stick out of the ground and set the meaty end of the stick on a piece of coconut leaf.

"Let's eat," he said as he peeled a sliver of crab meat off his chunk and popped it into his mouth. He moaned.

"Mm, that's tasty, just what I needed. That was a piece of good fortune, finding mister crab up that tree."

Amelia pulled up her stick and set hers down and used another small stick as a make-shift fork. She chewed a bite, and then sighed, and grudgingly admitted that it was delicious. She decided that the crab was a godsend, just as long as they didn't get sick from it.

"I have to admit, Noonan, this is first-rate eating."

Amelia watched Noonan from across the campfire. He wolfed down his crab like an animal. He probably thought that she was eating her daintily, whereas the truth was, she was deathly afraid that it was poisonous and would make her sick. The problem was that her famished body overrode her logical mind. Within minutes she was tearing into her portion just as greedily as Noonan devoured his.

They'd agreed that she would take first watch, and keep the fire blazing through the early hours. Later on she would wake Noonan and he would take over keeping the fire stoked until morning. He'd grumbled about it, still insisting that they weren't going to be rescued, but Amelia had insisted. He had only relented when she had reminded him that the fire kept the rats away from them. He seemed more worried about the rats that food, water, or shelter, so she played upon his fear to get him to acquiesce. He'd half-heartedly given in and the watches were set.

The crab had been delicious and Amelia now understood why it was considered a delicacy. So far, there had been no ill effects from their having eaten. Once it had cooled, the boiled sea-water had finally quenched her thirst and now that Noonan was sleeping, and there was no one to talk to, she found herself nodding off.

Several times her chin dropped to her chest and she jerked awake. She shifted her position on the ground, with her back against the trunk of a coconut palm tree and tried to occupy her mind in a way that she would stay awake.

•••

Noonan felt like he'd only dozed for a moment and when he opened his eyes Amelia was staring at him from across the fire. He took notice that there was something odd about her. He squinted and saw that she had a crow sitting on her shoulder. He was about to tell her that she had a bird on her shoulder when he realized that she was talking to the bird. He couldn't make out what she was saying, because she was whispering. The crow seemed to look at her, and listen as she whispered, and every now and then the bird would look over at him. Finally, Amelia pointed at Noonan and the crow began flapping it wings, taking off and flying from her shoulder, through the fire and directly at him. Noonan screamed and threw his arms up to protect his face but the bird never hit him. Noonan took his hands down, and then he saw why; the crow was sitting on his legs. It tilted its head, and Noonan could see its beady little yellow eye. Then the bird began pecking at his crotch. Noonan yelled, and slapped at the bird, but it flapped its wings and hovered over his crotch, with its claws holding onto the fabric of his pants. He felt the crow's sharp claws cutting into his penis. He screamed.

•••

Amelia knew she was dreaming when she saw her father standing before her. She was four years old again, and her father was holding her in his arms. She had skinned a knee and he was comforting her as she cried, holding her head against his chest and cooing softly, patting her head. They were on the front porch. She knows that in a few moments, when her tears are gone, he will take her by the hand and lead her into the kitchen and take a long black string of licorice from the cabinet. It is stored in the highest cabinet, where she cannot possibly reach. This was her fondest childhood memory. She loves the licorice, and it is the only candy she is allowed, and only very rarely does he give it out to her.

Amelia feels warm, protected in her father's safe and loving embrace, and she wants to stay here forever. But her mouth waters now, in anticipation of the licorice.

She smells his musky fatherly smell, part outdoors, and hears him comforting her, "its okay baby. It didn't hurt that much, you'll be okay, just let the sting fade away, you'll forget all about it in a while . . . it's just a knee-scrape after all. That's right, you be a good boy for your daddy."

Amelia pulled away from him, a frown on her face. "Don't be silly daddy, I'm not a boy!"

Her dad turns without a word and walks into the house. She goes to follow him but when she opens the screen door; a woman opens the door and steps in front of the opening so that Amelia cannot pass. The woman is pretty, but in a slovenly worn-out way.

"Who are you?" Amelia asked the woman. The woman shakes her head side to side slowly, and opens the door wider. Amelia looks past her into the room and sees many women. They all seem to be the same type of woman as this one at the door. It dawns upon Amelia that these women are what she has heard referred to as harlots, trollops, or courtesans. She is shocked to see them in her house. And her father is in there with them? There must be some sort of mistake.

She tries to step into the room, to follow her father and find out why these women are in the house, but the woman gently waves her hand towards Amelia, telling her to back up, and then she is closing the door in her face.

Confused, Amelia opens the screen door and places her ear against the door. She hears some muffled laughing and giggling. She puts a hand on the doorknob and twisted but there's no movement, she's been locked out.

She closed the screen door and walked around the porch to the side and peered through the window. The thin white curtains have been pulled across the window and all she can see is gauzy shapes and shadows. Laughter and giggling emanated from the room. One tall shadow, her father, glided across the room and joined another shadow. The two shadows merge as one, and then melted into a third shadow horizontal on the floor. Amelia knows this is the couch. The giggles began evolving into more animalistic sounds and Amelia wonders what type of game it is they are now playing. She taps on the window with her knuckle.

"Father?"

"Go away, son!"

Amelia frowns, "But it's *me*, father, Amelia!"

"Yes, Amelia, I know. Now go away, son. You father is busy."

Amelia shakes her head. Maybe she is not hearing him correctly through the window. There is more giggling from the women, and she hears a man grunting. She has never heard her father making these noises.

"I want to play too, father."

"No, Amelia, you don't know how!"

"But I can learn, please, *pretty* please?"

Now she hears a growling of anger, muted words, and then the curtains fly open and her father is standing there.

"Amelia, get out of here! Leave us alone."

"But father, why can't I come inside with you?"

Her father's face reddened in anger, and then he grabbed a fistful of his hair and ripped it out of his head and shoved his fist through the window. His hand came through the window without breaking the glass and the hair is in his hand. He shook it at her.

"Go on, take it and leave us alone!" the apparition that was her father yelled at her. He faded back into the house.

Scared, she looked down at his hand and saw that the hair he'd pulled out has become a long black strand of licorice.

●●●

Noonan screamed, seeing the crow ripping his pants away from his body in long strips. He screamed loudly,

"Help me, Amelia!"

He could see his underwear beginning to show. Every time he tried to grab the crow with his hands, the crow would peck at him, and his hands were bloody from the pecking. He suddenly realized that he could just get up and run from the bird. By the time he got to his feet, his pants were in tatters and the crow was starting to peck at his groin. Looking over at Amelia he could see that she was asleep.

How could she sleep through this? He'd been screaming for help at the top of his lungs.

He took off running, heading directly into the jungle. Seeing a worn path, he followed it, the crow flying directly behind him cawing and screeching.

Something in the path tripped him up and he went sprawling onto the ground and the crow was upon him immediately, pecking at his groin. Screaming when he felt a stab of pain in his penis, he looked down to see that the crow had his penis in his beak. Noonan stared, horrified at the crow and his bloody penis and the crow's unblinking yellow eyes. The crow tilted his head at him one way, then the other, as if trying to figure out what kind of animal he'd been pestering, then flapped its wings and flew off into the jungle, with Noonan's penis in its beak.

Noonan scrambled to his feet and took off after the crow, hoping he didn't lose sight of it as it flew through the dense jungle foliage.

The crow settled on a limb and looked down as Noonan came to a stop across the clearing from it. Beneath the tree limb where the crow was perched were millions of the rats. The crow dropped the penis into the rats and they swarmed it.

Noonan screamed and waded into the roiling mass of rats to retrieve his member.

●●●

Amelia stepped off the porch and walked through yard and sat down at the trunk of the big tree. There was a tire swing that she enjoyed as a young girl, but she knew that she was too old for that now. She looked at the licorice string and then at the house. She could still hear the sounds coming from in there, but they had changed from giggling and laughing and the occasional grunt, to full-fledged screaming. She thought she heard her father calling out for her, but she ignored it. She was now fascinated by the licorice.

Her mouth watered in anticipation of it. She rolled it between her fingers, feeling its ropy, slightly greasy feel, and with a sigh she reached up and put it in her mouth. She didn't chew on it right away, and she didn't place the end of it in her mouth. Instead, she placed the middle of it in her mouth, so that the ends hung down on either side. Her mouth salivated immediately, the juices rolling back down her throat and she could taste the anise and grape taste as she lightly rolled the strand between her teeth. She began chewing in earnest and both ends of the licorice rope came alive.

It was when she came fully awake that she realized that she still had the licorice rope in her mouth and the fire had gone out. The she saw that she was covered in rats, and *the licorice rope in her mouth was the tail of a rat.* She moaned in terror and began spitting the thing out of her mouth, thrashing around on the ground as the rats jumped away from her and scampered back into the jungle. She could hear their squeals over her own moaning and she finally got free of them and stood up, and a shiver went through her body at the thought of having been covered in rats. Realizing that she'd had the tail of one of them in her mouth, she bent over and retched, but nothing came out. She kept brushing at her face, her head and legs because she still felt them crawling all over her, even though they weren't. She looked towards Noonan, who was just coming awake. Realizing he was covered in rats, he began screaming. Jumping up, he looked down at his legs and then ran into the jungle while looking behind him as if he was being chased. He was screaming, "*give it back!*"

Amelia took off running after him.

He ran way ahead of her, but as she ran she noticed that there was a slight path through the jungle that they seemed to be following. After running a hundred yards or so, she burst into a small clearing and was astounded at what she saw.

Noonan has stripped off his pants and was dancing around frantically, "No! No! Give it back!"

"Stop, Noonan, calm down, it was just a dream!" Amelia yelled as she slowly approached him.

"No, stop them! They'll eat it!"

"Noonan, snap out of it! What is it you're talking about?"

He looked up at her, and his eyes cleared, and Amelia realized immediately that he'd just woken up from the dream.

He looked down and then jumped, as if scared by something, then looked all around him, muttering "where is it? I have to find it!"

"Find what Noonan, what did you lose?"

"They took it, the crow, the rats. . . they'll eat it!"

"Eat what Noonan? What did they take?"

He looked up at her again, as if seeing her for the first time. Amelia cocked her head and waited for him to answer. She was shocked when he pulled down his underwear and looked at his groin area. He stood there looking down at his member. Amelia felt her face redden at his impropriety.

She was even more shocked when he reached down and wrapped his hand around his member.

"It's still here. The rats didn't get it."

Amelia looked down at the ground, unable to keep standing there in front of a man who had his hand on his *parts*.

"For God's sake, Noonan, cover yourself up. It was just a bad dream, that's all."

Noonan looked back down and saw that he was holding the hand-bow from the fire making kit. He looked back up at Amelia who was giving him a funny look. He blinked and then looked back down and was relieved to see that he still had his manhood.

•••

Noonan came awake for a moment and he looked down at what was in his hand. He heard Amelia's voice saying something and he looked over at her. They were no longer on the beach. They were in a clearing in the jungle. He looked around, confused at the surroundings.

"Cover yourself up, Noonan. It was just a bad dream, that's all."

He looked down and was surprised to see that he was fully erect. He looked back at Amelia, but she was bending down looking at something on the ground.

"Cover up Noonan, and come look at this."

Noonan pulled up his underwear and then his pants and he walked over to where Amelia was on her knees looking at something on the ground.

"What is it?"

"A mud hole," she pointed, "but do you see how much water is in there? A few gallons at least, and I bet it's not sea-water either."

Noonan looked at her blankly, "What happened?"

"You had a bad dream, and I think I did too, but now we have drinkable water."

They spent a few minutes walking back to the campsite to get the bowl for the water, and along the way, Amelia tried to get him to talk about his dream, but he refused to say a word about it. He asked her to relate her dream to him, but she told him that she could never remember her dreams upon waking.

The rats seemed to fall back deeper into the jungle with the advent of more and more daylight.

CHAPTER 6

With sunup, the heat intensified, but Amelia felt better today, knowing that they'd found a source of drinkable water. They'd still boil it just as they would have done the sea-water, and she felt that a choice between the two water sources was that the water from the mud-hole was better for them. She noticed that her pants were beginning to rot away at the bottom of the legs. This climate or salty air, or something on the island was eating away at the fabric. She also noticed that she had ugly black bruises on her ankles. She pulled up her pants legs and could see that the bruises went all the way up her legs. She used a fingertip to press on one of the bruises and felt no pain, but the area underneath her fingertip felt squishy. The feeling sickened her and her stomach tossed and she had to fight the urge to vomit. She smoothed her pants legs back down and tried not to think about the damage that was happening to her body on this island. She was glad she didn't have a mirror, for she was certain that the sight of what she looked like would have positively horrified her.

She stoked the fire to a blaze while Noonan took the bowl back to fetch water. She could see that he feared the rats in the jungle, and she didn't blame him, but there was nothing they could do about it.

She'd now taken to looking up and scanning the upper tree trunks for more of the enormous coconut crabs, but didn't spot any. The last thing she wanted was for one of those hideous monsters to fall on her head. She wondered if the huge crabs were rare and they'd just gotten lucky in finding it or if there would be others.

Suddenly, her body tensed up and she came to a full alertness. She listened for the noise again and heard it again, a droning noise. That was the sound of an airplane. She jumped to her feet and ran out onto the beach. She yelled for Noonan but he was no longer in sight. She brought her hand to her brow to shade her eyes and scanned the sky for the airplane. There! She spotted a dot in the sky, on the horizon. She began jumping up and down, screaming at the top of her lungs, and waving her hands. But the plane was so far away. It was definitely too far away to have seen her. But she knew from her own flying experience that, at that altitude they would surely be able to see the island. She stopped jumping up and down as the speck in the sky slid over the horizon west of them. She stayed and watched for another half hour until it was clear that they weren't coming back, and her face was beginning to burn from the sun. She made her way back to camp and stoked the fire again and made sure that there was a huge billow of thick black smoke.

She leaned back against the trunk of the coconut palm and scanned the horizon as she waited for Noonan to return. She hoped the spotters on the plane would tell the rescue ship to check out the island.

The ocean, further out, was brilliant blue, and the water closer to shore was a milky-green. She looked toward the area where the Electra had been and wondered how it could have just disappeared. Being a weak swimmer she knew she would never venture out that far to look. Even if she did, what good would it do? Noonan though, could check again, and if the wreckage was not too far below the surface, might be able to dive down and salvage something usable for them. She considered what items they could use, and how they could be used, and then realized that she had no business thinking like this. They would probably be rescued today, so what was the point of trying to salvage anything from the sunken Electra?

Amelia chided herself for falling into the trap of feeling discouraged, and then came out of her reverie when she saw Noonan walking towards the beach about fifty yards away. She saw that he'd set the bowl down at the edge of the jungle.

She stood and called out, "Noonan? I heard a plane earlier!"

He ignored her and walked into the rolling waves.

Amelia put her hands and her hips and watched as he waded out waist deep into the surf. She wondered if maybe he had had the same idea as she did, about swimming out to look for the sunken Electra. But he stopped when he was waist deep. She cocked her head to one side, and then brought her hand to her brow to shade her eyes from the relentless sun.

She watched as he knelt down and using both hands to cup some water, brought them up to his mouth and began drinking. Amelia's mouth dropped open.

Why on earth would he do that? They'd both drank their fill last night from the boiled sea-water, and he was carrying at least a gallon of water in the bowl that could be drinkable within a half-hour. So why drink the salt water? She was convinced that Noonan had gone off his rocker.

He turned and started walking towards shore and once he was back on the beach, he bent down and picked up something. Amelia squinted, trying to make out what it was he'd found. Was it some debris that had washed ashore from the Electra?

She took a few steps forward and watched as he held up whatever it was he'd found, as if to examine it in a better light. Now Amelia could clearly see that he had nothing in his hands, yet he was holding his fingers as if he were examining an object very closely.

Whatever it was that he was pretending to examine must have pleased him because he smiled, bent down, place the invisible object on the ground and then he stood up and proceeded to strip off all of his clothes.

For the second time in one day, Amelia was subjected to the sight of him completely naked. Once stripped, he bent down, picked up his imaginary object that he'd found on the beach and then walked back into the surf.

Once he was into the incoming rollers waist deep he began using his new-found object to soap himself down. Amelia watched as he raised and arm and then used his invisible bar of soap to scrub his underarm, then he rinsed, and then raised his other arm and repeated the process. After his underarms, he did his chest, his legs and feet, and then his hair.

Amelia watched in horrific fascination, wondering if Noonan had gone completely insane.

When he'd finished his 'bath' he walked back up the beach, and proceeded to slowly get dressed again, and once again Amelia was subjected to seeing all of his manhood. It was impossible not to notice that he was aroused and in a fully erect state. Amelia blushed and turned away. She was obviously going to have to have a talk with him about his inappropriate behavior. She certainly didn't see why she should have to be subjected to seeing all of him so often, and especially when he was in a state of arousal. It was completely vulgar.

She had been very careful to make sure that when she needed to take care of her biological needs that she walked away from him and found an area of privacy. It wasn't that hard to do seeing as how they were the only people on the island. He should respect her sensibilities just the same.

Bewildered by his strange behavior, she watched as he marched back up the beach, picked up the bowl with the water from the mud hole and walked directly towards her. She couldn't detect from his expression whether or not he knew she'd been watching him, and he definitely showed no embarrassment at having stripped or acted inappropriately in any way. He set the bowl down in front of her.

"There's your water."

"Thanks, Noonan."

"Sure feels better having had a good meal last night, doesn't it?"

"Yes, Noonan, it does," she watched his face carefully, "and I see you had a nice bath. Did you get good and clean?" she joked, "I see you're all turned out in your Sunday finery."

She hoped her faux flattery would cause him to revert to good Noonan for a while.

He grinned, "I sure did! You should do the same, you know, you really are starting to smell. You have quite a strong funk."

Amelia felt her face flush and she took a deep breath,

"Noonan, I saw you drinking sea-water again, and I was wondering why you'd do that? You know it's bad for you. All you have to do is wait a few minutes until we boil this water."

He shook his head, "Amelia, that water is filthy. I told you anyway, there's nothing wrong with the sea-water. I'm drinking it and I've never felt better."

Amelia shook her head, "I see you found some soap, didn't you?"

He glared at her, "I found it, and you know the saying; it's *finders-keepers!* So, just stay away from it, or go find your own."

Amelia crossed her arms across her chest, "There's another thing we need to talk about Noonan."

He blinked several times and his body seemed to relax a bit, "Yeah, what's that?"

Amelia would have sworn that he had just changed back to the old Noonan, the man he was before the island, "I would appreciate it if you would stop parading around in front of me with no clothes. The fact that we're stranded here for a couple of days is no reason to forgo all attempts at decency. I am still a woman after all, a married woman in fact, and am accustomed to being treated with some small amount of decency and respect."

"What's the difference anyway? It's not like anyone can see us here, we're all alone."

"Well, Noonan, I can see you when you are naked, and I don't like it. That's something that only husband and wife should be privy to. We are not that, so I expect you to show some restraint, out of respect for my having requested it of you if not for the simple act of decency."

Noonan huffed at her, "Look, little Miss High and Mighty, you may think you're the queen around here, but it's like I said *after you crashed us here,* I no longer take orders from you."

"But Noonan, It's simply a matter of acting civilized."

"Civilized?" he spread his arms and whirled around to the beach, and then back to face her, "*civilized?* Where's the civilization, Amelia? Where are the restaurants, the schools, the roads, the police, and the houses? There is no civilization here, we left that behind and we'll never see it again!"

"It's not a matter of being *in* civilization, Noonan; it's a matter of *acting* civilized and proper, just because it's a decent way to act. Can't we still respect certain conventions?"

"Why act civilized, Amelia? If I do something wrong, where's the police to arrest me? If I do something right, where's my reward? Answer, there is none of either. I can do anything I want and I'll never get arrested. I can do everything right and I'm still going to die in a matter of days. So what's the use?"

"What about the basic respect of one human being to another? For that alone can't we help each other be comfortable and maintain a certain degree of civilized behavior? I remind you Noonan; we are going to be rescued, any day now, heck, any minute now. And what will the real world back there think when they hear about the way you've acted? They'll put you in a loony-bin, that's what!"

"You just don't get it, Amelia, Civilization and basic respect? Throw it all out the window, because those things are gone. It's down to survival of the fittest, where the strong survive and the weak perish. In fact, the strong overpower the weak just *to* survive."

Amelia knew that she had a look of shock on her face, but she was completely unprepared for the brutality of Noonan's outlook of their situation. She knew that he was forever changed. But there had to be some slim hope that she could talk to him, reason with him, and get him to calm down and be hopeful for their rescue. She realized that the sooner the rescue arrived the better it was for her, the longer it took, the worse it would be, for Noonan's sanity seemed to be deteriorating rapidly.

"You see, Amelia. It really has come down to the basics of survival. Only the strongest survive. What that means is that, in a matter of days, one of us, the lucky one, will be able to fend off death a few more hours, or maybe a few more days, by making a meal of their fellow castaway . . ."

Amelia shrieked and brought her hand up to her mouth as her stomach lurched in revolt at the image of atrocity he was painting.

"... now, I hope it's *me* who does the dining, but if some sad fate befalls me and it's you, then I bid you no ill will. Of course, you'll have to rid yourself of some of your more *genteel* refinements."

Amelia stared at him.

He cackled, "Now, how's *that* for respect and civility?"

•••

Noonan walked away, claiming he was going to circle the island just to explore. Amelia let him go without asking him to stay to help tend the signal fire she was keeping going. The fire during the day needed more branches and leaves from the trees, in order to keep a lot of smoke filling the sky. She didn't mind not being able to doze while he was gone, because she doubted she'd be able to sleep after having heard his speech regarding cannibalism. She sincerely doubted that he truly believed in some of the things he said. She decided that he had been rendered insane by the entire experience, the crash, and now the conditions that they were forced to live in. When she'd first met him he hadn't seemed like such a bad egg, but then, those circumstances were hardly as severe as these.

She considered going to the other side of the island and leaving him to his own devices, but she wasn't ready yet to do such a thing. She had reprimanded him for his lack of willingness to help them as a team therefore she couldn't run off and leave him alone either. She didn't want to be guilty of the very thing that she felt made him seem uncivilized. She still felt, in her heart, that the only way to survive this was to work together. They came to the island as a team, and they should live here, throughout the duration, until the rescuers came, as a team. Every task, every situation was made easier by the fact that there were two of them.

Even though she was stranded on an uninhabited island with one other person, she now felt even further stranded because of Noonan's mental state. He was obviously becoming unhinged. She didn't think she could bear it if she was on the island alone, yet Noonan, in his current state, was also not her idea of good company. It may be a miserable, even lonely day or two until the rescuers came to get them. She'd doggedly bear it though, half the battle was in knowing that they would be back to civilization soon.

She wondered if she should begin considering Noonan a threat. Was he an actual danger to her?

She decided to follow him. She needed to know if he was really a threat, or if he was just being difficult because he was jealous of her success. She tended to believe that that's what it was, his jealousy of her fame. Even here on the island, she outshone him. She could make fire, he couldn't. She was calm and unwavering in her belief that rescue was forthcoming. He was filled with dire predictions and saw futures of dreaded outcomes. She saw this as a detour with eventual rescue, and a return to civilization and happiness. He saw this experience as a fight to the death in a culmination of savage strength and brutality.

She heaped everything she could find in the area onto the fire and set out in the direction that he'd taken.

Following the shoreline a few yards away from the edge of the jungle she followed in his footsteps. His tracks carried on in a fairly straight line with no deviation of going closer to the jungle or closer to the shoreline.

After a while she caught a glimpse of him. He was just beyond a curve at the edge of the jungle. This was the farthest point of the island, the sharp end of the comma-shaped island before it turned back to follow a line horizontal to what she'd just walked. She was now on the opposite side of the island, and it was easy to see that their camp was on the nicer side of the island, if either beach could be considered nice. Amelia, like most people, had always assumed that islands were calm, peaceful, beautiful bits of paradise. The truth though, was quite the opposite. Offshore a few hundred yards, or a few miles, the island must have looked a beautiful little paradise, but up close it was too hot, hostile with rats, snakes and lizards, and without water, a veritable hellhole. It was difficult to believe that something so beautiful could be so deadly.

She peered around the group of trees at Noonan. He was squatting down, and for a moment, she was embarrassed, thinking that she had caught in the middle of answering a call of nature. She was partially correct, and when she saw what he *was* doing, she was disgusted. He was cupping his hands in between his legs as he urinated, and then holding his cupped hands up to his face and drinking it. Once again she had to see his privates.

She had no medical training, but wondered if maybe his consumption of the sea water had dehydrated him even further. Or maybe the dehydration was causing his mind to deteriorate.

When he finished drinking, he zipped up his pants and continued walking. Amelia followed along behind him a hundred yards of so behind him. She tried to stay close to the jungle tree-line, so that if he turned around she'd be able to step into the trees and remain hidden.

She followed as he walked back towards the mid-point of the island and Amelia guessed that they'd gone about half the length of the island when he stopped. She watched as he walked towards the tree-line and then stepped into the jungle. Now that he was out of sight, Amelia ran forward about fifty yards and then stepped into the jungle, hoping that she had not lost him. There seemed to be far fewer rats on this side of the island, or maybe it was just because there was more sunlight coming in through the trees. Whatever the reason, she was glad that they weren't underfoot. She crept forward until she saw him again, and now they were about twenty or thirty feet apart. He was kneeling and watching something.

Amelia crept closer and closer until she was afraid that he'd be able to hear her breathing, and she stopped, waiting to see what he was up to. She was still behind him, so she couldn't make out what it was that he was looking at so intently. She decided to move to the right so she could get a better look and pushed her way through the thick undergrowth, the sand here feeling much cooler on her feet than the sun-heated beach sand. She moved slowly, and when she was ten yards further to the right she squatted and watched.

Noonan was squatted on his heels and watching one of the huge coconut crabs in a small clearing. The crab was holding a coconut with its front claws. Amelia was trying to figure out what the crab was doing when Noonan's voice made her jump.

"He's going to open it and eat the coconut meat on the inside. I'm not sure whether or not they drink the coconut milk itself or eat the meat inside."

At first, Amelia wasn't sure if she'd caught Noonan talking to himself or if he was actually had addressing her.

"Yes, Amelia, I know you've been following me, I'm not stupid."

Amelia stood up and walked over to where Noonan was, "So why are you sitting here watching this?"

"Because I want to wait for him to get it open, then I'll get the coconut milk. It's supposed to be very good for you, and it beats boiling water," he laughed, "and of course, after he is kind enough to open it for us, I'll take him for dinner. Dinner and a drink from one source, now that's efficient; like I said survival of the fittest."

Amelia noticed that Noonan sounded like his 'old self' and that he used the word 'us' when talking about dinner. She took this as a good sign. More food would help both of them.

Noonan seemed to notice something else, and he whispered to Amelia as he pointed, "Look, he brought his friends."

Amelia looked to where he was pointing at the edge of the little clearing, and saw that there were five of six more of the giant crabs at the perimeter, all of them almost concealed by the underbrush. They seemed to be watching the other crab's progress with opening the coconut.

"Do you think they'll all share the coconut once he gets it open?" she asked Noonan.

"I don't know. This is the first time I've ever seen more than one of these things at one time. Plus, I don't know just how much juice is in one of those things. Not to mention the coconut meat itself. They might like the meat more than the juice, or vice-versa. Who knows?"

"Well, I guess we'll find out in a moment."

"No Amelia, we won't."

"Why won't we?"

"Because, the second he gets that thing open, I'm taking it from him. If I let them get to the meat and the milk, we will lose out on a meal, right?"

"You're right, Noonan. That makes sense. How many legs and pinchers do those things have anyway?"

"Well, they're decapods, so that means they have ten legs. The front pair of legs has those large claws, and I always heard that on crabs the left claw is larger than the right."

"Strange."

"Peterson says these things can lift up to seventy-five pounds. They carry the coconuts back up the trees and then drop them, hoping to crack them. Once they crack them, they have a way to get them open more easily."

"The third or fourth pair of legs has claws, but they're much smaller than the front claws."

"Look, I think he pierced it. See the liquid coming out?" Amelia pointed out.

They watched as a tiny bit of whitish liquid dribbled down the outer shell of the coconut, and then Noonan sprang out of their spot and advanced upon the crab. The crab, immediately began backing up and pulling the large coconut with it.

"Noonan, be careful!"

He laughed and bent down and grabbed the coconut from the side facing him, careful to keep his fingers out of reach of the crab's claws. The coconut was enormous, so there was plenty for him to grab without coming into contact with the creature.

Amelia shrieked, "Look behind you Noonan!" and Noonan whirled around to see the five other crabs coming out of the underbrush, quickly advancing upon Noonan with their claws raised.

Noonan's eyes widened and he let go of the coconut and backed away. "Aggressive aren't they?"

"Getting pinched by those claws could be painful Noonan, so you better be careful."

"It's probably no more painful than a bee sting. How much damage could they possibly do?"

"Just watch out."

Noonan walked back into the brush and reemerged a moment later with a small stick. He walked towards the crab and when he did, the other crabs began advancing on him again.

He brought his arm back and smashed the crab with it, but the creature held on tightly to the coconut. Noonan reared back and smashed the crab again, but the coconut remained firmly in the grasp of its claws.

The other crabs advanced a few feet further and Noonan was now in danger of being surrounded.

"I've got a better idea now," he proclaimed, and he used the stick as a spear, and inserted it in between the crab's arm and the coconut and then pushed the end of the stick into the ground, then he grabbed the coconut and pulled, while pushing against the stick, causing a lever effect to pry the coconut out of the crab's grasp. The coconut rolled free and Noonan walked over and picked it up. He held it in both hands and lifted it up, tilted his head back and allowed some of the milky fluid to pour into his mouth. When he finished he walked over and handed it to Amelia.

Noonan whirled around as he saw the crabs all advancing on him.

"Jesus!" he screamed, as one of them reached a claw out and pinched his calf. He stumbled away from the group and fell backwards onto the ground. He immediately sat up, and then looked at his leg. There was a small trickle of blood running down towards his ankle. A superficial wound, but Amelia could see that it had scared him.

Enraged, he jumped up and grabbed the leverage stick he'd used on the first crab, and ran towards the leader of the pack that was moving towards him, and he stabbed downwards with it, this time the pointed end went into the body of the crab and it pinned the crab to the ground.

He whirled around and walked towards the other remaining crabs and a foot or two away from the next one, he began kicking sand over the crab as fast as he could. The crab immediately began backing away from the avalanche of sand being dumped upon it, but when it backed out, Noonan reached down and grabbed it by its non-clawed legs on one side and in one swift movement, and he slung it around in an arc and smashed it against a tree trunk. The crab dropped dead to the ground, and Noonan ran towards the others and quickly and, one after another, used the same technique to kill them all.

Amelia was surprised by his animalistic display of savagery but said nothing.

Noonan grinned at her, "I guess we'll be feasting high on the hog now, huh?"

"Most of it will go to waste Noonan. They won't keep, and we can never eat all of that meat," Amelia said even though she secretly was pleased that they had full bellies for the next day.

Noonan glared at her, hatred in his eyes, "Too bad, but there's always more where these came from."

He held his hand out.

"What?"

"Give me the coconut, I'm thirsty and want more of that milk."

"Shouldn't this be mine? Aren't we sharing it?"

"No, Amelia, we're not."

"And why aren't we?"

"Because I'm the one who had the idea, and I'm the one who took it away from the crab. I fought for it, so it's mine, pure and simple. You can go paddle your own canoe," he snapped his fingers at her, "now give it up."

"But Noonan, you gave this to me."

"I only asked you to hold it for me."

"That's a lie, Noonan and you know it!"

He grabbed for the coconut, but Amelia was ready for him and when he lurched forward and grabbed for it, she hugged it tightly to her chest.

He forced his hand down, in between the coconut and her chest, but his hand went in under her shirt and came to a stop. She could feel the back of his hand against her bare nipple. He grinned.

"Stop that, Noonan! It's improper and you know it!"

He leaned in close to her and grinned, and she could smell his foul breath.

"Give it to me."

"No, I'm not giving up my coconut milk. You said 'us' earlier when you said we'd have a good meal, and this is a part of that meal."

Suddenly, a shock went through her as Noonan turned his hand around and was now firmly and somewhat painfully, squeezing her breast in his hand.

"Noonan, that's enough of that, you have no right to lay a hand upon me! It . . . it's wrong. Do you know what G P would do to you if I told him about this?"

"Call the law if you don't like it. Call the famous George Putnam too. Lot of good it's going to do out here. In the meantime, give it up and I'll let go. Of course, I could stand here all day if you want," as he spoke he began squeezing his hand, using it to massage her breast.

"Stop it, I won't stand for it you impudent bastard!"

"It's your call, Lady Lindy," he leered at her, their faces so close she could smell his rancid breath, "I'll get my coconut back, or you'll give yourself to me."

"Noonan, can't you suppress, even for a moment, your . . ." she grunted, trying to pull away from him, "your baser, primal urges? What kind of a man are you? Don't you have a backbone? Only a pathetic weakling would simply *give in* every time an urge rises up."

Her words must have hit home, because he gritted his teeth and squeezed her breast in his hand. Now the squeezing was so tight that tears welled up in her eyes.

She tried once again to pull away from him, but when she did, it gave him a chance to get a better grasp on her breast. He squeezed the nipple in between his fingers.

Amelia whimpered, "Stop it, Noonan. It's . . . its *rape* you know. When we get back I'll see to it that G P has you thrown in jail, you miserable varmint."

"We're never *going* back, Amelia, now stop being such a petticoat and relax," he said as he squeezed so hard that Amelia cried out. They grappled for a moment with Noonan grunting and Amelia breathing hard, fighting against him, and finally with a furious shove over her arms, Amelia let go of the coconut and grabbed Noonan's arms and brought her knee up as hard and fast as she could. Noonan grunted and she heard a whoof as he exhaled and bent over, grabbing his crotch.

"There you go; just desserts for a man who acts like a cur!" she spat at him.

Rubbing the pain out of her breast, and glaring at him, Amelia walked through the little clearing, reached down and picked up a crab for herself, and began her solitary walk back to the other side of the island. She was shaking all over and tears were running down her cheeks.

Amelia realized that she'd just seen him change back to the newer crazy Noonan. But crazy or not, this time he'd gone too far and she intended to do something about it. She hoped that sooner or later starvation would dampen his indomitable sex drive, but it seemed to have done the exact opposite. For now, it was her burden to be saddled with, but woe to the miscreant when they arrived back in civilization and Amelia portrayed their experiences to G P and the authorities. G P would pluck the buzzard named Noonan until he was featherless. He'd never fly again. Until then though, Noonan was vermin to her, just like the many rats on the island, just another species to be avoided. It was just before she stepped out of the jungle onto the beach that she saw it in the underbrush. A sauce pan, with its handle intact. She bent down to pick it up, looking around first to insure that Noonan wasn't watching. She examined it. A one-quart sauce pan. She couldn't possibly have found a more perfect dish for boiling water. Now she didn't need Noonan's bowl. For the first time in a long time she smiled, and then wondered how long she could keep it hidden from Noonan.

CHAPTER 7

By the time she made it back to her camp it was mid-afternoon and she wanted to get the fire started blazing again and she needed to gather wood and leaves.

She got the fire started and managed to get lost of thick black smoke billowing up into the sky, and she sat down with her back against the tree trunk. She wanted to think over her situation and make a decision on how to proceed.

Before sitting down she carefully inspected the trunk all the way up, looking for any crabs that may have climbed up there. She didn't want to be surprised by one of the ugly creatures. Then she found a stick to cook her crab meat on, and found a wide leaf to use as a plate.

Once she sat down she speared some of the meat out of the inside of the body of the crab, jammed the end into the ground, and then carefully pushed the top end with the meat on it over the flames. Soon the juice was running down the stick and dropping off into the flames with spatters and crackles. Her long walk, the fight with Noonan, and the heat had exhausted her and she was ravenous. With her back against the tree she was facing the beach, and the ocean's horizon spread out before her. The scene before her was beautiful, but she knew that she need only rotate and face the other direction, and the scene became one of disgusting loneliness and horror.

After a few minutes she pulled the stick out of the ground, placed her cooked meat on the leaf, and began to eat. The crab had yielded about two pounds of meat, and she ate as much of it as she could. There was no point in trying to save it. The rats, or crabs, flies and other vermin would get it, or it would rot in the sun, before she could eat again. It was a waste really, but there was nothing she could do about it.

It was then that she got an idea about what to do with Noonan. She would only do it if it became necessary, but, one more incident like today's and she would consider him dangerous and an impediment to her survival. If he wanted to act crazy and sully his own chances of survival, that was one thing, she couldn't stop him, but when he assaulted and became a physical threat to her then he was declaring war. In the sense of helping her fellow man, who was here in part because of her actions, she would give him another chance, but after that, she would not be liable for him in any way.

She tried to calm herself by looking for the outline of a ship on the horizon. The sun was setting and it was beautiful, but she knew that the darkness brought out the rats on this island, so the beauty did nothing to uplift her spirits. She decided that she would have a heart to heart with Noonan, to see if she could convince him that there should be some sort of rules of conduct between them for as long as they were on the island.

•••

Noonan rubbed his crotch. She had kneed him pretty good, and had almost hurt him for real. True she had caught him off guard, mostly by surprise, and he'd felt a little pain, but mostly on his upper thigh. If she'd really racked him, he'd of gone after her with a vengeance. Mostly, his letting her see that he was injured was a ploy. Let her think that she had the upper hand. Never show your adversary your true strength.

As he made his way back to their camp, he became more and more furious with her. She was so precious, the famed Amelia Earhart, with all her flying records, her derring-do and her gallivanting around with all the famous society people, wives of presidents and what-not.

He quickened his pace, hoping to get back before the sun set completely, because he wanted to be near the fire when the rats came out of hiding with the advent of darkness upon the island. He was carrying two of the giant crabs and that was slowing him down, but he resisted the idea of leaving one behind. He felt that he was hungry enough to eat both of them, but knew he'd be unable to. Amelia had been right about that. They would go to waste because there was no way to store them. They'd rot in two hours in this fierce sun, and trying to store them would just be inviting the rats to a free supper.

The day before Noonan had taken a look at himself over. His pants were frayed at the cuffs, and the seams were getting loose. Probably from being constantly exposed to the elements. There were holes here and there from jungle rot. The knees of both pants legs had large holes that had been torn open at some point, and they were getting looser and looser as his starvation diet caused him to lose weight in his waist.

His exposed skin was red and peeling all over and he had several dark black spots. He didn't want to know what they were. His hair was stringy and getting long. He could only imagine what his face looked like. He knew he stunk too, but there was nothing he could do about it.

A scab on the side of his leg was green, edged in black, and oozing a sort of white fluid. He'd touched a finger into it and wiped the ooze into the sand. The sand was warm, almost hot so he'd scooped up a handful of the sand and patted it down over the wound. The heat had seeped into the infected area, and it had begun feeling better almost immediately. He knew he was a wreck, but there was nothing to be done about it.

He remembered how it had felt having his hand on her small breast, her hard nipple between his fingers. He'd never thought of her as a real woman. She was not his type. She had no bosom to speak of, and her tall angular body gave her a mannish look.

Images of his first girlfriend flitted through his brain. He had been a virgin, and she had been somewhat like Amelia, which is to say, she was tall and bony. Later on he'd developed a taste for a more voluptuous woman. But his choices were now rather limited. Knowing that he would die soon, never having another chance to be with a woman, made their predicament more real to him.

He pulled his pants down to see if his groin was swollen from her kneeing, and he wasn't. He walked into the jungle a few yards to defecate and noticed that his stool was bloody and runny. Just the day before he'd felt a pain in the knuckle of his hands. He pressed on his pinky finger and the knuckle was mushy and squishy, as if there were no bones or cartilage in it. The idea that this island was eating him from the inside out had caused his legs to tremble and he'd felt faint. After a few minutes though, the feeling of disgust was gone, when he realized that there was very little he could do about it. He decided not to bother with any more close inspections of his body, out of sight, out of mind. One thing he couldn't help noticing though was Amelia's bedraggled appearance. She was skinny to begin with, and a week on the island had turned her face a dark red, and she was losing weight that she couldn't afford to lose. Her face was gaunt and pinched, and her legs and rear end were becoming bony. She was a wreck. Her hair was wild and frizzy, and she was covered in dirt. Noonan always imagined he was seeing an attractive woman when he looked at her. It was the only way he could justify feeling the 'urge' when he saw her. Under all the grime, sunburn blisters, peeling skin, bruises and skeletal looks, she was a biological woman, and coupling with her should still produce the same sensations, as long as he closed his eyes and thought of a beautiful woman when he took her. And, he would take her, *soon*.

As he walked, he could see the billowing smoke rising from the campsite. It was plain that Amelia was there, tending her precious fire. Why didn't she realize that rescue was impossible?

He would need to have a serious talk with her, and help her get over her misguided hope of rescue. The sooner that he could get her to that point, the easier it would be for them to survive. Not that he needed her to survive, but she was capable of providing for him one thing that he needed. Furthermore, as a man, it was his right to claim it, and her duty to provide it. He didn't care if she got mad as a wet hen. They needed to settle on a compromise of how things would be.

●●●

Amelia dozed off and on as she rested her back against the tree trunk. At one point she opened her eyes and saw Noonan making his way down the beach towards her, and she noticed that he was walking strangely. He was probably a half a mile to three quarters of a mile away. She squinted and put her hand up to her brow to shade her eyes. When she saw that it wasn't Noonan she jumped to her feet and gasped. Her knees went weak and she wanted to cry out, but she had no voice. Her emotions were so strong that she was simply unable to speak.

Her father! He was here. He must have landed with a rescue party. She looked quickly, up and down the beach to spot the ship but there was none. Maybe they had anchored on the other side of the island. Where was the rest of the rescue party? Maybe he alone had seen the smoke from her fire and had come on ahead of the others. That must be why Noonan wasn't back yet, he was with the other rescuers on the other side of the island.

Amelia wanted to run towards him, but for some reason she was frozen in place and unable to move.

Oh how she wanted to run and throw herself into her father's arms! Relief flooded through her body and she grinned so widely she thought her face might crack. Rescued, finally! She couldn't wait to see the look on Noonan's face when he saw that she had been right about the-

Amelia frowned suddenly. Something was wrong. Her father was gone and Noonan was walking towards her. She looked around, thinking she'd gotten mixed up. Surely her father wouldn't let Noonan be the one to come fetch her back to the rescue ship! And where's G P? He would be here too!

She watched as Noonan made his way towards her, and then she realized that she must be dreaming. Because Noonan did look a little bit like her father now. She was filled with a strong emotion for her father, and she wanted nothing more than to throw her arms around this man and hug him fiercely for a long time. But, seeing that it was not her father, but Noonan, scared her. Then she remembered the strange dream, of her father in the house with all those women, and how she wanted to be in there with him, and she shuddered with revulsion. How could she feel so repulsed by her father because of a dream, and yet still want to go and throw her arms around a man she despised, simply because his gait happened to remind her of her father. It was an optical illusion, and a mental trick and bad dream all in one.

Noonan strode forward until he was just a few feet away and passed her without saying a word. He plopped down in front of the fire and began his preparations to cook his crab.

That's when Amelia realized that she wasn't dreaming, and the last of the daylight vanished as the sun dropped below the horizon and night fell upon them.

•••

Amelia said nothing as Noonan cooked and ate his crab. She kept the fire stoked with wood, so that it burned brightly. One thing was for certain, that they could live here for years and have plenty of material for fires. But Amelia knew that their rescuers couldn't be too far away after three full days. There had probably just been some annoying mechanical hang-up, or worse, some sort of bureaucratic nonsense that had slowed down the rescue team.

"Do you want to take the early or later watch for the signal fire tonight, Noonan?"

He laughed, "Neither, Amelia."

"Neither?" Amelia turned to face him, "you can't expect me to stay up all night. That's hardly fair."

"Just as it's hardly fair to make me take a watch when I know that there will be no rescue. I don't believe in the idea that we will be rescued, therefore I refuse to take part in the signal fire maintenance."

"Noonan, what you *believe* or *do not believe* is hardly the issue here."

"And why isn't it?"

"Because, *Noonan,* whether you *believe* it or not, *if,* no *when* we get rescued, you will benefit greatly from *that.* Unless you plan to tell them that you want to stay here."

"You're wrong, Amelia. There will not be any rescue and the sooner you come to grips with it, the better off you'll be."

"Noonan, they knew our last position from the radio transmissions. They know the area that we're in. They are, *undoubtedly* on their way here at this very moment."

"You are wrong, Amelia."

"Is it wrong to have *hope,* Noonan? Hope that we will persevere, and we will fight hard and long, and eventually, we will have the best of this situation."

Noonan was shaking his head, "Look Amelia, let me give you an illustration."

"Okay, go ahead."

Noonan made a show of putting his hand up to his mouth, and biting on a fingernail. He used his other hand to pull the sliver free from his finger and he held the tiny sliver up in front of her face.

"See that tiny sliver of fingernail?"

"Yes. What about it?"

He tossed it over his shoulder.

"Now, even though you know the exact vicinity in which that sliver has been tossed, you'd still be hard pressed to find it. Wait until tomorrow and look while's there's good light to search in, and you'd still be hard pressed to find it. Now, just imagine that you didn't see me toss it over my shoulder and that the only thing you knew was that it was here on Rat Island. You are told to go find it."

"So?"

"Okay, so you've got just a few days to find a tiny sliver, maybe three-quarters of an inch long, by an eighth of an inch wide, and you have to find it, not one that looks just like it, but you have to find the *exact same one*

. . . on an island that is four miles long and a mile and a half wide. Now, to make it even more difficult, there are predators on the island that will eat that sliver if you don't find it soon enough. Snakes, lizards, crabs, ants, rats, birds and so on. Also, the living conditions themselves, the heat, lack of water and so on, might kill them before the predators get to them. So the chances that the rescuers are even in the correct vicinity are almost nil. Even if they are here," he held his arms up towards the sky, "flying overhead, if they blink one time, or happen to be looking out the other window, they'll miss us, and once they cross off a grid that has already been searched, they'll never re-search that same grid, because there's too many grids to go to next."

Amelia looked down. Noonan was making out a stark picture that she just as soon would not have imagined.

"Are you getting the picture, Amelia? I'm not being negative or despondent; I'm just being brutally honest and logical. This is why I reject it out of hand, that we'll be rescued. We're a tiny, microscopic needle lost in a universe of straw."

Amelia sighed and looked down at the sand. Was Noonan right? If he was it meant that she'd never fly again. She'd never see G P again. She'd never eat a real meal, sleep in a real bed, never have another bath with real soap and she'd never see her family again. It was too sad to contemplate.

It wasn't his blanket statement proclamations that they'd never get rescued, or the finality he spoke with that proved his own belief that they'd never get rescued that troubled Amelia. It was the one statement that he'd made that struck her like a blow to the stomach, knocking the air out of her lungs and doubling her over with pain. It was his explanation that, 'once they search a grid and cross it off they will never come back to that grid to search it again.' That had stunned her with its simple logic. When he'd made that statement, she'd seen, in her mind's eye, a man crossing off a sector on a map. Someone had been looking out of the wrong side of the airplane when they'd flown over, and because of that, they were written off.

Her sudden belief in that exact chain of events stunned her. It was true. There was no rescue coming for them. They had been skipped over. She remembered having heard the droning sound of the plane yesterday. That was the plane of searchers that had missed them, and now they weren't coming back.

Tears streamed down her face and she lay back on the sand and stared up at the stars. She had never felt so small, and so alone. The hope she felt, the hope for rescue, was the one thing she could cleave to in these horrific conditions that helped her keep her sanity about her. Without that hope, she was doomed. She wanted to stand firm, and keep her spirits up, keep the hope alive, but Noonan's dire assessment had outstripped her positive outlook. Now her world was gloomy. She had no rebuff for him, no positive platitudes, no plucky courage; she was no longer some dauntless heroine who would overcome all odds to survive. Now, she was nothing more than scared and beaten.

She cried harder than she'd ever cried in her life, and Noonan came over and lay down beside her and cradled her head against his chest and petted her softly on her back. She allowed this although, in her mind, it was just her and her father; she'd just skinned her knee and he was making the hurt go away. She fell asleep crying.

●●●

CHAPTER 8

Amelia slept through the night curled tight against Noonan. She woke up in the deep of the night, and she told herself, dreamily and thick-headed with fatigue, that she was not becoming more accepting of Noonan in any way, not in any philosophical sense, and certainly not in any physical way. That she slept next to him for one night meant nothing. She was just allowing herself one night, not even a full day, in which she was allowing him to comfort her in the depths of her despondency over her new-found understanding of their situation. It was simply a case of she had need of being comforted by another human being's closeness. That's all.

Her dreams were strange and confusing. She and Noonan were sitting on the beach, and the incoming waves were lapping at their toes. She realized that they were lying down and that Noonan had his hand on her bare skin, on her stomach, and it was moving down towards her pelvic area. She became anxious again, and she reached down with her hand to grab whatever it was that was moving there, and when she touched it, she realized that it was something that was thick and moving, something like a snake.

Amelia started and came awake, breathing hard. The dream had disturbed her, it had been so realistic. She could still feel the snake on her bare midriff, she reached down to pull her shirt down across her stomach, and what she grabbed wasn't a snake, but Noonan's hand. His fingers were under her pants! He jerked his hand back up and when it stopped moving it was back on her breast, rubbing her nipple between his fingers.

Amelia yelped and began thrashing around, throwing her elbow into him and trying to wriggle away from him. He tried to grab her but she rolled away and pulled herself up into a sitting position.

"How dare you, Noonan, trying to take advantage of me, in my, my, my *helpless* state!"

Noonan sat up and scooted back until he was leaning against the tree trunk, "I was just trying to make you feel better, that's all. You should be thanking me for my concern."

"Thanking you for your *concern*? You were trying to, to *rape* me!"

"That's impossible, Amelia."

"Impossible?" she sputtered, "Noonan, I woke up and you had your hand down my . . . close to my . . . *womanly area*. I'm a married woman and you have no right to attempt familiarity with me and by *force*, well that's rape!"

"Look Amelia. You came to an acceptance, last night, of just what our situation really is. You understand now, that we are very unlikely to ever leave this island."

"I was despondent about why our rescue is taking so long. *That* doesn't give you the right to manhandle me."

"Well, the truth is, Amelia, what I explained to you last night, is just the half of it."

Amelia stared at him, speechless, trying to figure out what he was getting at.

He continued, "the fact is, even if we make this place into home sweet home, under the best of all circumstances we won't live another month. It's almost impossible."

"I think you're completely wrong about that, and what does that opinion of our circumstances have to do with your taking liberties?"

Noonan held up a hand to signal her to stop, "Just bear with me, Amelia, I'm getting to it."

She nodded for him to continue as she crossed her arms across her chest.

"The fact is, one of us will get stung by a poisonous spider, or bitten by a snake, or we'll fall and break and arm or leg, or we'll get sick from something we've eaten. Or, we'll just flat out starve to death. Whatever it is, we aren't prepared for any medical catastrophe, heck we're not even equipped for a minor emergency."

Amelia was still vibrating with anger, "Noonan, all of this is neither here nor there. You were assaulting me against my will and we need to make some rules around here."

". . .and because we're not equipped for any major, or even minor emergencies, chances are that something will happen, and we're not going to come through it alive. Like I said, we'll be lucky if both of us, or even one of us, is still here in a month. I'm surprised we've made it four days to tell you the truth."

"That's a different conversation, Noonan. We need to, like I said, set down some rules of the island and rules of behavior."

"That's what I'm getting at, Amelia, rules of behavior."

Amelia was instantly suspicious. "*You* want to suggest some rules of behavior?"

"Yes," he nodded, "I am, Amelia."

Amelia didn't believe him, and she didn't trust him any further than she could throw him, but here he was about to suggest rules, so what could she do but listen? Maybe he was embarrassed about having gotten caught and was truly sorry? One could only hope.

"You see Amelia, it dawns on me, and I guess it has you by now, that there are many things that I'll never do again. I'll never have a good cigar again, and I'll never have a beer or a shot of bourbon again. I'll never get to fly again, or sail either, and I'll never get to sleep in a real bed, have a real shower, or listen to Bing Crosby or Amos and Andy on the radio again. I'll never get to wear a new suit, or eat another steak, or have ham and eggs for breakfast. I'll never see my family and relatives again, *ever*."

"If we are rescued, I'll never get to do those things again either, so what's the point, Noonan?"

"The point is this, Amelia" he paused, "there is one thing that we *can* do, and that we should do, to make our last remaining days here on earth more comfortable. We could bring a large measure of happiness to *each other* here by just agreeing to do one thing. Something that we might have even taken for granted the last time we were in civilization."

"What that?"

He paused for a long time with his eyes closed, and for a moment, Amelia thought that he might have dropped off to sleep. She knew that she certainly could, as tired and worn down as she was.

She whispered, "Noonan?"

He raised his hand, "Amelia, we have the ability, and some might say, I know I do, both the right and the obligation to do something for each other that we should consider."

"What?"

"Amelia, the whole world is out there, we are here. We might as well be on another planet. The rules are only good if we both agree to them, because there is no third-party law around to enforce the rules. But there is one rule that I believe that we should abide by."

"What's that?"

"The law that says a woman should be obedient to man and that she has a duty to offer up herself to comfort him to give him what he desires. A woman should be submissive."

Amelia shook her head. "That's for married couples, so I don't get it Noonan, what are you saying?"

"I'm saying that, even in the bible it says that women should be submissive to their husbands."

"Noonan, what G P and I do in our marriage is none of your business, just as what you and your wife do is nobody's business."

"But that's the whole point, Amelia."

"What is?"

"The fact that I'm never going to see my wife again and you will never see G P again."

Amelia felt tears streaming down her face again, but she still didn't get what Noonan was driving at, "Yes, we will. We *will* be rescued Noonan! What has all this talk of marriage got to do with the island?"

Noonan sighed and looked up at the stars. He reached over and grabbed two sticks of wood and threw them into the fire. An explosion of sparks flew into the air.

"The point, Amelia, is this; we are the only two people on this island. You can get down off your moral high ground and realize that we are very likely to die here very soon. I believe that God would look upon this situation as just, which is as if we were to consider our other-world marriages annulled, and that we should be, how shall we say, matrimonially-bound here on the island?"

Amelia's mouth dropped open. She started to speak but nothing came out. She blinked.

"You want to marry me? Is that what you're saying? Because if so; that's just absurd. I have no intention being part of such a farce. What's the point anyway?"

"You don't have an inkling of what I'm talking about Amelia. The point isn't about being married, Amelia. The *point* is that if we consider ourselves bound in that way, then we could assume the roles that are just and proper."

"And those roles are?"

"Well, you would be duty-bound in the eyes of God and man, when the time comes, to take care of my needs in a physical sense. You will acquiescence. Just remember Amelia, it's my right, as a man anyway."

"It's your *right?* Noonan are you crazy? I have no intention whatsoever of doing anything like that. Not only is it a crazy idea, it's repulsive."

"In the eyes of God, Amelia, we are alone here. This," he spread his arms, "is our Garden of Eden. God put woman on earth to please man."

"Noonan, you can talk until you are blue in the face, and you will never convince me that God summoned us here for this, and I certainly will never agree to this little scheme of yours. I will never, *ever* allow you to touch me again, is that understood?" she was upset and yelling now, and she could feel herself losing control, shaking all over.

"Amelia, before you say no, you should realize that as the man here, I am entitled to make the laws. We don't have to have an actual marriage ceremony, I just have to pronounce it in God's eyes, which I hereby do at this time. My previous marriage and yours too, are hereby considered null and void, and in the light of our present circumstances, our situation here, where we are the only man and woman on this earth, we are a prima facie, that means 'self-evident,' union of man and woman."

"Noonan, you should just be quiet and stop talking now, because I don't want to hear any more of this! I will not be a part of this! I shall not become bound by any misogynistic or medieval code of female servitude to any man not of my choosing, nor shall I consider myself bound to you similarly, or in any sense just because we are helplessly stranded visitors on this dreadful island. I will never knuckle under to your haranguing on the subject, so you might as well forget it."

"Let me finish, Amelia, in fact, I insist upon it. You see, as a lawful wife, lawful in God's eyes, you are under a duty, an obligation to attend to my needs. Doing so will only make me stronger, and if I'm stronger, our time here will be more comfortable. You have a *duty*, and I intend to see that you fulfill that duty. You cannot, and I repeat, you cannot deny that responsibility."

"Noonan, you are insane. The only way you will ever touch me like that is if you rape me. I'm not, nor will I ever be, your mate. I will always and forever spurn you, even if you are the last man on earth, which, apparently, for where we find ourselves, you are. And finally, I will not discuss this at length with you any longer. The very subject is one that I now consider taboo."

"That's where you are wrong, Amelia. You see, in the world we just left out there, it is legally, impossible for a man to 'rape' his wife. The Bible says as much too. A man may have to use force, but his wife cannot deny him what is his. So, while it may be forceful, it will *not* be rape. The Bible backs this up, from a moral standpoint. If you refuse, you are the one who is in the wrong, not I."

Amelia jumped to her feet and ran towards Noonan, "You're crazy, you son-of-a-bitch!" she kicked sand in his face and then, seeing that he was rolling over and about to get to his feet, she swung a kick at him and caught him full in the face. He yowled and fell down and Amelia saw blood spurting out from his busted nose onto the white sand. The redness of his blood stood in stark contrast to the tallow complexion he'd taken on since they'd arrived. After his initial sunburn, it had just become pastier. He had always been gaunt and now he appeared cadaverous.

She ran over to his crab-scraps and started pawing through the leavings and when she found what she wanted, she ran back to him.

She kicked him in the ribs and he flipped over onto his back and she pounced on top of his chest, sitting down roughly atop him. He grunted as the air went out of his lungs and he held his nose with both hands. Blood was trickling down his cheek onto the sand.

Amelia took the long crab pincher and then knocked his hands away from his face. She held it up in front of his eyes so that he could see what it was. Then she grabbed a fistful of his hair and pulled his head up off the ground. She held the pincher's sharp pointed end against his throat and pushed it in until a trickle of blood furrowed down to his chest.

"You ever try that with me, and I'll cut your throat. You hear me?" she screamed as she jabbed the crab claw into the skin of his throat again. He nodded weakly, eyes wide.

Amelia swung her leg off him and then pulled him up into a sitting position, and then held the crab claw in front of him again. There was a drop of blood on the pointed tip of the claw. She made a show of reaching down with it and jabbing him hard and upwards between his legs into the area of his groin.

She leaned forward into his face, "You ever get close enough to me again, or if you ever even let me see that thing again, I swear to you that I will cut it off."

He nodded and she let go of him and she stepped away from him quickly, just in case he tried anything, but he was too wounded to move.

Amelia backed up to her tree, and watched him for a moment. His nose was still bleeding, but that was nothing. She figured that she had probably broke a rib or two, and that wasn't dangerous either, and it would definitely slow him down for a few days. She walked over to the crab-dinner leavings and found another claw, and then she found two from the evening before. She would find some fibrous plants and make some twine and fashion herself a nice little knife and carry it with her always. She'd had enough. She saw his watch lying on the ground and she picked it up too. She thought it might come in handy.

Noonan moaned. That bitch had surprised him with her sneak attack. He wiped his face over and over, using the sand to scrub the blood from his hands, and a handful of leaves to clean his face.

He struggled to take a deep breath and moaned from the sharp pain in his chest. She had cracked a rib or two. That would slow him down for sure, but probably not as much as she might think. He was furious with himself for allowing her to get the jump on him. He just never expected a woman to be able to fight like that. Not that she was much of a woman.

As soon as he felt better, later today, or tomorrow, he'd show her what it's like to really get the jump on someone. Then he'd show her what it's like to have a real man take care of you. He sure wasn't going to be as gentle as G P probably was with her. Then, after she could see that it was useless to resist, he'd take her. Soon she'd come to realize that this was their home now, and she would do as any respectable woman would do; she'd be a faithful wife. When they both were working together to make their lives more comfortable, this place would become their new home. It would be slow going, but together they'd transform it into a home. Soon after that, they'd have one or two kids. They could make this work; all they had to do was get well, both of them, and then work towards a common goal, and that of course, was family. She would see. He'd make her understand that this was how it was supposed to be.

CHAPTER 9

Amelia made her way to the far end of the island, but stayed on the east side. It seemed logical to her that if they crashed on the east side of the island, that the rescue, if there was one, would come from that direction. She hadn't given up all hope, but she knew that with every passing day their situation became more and more hopeless. Her number one priority now was basic survival. With Noonan out of the picture it meant that she had to do everything alone.

One thing that Noonan said that made sense was that any small accident that befell them could spell disaster and death. If she stepped wrong and fell and broke an ankle or leg, it would mean almost certainly a much quicker death. The same thing applied to hundreds of potential disasters. A snake bite, a lizard bite, eating the wrong thing that would cause sickness, the island was a teeming mass of things lying in wait to destroy them and quickly finish them off.

She shuddered, having thought of snakes and lizards. She hadn't seen any snakes yet, but there were plenty of lizards, huge long green ones, red ones, and some black ones. They kept their distance, sunning on logs or rocks, and when approached they simply slithered away. Amelia had no idea if these things were poisonous or not, but she went out of her way to avoid them, just in case.

She didn't think that any of the birds posed a threat in any way, she didn't see how they could be, but she also knew, or had been told when she was younger, that birds carried diseases. She didn't know if it was true or not, but it hardly seemed to matter as there was no way that she could come into contact with them.

She remembered that Noonan had said that there were a few feral pigs on the island. She had no idea if they presented a threat in any way or not, but since she hadn't seen them she could only be glad that it was a problem she wouldn't have to deal with. You'd think that the pigs would feed on the rats, but who knew? Of course, Noonan talked about catching them and eating them, and while she had no problem eating swine, catching, killing and cooking them was, as her father used to say, *a whole other kettle of fish.*

With physical barriers and accidents and the dangerous animals accounted for, that left only one danger that was represented on the island and that was man. That man of cour.se, being Noonan. Amelia was convinced now that he was truly insane, and whether that insanity was a result of a bump on the head from their crash, or whether he was losing his mind due to the salt-water he was drinking, or if he had simply gone over the edge due to their situation she had no idea. Not that it mattered, because even if she knew, there was nothing she could do about it. Her best bet was to avoid him and deal with it in that manner. If she avoided him, then he'd be unable to do anything to shorten her survival.

One thing that Noonan hadn't said about the rescue was that if they didn't find anything they would keep on looking. There were three reasons they'd stop. Obviously they'd stop if they found them. They'd also stop if they found wreckage, the Electra, and if they found the wreckage and no bodies they'd assume that they'd drowned. Of course, if they found the Electra, they'd be rescued since the Electra was thirty yards offshore from the island. The final reason to stop looking was when they assumed that the survivors were no longer alive.

The authorities would stop looking if the costs of the search became too much, and the search dragged on for too long, but Amelia knew that G P would have no problem funding a private search, so she knew that the search would go on.

Amelia knew that the chances for rescue were still good, despite how Noonan had made her feel. Mainly because the authorities knew about all of these small islands, and they'd have to assume that they could have landed on one, or ditched into the ocean and then swum to shore, which was the truth, so, Amelia had a slim amount of hope still left, but in her darker moments, she had to admit that it was a longshot. In the air, even if you were looking for one of these tiny islands, they were hard to spot.

It was going to be difficult for her to keep a signal fire going all the time. Plus, she had to feed herself, and the most difficult problem she faced now, was that she had to defend herself against Noonan.

She was certain, beyond any doubt, that Noonan would be coming after her. In his twisted mind, he intended to rape her. Whether he was serious about considering them as husband and wife, or whether he was just using that as a way to justify his savage behavior she didn't know, and it didn't even matter. What mattered was that she be prepared to defend herself against his attack.

Why was it so important that he have relations with her? He must know that she'd resist. Surely he couldn't find romance in the act know that she despised him? Did he simply want to use her for his sexual release? She shuddered at the thought. Why couldn't he simply take care of the urge in the same manner as teenage boys all over the world, masturbation? She knew that grown men did that too, because she had walked in on G P once. A most embarrassing moment for both of them, and after G P's explanation, Amelia decided that it was a good thing because it lessened the number of times that he would come to her for the 'act'. Amelia had no idea why everyone enjoyed the act so much. In her opinion it was boring and being that close to someone was a disturbing feeling. She could do without it. G P had explained to her though, that social conventions dictated that, as man and wife, they were supposed to take care of each other. He also explained that it was important that they put forth the illusion to family, friends, and the public in general, that they were intimate. Amelia understood, though it was perplexing in complex ways that she had no interest in exploring further. So, she had told G P that he was relieved of his burden of being 'faithful' to her, in that sense, just as long as he didn't allow his dalliances to become public knowledge.

G P had agreed, and in that vein they'd cemented their marriage. Not exactly a marriage of convenience, but a close enough twin.

The problem Amelia now faced was in keeping Noonan at bay. IF he began an all-out war upon her it would be deadly for both of them. There was no way to provide for oneself, all alone, and defend oneself from a deadly enemy at the same time.

She hoped that if he could see that she wouldn't just willingly submit to his advances, that he'd give up and concentrate upon providing for himself, thus leaving her alone. Otherwise, the situation would become deadly in that it would pit them against each other physically. That was something that she wasn't ready to do. Sure, she had pummeled him earlier, but going any further than that was to consider killing him. She wasn't sure she was up to that, murder. Not just murder, but it meant getting rid of the only other person in your little world? It was too much to think about, and she wondered if he felt the same way. Surely he was not willing to go that far in his lust for sexual gratification?

You'd think that he would have enough to do, scrounging food for himself, rather than wasting time coming after her. Amelia realized that she had just given herself the answer of how to deal with Noonan. Her goal was to survive, to live long enough to be rescued. That was all it would take. She wished that Noonan could straighten out an help her to help them to survive, but it seemed that he had his priorities set on different things; things that Amelia had no interest in. She focused all her thoughts on one thing, and one thing only, survival. With or without Noonan, no matter what it took, she would be there on that beach when the rescue ship arrived.

She sat on the beach with the ocean on her left and a view of the jungle to her right and the long stretch of beach directly before her and thought about what to do next. Her new campsite was a mile or so from their original 'landing' spot which is where Noonan was staying. Her little cove was at a point where the beach met a rocky outcropping. The waves crashed up against the dark brown rocks, but not with any great force and the jungle jutted out almost to the back side of the rocky area. The shallow water just beyond the rocks seemed as if it might be a good place to find mussels or clams and since it was only ankle to knee-deep in places, Amelia knew she could get in without having to resort to swimming. She saw a conch shell, and realized that if she had seen it as a youngster, she would have squealed with delight and would have wanted to take it home and put it on a shelf. Now, she looked at it dully, and wondered if there was anything inside that she could eat; probably not.

Hopefully it was too shallow for the sharks, but if and when she got into the tide-pools area, she would still keep a sharp lookout for the sinister fins. The distance from the rocky area to the jungle was only a few yards, but it seemed enough that once she built a fire and the landward side of the rocks, it would be enough open space to deter the rats from crowding her campsite.

She jumped up when she remembered that they were eating when their fight had started. She immediately began walking back to the campsite.

•••

Noonan stood up gingerly and looked around. He needed to throw some wood on the fire and eat his crab. He picked it up from where it had fallen and brushed all the sand off of it. He stoked the fire and then threaded the meat back onto the stick. The food would do him good. The ground around the fire was dark from the blood from his nose. He kicked sand over the blood splattered areas. Not that it mattered, but seeing the blood on ground reminded him that he'd been bested by a scrawny woman. That did.

He stuck his meat stick over the flames and then walked over to the water bowl. He sat down and picked up the bowl and took a long deep drink.

He heard something in the jungle. The movement, probably Amelia, was about ten or twenty yards out in the thick of it. He hoped she was getting attacked by the rats.

"I can hear you out there, Amelia."

He cocked his head, waiting to see if she was going to answer. Maybe she was afraid, out there alone, and wanted to talk, maybe even to tell him that she was considering what he proposed earlier.

Something moved again, this time on the opposite side of the jungle, across the fire. He peered into the darkness, thinking he'd see her out there, lurking.

What was she doing? He knew it was her because there was no one else it could be.

Then he remembered the sound of the coconuts being dropped from the trees by the crab. It could be that too, or, it could be one of the pigs. How tasty would that be, to have roasted pork?

There was another sound, this time to his right. What the hell was going on? It had to be her. But what was her game? He should go out there, chase her down, and drag her back to the campfire. Show her just who is boss around here.

Then he heard a twig snap, and this time it was close, very close, just behind him. He whirled and ran into the brush quickly, saw movement directly ahead and chased after her. She eluded him though, and after twenty seconds of running, he stopped to listen but could hear nothing. She must be doing the same thing, stopping so she wouldn't give away her position.

He cupped his hands behind his ears, to pick up any slight sound of movement, and then he waited.

●●●

Amelia grinned. Her trick had worked perfectly. She stepped into the clearing and saw that his meat was cooked just about perfectly. She grabbed the stick out of the ground and ran away as silently as she could. She didn't want him to hear her crashing through the jungle and give chase. About halfway back to her end of the beach the meat had cooled enough for her to eat it, and she feasted.

●●●

Noonan made his way back to his camp after having given up on finding her, and could see that the rats had besieged the camp.

When he arrived and saw that the meat was gone, he was furious. His stomach growled. Now he would have to hunt down another one of the crab-beasts and he knew it would be more difficult what with his ribs crippling his movements.

●●●

Amelia ate half of Noonan's crab and then tossed the remainder into the waves. Now he would have something to occupy his time, finding food instead of finding her.

She decided to stalk him first thing tomorrow, and as soon as he had a crab she'd figure out a way to get that one too. The last thing a starving man would be thinking about was rape. Plus, every morsel of food that she stuffed into her body gave her more fuel to outrun him with.

●●●

CHAPTER 10

Noonan woke up just as the sun was rising and the fire was almost out. He stoked it and got some flames going, and decided that he would spend the day finding food. He could get one of the big crabs, as long as he didn't have to climb a tree to do so, and hopefully he'd be able to kill it without too much trouble. To kill it by slinging it against a tree trunk, with his ribs hurting like they did, would be impossibility. He decided that he would use a stick as a spear, and kill one that way. He also decided that he would find some fruits and roots by foraging through the jungle, if he could do so and avoid the armies of rats. He caught a scent of flowers in the air. A slight breeze stirred the leaves overhead. He sniffed the air again, this time when he turned to face the interior of the island. There was definitely the scent of something being carried in the wind. What was it, gardenias, lavender, roses? Whatever it was, the scent was strong in the air. After a few minutes the scent dissipated and he decided that the odor had come from another island. Perhaps there was an island just over the horizon from them, and island full of people, not rats and crabs, and the vegetation was lush and filled with flowers and whatnot. He turned back to his fire. Wondering about what was just over the horizon was a ridiculous luxury that he couldn't afford. If there was they'd probably never see it, and that was enough to kill Noonan's fleeting interest in it.

He really missed having coffee too. To think that he would never have a morning coffee against just made him madder at Amelia for being unable to land the Electra on the beach. Sure, it never would have flown again without any fuel, but it would have made an excellent shelter, and it would have made their rescue more probable just from the standpoint of being spotted from the air. He also might have been able to use the radio to signal for help. None of which was possible now, thanks to Amelia. Lady Lindy indeed!

It did him no good to sit around and think about what he didn't have, like coffee, bacon and eggs, and orange juice, so he stood and looked around, and decided to head into the jungle to try and find another crab.

He walked into the jungle and began searching up and down the tree trucks as he walked, hoping to spot one of the huge crabs. He used his stick as a swagger cane as he walked, knocking branches out of his way, and keeping it ready to use on one of the huge crabs.

As he made his way through the jungle, he noticed that the rats seemed scarce, and he wondered if it was due to the specific location in the jungle, or whether it was just that the rats seemed to be night creatures who rarely ventured out en masse in daylight hours. After giving it careful consideration, he decided it was the latter.

At one point he spied a coconut crab but it was too far up the tree trunk to safely climb up after it, so he watched it for a few moments, hoping it would scoot backwards enough that he could knock it loose. Twenty minutes later, the crab was still well over thirty feet up the trunk, and seemed in fact to be climbing higher rather than backing down, and Noonan gave up on it. He looked down, slowly straightening his neck back out, because it was cramping from having been angled back for so long. Leaning on the trunk of another coconut tree, he massaged his neck for a few moments to get the kinks out.

He noticed as he was rubbing his neck, that the trunk he was leaning against felt soft, as if it were hollow inside. He stood up, turned around and looked at it. The trunk was broken off at about three feet in height, and the inside seemed to be hollowed out. Inspecting it closer, he saw burn marks, and decided that lightning had struck the tree trunk and had either blown it apart, or set it ablaze at some point long ago. Peering inside the hollowed out trunk, he saw that it held standing water and palm leaves. Actually, the water seemed to be the color of milk, and it had a few leaves in it. Wondering if it was drinkable, he reached inside and dipped a finger into it, and then brought it out and tasted the drops on his finger.

He was rewarded with a pungent, yet sweet-tasting milky substance. It had a strongly fermented alcoholic kick to it too.

Smiling, Noonan reached in and put his entire hand into the liquid, just to test the depth of the liquid, and was surprised to find that he could reach in almost all the way up to his elbow! There was easily a gallon and a half or maybe two gallons, of the drink. He cupped his hand and pulled it out, brimming with the milky concoction. He picked the palm leaves out of it, and then brought it to his mouth and drank it as fast as he could. This set out a burst of hiccups and he laughed. He quickly slurped up five or six handfuls of the juice and then drunkenly stuck his face into the hollowed out trunk to ascertain just how much of the juice remained.

Laughing joyously, he realized that he had found a mother-lode of booze, manufactured by the jungle itself. He realized that it was fermented coconut juice, and made immediate plans to gather as many coconuts as he could, drain them of their juice and store them in the hollowed out trunk. In a few days, or weeks at most, he'd have another batch. He grinned at his luck.

In his weakened state the fermented coconut juice made his staggeringly drunk in minutes, and he sat back against the opposite trunk and languidly contemplated just how much nicer his discovery of the jungle juice had made his situation. Short of rescue, it was just about as much as one could hope for. Life on the island would be a sight better now that he had some island rum. He just wished he had a good wooden cask to store it in. Of course, the tree was that in and of itself, so that solved its own problem. Except that he'd have to trudge back and forth here to get it. Still though, booze on Rat Island! He giggled drunkenly; maybe he should name his new grog *Rat Island Rum*. He drank some more of his grog and headed back to his campsite.

●●●

Amelia had woken early, just before sunrise, and the first thing she saw was that the beach was twenty or thirty of the enormous crabs. She noticed that they weren't coming from the ocean. They were making their way from the end of the beach, a rocky promontory, and they were headed inland, towards the jungle. She walked over the rocky area and watched as several more crawled out of the cracks and crevices in the rock. She'd found their colony. She began walking back towards the tree-line at the jungle, and she noticed several hardened sand burrows where more of the giant crabs were coming out. She'd never seen one of them in the water, which proved that Noonan's friend had probably been correct, that sea-water would kill them. But now she knew where a food source was located, and that would save her a great deal of time.

She wondered if she should share this secret with Noonan. She knew that she'd have to eventually, but for now, it would be her secret. If he began acting more civil, she'd tell him, if not, let him find it on his own.

About halfway back to the camp, she came upon a strange sight. One of the giant crabs had one of the large island rats in its claws, and was making a meal of it. It was disgusting, but Amelia knew that the crabs had to have a large supply of food, and there was one thing that this island had in quantity, and that was rats.

Amelia had another problem to solve too, and that was the fact that Noonan had the bowl for the water. She knew that she had a supply of fresh water, but it still needed to be boiled. Once it was boiled she could keep a supply stored in hollowed out coconut shells, of which there were plenty around, but the fact remained, the water had to be boiled. She knew Noonan would miss the bowl if she took it but since he seemed to have no problem drinking the sea water, he might not care if she took the bowl. He'd probably deny her out of pure spite.

Amelia arrived at the campsite and the moment she saw him she realized he was sloshed.

"Noonan, you're completely soused.'

"No, Amelia, I am not!"

"Yes, you are, you're practically nose-less!"

"Nope, you're wrong Amelia, see? I'm not drunk," he reached his hand up to touch his nose "I can still feel it."

Amelia smirked, "But you had to check, didn't you? See Noonan, I knew you were foundering the moment I saw you!"

"So what, Amelia, what's the big deal? Who are you now, Carrie Nation? You heading up a new chapter of the Temperance League?"

"Where'd you get it Noonan? The hooch, the sauce. Where? How?"

"None of your bee's wax, Amelia. It's not like I had to *take the pledge* when we got marooned here. I found it, you want a taste, go find your own."

"I don't want any of your stinking rot-gut Noonan. I only asked because it surprised me, that's all."

"Well, of course you wouldn't have a sip. Not you. Not the high and mighty Amelia Earhart, the famed *Lady Lindy*. Look at you, putting on airs, acting like you're to the manner born."

Amelia started to argue, but closed her mouth, realizing that it wouldn't do any good. She walked away, and when she glanced over her shoulder to see if he was looking; and he wasn't, he'd already begun stumbling off into the jungle.

She followed him into the jungle, hoping that he was so soused that he wouldn't realize that she was following him.

•••

The further into the jungle Noonan walked, the more sober he became. After a while he came upon a crab just as it was starting its climb up the trunk of the coconut tree. Using his stick he stabbed through it, right there on the tree, and when he pulled the spear stick out, the crab fell to the ground with a wet plop.

He picked up the carcass and turned to head back to his camp. His stomach was grumbling and he knew that he could get back to his camp before the fire burned out, He would be eating within an hour.

Amelia watched Noonan find and kill the crab and then she crouched down into the brush as he walked by, obviously heading back to cook and eat the crab. As she crouched he felt a furious itching on her foot, and she pulled her shoe and sock off to scratch it, and was horrified to see that one of her toes was completely black and swollen. Her stomach flip-flopped and she felt a wave of nausea. When it passed, she put her sock and shoe back on and promised herself that she'd stop inspecting her body so closely. It sickened her to think that the island itself was eating away at her in some way that she couldn't battle. Ignorance was bliss until she was physically disabled by some ailment or accident.

Amelia walked out a ways in a ninety degree angle from the direction he was heading, and then she began running back towards the campsite, hoping she could get there before him. When she arrived, she ran quickly to the water bowl, picked it up and ran out onto the beach, and then down the jungle tree-line for fifty yards or so. She hid the bowl out of sight, and then headed back to his campsite.

She arrived just as he did, and once again, she squatted down on her heels and watched as he began cooking his crab. He jammed the stick into the sand, and then angled the stick forward so that the meat was just above the flames. He leaned back against the tree trunk to wait for the meat to cook. Amelia wondered what she could do this time, to get him away from the meat. She would be unable to draw him out like she did last time; he wouldn't fall for that trick again, so she racked her brain trying to come up with some sort of ruse to get him away from that fire.

She heard a noise, and looked at him, and was surprised to see that he had fallen asleep! He was snoring. He was probably tired, and after having been loaded the natural inclination was to doze. Either that or he was passed out cold.

She crept forward and approached from his side.

Noonan heard a noise and jerked awake. He had dozed off, waiting for his meat to cook. He was completely exhausted. Keeping the fire going meant feeding it every few hours. The lack of sleep was beginning to wear on him. His trek to get the crab had exhausted his store of energy.

And being drunk had taken it out of him, too.

He figured that the noise was probably Amelia, out there in the jungle, a few yards away, watching him.

His mouth dropped open when he saw that his meat-stick was gone. His crab! He jumped to his feet, his ribs screaming in pain as he did.

"Amelia! You bitch! You bring my food back right now! If you don't... I swear I will track you down and-" He stopped in mid-sentence when he saw that it was gone too. The water bowl was gone.

He suddenly realized what she was about to do, and exactly where she'd be. He took off running through the jungle.

•••

Amelia wasted no time when she stepped back into the jungle and away from his campsite. She took several huge bites of the crab and kept chewing and swallowing as fast as she could. Finally, seeing a horde of rats in the bushes, she tossed the remainder of the crab into their midst and the entire dark gray mass began swarming over the meat. She could actually hear them tearing into each other as they fed in a frenzy. She shuddered.

She went to the spot where she'd hidden the water bowl, picked it up and set off through the jungle. She heard Noonan, off in the distance, screaming and cursing at her, and she picked up her pace. She hoped that he didn't notice the missing water bowl, and if he did, that he wouldn't figure out what she was going to do next. Her survival would be severely limited if he figured it out and found a way to stop her.

She found the trail and realized that Noonan's camp was far closer to the mud-hole than where she had started out. Of course, he would have to have immediately realized what she would do, and have set out at that moment, if he was to beat her to the spot. She seriously doubted that he would do so.

She came to the crossroads of the two trails and she was about to congratulate herself when she saw him. He was bent over the mud-hole, and at first she thought he might be getting a drink, even though it was muddy, the water was still good water, which is to say, not salt-water. But then she saw that he was not bent over and drinking, but squatting down next over it. She changed her position in her cover, she didn't want him to know that she was here, and then she saw what he was really doing.

He was squatting down directly over the hole, and he had his pants around his ankles. He was defecating in the only fresh-water supply on the island!

She jumped when he laughed.

"I know you're out there Amelia."

Amelia watched as he looked around, obviously hoping she'd show herself. When she didn't, he spoke again.

"You keep getting my dinner Amelia. So I decided to spice up your precious water supply. If I can drink sea-water, so can you little Miss High and Mighty, and until you decide to leave my food alone, this will be where I take my daily constitution."

Amelia was disgusted by him, but said nothing and stayed hidden.

"Amelia? Do you hear me?"

Amelia slowly backed out of the area and went back to her end of the beach.

•••

Noonan made his way back to his camp, doing his best to avoid the hordes of rats, and along the way he stumbled across an unusual sight; a swarm of rats feasting on a crab carcass. There was no outer shell, and Noonan realized that Amelia must have grabbed his meat stick and flung it into the jungle, and the rats had found it. He watched as they swarmed over it and at one point the roiling mass of rats thinned out and he saw his cook-stick. So, that was exactly what had happened. Amelia had tossed his dinner to the rats. He waited a while until they scattered, all the crab meat gone now, and he retrieved his sharpened cook-stick. AS he walked back to camp he thought about what he must do. He must figure out a way to neutralize Amelia from stealing his food and he must get his water bowl back . . . and he decided that he must try a dinner of rat meat.

It made sense too, since the rat population was large enough that he would always have meat at hand. The supply of rats on the island would never be exhausted. If the meat was edible, he would just need a way to trap and kill them.

•••

Amelia sat back against the tree trunk and looked out over the ocean. She had set up at the south end of the island and on the east shore. Halfway up the beach, maybe two miles or so was where they'd crashed and where their original camp was. Noonan still occupied that camp, and she doubted that Noonan would ever change camps.

She liked being able to take in the entire beach, their crash spot just offshore, and Noonan's camp in one look. Even though she had invaded and had stolen from his camp twice, he had never attempted to come to her camp. She didn't know if it was because he was afraid to venture out away from the fire at night, or if he was just being lazy. Maybe he was afraid of her.

She stoked her signal-fire, just in case there was a ship out there near the horizon, and she looked up at the stars.

She dreamed that next to the rats there were hundreds or even thousands of the giant crabs. The rats were crawling all over each other as if they were somehow being held back and they seemed to want to be loosed so that they could get her. The crabs were waving their pinchers in the air and snapping them.

Then she woke up with a headache.

She remembered very little about the dream, but she wanted to ask Noonan if he was having bad dreams, but she didn't know from one minute to the next which Noonan she'd be talking to, the boring, average co-pilot, or the raving madman. He seemed to flip from one to the other in an instant.

•••

Noonan woke in the middle of the night and the fire had died away. He glanced around quickly, afraid that he would find himself surrounded by the rats. They were still staged at the edges of the jungle tree-line, just about ready to burst forth from the shadows. The only thing which hindered their attack was that the embers of the fire still were glowing. The light was fading fast though, and Noonan rolled to his feet and ran out of the area as fast as he could. Reaching the middle of the wide expanse of beach, he paused, his eyes being drawn naturally, in the darkness of the night, to the only light that shone, other than the moon. Amelia's fire was blazing properly, acting as both signal fire for any would-be rescuers, and also as her very own security against the marauding hordes of rats. Noonan stared wistfully at the warm yellow light just a mile down the beach and he had an idea. He thought it over and it brought a smile to his face when he realized that it would work.

He started towards her camp.

•••

Amelia slept a dreamless sleep, waking every two hours to check on her fire, and readjust her position to get comfortable again. Sleeping on sand was okay, it was soft and warm, but she found that she had to have some sort of cloth between her body and the sand. As she slept she moved around, and every time she woke, she needed to re-position the shirts she was laying on.

At one point though, she awoke due to a sound. She was sure it was a man-made sound too. Her head came up off the sand and she saw a movement. Afraid that the rats had braved the firelight and attacked, she sat up and drew her legs in underneath her and snatched up the shirts she'd been sleeping on, and held them across her body. The movement, whatever it had been, stilled. Something was over there, on the other side of the fire. She willed her body still, and even pretended to close her eyes in an attempt to appear as if she was drifting off to sleep again. Then, from under her lidded eyes, open just a sliver to spy whatever it was, she saw it. A stick from the fire being pulled out slowly. Then the form rose up from the sandy beach, the end of the stick fiery and glowing. Noonan! She wondered for a moment if he was using her fire to cook something on the stick, and then she realized what his intent was. Her suspicions were confirmed when he turned and walked away from her campsite. He wasn't cooking, he was stealing fire! She wanted to chase him down and throw the fire-stick into the ocean, but caught herself short; realizing that doing so would have the opposite intended effect for her. For her to take the fire away from him would only mean that he would find some other reason to come back. If her allowing him to have fire due to her efforts meant that it would have the effect of keeping him away from her, then so be it. That was a deal she could live with. Sooner or later though, she'd find something that he had, and she didn't, and she'd demand her quid pro quo trade.

CHAPTER 11

Two days later Amelia opened her eyes at sunup and immediately noticed the debris strewn all along the beach. She jumped up and ran towards it. It was scattered for a couple hundred yards along the shore, and as she approached it, she was aware that it was from the Electra. Of that there was no doubt.

Not much of it was usable though, it was mostly just waterlogged papers, maps, and two seat cushions and lots of other debris.

She was setting aside two seat cushions when Noonan come running out of the jungle. He had obviously just seen the bounty that had washed ashore. Amelia began running towards a suitcase that she recognized as hers, so that Noonan wouldn't get it before she did. Any clothes would be valuable, both for wearing and for the utility of the cloth itself. Their situation had neatly turned both of them into mendicants, but it was too late to complain about it. The last thing she wanted was to turn into a malcontent like Noonan.

Noonan was running towards several pieces of metal that were still being washed over by the waves. Amelia had no idea what use he'd have for them, but she was focused on her own efforts to gather useful items.

They each began scurrying back and forth, from the beach to the tree-line each grabbing an item that caught their eye and then taking it back to the tree-line to hide it. They rushed to and fro for almost an hour until the beach was once again clean of foreign objects.

Noonan disappeared after that, obviously ferrying his new-found treasure back to his camp site, and Amelia began doing the same.

Amelia had found her suitcase and a few shirts, three pair of pants, no more shoes though, which was especially frustrating, since she knew there was two more pair on board. However, her best find was a small knife.

Amelia opened the knife, inspected the blade, then folded it closed and slid it into her back pocket. She had two seat cushions, several maps, two packs of waterlogged cigarettes that she planned to barter to Noonan, and some of the beechnut gum. She'd have to hide everything very carefully though, because she knew that as wily as he was, she could lose it all if she wasn't inconspicuous about where she hid her treasures. She decided to lead him on a chase, willy-nilly, go into the jungle a few times and act as if she were digging holes at random, all the time knowing that he was spying on her, and then wait for him to go on a surreptitious treasure hunt. It would take him awhile before he realized that something's afoot.

During their scramble, she'd seen Noonan pick up one of his flasks of whiskey which apparently was still full. She wondered just how many of those flasks he'd brought with him. She knew he'd been drinking the hooch when they'd crashed because she'd smelled it. Therefore, if he'd found another flask, then he'd started out with more than one. He'd whooped for joy when he found it, and immediately unscrewed the cap and took a deep slug. The alcohol must have hit him hard because he staggered around drunkenly for a couple of minutes.

Amelia had found a bra, which she decided would come in handy for straining water before boiling. The only problem with that idea was that Noonan had reclaimed the 'bowl.' Either he'd come to her camp and stolen it back, or the crabs had dragged it away and he'd come across it and reclaimed it.

The only other item of interest was a long steel rod, about five and a half feet in length which Amelia had seen Noonan pick up as his first choice when he'd hit the beach, and she figured he would use it as a spear for fish, and crabs.

She'd found several flat pieces of metal, one of which she'd grabbed because it would make a serviceable skillet. She knew that Noonan had taken two more of the pieces too, and she realized they must have been part of the fuselage that had been torn away on impact, or when the Electra ground against the coral under the waves. There were tell-tale scratch marks on the underside of the pieces.

Noonan stowed his new possessions and picked up he long steel rod. The end of it had an eyelet, which was big enough to loop a finger through, and would give him something to use as leverage when throwing it as a spear.

The end was blunted, but the rod was such a small diameter that it still made a nice spear. It would never break like wooden ones and it had enough tensile strength that he could use it to pick up the rats he speared, with no fear that it would break.

He began his rat hunt in earnest.

•••

By the end of the day, the refuse from the beach had been plundered and Amelia took her bounty and made her little camp as comfortable as possible. Even with the extra items she had very little in the way of possessions. She was glad that they'd found the clothes though. There were no shoes or shoelaces but she could use the knife to cut roots and make bow-strings for several more fire-kits if needed.

The whole incident had taken just a couple of hours. Amelia took the watch from her pocket and carefully wound it. Despite having been in the water, it still worked perfectly. She wondered if Noonan had noticed that it was missing. Not that it mattered. One could easily look up at the sun and tell what time of morning or afternoon it was. It wasn't as if the exact hour or minutes mattered here on the island. Still, it was a piece of civilization, and because of that alone, it mattered to her.

Amelia had wanted to ask Noonan if he'd had any strange dreams during the night, but she had decided to wait and ask later.

She watched as the afternoon drifted slowly away, and she realized that she wasn't even hungry. She'd eaten so much crab that she was actually full.

She did wish that she had some tea. Maybe tomorrow she would try to find a plant that would yield some tea if she boiled the leaves. It would be nice to sit here and look out over the ocean and have a cup of hot tea.

Amelia knew that the best find had been their suitcases, full of clothes. Now they each had three or four changes of clothes. The only thing that the debris could have yielded that would have been more surprising would have been a working radio, or flashlights.

She decided that the first thing she would do is whittle a few spears. The blade was sharp and would make a great weapon, and it should be useful in helping her make some other tools.

She spent the rest of the day and the following days admiring her new possessions, setting up her camp, and trying to figure out new uses for the bounty she'd gathered. She didn't see Noonan for the entire three days.

Amelia's days had become monotonous with drudgery and routine. Lying in her camp, lethargic, fatigued, sunburned, starving and sad. She avoided the sun when she could, and racked her brain for ways to procure food. Her body was sloughing skin like a shedding snake from her extreme sun burn and she itched all over. The area over her stomach was bruised an enormous blotch of ugly purplish and black. She had no idea what had caused the discoloration. Her clothes were almost all rotted now, they hung in tatters off her skeletal body, and she knew that the day would come soon that both she and Noonan would be reduced to walking around sans clothes of any sort. Unless of course, they could fashion something out of leaves and bark. Rat hides sewn together maybe? She shook her head to dispel the image of her and Noonan on the island, nude and helpless, like wild animals, a modern-day Adam and Eve.

She tried the tide-pools, looking for some sort of shellfish, but couldn't find anything. The two sharks appeared on the second day, menacingly swimming in and out of the shallows, and that was enough to keep her out of the water for good. The sharks were about five feet in length, and they always seemed to be together. Watching them swim in and out of the shallow area and along the length of the beach on this side of the island convinced Amelia that there were no safe areas in the water. They were fast swimmers too, appearing in minutes from one end of the island to the other. She couldn't be sure it was the same two sharks, but it didn't matter either. They guarded the water, and dared her to enter their realm. Amelia had no desire to test them.

CHAPTER 12

Noonan hadn't seen Amelia for two days now. Other than the times in the night when he'd creep up on her camp in the dead of the night and steal a stick of fire and run it back to his own camp. He did this in the middle of the night, but decided that he needed to figure out a way to keep his own fire going longer during the night. Maybe he'd search the jungle for larger logs, or figure out an arrangement where the firewood could be laid out to burn longer.

As he walked through the jungle, looking for both firewood and crabs, he came across a spot where the jungle canopy overhead was thinnest, and more light shone down onto his trail than in other places in the jungle. He used this spot as a place to rest his legs and catch his breath. Going without food and water was taking its toll on him physically. As he sat and caught his breath and looked around, the sun shone directly through the palm fronds overhead and he was suddenly struck by a profound thought; that God was testing him. He ruminated the idea over and over in his mind, trying to follow the trail of thought to its logical conclusions. An hour passed and he was deep in thought, and finally tears began to stream down his face and he lowered himself to his knees and he looked up to the sapphire sky showing through the palm fronds overhead and he began to pray.

•••

Amelia sat with her back against the rocks, her body facing seaward, and she let her mind drift as she gazed out at the empty wide expanse of the blue waves and cloudless sky. She tried to will herself to dream of G P and her home, her family and friends, but no images would appear in her mind. It was as if her entire being-ness had shrunk down to this tiny spit of land, thousands of miles away from all others. This island had become her universe; one within a mother universe, with no way to communicate with any other inhabitants.

•••

Noonan walked through the jungle until he came upon a large massing of the rats. He had brought an extra shirt with him, and using it as a sling, had filled it with six or seven smaller coconuts. He had his steel spear, and also his wooden stick, which he'd wield as a club. The rats were large, for the most part, about twelve to fourteen inches in length, not including the tail, and they probably weighed on average maybe two or three pounds. After gutting one, he figured that the actual useable meat would be about one or two, maybe as much as six or eight ounces. So, he figured that if he got five or six of the larger ones, then he'd be able to make a decent meal.

He jammed the end of the rod into the ground and it wavered as he stood next to it. Hefting a large coconut, he set his feet, and then threw the coconut at the thickest clump of rats and the injured ones immediately began squealing and the others fled outwards. The four or five that had been stunned by the coconut were flopping on their sides and trying to regain their feet. Noonan grabbed his spear, pulled the end out of the ground and stepped forward and made a stabbing motion. The speared rat slid up the rod, and he jammed downwards again and speared a second one. He put a foot forwards and placed his shoe above the two speared rats and pulled the spear upwards using his shoe to clear the rod of the two dead rats. Then he speared three more that had been stunned by the coconut. When he was finished, several rats came in to try and eat their dead and fallen comrades, and he speared them too.

When he was finished he had eight large-sized rats. He scooped them up into his extra shirt and headed back to camp.

Upon arrival back at camp, he stoked the fire and then began gutting the rats. When he finished them he speared the meat onto the stick and put it over the flames. He jammed the end of the stick in the ground and waited for the meat to cook. Since he'd never cooked rat, and had never even seen it cooked, he had no idea what it would look like, so he decided to make sure that he cooked it very well done.

Without a sharp knife, he'd been unable to get all the fur off the skin, and his meat was one-sided with meat, and the other side was still dark gray, almost black, and furry.

The smell of the burning rat hair was almost enough to make him nauseous, but he had no choice but to endure it. What he wanted was a hot meal, and protein. Obviously, if the taste was anything approaching edible he'd be happy.

After the rat meat had cooked for a while, he found a flat rock and used a stick to push the sizzling steaks off of his improvised kebab stick. His mouth watered, but his stomach was doing flips as he picked up a piece of the cooked meat and took a bite. He gagged at first, because the meat was extremely greasy and gamey tasting. Once he began chewing though, he found it to be likeable. What he needed was some sort of spice, or something to go along with the meat to disguise the gamey taste. Maybe coconut or perhaps he could search the jungle for some sort of berries, or roots or something to add to it. Even if he had to always eat it as a single dish he would do so, simply because he needed the protein. The taste was not bad, and certainly a welcome alternative to crab.

He wondered if any of the birds on the island were edible. The steel rod would make a great spear, and if he could sneak up on one . . . then he remembered the two wild pigs he'd seen. With the steel rod, he had a chance of bringing one of them down. A wooden spear would never do it, because even though the pigs were small, he would never be able to fashion a spear that would puncture them deep enough without breaking. Using the steel rod though, he should have no problem in spearing one. He smiled at the thought of roasting pork over his fire. Of course, most of it would go to waste, but for a day or two he'd feast mightily.

●●●

Amelia hid in the bushes spying on Noonan. She felt like she'd spent half her time on rat island huddled in the jungle spying on Noonan, and she knew that he tried his best to spy on her too. She tried to imagine what it would have been like to be marooned with someone who worked with her as a team. Their survival would be much easier, and profoundly more comfortable.

Now, he was eating something. She couldn't tell what it was, but he had a lot of it. She could tell that it wasn't crab because she didn't see any of the crab shells or claws strewn about. The crab meat was whitish and pink, and whatever it was Noonan was roasting over the flames was dark. Had he found an edible bird, or some sort of pig that he'd killed and cooked? She hadn't eaten in almost three days and she was trembling with hunger, and faint, her body drugged with fatigue.

The slight breeze shifted and Amelia caught a whiff of the meat. Whatever it was, it smelled rank and had a hint of singed hair.

She watched as he ate, and then he leaned back and closed his eyes and drifted off to sleep. No doubt his full belly and fatigue lulled him into a peaceful sleep. Amelia thought about what she was going to say to him, in her appeal to him to work together with her in making their stay here as comfortable as possible until the rescue, if there was one. She frowned and chastised herself; Noonan's pessimistic thinking was already rubbing off on her. She corrected herself, *when* their rescuers arrived, not *if*.

She fell back from her hiding spot and then walked slowly into Noonan's camp, and what she saw troubled her greatly. The smell too, was indescribable. It was of burnt flesh, greasy, gamey and rank. Like burnt oil and singed hair. The odor alone almost made her swoon. Seeing what it was, she realized it for the wicked scene that it was. She was profoundly shocked at just how far Noonan's grip on reality had slipped.

"Noonan, wake up, it's me," and she looked down and saw the rat carcasses, "oh Lord, Noonan, what are you eating? What have you done?"

His answer was a loud snore, sated no doubt from his repast, so Amelia sat down on the opposite side of the fire and waited for him to wake up. Her own stomach, enticed by the idea of food, rumbled, yet she knew that she could never get it down without getting sick and throwing it up immediately. She simply couldn't eat rat.

•••

Noonan felt drowsy after eating the rats, and he leaned back against the tree trunk and looked down at his legs. The cloth of his pants was more holes than fabric; something on the island was eating away at their clothes at an alarming rate. He noticed also that his toenails were all purplish-black and two were a sickly yellow. He was rotting from the inside out. His shoulders were achy and tight, as if the muscles in his back were drawing inwards. He was constantly tired, and if he'd had the energy he would stretch and work out the pain, but it was difficult to think about exercise when it took major effort to stand and walk.

He finally allowed himself to surrender to the deep, low pull of sleep and his eyes closed slowly and he drifted under. In his dreams, God spoke to him and told him not to worry, that he would save them.

Awhile later Noonan awoke when he heard a noise.

Amelia walked around the fire to his side,

"Noonan," she waved her hand at the rat carcasses, "have you been eating rat?" she looked at the twenty or thirty furry carcasses strewn around, grisly and singed, some with pink entrails spilling out.

"Noonan, there's no excuse for that. Eating vermin, especially rat. That is so *uncouth*."

He nodded, and smiled,

"God saw that I was hungry and HE provided, in abundance. Ask and ye shall receive. He came to me in a dream and said that he would take care of us. In the meantime, he provided for my sustenance."

"*He* provided?"

"He is watching over us, Amelia."

"Noonan, have you been having odd dreams again. Those dreams are from some other source, maybe from the crabs we're eating."

"Don't be smart, Amelia."

"Noonan, your strange dreams are digestive in nature, not biblical. Those crabs are freakish anyway."

"It's not the crabs, Amelia, it's a miracle, and we're saved!"

She looked at him long and hard. He was gaunt and cadaverous, yet his stomach was pooching outward, just a circle under his belly-button and over the belt of his pants. Not fat, but as if he'd swallowed a very small melon. Just enough bulge to cover with one hand. He must have been eating more rat than he was admitting to.

Amelia lifted her arms, palms upwards, "Then why are we still here, Noonan? If we're saved, then why are we still here?"

A dark look came over his face, "don't mock the Lord Amelia, that's not right, it's blasphemous."

"Noonan, you can't be serious."

"He needs something from us, Amelia, and as soon as he gets it, we get to leave. So, we need to be respectful."

Amelia shook her head and sighed, "Noonan, what could the Lord possibly need from us? Wouldn't he be more powerful than two castaways on an island who are wearing rags and eating rats and drinking fouled water?"

"You don't need to be talking like this Amelia. I won't have him angered because of your insolence."

"Well, Noonan, if he's going to be angry with me that's just too bad."

Noonan's eyes widened and he physically shrank back from her. "You really shouldn't talk like that Amelia."

"Noonan, I have no fear of your," she waved her hand as if swatting away a fly, "*dreams*. Why should I be afraid?"

"Because the Lord can save us, and get us home."

"If he could do that, then why hasn't he? Face it Noonan, your dreams were just that, dreams."

"That's typical of you, Amelia. A headstrong woman, trying to live your life as a man, and expecting everyone and everything to just get out of your way, or help you, or better yet, to help you and then get out of your way. The Lord has his reasons Amelia, and you can bet that it has nothing to do with furthering the legend and the fame of the great Amelia Earhart. Believe it or not, Amelia, the world does not revolve around you and your silly shenanigans."

"My silly shenanigans, that's what you would call all of my accomplishments?"

"Amelia, hearing your talk, it seems you believe that you can simply flap your arms and fly, without a plane. What will you think if he saves me and leaves you here alone on rat island? You'd be in a pickle then, wouldn't you?"

Amelia sighed again, she was getting nowhere with all this talk of dreams and angels, "Look, Noonan," she softened her tone and plead with him, "We need to work together here. On this island, as long as we're here, we need to work together. We can't be arguing and fighting any longer."

Noonan smiled, "I know that Amelia," his voice and I forgive you for everything. You're right; we do need to work together. We need to conserve our energy, and get comfortable and plan to use what we've been given to the best of our ability."

Amelia nodded; stunned at his inexplicable and sudden change of heart. She still thought he was drunk, although God knows where he would have found booze on this island. She realized that tomorrow there was a good chance she'd probably see the other, mean version of Noonan again.

He walked off into the bushes to take care of nature's call, and Amelia was glad that he wasn't going to take care of his needs oblivious to her again. Being in sight, sound and smelling distance of him when he was taking care of these bodily functions was an odious thing. He'd relished in making her uncomfortable with these foul displays, and she was grateful that he seemed to be over such behavior.

Another thing that was bothering her was the fact that their clothes were beginning to disintegrate. Whether it was from the fact that they wore them day and night, or that there was something in the tropical air that ate at them and caused them to fall apart, she didn't know. But their shirts and pants and for Amelia at least, her undergarments were simply rotting and falling off their bodies. Amelia realized that if they were somehow stranded on this island for another month or two, God forbid, they would be without any wearable clothes. Noonan was already starting to go about with no shirt and with his modified pants, which he'd simply turned into shorts by tearing off the lower leg portions. She had no idea what he'd done with the fabric that had once been the lower legs, it must be useful for something she decided, but she had seen no scraps of fabric after he'd altered the pants.

As for herself, she knew that sooner or later she'd need to come up with something to wear. She had no intentions whatsoever of parading around naked in front of Noonan. It was unseemly.

While he was away from the campfire she leaned back and let her head rest back against the tree and allowed the pull of fatigue and the warmth of the fire and the spinning of the stars overhead to lull her to sleep.

●●●

The fire popped, hissed and crackled, but with no one to tend and feed it, began to slowly die out. The flames, at one point blazing as high as four or five feet now were just a few inches and every now and then and flame died and settled down into the white hot coal casings and began glowing with an internal orange hue.

At the edge of the jungle tree-line, ten feet away, the swarming mass of rats pushed forward as the darkness of the jungle and the night on the other side of the fire crept closer towards each other. The smell of meat emanating from the circle of light that the fire produced was growing stronger and stronger as the circle of light shrank and the circle of darkness grew. Soon, the rats from the jungle were swarming all over each other, some poking their whiskers into the light, and then pulling back, as centuries of training had imprinted upon their minds to avoid light, for the safety lay in darkness. On the beach side of the campsite, the crabs scuttled forward, hundreds and hundreds of them, for they fed upon the slower rats, and their sense of smell had been refined enough to know where the odors were emanating from, and that was the circle of light that was progressively growing smaller, being transformed into the inky blackness of night that they too had been trained to exploit. They were swarming out of their rock and sand caves in droves and making their way along the beach at the edge of the jungle tree-line where the rats swarmed in anticipation.

CHAPTER 13

Amelia was dreaming of her sister, Grace. They were five or six, and they were playing outside. Amelia remembered the day clearly, and was somewhat amused by the fact that she was dreaming of the incident so clearly. They were chasing each other around and Gracie had fallen and scraped her knee in some gravel. She had cried, and Amelia had put her arms around her and they had walked back into the house to allow their Mom to take care of the scrape.

This time though, Gracie wouldn't stop crying, and Amelia wanted to go to her to put her arm around her and hug her, and tell her that everything would be okay, but in the dream, Amelia couldn't move. She was frozen, paralyzed with fear. Gracie looked up at her, and then screamed loudly, her scream passing from what was an innocent crying to that of a full-fledged scream of horror. Amelia's heart started pounding and Gracie's scream became even louder, and Amelia put her hands over her ears, and it felt as if a blanket had been draped over her head. Then she woke up, and the screaming was even louder. She realized that it was Noonan!

Amelia opened her eyes, and realized that the blanket in the dream was a swarm of rats that now covered her. She flung her arms out scattering rats everywhere, fell away from the tree trunk and began rolling over and over to escape the swarm of vermin. She felt rats wriggling beneath her as she rolled, crushing some of them, and causing the others to panic and bite and claw to get away from her.

She scrambled to her feet using her hands to slap away rats clinging to her hair and clothes. Noonan's screams became more and more high-pitched and frantic. A shiver went down her spine. He couldn't be screaming like this just from a bad dream, it sounded as if they were killing him. Was it possible that the rats were killing him?

Having brushed the rats away, she bent down and put her hands on her knees, and bent over, she heaved and threw up onto the sand. Her vomit was viscous and stringy, and greenish-yellow. It ran out her mouth in long stringy snot-ropes and felt rubbery and tough when she used the back of her hand to wipe it off the corners of her mouth.

The adrenaline, the fear, and the harrowing screams coming from Noonan had turned her insides out. She gasped a few breaths to steady herself, and then grabbed a few sticks and ran to the fire and began poking at it to get the flames up. She grabbed an armload of wood and tossed it into the fire and the flames immediately began blazing higher and brighter. She looked around, with horror and saw the hundreds of crabs, they'd advanced all the way into the camp and now they were everywhere. Some had large rats caught in their claws, and behind Noonan was roiling mass of black, rats, making their way back into the jungle and away from the light. They were crawling all over each other, and the chattering sound they made in their nervous escape set Amelia's teeth on edge.

Noonan was scooting backwards on his rump, pushing with his heels in the sand to propel himself away from an exceptionally large crab. The crab was easily four feet across, and two feet in height. Every time Noonan pushed his legs out and scooted backwards, the crab advanced upon him at the same rate. Noonan screamed bloody murder, and then Amelia saw what was happening. The giant crab had Noonan's hand in its mouth, and a claw pinched across his hand. The crab too, was dug into the sand and pulling backwards. Every time Noonan pulled back, the crab pulled Noonan just as far backwards. It was dragging him away, back to its lair probably, and it was large enough that Noonan was locked in a tug-of-war with the creature. If Noonan had been dead-weight, the crab would have easily pulled him away.

Amelia was stunned, and frozen with fear. She had never imagined seeing what she was seeing, and an odd thought flicked through her mind. This island was a living hell. Noonan's screaming again gave her a jolt. She had to do something to help him.

She looked around and saw the long steel rod. There were still several cooked rat carcasses speared on it. She picked it up and walked towards Noonan and the crab.

Noonan was sprawled out on the ground, one hand in the beasts mouth and the other thrashing and beating at the creature, kicking his legs at it too. He looked up, tears rolling down his face, fear written on his face and screamed at her, "Do something! Help me!"

Amelia stepped forward and raised the rod and jabbed forward and down, and she felt the sickening crunch as the end sliced through the bony carapace and the end of the rod sank into the sand under the crab. All movement stopped. She had effectively pinned it to the ground.

Noonan was still screaming and pulling backwards on his hand but the crab, still alive, wouldn't let go. Its eight legs were still scrabbling backwards, but, pinned to the ground, it was going nowhere. One of the other two legs, the giant pinchers, was clamped onto Noonan's hand.

The claw opened and reached around and Noonan screamed when the second claw clamped down on his little finger. He began thrashing around on the ground now, moaning in pain, but his hand was pinned and it stopped him from rolling away from the crab. The crab was still trying to scuttle backwards, but could no longer move since it was pinned by the steel rod. Noonan's thrashing was severe, but it was not enough to allow him to work his hand out of the crab's grasp.

"Do something now, you stupid bitch, don't just stand there!" he screamed at Amelia.

"Oh, quit your squalling, Noonan! Just give me a second to get this figured out."

"Hurry up, it's killing me!"

"Pipe down, Noonan. Let me think!"

"Don't think, just kill the damn thing!"

Amelia decided that she couldn't use her hands to grab the creature or she might end up just like Noonan, caught. There were no weapons, except her knife, and it was back at her campsite. She glanced around, hoping to spot something else to use as a tool. She felt helpless. She saw that the sun was coming up now and the area was slowly getting brighter.

She grabbed the rod using both hands, and put her foot on top of the crab's exterior shell covering, and she pulled it out. The crab immediately began pulling Noonan backwards again and he screamed,

"What did you do? No!"

Amelia raised the rod with her hands over her head and then swung downward and when the rod slammed across the back of the crab, she knew she could kill it. She raised it again and brought it down again, and again, and again. Noonan was screaming bloody murder now and Amelia felt her nerves tightening even more, as if they were being wound around a stick inside her. She felt like that stick might snap at any moment.

After several more blows, the crab stopped moving, but Noonan was stick caught by the pinchers. Amelia positioned the rod underneath the crab, and leveraging it against the ground she lifted up and flipped the crab over on its back. Noonan howled in pain. His forehead was covered with sweat and his eyes were slits.

Amelia placed the end of the rod on the center of what she assumed was the stomach of the crab, and was about to drive it through, but the instant the tip of the rod touched the soft underbelly, the crab's claws opened and Noonan jerked his hand away from it.

Amelia, exhausted, bent over and vomited again after seeing that Noonan's little finger stayed behind in the creature's mouth, the dirty fingernail protruding from the pinkish mouth. She wiped her mouth and looked over to see that Noonan had passed out. She knew this was a disaster.

She was dog-tired, and felt as if she could sleep for a week.

This was just the type of disaster that he'd predicted. She looked through his luggage bag that they'd found, and found a white undershirt. She ripped it into a strip, and then she took the bowl, made a trip to the mud hole and dipped it into the murky water. Back at the camp, she used a piece of cloth to strain the dirt from the water, placed the bowl at the edge of the fire, and dropped in the cloth and allowed it to boil for a few minutes. Then she allowed it to cool enough to pull the cloth out, it was steaming, and she wrapped it around Noonan's finger. He moaned and whined constantly in his delirious state, Amelia ignored his protestations. When he finally passed out, Amelia was glad.

Amelia pulled the rod away from the crab and scraped the last three rat carcasses off it. She stuck the end of the rod into the white coals down in the fire and waited for the tip to begin glowing red. After it began glowing she pulled it out if the fire and walked over to Noonan. She dropped to her knees and pulled his mangled hand into the sand in front of her. The white bone of the knuckle was showing, and the sand all around him was stained with his blood.

She steeled herself and then quickly pressed the red hot tip of the steel rod against the end of the sliced finger. At least this way, there'd be less chance of it becoming infected. Noonan's body jerked violently and then slumped back into the sand. When she heard the sizzle of the hot steel tip against the bloody flesh she almost fainted. When she caught the smell of the singed flesh she fought the urge to vomit.

She pulled the tip away from the finger, but it was fused with the flesh and she had to pull it abruptly to tear it away. She bent down to get a closer look, and gagged, almost vomiting, and when the sensation passed, she inspected her work. The end of the finger was no longer seeping blood, so she decided that she had done something right. If she hadn't it would still probably be the least of their problems. She looked over her work, both admiringly and with a degree of nausea and declared the incident finished.

Exhausted, sweat pouring from her body, she slumped against the tree trunk and looked at the carnage around her. Rat carcasses, cooked and uncooked, some partially eaten by man, and some partially eaten by the crabs or even other rats, were everywhere. Several of the huge crabs were scattered around, they must have been Noonan's supply. If that was true though, why was he eating rats? And then there was herself and Noonan. She had no mirror, but she figured anyone walking up to this scene now might just as well see them and believe them to be corpses too. All told it had been a strange incident, a man almost dragged into the jungle by a crab. How many times had she eaten crab in a restaurant, and had never suspected that they grew this large, or that they would ever be considered aggressive. But, that was life back in real civilization, not here on Rat Island.

Her eyes stopped at the enormous crab that had been doing battle with Noonan, his pinky finger still protruding from the creature's mouth, the finger was already turning black, and Amelia swore to herself that she'd never again take another bite of crab. She wouldn't stoop to eating the rats either, so that meant that she would either catch and eat fish, which was next to impossible considering their limited store of tools, or she would get into the jungle and find roots or something edible. Hopefully she could find something that wouldn't bite back.

•••

"You stupid bitch, what have you done?" Noonan screamed at her when he woke up. He was holding his hand up in front of his face.

"Oh God, he moaned in pain, holding his hand, and rocking back and forth, "the jig is up. I'm done for. All washed up."

Amelia came awake with a start. His yell had caught her just as she was about to drift off to sleep. She looked over at him, muttering and bemoaning his fate.

"I did the best I could, Noonan. *That,*" she pointed tiredly at the huge crab between them, "that *thing* was dragging you away. I saved you."

"What did you do with my finger?"

"I stopped the bleeding as best I could, that's what I did, Noonan. You should be grateful to me."

"You dumb bitch. Why did you do it?"

"I told you, Noonan. I tried to help you. I had to kill that crab, and then I needed to stop the bleeding, so I used the only tool I could find."

"No one told you to do that! Why on earth did you think you could just *operate* on me?"

"No one asked me to do it? Noonan, you were crying like a baby, and I had to do *something*. You should be thanking me for my efforts. I cauterized it. Now, hopefully it won't get infected."

"Where is it, my finger?"

Amelia wrinkled her nose and pointed at the crab, "He still has it."

Noonan leaned over and used his elbows to pull himself closer to the crab. Using his good hand, he tried pulled the severed finger away from the crab's mouth but was unable to pull it loose, so he sat back up, his back against the tree trunk. He looked across at Amelia.

"It could have been fixed you know."

"What are you talking about, Noonan?"

"I'm talking about my finger! You should have awakened me, so I could have talked to him, and *he* would have made me whole again, but now, now that you've interfered . . ."

Amelia's mouth dropped open in surprise, "Made you whole again? Who could do that, Noonan?"

"God, Amelia, that's who."

"Noonan, those were *dreams*, nothing more."

"You're wrong, Amelia."

"You're saying that God could reattach your finger?"

"Of course he could, Amelia. He could do anything, if he wanted."

"Noonan, if he is watching out for you, then why didn't he save you from the crab in the first place? That was *me*, not your God."

"It was because of *your* lack of belief, and your blasphemies that this happened. You just need faith, Amelia."

"Noonan, you've lost your mind."

He stared down at his hand, cradled his injured hand with his good one and moaned, "It hurts, oh my God, it hurts so bad." He leaned back against the tree and seemed to pass out.

Amelia stared at him, wondered just how much more insanity he would show, when she realized that he had set his severed finger on his knee. It was turning even blacker now, and Amelia felt her gorge rise and she turned away from the sight.

She wanted desperately to get away from all of this, but until they were rescued it was inevitable that she and Noonan were paired up in a fight for survival.

She didn't want that fight for survival to be a fight against the only other person on the island though. She still felt that they needed to work together, yet it seemed that working together just simply wasn't going to be feasible.

Would she feel guilty about abandoning Noonan? Leave him to his own devices, let him eat his rats and make it on his own?

Would it be right to consider him a threat to her survival and just abandon him, or would that be considered a crime back in civilization? She herself had warned Noonan that when they got back to civilization, that any word of unrespectable behavior on his part would be spread and he would be publicly shamed. Now, with the shoe was on the other foot, it was she who could be publicly shamed because of her actions.

There were no real answers. To make any mistake on this island could cost them their lives. Actions taken that would enable her to live long enough to be rescued could cause untold problems for both herself and Noonan when they get back home.

On the other hand, not making the correct decision here could also mean her death here, even though she might very well know that her actions may cause further anguish once she was safely back home. Any explanations and justifications for actions made here may be misinterpreted and cause grief back in civilization.

Amelia shook her head. There was no way to know whether she was making a decision that would save, or prematurely end, her life here. Whatever 'civilization' thought of her actions made no sense in the context of what she actually did here. Her main focus was to live to be able to see civilization again. That meant making serious decisions here and now.

She decided to play it by ear. She would have one more talk with Noonan, and try to reason with him, and see if they could work things out so that they were comfortable, for however long it would take for their rescue to arrive. If he refused to act normal or if he insists in blaming her for things that are completely out of her control, then she would tell him that he was on his own. And next time they separated, she would not come back, no matter what. Nor would she allow him to come to her for fire. That threat alone should be enough to keep Noonan in line for quite a while, unless he learned how to provide his own fire.

If there was no rescue, what then? She couldn't imagine the idea of being all alone on this island. She also couldn't imagine what it would be like living here for months, or even years with Noonan in his mental state. Living here for an extended period of time as his wife, which was something that she would never consider, under any circumstances whatsoever. She'd die before she gave in to him regarding that.

Back at her camp, she walked the shore and was surprised to see three fish washed up ashore. She ran to them and knelt down over them. She had no idea what type of fish they were, but in size two of them were about six inches long, with silver scales, and thin bodies. The other was a small octopus that was probably ten inches in length. She'd never seen an octopus up close. She knew they were edible, and had never tried one, but decided she would definitely eat this one. The two smaller fish weren't even worth messing with. They were more scales and fins and head than body. She tossed the two smaller fish aside and took the octopus and made her way back to her camp. She had nothing to cook it in, but was able to gut it with her small knife. Using a stick she speared it, and wrapped it's appendages around the stick so that they wouldn't be hanging down in the flames. She placed the stick full of meat over the flames. A few minutes later she decided to try it. It probably wasn't cooked enough, but her stomach wasn't willing to let her wait. She brought it up to her mouth and took a bite. It was rubbery, extremely salty, and unbelievably bitter. She ate as much as she could anyway, she needed the nourishment, and it was made slightly more palatable by concentrating on eating the flesh and not the skin. By the time she'd finished a little more than half of it, her stomach rebelled. She cramped up suddenly, and doubling over in pain, she began violently retching. Nothing was coming out though except a small watery glut of black bile. The cramps were so severe that she grasped her stomach and fell to the sand, curling up in pain as she retched and retched. Her face felt hot as fire and her throat tightened up. She was sure that she was about to die. After a few minutes the choking sensation ebbed and she lay in the sand, cramping and retching. After two hours, she dragged herself down the beach to where the waves were rolling in and she allowed the waves to cover her body. The coolness of the surf revived her a little bit, and she crawled back to her makeshift camp and passed out.

●●●

CHAPTER 14

Daylight came, and Amelia felt a sense of relief. She had been sitting with Noonan for three days, nursing him and his hand. She felt that she could leave him on his own now, and he would be okay. She needed to eat and sleep. It occurred to her that the rats and the giant crabs were night creatures. She didn't have the child's imagination that made nights seem scarier. The fact was that the rats and crabs were more plentiful, mobile and much more aggressive at night.

The last time she'd seen Noonan in an amiable mood was when he'd been drunk. He'd probably found a flask of bathtub gin in the wreckage debris that had washed ashore. Unless he'd found some way to make some sort of crude hooch with something on the island. That seemed unlikely though.

Otherwise, he was running through the jungle screaming and checking his privates to see if they'd fallen off, or he was suggesting to her that they take up relations as husband and wife.

Amelia had no idea what was causing his mental states; the crash, the diet here on the island, the very air they were breathing, or whether his brain was fried from the relentless sun. Whatever it was, she just hoped that she could help him keep his wits about him until a rescue ship sailed into view.

She needed to keep an eye on him at all times. She couldn't allow him to poison their water supply again, and as distasteful as the subject was between unmarried couples, personal hygiene was going to have to be brought up again. There was simply no way to avoid it any longer. Unless they kept to their own separate campsites, they would simply have to come to an agreement about certain things.

They would have to, without a doubt, figure out a way to work together to monitor the fire. One would sleep, and the other would feed the fire. This was an unconditional point. She doubted she'd have much trouble convincing Noonan about the fire though. After losing a finger to a crab, she doubted he would ever want to spend a night in darkness again. Plus, she knew he would just as soon not have to creep over to her camp every night and steal fire. It was a waste of time and energy.

If she stayed in her own camp, she'd have to tend her own fire. That meant training herself to wake up every couple of hours, unless she wanted to go through the process, every day, of assembling the fire-kit and starting over every time the fire went out. Not to mention the fact that when the fires did go out, they were besieged by rats and crabs. Her camp was rat-free, but his was constantly besieged, with only the fire keeping them at bay.

Waking up often enough to tend the fire was already taking its toll on her physically. Malnourishment, lack of clean drinkable water, little or no food, relentless heat, no soap, and no medical supplies at all; it was an untenable situation that would surely reach a breaking point if Noonan wasn't willing to cooperate with her. She was already fatigued beyond belief, and stretching herself even further would push her already body to the breaking point.

The big issue, with her though, was food. She had no intentions whatsoever of eating rat. She'd been tall and lean all her life. Now, in this horrific situation, she wished she'd had a few more pounds packed onto her frame before they'd gone down. There were simply no reserves of fat on her body that she could afford to lose. Noonan was the same way, tall, rangy and skinny; he was already looking decimated and gaunt, skeletal even. She shuddered at what her own appearance would be if she happened across a mirror. Luckily, that was one indignity that she could spare herself. She would just have to give her all in convincing Noonan to cooperate. She might try to talk him into wading out into the surf and use the steel rod as a spear and get some real fish. The fish she'd eaten had been wonderful. Maybe he could even use it to spear a bird or two, or one of the wild pigs he claimed to have seen.

She decided to spend the day looking for roots, fruit, or anything edible she could find in the jungle. Surely there were more edible things on the island other than rats and crabs.

Amelia picked up the steel rod, it really was a useful tool as a weapon of sorts, and with the knife in her back pocket as an added tool, and she set out into the jungle.

Making her way to the opposite side of the island by walking around the perimeter, she chose a spot in the middle and thickest part of the island to start into the jungle. With that much jungle to cover she figured that she'd come across something that they'd hadn't yet seen; any edible plants, insects, small animals.

On her one trip around the perimeter of the island on the beach, she'd kept a lookout in the rocky areas and further inland towards the trees, looking for caves and hideouts the crabs used. She knew they wouldn't be right on the beach where the sea-water could get to them, but they would be close. She saw only three crabs on her walk, and decided that her theory that the crabs and rats came out more at night than daylight was essentially correct. The further one went into the jungle where the sunlight was unable to make its way down through the overhead canopy, the more rats one would see.

She and the girls of the Ninety-Nines, on one of their weekend camp-outs had dug up many roots and learned to recognize several edible plants. She'd found the aloe plants and had broken the broad rubbery-looking leaves and rubbed the cooling gel all over her and had felt immediate relief from the constant sunburn. Noonan had taken to using it too.

Unfortunately for her though, none of those plants that she and the Ninety-Nines learned to identify were found on Pacific islands, but maybe her base knowledge would help her in some way. With her scant knowledge, guesswork and luck, she hoped to be able to find something.

By the time the sun was directly overhead she was sweating from her exertions, even though she was deep in the shade of the jungle. She'd remembered to bring along an older shirt from her bag. The shirt looked much worse for the wear than she remembered, and she thought that the day or two of being waterlogged in the ocean had almost ruined it for wearing in civilization. Now though, it made a nice bag which she packed full of palm tips, seeds and roots. With the knife, she had cut open several coconuts and drank the sweet milk, and after tasting and eating several roots and handfuls of seeds, her energy picked up. She decided that she'd wade out into the surf and give herself a good bath. She wouldn't do it unless she was sure that Noonan was far away, or asleep. Knowing he was nowhere in the vicinity now, she stripped down and waded out waist-deep into the surf. Keeping a wary eye out for the two sharks that always seemed to be lurking in the shallows she used her hands to rub her body down, using handfuls of sand as an improvised bar of soap. When she'd finished her legs, she knelt deeper into the water and used her hands to vigorously scrub her face, neck, chest and arms. When she finished she allowed herself to turn her back to the ocean and she looked landward. Gazing at the island from this perspective, it appeared as a veritable paradise. The beach was white sand and with the blue sky above it, perfectly framed the tall swaying palms with their bursts of green fronds at the tops. Idyllic and gorgeous, the island perfectly hid its own secrets; that being the dangers posed by the non-human inhabitants therein. A view of Paradise itself on the outside, absolute hell once its inner secrets were discovered by the person unlucky enough to make the discovery.

She made her way back onto the beach, dressed quickly and spent the rest of the day searching for edible plants and didn't worry about, or even think of Noonan for the remainder of the day; out of sight, out of mind, as the saying went.

CHAPTER 15

Noonan woke up around mid-day whimpering with a throbbing hand. He knew that he had no recourse, other than to tough it out, since they had no medicine or painkillers on the island, but what he really had an urge for was a shot of whiskey.

He decided to get up and walk around, just to get his mind off of the pain in his hand. He wondered where Amelia had gone, but decided that he didn't really care, she did nothing but hold him back anyway, and he was glad that she wasn't around. He looked at the dead crab laying neck to him, and his stomach lurched when he saw that the creature still had his little finger in its mouth. The finger was decaying rapidly in the heat. It was almost totally black now, with a purplish streak on the outside edge. There were insects all over it, and he wondered why the rats or other crabs hadn't come for it.

He got to his feet and walked out of the camp and onto the beach. There were still remnants of Amelia's 'help' sign on the beach, but the individual letters had been smoothed over, and the leaves and branches that had filled the letters were strewn all up and down the beach. This puzzled Noonan initially, but then he saw that the crabs were to blame. They had crawled across the beach, not stopping for the letters, and their bodies dragging across the sand had acted as brushes to wipe out the letters.

He saw something moving further down the beach and he went to investigate, hoping that it was a crab. He wished he had the steel rod. Then he realized that he hadn't seen it since Amelia had bandaged up his hand.

When he got closer to the moving object, he saw that it was not a crab, which he would have enjoyed. He was starving. It was a turtle, and it was heading back towards the ocean. He knew their meat was edible and very rich. He also knew he must make haste and grab it before it made its way back to the ocean. He felt a surge of energy as he ran towards it.

•••

Amelia bent over and spit out the seeds she'd just tried to eat. She had been searching for seeds and roots almost all morning and now after testing some she'd found, her mouth, lips and gums were burning with the bitter taste. The palm that she'd taken the seeds from was squat and had a large crown of compound leaves. The seeds were dark, almost blood-red, and when she'd started chewing them, it felt as if she'd taken a drink of bitter acid. She'd immediately begun spitting out the seeds and retching. Now, the skin on the inside of her mouth and her tongue was burning. She retched several times, but there was nothing in her stomach to expel, so it was nothing more that dry-heaving. She used her fingers to wipe out all traces of the partially chewed seeds from her mouth, and the dark red juice even numbed her fingers. Uppermost in her mind was Noonan's dire warning, that the slightest accident could spell disaster for them. The smallest accident, cut, scrape or ingesting something very bad for you, could mean imminent death. It was singularly the most auspicious truth that had been uttered in regards to this island; in that their lives here were tenuous at best. Noonan had been annoyingly correct in his harsh assessment of their new lives.

She gurgled down some of the coconut milk and washed her mouth out with the cool juice and then spit it out. The burning sensation subsided and she noticed that her forehead had broken out into a sweat. She made a mental note that the seeds were poisonous. She also made a note to never begin chewing and swallowing anything without first trying a very minute amount of it beforehand. From this point forward, anything she decided to eat would be tested; just a small trifle on her tongue for taste, and a small amount after that to see if any ill-effects were caused by ingestion.

She gathered a couple of handfuls of the seeds, because she thought they might be good as a way to numb a cut or sprain, and so that she'd have some on hand for identification purposes. Her enthusiasm for seeds and plant hunting for the day had been cut short by her near-poisoning.

•••

Noonan flipped the turtle over on its back so that it couldn't get away and immediately began searching for a way to kill it. The turtle's began waving its flippers and it used its back foot to gain a hold in the sand. Slowly, it started turning itself over. Noonan grimaced. It wasn't a large turtle, at about sixteen inches across it certainly wasn't as large as some of the big ones that were hundreds of years old. Those were four or five feet across and weighed hundreds of pounds. This one would make a nice meal though.

His hand had throbbed when he'd flipped the turtle over, and now the pain was beginning to pulse through his arm in waves now. He wished they had some sort of painkillers, but that was another luxury they'd never have again.

He ran back to the edge of the jungle, looking back twice over his shoulder to see if the turtle had righted itself. He couldn't let it get away and into the ocean.

As soon as he reached the edge of the jungle he spotted a decent size piece of wood, picked it up and started running back towards the turtle. It had righted itself and was making a dash for the water.

Falling upon the turtle and his hand too, which caused him to yowl in pain, he started jamming the stick down into the wedge between the upper and lower shells as the turtle pulled its head and legs in for protection. Even closed up there was a small space that he could jam the stick into, and after a few minutes, he'd pried the edges of the shell apart just enough of a chink to insert an edge of the wood and that gave him leverage enough to rip it apart. Once he'd killed it he immediately realized that the top shell, the carapace was going to be a useful tool. Right off the bat he knew it would become a great plate, and he'd probably find other uses for it as well. He left the head, tail, feet and the guts lying in the sand, and headed back to his camp with the carapace and the meat that he intended to cook over the fire, just as they had done with the crab. He wondered if it would be better cooked directly over the flame, or boiled in water.

When he got back to the campsite he speared a chunk of the meat on a stick and positioned it over the flames.

He noticed that the meat had a thick film of whitish fat all over it, and as he was scraping it away from his first steak, he realized how cool and soothing the white greasy fat felt on his injured finger. Having an idea, he un-wrapped the finger and stuck the bloody end of it into the fat. The make-shift salve made his finger feel better almost instantaneously. He smiled and congratulated himself and then began wrapping the cloth back around his hand. His mouth was watering now, in anticipation of his turtle-meat dinner and he watched it as it cooked over the flames.

Hours later, after he'd eaten, he noticed that as soon as he'd finished eating the turtle meat, he'd fallen asleep. He attributed it to the fact that it filled one's stomach, and the body needed to process it and that caused one to become soporific. He enjoyed it and the sleep he endured after eating the turtle was deep and full.

CHAPTER 16

Amelia had stowed her seeds in a hiding place near her camp hoping that she'd hidden them well enough that Noonan couldn't find them, and also well enough that the rats couldn't get to them. She'd spent several full days now, finding and storing seeds and roots and leaves that were edible. Tonight, she wanted nothing more than to simply sit and stare placidly out at the ocean and watch for a rescue ship, and be lulled to sleep by the hypnotic sound of the waves ebb and flow on the shore but then she heard Noonan walking up behind her.

He came into view by taking a wide detour from around behind her, as if being cautious so as not to seem like he was sneaking up on her and coming into view from her right by the incoming waves rolling up the beach. It had been two days since they'd seen each other.

"Hello Noonan, how's your hand feeling?"

"It feels okay, Amelia, thanks to your wonderful bandaging. I think it will be all right."

Amelia was instantly suspicious. Noonan had never been one to say thanks, nor to sound so cheerful. She looked him up and down. She was startled by his appearance. He looked absolutely vibrant with life. He looked *healthy*.

"What is it that you need, Noonan?"

"I came to invite you to dinner."

"You want to invite me to have dinner with you?" Amelia frowned. This was, to say the least, incongruous of his usual manner. His tone of voice was downright cheery. It set off alarms in her head. But maybe she had just grown too suspicious of him.

"Yes."

"Noonan, you know I've lost my taste for crab, and I will never eat rat, so if you-"

"Amelia, I have been eating turtle, and it's quite good actually. Lot of fat, but that won't hurt either of us," he explained as he patted his gaunt stomach,"and yes, I have been eating some rat too, there's so many of them, and the taste is not all that bad either. But I just eat the rats when I run out of crab and turtle."

"How do the turtles taste?"

"They're very good. Nowhere near as gamy as rat, and nowhere near as fishy tasting as the crab. It's a great alternative though, which you'll admit, is something we can use on the island. You'll fancy it."

Amelia stared at him. He appeared to be telling the truth, his sincerity was genuine. Maybe bad Noonan had been replaced by a nicer one?

Amelia wanted to ask him,*'So what am I going to owe him, for being the recipient of such provident largesse?'*

She decided to bite her tongue though, because if he was being truthful, she would really kick herself if she said something to queer the deal.

Amelia's stomach had been growling furiously all day long. Her new diet of seeds hadn't been one that allowed her to keep up her energy levels. It took too much time and energy to find the seeds. The small amount of nourishment, energy and nutrients that the seeds contained weren't enough to make up for the massive amount of energy it took to procure them. The idea of meat sounded very good suddenly, as long as it wasn't rat.

"Okay, Noonan. I'm looking forward to trying the turtle meat. How did you get lucky in finding the turtles? I've only seen one or two, and they were going back into the ocean when I saw them, so there would have been no chance to catch them."

As they walked back to Noonan's camp he told her how he caught, killed, and cooked them. He warned her about the bland taste, but assured her that she'd like it better than the crab. Amelia was interested in hearing this, because there may come a time when she needed to catch a turtle and cook it on her own, but what she was more interested in, was the fact that Noonan seemed completely changed.

•••

Two hours later Amelia leaned back against the tree trunk and sighed.

"Now *that* was ambrosia."

The turtle meat had been excellent, and Noonan had been a perfect cavalier throughout the evening. She couldn't remember feeling this contended and well-fed since before coming to the island. It was amazing. She allowed Noonan to talk on without interruption; he was going on about how he had been exploring the island.

At one point, Amelia noticed that Noonan had stopped talking altogether, and she allowed herself to slide down and away from the tree trunk and stretch out on the sand on her side, her body curled up slightly, and she allowed sleep to overtake her.

•••

Noonan had fallen asleep while he was talking to Amelia after they'd finished their turtle meat. One moment he was talking, and the next moment he was asleep and in a dream.

In the dream he was sitting next to a tree. His hands were tied behind his back, and his legs were tied to stakes in the ground. His legs were spread apart and he was in his underwear. He looked up to see Amelia standing over him.

"Now I've got you, Noonan."

"What are you going to do, Amelia?"

"I'm going to do to you what your mother should have done a long time ago, Noonan," she said as she pulled out a large butcher knife and knelt before him.

"What's that for, Amelia? What did I do?"

"It's not for what you did, Noonan, it's for what you could do, but I'm going to fix that."

"Fix it, how?"

"I'm going to fix you, in a manner of speaking."

"How will you do that?"

"By gelding you, Noonan, that's how."

She reached down and grabbed his manhood and used the knife to start cutting.

When he awoke he was sweating.

He walked over and stood over Amelia, who was sleeping. His ploy had worked perfectly. He knew that the meal of turtle meat would put her to sleep.

•••

Amelia was dreaming of her father again.

Her father and G P were cooking meat on sticks over a fire, but their pieces of meat were much larger than the pieces of crab and turtle that she and Noonan had cooked on the island.

She noticed a movement on the other side of the semi-circle and she smiled when she saw Noonan sitting there.

"Hello Noonan. Have you taught your friends how to cook?"

Noonan shook his head, and Amelia wondered why he wouldn't talk to her. As if to explain he nodded at her father and G P and Amelia looked back at them cooking over the fire. She noticed that one of them had a very small piece of meat on his stick, and as soon as she focused on it, her father pulled the stick away from the fire and put the stick with the cooked piece of meat speared onto the end of it, in front of her face. The aroma of cooked meat made her mouth salivate, and she looked back at Noonan, hoping that he would tell her if it was okay to eat with them. Why didn't he join them around the fire? She wondered. He was sitting with his back against a tree and leaning over on one side.

She also noticed that it was cold, her legs were freezing, but the warmth of the fire felt nice against her skin.

"Noonan don't you want to eat with your friends?" she asked, and when she looked to him for the answer, he opened his mouth and screamed a silent scream, a long grunt of sorts. When his mouth opened, she saw the ragged bloody edge of flesh where his tongue used to be, and she turned back to piece of meat on the stick that her father was offering her. It was then that she saw the meat on the stick in front of her face was Noonan's tongue.

She shook her head no, that she didn't want to eat, and then she saw what else was cooking.

It was a leg and an arm. She looked back towards Noonan and saw why he wasn't joining them at the fire. He was slumped over on the ground, minus an arm, and a leg.

Amelia turned back to G P and her father and saw that G P had one of the shells from the turtle. Holding the carapace in his hand, it reached the other hand into a liquid that was in the carapace, and then pulled the hand out, and Amelia saw that its finger had a drop of blood on the end of it. It reached forward with the blood on its fingertip and touched the tip of the finger to Amelia's forehead, to a spot over the bridge of her nose, in between her eyes.

Then she backed away from the fire.

She woke up. Her legs were still cold and she was suffocating.

She gasped, trying to get a breath, but it was like trying to breathe through a piece of cloth. She opened her eyes from the dream and realized that she was suffocating because Noonan was on top of her and had his hand across her mouth. Her legs were cold because Noonan had pulled her pants down. When she felt him start bucking and thrusting into her she screamed and began bucking side to side in order to throw him off. He had her hand in his free hand and his bandaged hand was across her mouth. Because he was unzipped and positioned in between her legs, he had her pinned to the ground, but he hadn't expected her to resist this much.

Drawing upon every ounce of energy she possessed he pulled her head up, then fell back, and when she did his hand came away from her mouth. She opened her mouth to gulp a huge breath, and as soon as she did his hand came back down over her mouth. She bit down as hard as she could into the bandaged hand, and she felt her teeth sink through the flimsy bandage and into the fleshy part of his hand. His body jerked as if an electric current had been discharged into it. He pulled back and that was all Amelia needed. She rolled to her side and in one swift movement jerked her knee up as hard as she could. She made perfect contact this time with his privates and he howled in pain and rolled off of her.

She scrambled backwards away from him. He pants were down around her ankles which made it impossible to get to her feet to run. She bent over and grabbed at the waist of the pants and began frantically pulling them up. Out of the corner of her eye, she saw Noonan roll over into a crouch on all fours. He kicked with his foot and his bunched up pants came off of one foot, the other pants leg still caught around his other ankle, and he sprang at her before she could get to her feet.

He landed upon her and forced her back down onto the sand, wedging a knee in between her legs, and started the process all over again.

This time she'd grabbed at his neck with both her hands, but when he landed on her his weight effectively pinned her hands in between their bodies. All he had to do now was not pull back and she was trapped. He began thrusting and Amelia screamed in his face, hoping to back him off with her rage. He leaned forward, inching his face into hers.

Oh my God, Amelia thought, he's trying to kiss me! She closed her mouth into a tight grimace and forced her lips together. She turned her face to one side, unwilling to submit to any more indignities and she felt his hot breath on her cheek and he was kissing her anyway. His tongue began licking at the line where her lips meet, and she feels so repulsed that she feared she would vomit.

Then his hand came out from between their bodies. He was grunting and angry now and she felt his hand at her throat, just up under her jaw, and he started squeezing.

"Dammit, Amelia, I told you, this is not-" he grunted with his effort to control her as she bucked underneath him, but he had her pinned too securely this time, "-this is not something you can refuse. It's your wifely duty-"

Amelia grunted as she fought him, and then she realized that he was going to get what he wanted even if it meant killing her. She stopped squirming for a moment, hoping that he'd try to reposition himself, and in doing so give her an opening to fight more effectively.

Instead of repositioning, he leaned in closer, thinking that she was finally giving in, and once again she turned her face to the sand, thinking, *rape me if you must by force, but I'll not allow you to kiss me!*

He kissed her cheek and the grimaced line of her mouth, and then reapplied pressure with his thumb and fingers at her jawline, and in one hard movement jerked her so head so that they were nose to nose. She squirmed again, trying to wriggle out from underneath him but her results were negligible.

He laughed at her discomfort.

"You're in hot water now, huh? The fancy-pants hero is finally in a spot she can't fly out of!"

"Let me go, Noonan! I'll never give in to this, I'd rather die than submit to you that that's how repulsive you are, you . . . you disgusting besotted lush!"

Grunting, he leaned closer, and pushed his face in towards her until their lips met, and then she felt his tongue poking, at her lips, trying to force them apart. His hand applied even more pressure, cutting off her windpipe now, and she was forced to open her mouth in order to gasp for air. When her mouth opened he shoved his tongue inside her mouth and she felt his slimy tongue against hers, and she took a deep breath and clamped her mouth down, hard, and she felt the blood from his burst tongue squirt into her mouth. He screamed and fell back away from her.

Amelia immediately began kicking at him and scrambling backwards from him as he covered his mouth with his hands, howling in pain.

"Oo doo ped *itch*! Oh my *gaaa*!"

"Get away from me you maniac!" she screamed at him. He was shaking his head side to side, blood dribbling out of the corners of his mouth.

"awl kee yoo . . . yoo itch!"

"Stay away from me you lunatic. Don't ever come near me again! Ever! I'm going back to my campsite. You stay here. You are not welcome over there!" Amelia screamed at him.

He repeated his earlier threat, "awl keel oo . . . oo itch!"

She looked around, and scrambled over to her shoes, and tried to make sure she gathered everything that was hers before she left. She kept one eye on him in case he got to his feet to attack her again, but he was no longer in the mood to fight, he was too busy tending his wounds.

Amelia got dressed, as quickly as she could, while watching him out of the corner of her eye. Luckily, she could still say that she had fully resisted his advances, which is to say that the rape had been unsuccessful. She turned to go and then something registered in her brain, and she turned around again to see if she had seen exactly what she thought she had. She stayed on the other side of the tree trunk that grew horizontal to the ground for four feet before angling up to the sky, and she looked closely at him.

He had unraveled the make-shift bandage that she'd made for his hand, days earlier, and was using it to blanch the bleeding in his mouth. His hand was in his lap, and he was slumped against a tree trunk on the opposite side of the clearing. She waited a few moments and they glared at each other with a murderous rage.

Then he raised his hand with the cloth to dab at the blood in his mouth and Amelia saw it again; clearly this time.

His little finger had completely grown back.

Amelia ran back to her campsite and found the knife that she'd hidden and ran back towards Noonan's camp. Her mind reeling at what she'd seen. She wanted to talk to him about it, but in his current mood, he was unlikely to act civil towards her. Not that she wanted to be anywhere near him either. She made a promise to herself that she'd never go anywhere again without the knife. From this point on, no matter where she went on the island, she'd have the knife in hand. Just in case.

She arrived back at his campsite. He was sitting near the fire, poking at it to get the flames up. It was full-on darkness now, and the rats would be out in force.

She hid behind a tree, watching him and at the same time, keeping an eye on the ground around her feet, watching for rats. They hadn't found her yet. She looked up the tree trunk, her eyes running up its full length until she saw the fronds at the top. No crabs scaling the trunk. The last thing she wanted was one of those things dropping down onto her back. Seeing the bare tree trunk gave her an idea, and she hugged the tree trunk and slid her legs around it and slowly began pulling and scooting herself up the trunk. Like many of the coconut trees on the island, this one did not grow straight up, but instead rose up at a slow angle, with the first twelve to fifteen feet of trunk rising from an almost horizontal position to straight up. Amelia guessed it might even be seventy or seventy-five feet high at the top fronds. Many of the coconut trees on the island grew the same way.

She scooted up slowly and quietly, always keeping her eye on Noonan down below. When she was high enough that she thought he wouldn't dare come after her she stopped. She thought that she was probably fifteen feet up the trunk, maybe even twenty. She was at the curve in the trunk where it straightened out from its horizontal position to where it started going straight up. She straightened up and was reminded of sitting in a saddle.

She watched him for a few minutes from the upper vantage point. He was moving around now; seemingly oblivious to the injuries that she'd given him. Maybe her knee hadn't connected as well as she'd thought. She tried to watch his hand, and several times he used his hand as if there had never been a problem. Days removed from losing a finger, with no medical supplies whatsoever, and he is acting as if it had never happened. The hand itself, the finger in particular, seemed almost untouched from its original state, before the crab had sliced the finger off.

It seemed impossible, but there it was. Amelia could only believe what she could see with her own eyes.

She decided to see what he would say about it.

"Noonan!"

He jumped to his feet and spun around looking for whoever was behind him, and seeing nothing in front of him, he stepped forward a few steps and peered into the dark bramble of jungle.

His voice trembled and he whispered into the darkness of the jungle, "Have you come to take me away?"

Amelia watched him for a moment, and was alarmed at just how far his sanity seemed to have slipped. Did he really believe that seeing God in his dreams was real, and that God was going to save him? His dreams of God were simply that, dreams.

She felt that if she could appeal to something in Noonan's reasoning, or to touch him in some way on a personal level, maybe get him to thinking about his home, his wife, his work, then maybe he would have some perspective that would bring him back to sanity. She still firmly believed, even after all that had happened that their key to survival was to work together. If they fought, they would perish before the rescuers arrived. This island, and their precarious position on it, was too dangerous to try to survive without help.

As much as she despised him and would happily see him sent to jail for what he had attempted to do to her, she knew that she needed him, and whether or not he knew it, he needed her.

She would keep the knife nearby, for protection and for other survival needs, and she would attempt to reason with him again. Their very survival depended upon it.

"Up here, Noonan."

He spun around as if he'd been goosed from behind.

"Look up, Noonan."

He looked up and then stepped back a few feet to get a better look at her.

"What the hell are you doing up there, Amelia?"

"I'm watching you, Noonan."

"Watching me? Why?"

Amelia was about to tell him that up here, he would be unable to attack her again, but she wanted to keep things on a civil level, so she ignored the question.

"We need to talk, Noonan."

He looked around again, and then back up at her, "Okay, come on down and talk."

"I am quite comfortable right here, Noonan."

He seemed to accept this, "Okay, what do you want to talk about?"

"We need to stop fighting, Noonan, and we need to start working together, if we're to be rescued. It looks as if it will take longer than we expected for the rescuers to arrive and-"

"There's not going to be any rescue, Amelia."

Amelia sighed. He was not going to make this easy.

"Look, Noonan, can you just agree that there is a *chance* that we will be rescued, just a slim chance?"

"It's possible, but not probable."

"But *if* it's possible, no matter how slim a chance, don't you want to be ready, and do everything we can to bring it about?"

"We already have everything we need to be rescued, and we *will* be rescued. *He's* going to save us, Amelia."

"Who is, Noonan?"

He waved his arm out towards the jungle, "God of course, *that's* who, I spoke with him again."

Amelia closed her eyes, and sighed, and decided that Noonan was to the point where he was almost beyond help.

"You *talked* with him?"

"Yes, Amelia, I did."

"Noonan, you're just having a strange dream, that's all."

"You're wrong, Amelia. He's real."

"Noonan, it was *just* a dream."

"We talked about this Amelia. God was *punishing* us."

"Well, I'd say he did a good job, stranding us here on this island."

"You don't mock *God*, Amelia. He put us here for a reason."

"What reason, Noonan?"

"He said that everything would be okay, if we both would do as he instructs."

"What *exactly*, Noonan is it that we should *do?*"

Noonan started to speak, and then stopped. Amelia was uncomfortable, pushing him like this, but it needed to be done. She needed him thinking clearly, in order to help her survive this place. She couldn't have him spouting nonsense about God and claiming that she should be his wife and perform her 'wifely duties.'

"The first thing we need to do, that you need to do, is to believe in him. You can't be helped if you do not believe. Once you believe, as I do, and as you *should*, then everything will be all right."

"Noonan, if believing in him keeps you safe, then why did he allow you to lose a finger? Why hasn't he taken you off this island? You're not a true believer are you?"

He immediately straightened up and glared up at her,

"Amelia, you'd better watch what you say, there will be no blasphemy. You've already angered him."

"What about you, Noonan? What about your hand, and the fact that I fought you, and what about the fact that you are still stuck here on the island? If you are protected you because you are a believer, then that protection is not very good, is it?"

"Shut your mouth, Amelia!" he looked around fearfully, "you are being blasphemous and he will *not* stand for it!"

"Answer my question, Noonan. What about our fight? I broke a rib or two, and you lost a finger to the crab, and you're still stuck here, just as I am, on this hellish island. What has he done for you, Noonan? Nothing, that's what, he's done nothing because he doesn't interfere. He helps those who help themselves. You had a *dream* Noonan, *God* didn't appear to you!"

Amelia watched as, Noonan, infuriated at her blasphemy, held his hand up for her to see.

"My finger? Here, take a look, Amelia. There's nothing wrong with my finger, looks good as new to me, what do you think?"

Amelia's eyes widened when she the hand, unmoving, fingers spread, and watched as he turned the hand around, back outward, and then palm forward for her to get a good look. The hand looked perfect in every way. The little finger was fully restored without even a scratch. Her question was now answered, she hadn't been imagining it. His finger really *had* grown back.

Amelia slid backwards down the tree trunk a few feet in order to have a closer look at the hand. She was in disbelief of what she was seeing, but there was no doubting that the hand she was seeing was perfect, and showed no sign whatsoever of ever having had so much as a scratch.

"Now do you believe?"

"I've always believed, Noonan," Amelia shook her head, "but not like you think. I believe that God exists, but what's happening to us here is not his doing. We simply got unlucky, and now we're going to have to deal with the situation. God may be watching, but he is not interfering, and neither helping nor hindering what we do."

"Explain this then!" he shook his hand at her.

"What I see, Noonan is incomprehensible to me, and it defies the imagination, and what is known medically as fact, but there must be scientific reasons for it; all the more reason for us to live through this and make it back to civilization, and show others."

"There are no *scientific reasons* Amelia, it's a *miracle,* pure and simple."

"No, Noonan, it is *not* a miracle."

"Amelia, your blasphemy is not needed, nor wanted, on this island."

"Noonan, I'm skeptical of your claims, but I do not disbelieve. Furthermore, you and I are alone on this island."

"No, Amelia, we are not. Just because you don't see something, doesn't mean it doesn't exist. Have you ever seen God?"

"Noonan, I have always been a Christian, and I know that one doesn't *see* God, but -"

"Amelia, you should not speak about things lightly, things which you have no knowledge of."

"Look, Noonan, why hasn't God saved you yet, from all this pain, suffering and danger?"

"He is testing me; to ascertain that I'm worthy. He has instructed me to do certain things and once I've accomplished what he asks, I *will* be saved. It's very illuminating, Amelia."

Amelia shook her head and looked around. She was world-famous, wealthy, young and in good health, and she had a wonderful life ahead of her. Yet here she was, stranded on a deserted island, halfway up a tree, carrying a knife for protection against rats, crabs and a crazy man, while absurdly arguing about God! She wanted to scream.

She sighed again, and as much as it vexed her to give in to his delusions she felt compelled to ask.

"What is it then, Noonan, what is it that he wants you to do?"

"I am to become Adam."

"You are to do what?"

"And you, Amelia, are to become Eve."

"What?"

"It's what we are chosen to do, Amelia."

"Adam and Eve? What on earth are you talking about, Noonan?"

He seemed exasperated at having to explain it. "It's simple, Amelia, you and I are chosen to start over."

"Start over? What are you suggesting, Noonan?"

"Well, *he* wants us to start anew. Obviously, I am Adam, and you are Eve. How much more plainly can I say it, Amelia?"

"Noonan, that's insane. What is the point of you and me playing Adam and Eve?"

"It's not for us to question him, Amelia. He has asked this of us, and it's up to us to do as he wishes."

"I thought you said that he would have us rescued."

"He will."

"According to what you're saying, Noonan, we're supposed to live here, together, as Adam and Eve? And the island is the Garden of Eden, I suppose?"

"Yes, Amelia, that's it exactly."

Amelia snorted, "Look around you, Noonan. This is not exactly a *garden* of any sorts, now is it? If we're supposed to live here, then when is the part about us getting rescued and *taken off* this island?"

Noonan shouted angrily, "You're not a believer! You shouldn't question what you don't understand!"

"But Noonan, *you're* a believer, why don't *you* explain it to me?"

Noonan's face reddened, "*You* wouldn't understand, Amelia, being such a dissolute *blasphemer!*"

They were quiet for a moment, and Amelia tried to think of what to say. What Noonan claimed that God was proposing was so ludicrous that it made no sense.

Obviously, Noonan was too far gone to reason with, but she had to try to reach him, some way or another. What she would not do, would never do was to be a party to such madness. She realized that he needed to be stopped; otherwise she would have to live in fear of him at all times. She wondered if it would be possible to catch him. Sneak up on him, capture him, tie him up, and keep him immobilized. That would ensure her safety. The problem was that he would overpower her if she failed at any point in disabling him. She couldn't kill him. She had no way of doing it, plus, it was easier for them to survive if there were two of them to hunt for water and food while they waited for rescue. If she couldn't talk sense into him, convince him to work with her rather than against her then she would have to come up with some sort of plan to do just that, immobilize and capture him, just to ensure that he didn't hurt her. He was precariously close to being a constant danger to her. Now, all this Adam and Eve and God nonsense was making him more and more unstable to deal with. She couldn't find food and water on her own, keep a signal fire going, and fight Noonan all at once. It was exhausting enough just to make it through a single day doing any one of those things.

"Noonan let me ask you a question, in all seriousness, and I want you to know that I am *not* ridiculing you or God when I ask this. I *really* want to know the answer to this question."

He nodded at her to continue.

"What would change? For instance, if, and I say if as a theoretical only . . . if you and I started calling ourselves Adam and Eve . . . what would change? Would the island suddenly have lots of easily available drinking water? Would fruit appear on the trees? Would the fire burn always without our having to tend to it? Would a rescue ship, or plane, suddenly appear? I mean, seriously, Noonan, what would change and be different around here from the way things are now? Would this place suddenly become a real Garden of Eden?"

She watched as he digested her question, and hoped that the sheer logic of the question would override his fanatical-fervor and the logical side of him, the *engineer* in him would reassert in his mind. The answer being of course, that *nothing* would change just because they indulge in a ridiculous fantasy.

He looked up at her in her tree perch and spoke,

"Nothing would change as far as I know, Amelia. Maybe we'd still be on the same island, and we'd have all the same problems,-"

Amelia thought, from his answer, and the tone of his voice, that maybe she'd finally gotten through to him with cold, hard logic.

"-with food problems, fire problems, and just general discomfort, *but*, there is one very important thing that would change, and I think it's what he wants."

Amelia frowned, she'd thought she'd finally broke through to him but she realized that her hopes were about to be dashed.

"And what is that, Noonan?"

"We'd be husband and wife, just as God willed it for Adam and Eve."

"That's preposterous, Noonan, and you know it. We've already talked about this. I will never agree to that. I am *already married*. We have more important things to consider, Noonan. We need to *survive*, not think about, you know, *marital relations*."

"And as husband and wife," he continued, as if he hadn't heard a word she'd said, "You are to be with child, of course. After all, we are supposed to start anew."

"Noonan, that's the craziest thing I've ever heard in my life. There is no way we are having a child. I would never do that with you as the father, and besides, a child on this island? The very idea is clearly insane and you know it!"

"Think about what you're saying, Amelia. Not only would we be doing as he asks, but we would also be solving our own food problem too."

Amelia cocked her head, thinking she must have misunderstood him.

"Solve our food problem too? How do you figure that, Noonan? The child would take years of upbringing before the child would be able to help us with any kind of food procurement. And you yourself, with your dire predictions once stated that we'd both be dead with seventy-two hours at most. We've bested that guess by many days and we are nowhere near death. We just need to hang on, and survive until we are rescued-"

"You misunderstood me, Amelia."

"I believe that I heard you very clearly, Noonan."

"No, you didn't."

"Well then, by all means, set me straight, Noonan. This should be rich."

"We are not to raise the child, not to adulthood anyway."

Amelia blinked. She was stumped at finding his meaning, and decided that maybe she'd misunderstood him. She had thought that he'd meant that they should have a child, literally. Maybe he had meant in a figurative sense, somehow.

"I suppose that God himself would take on the task of raising the child? Is that what you mean to say?"

"No, Amelia, what I meant is that the child would never become an adult."

Amelia felt a chill run up her spine, "Well then I guess I don't understand. So, Noonan, what *are* you saying?"

"I'm saying, Amelia, that the child is to be a source of . . . *nourishment* for the both of us."

Amelia squinted at him for a moment, thinking that he was talking in a figurative sense, but then it dawned on her just what he really meant.

She gasped, "What kind of bloodthirsty fiend are you, Noonan?"

She leaned forward to brace herself on the tree trunk for fear that she might fall off. Her head swam. After a few moments she was able to speak again.

"Noonan, that is the most horrifying thing I've ever heard. Surely you're not suggesting that we, that we," she forced herself to voice it, "that we, *consume* a child?"

"That's exactly what I am saying, Amelia, and we should."

"The very idea is just . . . *evil*. How could you possibly even *think* of such a diabolical thing?"

"Do you know what the nutritional value of human flesh is, Amelia?"

Amelia screamed, "Stop it, Noonan, I won't listen to this devil talk!" she covered her ears with her hands. Whether she fell or not, there was no way she could listen to such vile and evil things.

She looked at Noonan who'd stopped speaking and she pulled her hands away from her ears.

"Noonan, you can't be serious. Not to mention the fact that you'd have to wait nine *months* for such a thing, did you think of that? You are insane for even speaking of such a vile atrocity."

"You don't get it Amelia. If it comes *from* us, we can do with it as we please. Eating of our own flesh, or the flesh of our own flesh . . . such a thing is . . . *permitted,* and in fact, advisable. And it will not take nine months. You'll have it months early, when it's large enough to, you know, to be enough for us to consume."

"That's enough, Noonan. What you suggest is horrible and most vile and I will not even partake of such a discussion. Please do not bring it up again. It's inconceivable to me that a human being could even conceive of doing such a thing."

"The survivors of the Whale ship Essex in 1820 would disagree, as it saved their lives. Besides which, *he,*" he waved a hand towards the jungle, which was apparently his way to indicate God, "told me that consumption of the body is a very sacred thing and with the eating of such, there is no real loss."

"Noonan, again, you are insane for believing in your utterly villainous and particularly disturbing version of God, and to suggest what you say that he suggests . . . only proves that the *God* you've dreamed is a demon and not *the real God of all creation.*"

"But there is no loss, Amelia."

"Noonan, you're a skunk, a bounder, and a toad. A fink of the lowest stripe to even voice such evil depredations. God should strike you down at once, this very moment."

"And you're a harpy, a harridan, a reviler, and a vituperatist of the highest order."

"A vituperist? Noonan, your vocabulary is that of an intellectual pretender."

"And you're nothing more than a social gold-digger. You have no class, so you tried to marry-up."

Amelia seethed, and bit her lip while contemplating another comeback.

"But there's no harm in doing it Amelia. Because there's no loss," he repeated.

"No loss?" she raised her voice, "no loss except that of an innocents life! That is the highest loss of all, Noonan. What has happened to your soul, your humanity?"

"All loss, in that regard anyway, is replaced, Amelia, which means that we can eat our fill, and become healthy. There is no loss of body, because it is re-born, as it were. It grows back."

"Noonan, you're speaking gibberish now, you've become completely unhinged. Please, I beseech you to drop this ghoulish, evil subject. This is unfit for human ears."

"Amelia, I can offer proof."

"Noonan, what has blackened your heart to human compassion and decency? Have you lost the very thing that makes you human? You must have decided at some point that life is not real drink and the devil has done for the rest."

Amelia was so tired from grasping the tree trunk tightly to keep herself in her perch that she was beginning to tremble. She only wanted to get down from the tree and get back to her camp, and as far away from Noonan as possible. He was completely insane and there was nothing more she could do.

Now he was holding up his hand again.

"You see?"

"See what, Noonan?"

"Evidence that it works."

"What evidence are you referring to?"

"My finger, see?" he waved his hand at her, showing off his intact hand.

"I know that your finger grew back Noonan. I don't know *how*, but it did. But in the context of having a child, what does it prove, Noonan? Other than some sort of medical anomaly has taken place?"

"No, Amelia, it proves that consumption of the flesh is not evil, in fact it is to be recommended if we are to return to health."

"Noonan, the tip of your finger growing back proves *nothing* regarding, I shudder to even speak the word, *cannibalism*."

"Sure it does Amelia."

"How so?"

"Because Amelia, it never would have grown back had it not been consumed."

Amelia's mouth dropped open, "*What?* Noonan, are you saying that you? You surely *didn't*, did you? What kind of horrible stinking morass has become of your soul?"

"Yes, I did. I dug the finger out of that crab's mouth and ate it, and now I am complete once again."

Amelia's eyelids fluttered as she felt faint again, and then she had a vision in her mind. Of the crab, of the black, rotting finger, and she visualized Noonan pulling it out of the crab's mouth and . . . she retched and heaved, but was unable to empty her stomach.

CHAPTER 17

Amelia, frozen in an irresolute state, clung to the tree trunk until daylight. She was genuinely afraid to come down. Noonan's mental instability had slipped far more than she had guessed. She realized that after their rescue, he would have to be institutionalized for the remainder of his life. She felt a wave of intense loneliness pass over her. It was bad enough that they were stranded, far and away from all civilization, but now she was completely alone. The Noonan that she'd known had vanished into the ether. He was nothing more now that a blackheart, a monster. What was even worse was that he had not disappeared physically, just mentally. Physically, he was still here, and as such, a threat to her survival.

She watched him from on high, and he pleaded with her to come on down and sit by the fire with him.

She knew that his sudden amiable nature was calculated; he wanted her down out of the tree simply because she would tend the fire better than he could. For whatever reason, his fire-making and fire-tending skills were non-existent. He was simply unable to make fire.

She kept a wary eye on him and when he finally leaned back against a tree trunk and started dozing off; she climbed down and snuck away; not hesitating one moment to take a path through the jungle. She congratulated herself on her shrewdness in sneaking away. Then she realized how low she'd sunk in life. Where, in her sad state of affairs, dealing with hordes of rats was now a better option than dealing with another person.

Life had become much less noble. Instead of jauntiness and heroic action, she was reduced to skulking around Rat Island, looking like a skeleton, scrounging for meals and trying to avoid rape and death.

The sun was just rising over the ocean when she made it back to her camp, and she knew that she was probably safe from him until late afternoon or night. He seemed like a different person at night. Or maybe the island itself was different at night, because that's when the rats and killer-crabs came out and began foraging for their food. His fear was preyed upon by the dark, and she represented light, fire, and safety to his addled brain. Therefore, his personality, his demeanor changed with the onset of darkness.

She realized fully now, that she would have to advance her plan and capture him. If for no other reason than to insure her own safety, she needed to render him disabled in some way, knock him out and tie him up. She shuddered, remembering his insane conversation about impregnating her and eating the child. He was completely insane. Her plan was fraught with danger, and chancy to boot. If she failed, the tables would be turned and he'd have her captured. If that happened she swore to herself that she'd fight him to the death before she allowed him to impregnate her. Another problem would be that once she captured him she be forced to care for him. She would have to feed him and care for him; she couldn't just capture him and allow him to die. She would not be a murderer, unless she was forced to battle for her very life, and even then, the thought of killing sickened her.

She carefully concealed the knife under the sand behind and almost underneath her, and lay back to sleep. She made a promise to herself to never to let the knife out of her reach. Whether it was a horde of rats, a giant crab, or Noonan himself, she now needed the knife for protection.

That night she dreamed that she was talking to her father. He was asking her all sorts of questions about the island, and after a while she realized that they had been rescued and that her father was asking about something that had happened long ago. She was having problems answering his questions because that ordeal had been so long since she'd been on the island.

Her father asked her what they'd eaten, and she told him about the crabs. He had laughed and laughed about her answer, and when she asked what was so funny, he just pointed at her hands which had been folded and in her lap, the whole time.

She looked down at her hands and jumped in fright, because in place of her thumbs, she had crab claws. She held one up to her face to study it more closely.

"You see darling, you really do become what you eat!" he said to her and then began laughing.

Amelia, embarrassed, put her hands back together and placed them in her lap. She looked back up at her father's face.

"Daddy, why are you laughing at me? I had a terrible ordeal on that island."

"It's okay son, I forgive you."

"Daddy, I'm not your son," she plead with him, tears in her eyes, "I'm your daughter! Why do you always call me your son?"

"I am so sorry little *girl*, please forgive me," He said and he stood up to leave.

"Don't leave Daddy!"

He put his hand to his lips to blow her a kiss, as he'd done so often, but when he pulled his hand away, one of his fingers stayed in his mouth, the blood running down the corner of his mouth to his chin. He wiggled his remaining fingers at her, and instead of blowing the kiss, he was chewing on the finger in his mouth.

Amelia turned away and wondering what was happening, and then she looked back at her father, "Father, please don't go away, I love you!" but now, his face had changed into Noonan's.

●●●

Noonan trekked through the jungle back to the place that he now referred to as the crossroads, the place where the two trails intersected. He wanted to talk to *him*.

As he had walked towards the area, he found his steel rod and he wondered how it had gotten so far away from his campsite. He wondered if the crabs had pulled it away. He remembered that Peterson had told him that the crabs were just like raccoons in that they'd take shiny objects and leave them around their nests. Noonan didn't think that the rod wasn't exactly shiny, but to a crab it might be. He picked it up, glad to feel the power of the tool in his hand again.

Arriving at the crossroads he immediately noticed that there were a large number of rats and he could hear the crabs rustling through the underbrush. Noonan could hear them clicking their claw-pincers together. *Click-click-click*. Like someone was quickly opening and closing a pair of scissors. He also thought that he could hear the rats making little hissing sounds, but he knew that this could be a figment of his imagination. The rats also seemed to grind their teeth together when they were all massed up together. Noonan didn't know if they did this out of hunger, or if they were nervous, or just anxious to begin eating. Whichever, it was creepy. If the island was rat island, then the inner jungle area should be called crab jungle.

He called out for God. *God, it's me, Noonan!* No answer. He noticed scurrying rats in the jungle to his right. On the left he swore he heard the *click-click-click* of claws.

Standing in the exact middle of the clearing, right on the intersection of the crossroads, he yelled out several times for God, but there was no answer. Where was he?

He saw a blur, and a group of rats ran through the clearing, and brushed his legs as they passed on either side of him. He felt a panic rising. They weren't supposed to be here, the rats. This clearing, the crossroads, was off-limits to them. *Click-click-click*, he heard the crabs rustling through the underbrush, and then he saw that three of them were crawling right into the clearing and straight for him. These three were enormous, and their coloring was bluish tinged.

A huge group of rats scurried out of the jungle and began swarming next to the crabs.

Ha! Noonan thought, let *them* fight it out.

His smile vanished as both groups began moving towards him again, and he yelled out for God.

"Where are you?"

Sensing that he was alone, the rats and crabs advanced to within a few feet of him, and Noonan screamed and began slashing with the steel rod. He stabbed two of the crabs and then began jabbing the pointed end of the rod at the rats, spearing them one by one and the dead rats began stacking up on the shaft of his rod. Stab one, and then another and the newly killed one was impaled on the shaft, and its predecessor just above it, like a shish-ka-bob. He stabbed and stabbed, and the rod began getting heavy with rat carcasses. He stuck his foot out, caught the toe over the top rat on the shaft, and pulled back on the rod, and the dead rats dropped off onto the ground. Once the most aggressive of the rats were slayed, the remaining horde stopped advancing, and he turned his attention again to the remaining four or five huge crabs. They'd formed a semi-circle around him and one by one he stabbed them into the ground, and then trapped and pinned down they were unable to stop him from using a foot to stomp on the front of their heads, killing them. Then he'd repeat the process.

Then he saw a bigger animal rustling through the underbrush. Whatever was moving around back in there had to be a person, Amelia. It was too large to be anything else.

"Amelia!" he called out, "I know you're out there. Come on out and be seen, stop skulking around."

The only answer that came was more movement. Whatever it was, it still moved towards him.

Then Noonan thought of the wild pigs. Whatever was rustling around there was definitely large enough to be a pig.

He hoped it was a pig. That would be some good eating. He stepped forward to the edge of the clearing and tried to peer into the underbrush. There was movement, but he couldn't see what was causing it.

He was about to go in after it, when the creature made its way out of the underbrush and into the clearing.

Noonan's eyes bulged when he saw it. The biggest crab he'd ever seen. It had a bluish shell with claws as large as actual scissors, around six feet across the back, and it stood almost two and a half feet off the ground.

Without spoilage, this would provide enough meat to last two weeks. There had to be thirty or more pounds of meat, maybe more. Too much meat for one meal though. Even for both him and Amelia, it would be enough for a week or more. Without a way to preserve it though, most of it would waste.

Noonan was amazed, and a little intimidated. This thing was monstrous. It was singly above and beyond all the others in size and aggressiveness too. With that in mind, he knew it would make an enormous hearty meal. Heck, this monster would make enough meals for a week. Immediately, he named it Big Blue.

It kept lumbering towards him. The fact that it didn't seem afraid of him made Noonan angry. He was the man, and as such, the lord of all animals, yet this thing just kept coming towards him. As it neared him, it raised its claws and began clicking them in a pincher movement. Noonan raised his steel rod and thrust. The first thrust broke through the shell, and the beast turned and almost jerked the rod out of his hands. He moved to the side of the creature and began thrusting the steel rod in and out. The beast put up a good fight, and it took Noonan fifteen or twenty thrusts before the massive creature had stopped moving. Sitting down and sweating from his battle he looked at the carnage all around him.

"Survival of the fittest!" he said out loud, and then began laughing hysterically.

There were well over two hundred rats, and six or eight of the huge crabs, and 'big blue,' the monster-crab. His shook his head ruefully; it was too bad he had no way to keep the meat fresh.

He picked apart two of the crabs, and cut out a huge meaty portion of big blue, and that being all he could carry in his wrapped up shirt; he began the trek back to his camp. He looked back one time towards the clearing, wondering where God was. He was upset that God hadn't appeared, but then smiled, realizing that God *had* provided for him.

As he left the clearing he noticed that more crabs and rats were all massed together side by side back in the jungle. They seemed to be watching him as he made his way back to his camp. They weren't following, which was a good sign.

As he walked through the jungle he thought about Amelia and wondered why she resisted him without even considering his plan. He would just have to show her that he was in charge. His needs were paramount to hers, as he was the man, and she was, as a wife, supposed to be submissive. He realized that he should quit asking her to be his wife, and just make her do as he asked. Why pussyfoot around and beg her? He was the man, she was the woman. God put woman on earth to complement man, and to be submissive. She was supposed to honor him by doing as he asked. From this point on, he decided, he wouldn't ask, he would just *take*. If he had to subdue her, capture her and keep her tied up while he taught her how to be a good wife, then he'd do that. Once he had her captured, he'd impregnate her, and she would be powerless to deny him a child, their nourishment, their deliverance.

●●●

Amelia spent the day foraging through the jungle finding roots and seeds, stuffing them into her make-shift bag that she'd fashioned from a bra that she'd never worn.

At one point she saw something white in the underbrush and she immediately became excited because she knew that something that white probably meant that it was something man-made. She rustled the bushes around the object disturb and scare off any rats that may be nestled in there, and then she took a deep breath and reached into the bushes and wrapped her fingers around the object. She pulled it out of the earth where it was partially buried, and in doing so realized that it was larger than she'd initially thought. She looked around as she pulled it out; wanting to make sure that Noonan wasn't skulking nearby. When she cleared it from the bushes and saw what it was she shrieked and dropped it to the ground and stepped back away from it. A leg bone, still attached to the foot. The entire bone structure was still there. A leg and a foot. The bones had long since been bleached white by the sun. A crab had probably dragged it back here, probably before it was cleaned off of all the flesh and muscle; a gruesome find.

It occurred to her that she might be able to make use of it as some sort of improvised tool, and she picked it up and looked it over carefully trying to decide how it would be usable. After many minutes of theorizing how she could use it, she came to the decision that she couldn't, and she tossed it back, deep into the jungle. As soon as it hit the earth, she could hear some sort of creatures, rats probably, scurrying through the underbrush after it. She shuddered, and wondered just how many people had ever been stranded here as they were.

Going back to her original project, she knew that it would take a great deal of her roots and seeds to keep her fortified, since she had decided to never eat the crab or rat meat. She busied herself in building up her stores, and her knife came in handy for digging. She was smart enough to hide this store of food, just in case Noonan decided to raid her campsite.

On her way back to her campsite she saw a turtle heading back into the surf, and wondered if she might be lucky enough to find where it had laid its eggs. Of course, she'd have to split them with Noonan if she did, since she'd need his bowl to cook them in, but she decided it might be worth it. Otherwise, she planned on staying far away from him.

She walked to the beach and back-tracked the flipper marks that showed where the turtle had come from, and about fifty yards inland, about three-quarters the way up the beach towards the jungle, the tracks ended. She knelt down and used the knife to spread back the sand and found five good-sized eggs. She marked the spot in a non-conspicuous way and left them.

She wondered if she could find a flat rock to put into the fire, and scramble the eggs on top of the rock, that would allow her to have all the eggs to herself, and stay away from Noonan.

Looking out at the horizon she saw that three or four dolphins were splashing playfully in the area close to shore, near the spot where the Electra had once been. She watched as they jumped, hearing their playful squeaks when they danced on top of the waves. She noticed that, for the first time since they'd been on the island, the sharks were nowhere to be seen. She scanned the waves from left to right and back again several times, but there ominous fins were absent.

The scene made her smile, and she realized that it had been weeks since she'd smiled, and though she was smiling now, realized that it was a pity, to know that one may never again do something as simple as smile. Sitting back, she watched the dolphins and hoped that their presence was a harbinger of good luck as some sailors believed. She wasn't the least bit superstitious, but at this point she needed something to believe in.

•••

There were still some embers in the fire pit, and Noonan blew on them and was barely able to get the flames started, and when he did, he stoked the fire until it was roaring. Within the hour he was gorging himself on crab meat from Big Blue. He cooked the other two smaller crabs and ate until he felt as if his stomach would burst, and wrapped the leftover meat in a leaf and buried it in the sand under the tree. Hopefully later, he'd be able to unearth it, clean the sand off, and eat the meat. It would probably spoil but he had to try something, because there was no way he could survive by hunting down every meal. It took too much energy.

He rubbed his belly contentedly, thanking Big Blue and leaned back against the tree trunk and fell asleep.

•••

Noonan looked out over the ocean as they flew above it and turned to Amelia and grinned.

"We made it didn't we, Amelia?" he felt the wide grin on his face, and thought that he may look ridiculous, grinning ear to ear like this, but who cared? They were rescued, weren't they? He didn't care what anyone thought, now that they were off the island, he was happy again.

"I have to admit it, Amelia, you said we'd be rescued, and here we are. I guess you really know your onions after all!"

"Well, Noonan, the jury is still out on you. Being such a scaredy-cat the whole time we were on the island. You should be ashamed of yourself."

"Hold your horses there, Amelia. You weren't very much fun to be with either, Amelia."

"Noonan, you're so exasperating," she shook her head, "dealing with you is . . . it's enough to make a preacher cuss!"

Noonan laughed at her, "Well, I'm glad I was able to get your goat!"

Amelia turned away from him and slid back the window, and Noonan immediately felt the cool air rushing in. Amelia hunched over and began digging through her purse. Where had she gotten a purse? He didn't remember seeing her purse in all the time they were on the island.

"What are you looking for Amelia?"

She ignored him and kept searching through the bag.

"Amelia, what are you doing? Come on, forget about that, look out the window and enjoy the view with me. See? Look down there and you can see the entire island."

"Yes, I see it, Noonan." She had finished looking through her bag now, and was holding something wrapped in a piece of dirty cloth.

"Wave bye-bye to the island, Amelia," Noonan giggled as he said it, and he waved his hand.

"I will Noonan, but first I want to throw the trash out of the window."

"What trash?" he asked her.

"This trash, as soon as we get rid of it everything will be hunky-dory, Noonan," she said while she unwrapped the item in the cloth and held it out for him to see.

He screamed when she unfolded the filthy rag and he saw his bloody severed penis in her hand. She tossed it out the window and Noonan watched it dropping down towards the ocean and the island.

"Good riddance to bad rubbish!" Amelia chirped playfully, and waved bye-bye with her hands, "now, I'm as happy as a clam."

Noonan looked down at his lap and saw a bloody mess of rat guts and carcasses. He looked back up at Amelia, still waving bye-bye to his penis, but now her hands had turned into crab claws.

Gasping, he woke up and looked around. He was still on the island and it was getting dark.

●●●

Amelia fell asleep watching the dolphins jumping and playing offshore, and then saw a ship just offshore. The ship was obviously one that G.P. had contracted to join in on the search for them, because it was far too large to belong to any Pacific Islander, and it wasn't military.

She could clearly see the people on the boat, looking at the island with binoculars, and she knew that if she were to jump up and wave her arms and yell, that they would see her without a doubt. She also realized that the fire must have gone out because if they'd seen smoke from a fire, they would come onto the island to investigate. She watched, in her dreamy state, and wondered if she could make G.P. appear on the boat. It was a dream, so why shouldn't she be able to do that?

She conjured him into the dream. He stood on deck, she could clearly see him. He had a pair of binoculars to his eyes. She was looking at him, and she felt as if he were looking straight at her. She felt a tinge of sadness at being unable to signal him, and she watched as the ship turned away from the island and began moving away.

When she opened her eyes again, she could see that the ship was still there, and she hadn't been dreaming at all. Scrambling to her feet, she ran towards the waves. The ship was there, but it was too far away and moving away from her. Having spied no movement on the island, they'd turned away and were leaving!

She began jumping up and down and screaming, waving her arms, but it was too late, she realized. The ship was moving from her left to her right. After a few minutes she stopped yelling, and stood to simply watch as the ship sailed over the horizon. One moment it was there, and the next moment it slid over to the other side of the world, the side that was out of sight. The sun was beginning to set now, melting into a ball of orange into the blue ocean beneath it, creating a purple mélange, and now she sank, broken-hearted to her knees in the surf, and cried. She sincerely hoped that the waves would pull her out to sea.

Overhead the stars appeared, and silence fell over the island. A shooting star blazed across the sky and seemed to draw a curtain of darkness behind it. Silence reigned.

CHAPTER 18

Noonan kneeled in the sand and blew on the coals and fanned the flames with a palm frond. Soon, the fire was blazing and bright enough to keep the rats away. Hungry again, he'd uncovered his crab-meat stash, but it was covered on small white worms, and the meat itself was rotted and going black. He picked the worms off and then dipped the meat into his bowl of water, and then began eating. After chewing and swallowing a few mouthfuls, he felt his stomach lurching and he went to his hands and knees and, bending his head down, vomited onto the sand. The vomit was a white, lumpy, wriggling mass of worms mixed with a few chunks of the black rotted meat.

He felt immediate relief at having expunged the offending meal, and realized that his preservation experiment was a failure. He'd simply have to wait until daylight to go hunting again.

Leaning back against the tree trunk, he wondered if Amelia was watching him. He vowed to steer clear of her from now on. In the dream he'd seen just what her motives were. She wanted to cut his manhood off. She was crazy enough to do it too. Her mind had been poisoned by G.P. Putnam. He's the one who had put her up to this trip, and had probably been the one to suggest hiring him as her navigator. He was the cause of *all* of this misery. Well, he and his wife, whom, despite all the publicity and hero-worship to the contrary, was a sorry, amateurish pilot.

Another wave of nausea swept of him and he leaned over to his left, turned his head and vomited. There hadn't even been time to get on his hands and knees. Vomit ran down his shoulder to his elbow and dripped into the sand. His eyes swam and he went to his hands and knees, and started shuffling through the sand towards the bowl of water.

Halfway there, he fell over, felt the bile rising from his stomach up into his throat, and he opened his mouth and vomit poured out. He passed out.

•••

Amelia dragged herself up the beach and lay on her back, looking up at the stars. She stayed there for what seemed like hours, and then she realized that, because of what had happened, she was craving human companionship. She didn't really expect to get much from Noonan, but at this point she just wanted to be able to have human companionship. Even if she could just get him to talk, about anything except his crazy new ideas, it would be worth it. All she needed was to hear another human voice. Her own misery was such that she would expose herself to Noonan's insanity, just to be assured that she was not all alone on this island.

She started towards his camp, and noticed as she walked, that it was dark. He must be asleep, and had allowed his fire to die out. As she walked down the beach she forced herself to look inland, and away from the waves, fearful of seeing another rescue ship that would do nothing but cause her internal anguish, for she knew that God had forsaken her as a way of punishment for thinking she could fly into the sky like an angel.

The only thing left for her was her now infrequent and wildly optimistic hopes for rescue, but she was tiring of feeling forgotten and lost. So, her main occupation now, was to find food and stay out of the clutches of evil, which was personified by Noonan. She was having no luck finding food though. The biggest problem they had was that once food was found, it must be eaten immediately or it would spoil within an hour or two. If left uneaten, it would be devoured by pests, rats, crabs, birds or dozen other organisms. Every meal must be hunted, caught and cooked, and the amount of nourishment one took in was almost rendered null by the sheer amount of time and energy it took to procure said food. They needed a large source of food, or a way to store food for a day or two.

When she turned off the beach and began walking towards Noonan's camp, she found herself secretly hoping that she might find him dead, and she wondered what part she would eat first, if she could bring herself to eat human flesh. She wondered if she could somehow store some seawater in some sort of container, and place meat into the water to save it for a couple of days. Unfortunately she knew very little about cooking and even less about food preparation and storage, so she had no real idea just what was possible.

•••

Noonan moaned as Amelia held his head in her lap. She took the rag, the same one that had been wrapped around his damaged hand, so it was still blood-soaked, and she dipped it into the water bowl and dabbed his forehead. He was miserable and sick from the crab he'd eaten. He realized that 'Big Blue' had been what had made him sick. Maybe it was the older crabs, or perhaps just the big blue ones that were the source of bad meat.

He'd managed to blurt out the story, in between bouts of heaving. He'd thrown up everything in his stomach, and was now dry heaving every few minutes. He felt weak, feeble and he knew that he might die. For that matter, Amelia could very well do him in. He was in no condition to fight back.

She had come upon him passed out, and at first she'd simply thought that he was asleep, but then she'd smelled and seen the vomit, and knowing he was sick, she'd rushed in to help.

•••

Even though it was a simple case of food poisoning, Amelia knew that this was a serious situation. If he became too dehydrated, he would die. They were both already in weakened states and the smallest injury or sickness of any sort could kill them.

She remembered what Noonan had said, days ago, when he had been explaining how easy it would be to die on the island, when he'd told her that one of them would suffer a catastrophic injury which would be compounded by the general state of things here on the island, and they would perish. He was right, on the island, theirs was a precarious existence. The question was; was this catastrophic event the one that was going to kill Noonan? What would she do if she was alone on the island? Finally, the forbidden thought emerged, and peeked from a corner of her mind; would she be able to dine on his body to sustain herself?

She sat with him throughout the night, and she could see, beyond the ring of light that their fire provided, the reflected light in the eyes of the rats, massed at the edge of the jungle. She could hear the clicking, click-click-click of the crabs claws, to the side of the camp where the sandy beach met the jungle tree-line. If the campsite had been even a few feet deeper past the tree-line they'd have been completely trapped by the island's inhabitants.

She knew that they were waiting for easy prey to become their dinner. Fortunately, she was able to keep the fire burning brightly and they were protected. She thought back a few hours or was it days? She realized that she'd promised herself that she'd 'capture' him when possible and keep him tied up, but she couldn't bring herself to do it. It seemed unnecessarily cruel. He couldn't harm her like he was now, and maybe whatever it was that had made him sick now was what had caused him to speak such craziness? She knew she shouldn't, but she decided that she'd give him another chance before she enacted the plan to subdue him and keep him captured. She hoped that her good faith gesture wasn't going to end up being the harbinger of her own death.

CHAPTER 19

Sometime near dawn, Noonan took a deep breath and sighed, and Amelia was alarmed, thinking that he had died. She bent down over him and put her ear near his lips and felt a tiny wisp of breath. She realized that the worst had passed and that he was just asleep. She was so tired she could barely move. The emotions of the afternoon, and the scare with Noonan had taken all of her energy. Though she couldn't stand the man, she knew that survival on the island was easier for two than for one alone.

She sat and watched the fire, and without thinking, closed her eyes and drifted off to sleep.

She didn't wake up for hours, and when she did, she realized that her hands were tied and her pants were gone.

She screamed, "Noonan! You miserable, treacherous cur!"

She sat up. There was no way he could tie her down to the ground, and the vines holding her wrists together were not tight. He must have been planning to come back and finish what he'd started. Why hadn't she done what she'd planned? Her trusting nature had back-fired on her, and now she was in trouble. She cursed her own timidity and hoped that she hadn't sealed her own fate. She resolved that if she got out of this alive, that all bets were off, and that she'd disable him and capture him at any point that was feasible. No more believing that he would change, and no more missed chances. She would have to do it as a matter of survival.

She looked around and seeing that he wasn't in the area, began twisting and turning her wrists and working hands out of the twisted vines. Luckily for her, Noonan was about as adept at tying knots as he was at making fire.

Slipping the vines off, she stood up and ran towards her pants lying next to the tree opposite her in the clearing. She slapped them up and down to shake the sand out of them and had one leg in, and was about to slide her other leg in when Noonan came barreling out of the jungle with a rapidity that stunned her. She realized that he must have just returned from wherever it was he'd disappeared to, or he'd been napping out of her sight and had woken up just in time to see her making her escape. He hit her from behind, and they hit the ground and began wrestling.

"Get off me, Noonan!" she screamed, using her fists to pound his back.

He pinned her to the ground with his forearm, and then reached down and stripped the pants off her leg and flung them into the jungle.

He positioned his knees inside hers, and then used his hands to hold onto her wrists over her head, so she was now stretched out underneath him. He moved her wrists together, using one hand to pin both her arms by her wrists, and then used his free hand to reach down and free himself from his pants.

He was grunting and panting now, and Amelia kept jerking up with her legs, trying to get a heel-hold in the sand so she could leverage him over to one side, but he was too well positioned on her this time, and she couldn't wrestle herself free.

"I'm not going to gild the lily here, Amelia," he breathed in her face, their noses touching, "I said you'd be my wife, and as such," he jerked and grunted and she felt him enter into her roughly, "you will not, and *cannot* deny me. It is my right to have you this way, and you *will* submit! By this time next week, after we've been husband and wife a few times, you'll be *in an interesting condition*, as they say." He grunted and then bit his lip and began thrusting in and out of her.

Amelia fought him with her muscle, every nerve in her being, but he was too powerful for her. As long as he straddled her, she couldn't budge.

In a matter of seconds it was over and he fell off of her, and sat up. He laughed at her, and then stood up and pulled his pants up, but not before Amelia was treated to yet another look at his manhood. She felt nauseous.

He walked over to his tree and sat down in front of it, glaring at her.

"I told you, Amelia, it's the way it is supposed to be. There's no sense in fighting it. It's my *right*, as a *man*, and your *duty*, as a *woman*, and you'd best remember it from now on. Now that wasn't so bad now, was it? Easy as pie, I'd say."

Amelia felt a guttural growl erupt from her throat, so intense was her hatred for this pathetic man. He looked as if he might attack her again, so she did nothing.

She got to her hands and knees and crawled to the edge of the clearing and pulled her pants out from under the underbrush. She fell backward onto her seat and slowly pulled the pants on. When she got them to her waist, she had to stand up to pull them the remainder of the way on.

When she buckled the belt around her waist, she felt the knife in her back pocket.

She stumbled, in a daze, across the clearing, past the fire, and then stopped when she was standing next to where Noonan was sitting with his back against the tree trunk.

She looked down at Noonan, and he looked up into her face, his smirk still daring her to say anything, and she pulled the knife from the back pocket and opened it behind her back.

"Now, Amelia, we'll have our very own little Garden of Ed-" Before he could finish Amelia knelt quickly and grabbed a handful of hair and jerked his head to one side and with the other hand she shoved the knife blade up against his throat. His eyes went wide.

"*What the hell?*"

Amelia pulled the blade away from his throat and put the point a half inch from his eye.

The knife was small, but she had sharpened it on the coral, so it was razor-sharp.

"I've had *enough*, Noonan. The only reason I don't kill you now is that it takes two of us to survive this island. We *need* each other."

He nodded, and kept trying to pull his head back away from the knife point.

"I tried and tried Noonan. I keep telling you, we need to work together, but I am not, and *will never be* your wife; *never*. You ever so much as lay a hand on me again, and I will castrate you on the spot. Don't believe me, and you'll suffer the consequences, and *that's* the last word on the subject."

Noonan started to say something but Amelia jerked his head back with her handful of hair, and he gave a little yelp of surprise and pain.

Amelia felt his hair coming out of his scalp when she jerked his head. Tears sprang to his eyes.

"Stay at least twenty feet away from me at all times, Noonan. If you want to move to the other side of the island, go ahead and do so. But if you ever come near me again, near enough to touch me, I will cut off your most prized possession. You want to eat that and see if it grows back, be my guest, but stay away from me, from now on," she shoved him aside and she stood and headed back to her camp at the end of the island. She was shaking with rage as she walked away wondering what might happen next. Holding the knife to his throat had made her point, for sure, but there was no way she could have set that knife down to tie up his hands or feet. She needed to knock him cold and that would give her time to time his hands and feet. Then she could re-arm herself with the knife and once and for all, be safe from him. Still, she trembled at how close she'd come to being his captive forever. She cursed herself again for having thought that he could, or would, ever change if given the chance. If his knot-tying skills had been better, she wouldn't be walking away from his camp right now.

CHAPTER 20

Amelia spent the two days watching the ocean from her camp, and wishing the dolphins would return. Several times saw the two ominous shark fins slicing through the water in the area near where the Electra had been. The feeling of evil that they represented seemed perfect for what the day had become. She fed on seeds, and her stomach growled constantly as she wished for a substantial meal.

She thought about Noonan, wondering how a man in this situation be so focused on something that no longer mattered, that being sexual relations, and not seem to care about the serious issues that they were facing regarding survival?

Then she remembered some of the things he'd been saying, about marriage, and about a child. They were repulsive, sick, and mentally deranged thoughts. He was obviously insane, and she hoped to someday see him locked away in an asylum somewhere.

She thought about how she felt when he'd been on top of her, doing *that,* and how she'd so badly wanted to slice his throat when she'd had him against the tree.

She wondered what would have happened if she had used the knife to slit his throat. Would it have been physically hard to slice a throat? How much force would she have had to use? Would he have died immediately, or would it have taken a while? What would she feel like, after doing it? Would she vomit at the sight of his blood? Would she cry and feel miserable? She would undoubtedly feel guilty about killing someone in cold blood.

The other question remained too. Would she be able to kill him? Would he overpower her the second he realized she meant to do it, and then would he kill her? She realized that this was a possibility. Skinny as he was, he was much stronger than her. Simply because he was a man and she was a woman.

As for castration, she knew that had been a threat, but what if she did actually castrate him? She shuddered at the thought. Her stomach was too weak, and she was too timid for almost any type of violence to do anything like that. For that reason alone, she realized that she'd probably never really be able to kill him. She was completely abhorred at the very thought of violence in any way, shape or form. The fact is, Noonan had just pushed her too far and her temper had gone out of control. Never before in her life had she lost her temper like that, and her ferocity had surprised her.

If he attacked her again, she swore to herself that she would protect herself, and she hoped that it never came to the point where she would have to see if she had it in her to kill a man.

Then she wondered too, what would she do with his body? Give him a Christian burial? Leave it for the rats and crabs?

She remembered what Noonan had said on their first day here. She shuddered, remembering again, and allowed herself to think it again, to wonder . . . what *human flesh would* taste like. This was the second or third time she'd contemplated the scenario, and it scared her, that she was perhaps, becoming as insane as he had become.

She sat at her rock-couch, watching the ocean for any signs of ships on the horizon, and her eyes finally closed and her head dipped forward and her chin rested against her chest and she slept.

●●●

Amelia laughed as the puppy wriggled in her hands. A yellow lab puppy with floppy ears as soft as chamois-cloth, and a pink-speckled fat little belly, it yipped and yelped in ecstasy as she played with it on the bed. The puppy finally settled down and for some reason she was tired so she laid her head back on the pillow and fell asleep, dreaming of flying.

●●●

Amelia awoke to the puppy licking her bare toes. The feeling caused her to giggle, and she wiggled her toes which caused the puppy to playfully nip at her little toe. She admonished the puppy with a wagging finger, and the puppy gave her little toe another nip and this time it hurt.

She yelled at the puppy this time, and the puppy renewed its attack. It growled and bit down hard and Amelia's eyes flew open.

Amelia realized she'd been dreaming. She was on the island. The sun was coming up on her left. She thought about the puppy, the dream had been so realistic that it amazed her. She could even feel where the puppy had bitten her little toe. It actually hurt as if the dream had been real.

The light was just enough that she could make out the waves rolling up the beach a few feet away. Then she felt a sharp pain in her little toe, as if the puppy in the dream was still biting her. She looked down at her foot and shrieked when she saw the rats. She screamed and pulled her legs up towards her, and scrambled her way to her feet and the rats scattered, all of them scurrying back towards the jungle. One large crab was still facing her and she kicked sand at it as she scrambled back over the rock of her rock-couch. She fell backwards and landed on her ass onto the beach. She looked around fearfully for more rats or crabs, and seeing none, she looked down at her foot. The little toe was bleeding profusely, and a strip of skin hung loose off to the side. The toe, and her entire foot throbbed and stung. She shrieked and stood, looking around fearfully again for rats. The crab which had been tugging on the skin was skittering up the beach now, back to wherever the crabs hid during the daytime. Probably a crab lair back in the jungle. She was shaking uncontrollably from the fright of the experience and her knees felt rubbery.

Amelia hobbled towards the surf. When she came to the inrushing waves she plopped down in the sand and stuck her foot into the oncoming waves. The waves covered her foot and then receded and the cool water immediately gave her relief from the stinging, throbbing sensation. Looking out into the surf, she saw the two familiar shark fins. They were coming in closer and closer, and Amelia instinctively pulled her leg back when they came within a foot or two of her foot in the surf. The green foam at the edges of the waves covered her foot. She watched as the green foam dissipated in the air, and she waited for another incoming wave to bring more foam. She allowed the water to cover her foot again and she used her foot to filter the foam before it was pulled back out with the receding wave. She sat for an hour in the incoming waves and allowed the cool water to make the throbbing in her foot and toe to stop.

By the time she went back to her camp the toe was no longer throbbing, but there were still cuts and a piece of fleshy skin hanging loose. She wished she had something to cover it with, but medical supplies were a luxury she didn't have. She hoped that the island rats weren't carrying rabies or the plague or any other nasty diseases, but she knew they were covered in all sorts of germs, how could they not be? She shuddered, thinking about the vile rodents coming so far out of the jungle and into her camp, and in broad daylight too! The cool water had felt good on her skin, but it was pointless to even think about taking an ocean-bath, what with those two devilish fins constantly lurking just offshore. She carefully put her shoes on, and decided to hope for the best.

•••

Amelia spent the day with her eyes on the horizon and the sky above it, watching for ships or planes bringing a rescue party, but nothing appeared except for a bank of purplish clouds to the east and the two ever-present shark fins patrolling the water just beyond the beach. The clouds stacked up higher and higher on the far horizon, and when it seemed they would move closer they turned blood-red and then dissipated completely.

As the sun was setting Amelia pulled her shoe off to re-examine her morning injury and was surprised to see that her little toe was completely free of any scars or scratches. The skin that had been pulled back by the crab was not even broken. Amelia couldn't believe her eyes. Her foot was so perfectly unscarred, no scratches, no tenderness, no pain whatsoever, that she began to think that she'd hallucinated the entire incident. She looked around in the fading light to see if there was anything that she could see that would prove to her that the event had really ever happened, but there was nothing, although she knew with a surefire certainty that it had happened. Maybe she hadn't hallucinated the event but she *had* overdramatized the injury. Maybe the skin hadn't been hanging off, and maybe there really hadn't been any scars or cuts. She stared at her foot until the fading daylight leaked out of the sky and it was impossible to see anything except the whiteness of the beach and the incoming rollers, rising up the beach and then receding, leaving the fluorescent green foam in its wake.

●●●

Noonan spent three days searching for food but he didn't see a single crab or rat. He went to the crossroads and back, several times, and he could hear the rats scurrying through the jungle on either side of him, and when he stopped and stood still, to hear better, the sounds of the crabs clicking the claws together was unmistakable. Yet he never laid eyes on one.

On the previous day, he'd once again seen the rescue ship on the horizon, steaming from right to left across the width of his expansive ocean view, and he knew he was being tested by God. *Be patient, you will be rescued. This will all be over soon . . .* he imagined God telling him. He realized finally, that he was not on his own so much as he was in the process of being tested. So, there *would* be a rescue, but it was up to Noonan to remain strong and be ready for the moment God called him.

He carried the steel rod with him always now, for use as a hunting tool, and also for protection against Amelia, just in case she attacked him again. Because that's what she'd done, she'd attacked him out of the blue. He had done nothing wrong, and she knew it. He was fully with his rights to demand what he wanted from her, and she was forbidden by laws, both legal and moral, to deny him.

The crab and rat population seemed to be avoiding them now. Maybe they'd seen what happened when they got too close to man, and they'd spread the word and somehow knew now to avoid them.

Whatever the reason for the sudden change in the rats' and crabs' behaviors, it was serious. He was starving now. He wondered what Amelia was doing for food. If she was remaining true to her promise to never eat crab again, and God knows she wouldn't eat rat, then she must be eating something. He wondered if she'd found a new food source and was purposely not telling him about it.

That's probably what it was, she wanted to weaken him, and then she'd pounce on him in his weakened state, and castrate him!

He decided to go to her camp, and keep an eye on her. If she was eating, he'd find out what it was, and where she was getting it and his problems would be over with. Plus, if he kept an eye on her, she wouldn't be able to sneak up on him and use that knife on him. He could even wait for her to sleep, and then steal the knife away from her; if he had the energy. He was so fatigued and depleted of energy that he wanted to crawl, or just lay down and go to sleep and never wake up.

•••

Amelia knew that he was watching her, and that's why she decided not to go into the jungle to scavenge for more roots and seeds.

If she had food, and he didn't, then his weakened state would mean he would be less likely to attack her. Plus, she had several days' worth of seeds in her bag. She was resolutely content to let him sit out there and watch her doing nothing. She kept the knife in her hand, just in case.

After a few hours of watching the waves roll onto the beach, she stood up slowly and looked around. Noonan was gone. She knew that he thought he was clever, hiding just inside the tree-line of the jungle, but she knew exactly where he was.

She decided to go to her food stash and have something to eat. She looked around one more time to make sure he wasn't watching and she went to the spot where she'd hidden the bag. She was tired, but she knew that the seeds would give her some energy.

It was gone.

At first she blamed Noonan, thinking that he'd stumbled across it by accident, but then she saw the tell-tale scrape marks in the sand, with the tiny furrows made by the smaller tiny legs of the crabs, and she realized that she'd been robbed by the crabs.

She followed the scrape marks until they circled around a tree trunk at the edge of the jungle and then she saw the bag, which was nothing more than an old shirt, knotted and fashioned into a bag. She went over to pick it up, and when she touched it something in it moved, and she dropped it. A long, light brown snake slithered out, and she stepped back away from it. The snake undulated around for a moment, and the crawled back into the cloth.

Amelia's heart was beating fast. This was the first snake she'd seen on the island, but she'd once heard, and Noonan had agreed that it was true, that all sea snakes were highly poisonous. She decided that any snakes they came across on the island would be of the poisonous variety. She knew that if bitten, you'd die within a few minutes.

She wondered if she could stab it with her knife, but didn't want to get close enough to try. By her reasoning, if she was close enough to stab it with the short little knife, then it would be close enough to strike and bite her.

She was about to walk away, and she realized that she had another option. She searched through the jungle until she found a piece of wood large enough to crush the snake. She would drop the wood on the sack, crushing and killing the snake inside. She congratulated herself on smart thinking, and was about to pick up the piece of wood when she saw another snake slither under the wood she'd been about to pick up.

She stepped back and looked around. Was this part of the island home to all of the snakes? They'd been on the island two weeks and neither of them had seen a snake, and now, with a matter of minutes she'd seen two of them.

She left the cloth sack and got out of the area as fast as she could.

A wave of nausea swam over her, and she leaned against a tree for support as it made her knees tremble. Looking down at her hands she saw them shaking with hunger. She turned and looked back at the area of the jungle that she'd just fled from. Her hunger now was palpable. She wished she could chew the bark from the trees. She was surprised to feel tears running down her cheeks. So, hungry that she was crying with helplessness, yet she refused the idea of eating another crab, or God forbid a rat.

Her mind went back to the first day on the island and how shocked and horrified she'd been when Noonan had made his remark, and she realized that human flesh was probably *cleaner* to eat than rat, and probably better tasting. Would it taste like beef, or chicken? She'd had horse before, and it had tasted better than cow's beef, but hadn't enjoyed the meal just the same. Before she realized what she was doing, she'd pulled the knife out of her pocket and was looking down at the blade. She needed to sharpen it if she was going to use it to find more seeds, it was getting dull.

CHAPTER 21

Noonan's hunger was driving him into a panic and he was woozy with fatigue. This was the third day he hadn't eaten. He had spied on Amelia and from what he could see, she wasn't eating either. He wished he could find another turtle, but they weren't coming around anymore either. In fact, all of the wildlife seemed to have vanished. Except for the rats and crabs that stayed hidden in the jungle, he hadn't seen any live animals since his rat-massacre and the killing of Big Blue at the crossroads.

His legs trembled as he walked along the shore watching for turtles and crabs. His head was swimming with dizziness and he knew he needed water too, but it was the prospect of a meal that made him continue on. He watched as two shark fins made a figure eight, as if they were circling their own prey, and he wished he had a net, or some fishing line. He waded into the surf, thinking maybe his steel rod would make a good spear. Then he realized that if he threw it and the fish swam away with it, he'd lose the tool forever. That was something that he couldn't chance, the loss of his best tool.

Other than the two sharks, which he knew he couldn't tangle with, all of the island's wildlife seemed to be in hiding. The tiny fingernail crabs that they'd eaten on that first day, which usually washed in with every wave, seemed also to have disappeared.

He was despondent. He knew that he could walk inland and start digging in the jungle and find some sort of insects or roots to eat, but he just couldn't will himself to give up on the crab, turtle, and rats. Meat was good. On this island it was survival of the fittest, and right now, Noonan felt his fitness slipping away. Besides, he had no clue as to what roots, seeds and plants were edible.

•••

Amelia lay just beyond the jungle, past the rock lair that made up her camp, and almost at the edge of the waves rolling up on the sandy beach. She was too tired to move. Her energy was completely gone. She watched as Noonan somnambulated past her and continued on to the beach, tottering along, mumbling incoherently, and passing near enough to her that she could have swung a leg out and tripped him, but he never even noticed her.

Deciding to follow him, she struggled to all fours and

Slowly gained her feet and simply leaned her head forward, as if to fall down, and then allowed her feet to take over.

As he turned into the shallow indentation of the jungle where he made camp, she stepped into the edge of the jungle to avoid being seen, though it seemed unnecessary. She could have grabbed his shirttail and hung on and allowed him to pull her along and he never would have noticed her. So deep was his aura of fatigue. She felt the same way. Would this be how death overtook them, with a sleepy fatigued feeling? Sleep seemed like a delicious idea, but it alarmed her, because she was inexplicably certain that it she gave in to the fatigue and lay down to sleep that she'd never awaken, so grave was her state of starvation. She felt that they were both near the end. Their bodies were depleted of all resources. The human body was not made for this brutal existence. A feast of insects, rats and crabs would no longer sustain them. If a rescue was not on the immediate horizon, then death was.

She turned her mind away from morbid thoughts and watched as Noonan stoked the fire into flames and crawled on all fours, circling around the fire, looking for scraps to eat, no doubt. He'd become an animal in the jungle, foraging for sustenance, just like the rats.

•••

Amelia lowered herself to her knees while she watched Noonan. Standing took more energy than squatting and she needed to conserve every ounce of energy available. She leaned against the trunk of the coconut tree and wrapped her arms around it. She fought the fatigue, trying to stay awake, believing the sleep equaled death at this point. She must eat before she slept again. She also needed to know that Noonan was preoccupied before she attempted to eat. If she found food while he was looking on, he might steal it from her, and she hadn't the energy to double her efforts. If he slept, she would sneak away and try to find food. If he found food while she was watching, she would demand to share. Not that it mattered, because at this point, he was sniffing the dirt around his campfire, apparently trying to find food using his nose.

Amelia turned and began crawling away from his campsite. She was trying to be as silent as possible. By the time she got to the edge of the jungle and stepped out onto the beach, she heard him behind her.

"Amelia! What are you doing sneaking around my camp?"

Amelia turned to see that he was about fifty feet behind him, leaning against a coconut tree. He was exhausted as she was, apparently.

"Go away, Noonan. I'm not bothering you. I'm headed back to my camp, and you're not invited, so go away and leave me alone."

"You've got food, Amelia, I know you do."

"No, I don't Noonan."

"You look like you've been eating, Amelia. Have you found a secret stash of food, do you have a new food source? What is it? Plant, animal, fruits maybe? Or has something delicious washed ashore?"

"I don't have anything Noonan. I could ask you the same questions."

"That's the point, Amelia, you *weren't* asking, and that's why I think you've found something."

"I have nothing, Noonan, that's why I'm heading out to look through the jungle, to find something."

Amelia stumbled forward, wishing she had the energy to run away from him, lose him, leave him behind, but her energy level wouldn't allow it. She was now reduced to stumbling blindly about, her legs barely had the strength to hold her upright any longer.

"Don't run away Amelia! I'll just catch you and tie you up again! It won't be a pleasant experience this time either."

Amelia gasped and looked around. She saw Noonan a few feet behind her. His strength was ebbing too, because the little burst of speed he'd used to catch up with her had cost him. He was panting now, hanging on to a tree trunk, sunk halfway to his knees. She was shocked that he freely voiced the idea of harming her.

"*I have a knife,* Noonan," she yelled at him, trying to sound brave, "and I'll defend myself if you touch me!"

"I don't believe you, Amelia. You hold up and wait up for me! We'll find some food together. You know, like you used to always say, *teamwork*."

"Go away Noonan!"

On her knees now, she scrambled forward across the hot sand. She looked behind her as she scooted and hands and knees, and saw that Noonan was on hands and knees too. When she stopped to catch her breath, Noonan took a breather too, by sitting back on his bottom, legs splayed out in front of him.

Amelia looked towards the East. Her camp was a mile away. She had lied when she'd told Noonan that she had a knife. She'd forgotten to bring it. It was still at her campsite and now she needed it more than ever. Whether it was to hold off Noonan and protect herself from him, or to use for finding, killing or preparing whatever food she could find, it was essential. The one piece of equipment she should never be without, the most valuable tool on the island was hers, and yet she'd gone off and left it. A mistake like that could easily be a fatal one and in her case, it still might prove to be her final miscalculation. She wondered if she had the strength to choke him to death if it came down to a fight for survival between them. She doubted it. But, is she could find something heavy to use to bash him in the head, and stun him, maybe then she could choke him to death.

Was this what her life had come to? Deciding to kill the only other living soul just to ensure her own survival? She shook her head ruefully. She'd become an animal too, no better than the rats and crabs on rat island. They'd feasted on the vermin's bodies, but the very same vermin, the island itself, had fed on their souls. They'd both been reduced to vermin, albeit vermin of a two-legged variety.

Amelia yelled over her shoulder as she began crawling forward again on her hands and knees, "Find your own food Noonan, even if I had something I'm not sharing. I don't trust you anymore. I don't want you anywhere near me!"

There was no answer, so she looked behind her to see if he'd given up on following her.

She turned and gasped as she saw how close he was and she felt his hand wrap around her ankle at the same moment and she fell face-forward into the sand and he jerked her backwards.

His hand jerked again and she was pulled backwards a few inches. Amelia screamed and kicked down at him with her free foot and caught him in the face. She'd caught him by surprise with the kick and she heard *oomph* and the grip on her ankle relaxed momentarily and she jerked free and began scrambling away as he tried to regain his senses. He was bigger and more powerful than her, and she knew that the only reason she could have stunned him with the kick was due to his failing energy. He was in just as bad a shape as she was in at this point.

"Stop it, Noonan, leave me alone!"

"Slow down Amelia, let's be friends again. Just stop and talk with me, okay?"

"No! Go back to your own camp Noonan! I've got a knife and I'll use it if I have to!"

"We need each other, Amelia!"

"Now you say you need me? Go away, I don't trust you, Noonan, you're a devil!"

"Amelia, we need each other in order to survive. Just stop so we can talk about this!"

Amelia decided that it was no use to talk to him anymore, so she didn't answer. Instead, she put all her effort into scrambling forward towards her campsite. She was within fifty yards or so now. A quick glance behind her showed her that Noonan had given up on talking and he too was putting all his energy and effort into the chase. He was further behind her now; her burst of energy had paid off. She concentrated on getting to the knife before he overtook her again. She hung her head and put all her effort into moving forward. The sand was burning her hands it was so hot. She couldn't remember the sand ever being this hot before. The sharp glass-like granules of sand were rubbing on her knees against the fabric of her pants, and she knew that if she pulled her pants down now and looked, that her knees would be bloody. Still, a bloody knee was nothing considered to the alternative, death, which is what would happen if she stopped.

It was a race against death and she was determined to survive.

•••

Noonan had been caught by surprise by the kick. He didn't think she had that kind of power in her, or the energy, but she'd nearly rendered him senseless. It took several minutes to shake off the fogginess in his brain and the stars in his eyes that the kick had produced. Once he'd shaken it off and started after her again, she'd gained a ten yard lead on him.

He didn't believe she had the knife, but if she did, he'd definitely take it from her. A knife would be invaluable.

Then it dawned on him. She wanted to find food, yet she was heading away from the jungle? Why would she do that? The answer was simple. She wouldn't. Unless she had a cache of food at her camp, or if she really did have the knife secreted there.

His sudden understanding made him double his efforts and he willed himself to move faster. She was fifteen feet away from her camp now, but he was gaining on her.

•••

When Amelia looked behind her again, Noonan had gone silent in the past few minutes, she shrieked in surprise. He was gaining on her and once again was close enough, almost, to reach out for her leg. She felt his hand swipe across her leg and she spurted forward just out of his reach and then around the corner of her rock-couch and frantically began scooping through the sand to find the knife.

She was running her hands just below the surface of the sand, hoping to feel the handle when two hands clutched her leg, her upper leg, on her thigh and then she was savagely jerked backwards, and then he has his arms around her waist.

She screamed and flipped over on her back, hoping to get into a position where she could use leverage to kick him. Flipping over when she did was perfect timing because when they landed his back hit the rock and it jarred him loose and she scrambled off and away from him and sat down her back against the rocks opposite him, and she pulled her legs up and got ready to kick out at him if he moved towards her again. As she braced herself with her arms down at her sides, her hand felt the knife handle and she closed her hand around it and then brought it up out of the sand. Noonan was pushing himself up off the rock and moving towards her when she held the knife up in her hands, and he stopped cold upon seeing the weapon, not daring to attempt to take it from her.

"Stop right there, Noonan! I'm not kidding; I'll cut your throat if you touch me."

Noonan looked at the knife, and then at her eyes, and he knew she would do, or attempt to do, what she said.

●●●

Amelia was shaking with fright. She was afraid that he would foolishly attempt to take the knife from her and she'd have to kill him. She wasn't sure she could do that, but if he attacked her she'd have to try, wouldn't she, after all, he was certain to abuse her in some way if he was able to take her prisoner. The idea of murdering him was distasteful, even in the context of survival. She hoped it wouldn't come to that, but he had shown no inclination towards being civil, or even sane in the past month, so she knew it might very well come down to a physical battle. She wished she had a large rock in addition to the knife.

•••

Noonan watched her very closely. She seemed to be deliberating something. He knew she abhorred violence, and deep down, she'd hesitate to fight him. He seriously doubted she would use the knife on him. Kneeing him in the balls was one thing, she'd done that readily enough when threatened, but using a knife? He knew she was scared right now. Probably more frightened than she'd ever been in her life. He would use that against her. He would get that knife, and then what? He'd do the only left to do. He'd have his food, finally. She was scrawny, sure enough; skinny and boney all over, but there was enough meat on those bones to give him energy enough for a week, maybe two. Enough time to get out and hunt. With that knife, and no interference from her, the island was all his. He was king.

He watched her eyes; she was obviously internally deliberating what to do next. A distasteful thought must have crossed her mind, or she was falling asleep out of sheer fatigue, because she closed her eyes for a moment and that's when he made his move.

•••

Amelia shuddered when thinking about stabbing him with the knife. She just wasn't sure she could do it; in cold blood, or in self-defense. What if she only wounded him and then didn't have the guts to finish him off, she'd have to care for a wounded man, and for herself, and that was impossible. The other scenario would be if she stabbed him and wounded him, then he'd be in pain, and she'd have to cold-bloodedly finish him off. The though caused her to shudder and close her eyes momentarily. Suddenly there was hot sand in her face and he threw himself on top of her and they were struggling. He wasn't hitting her; he was reaching for the knife, and trying to hold her arms out so that she couldn't thrust downward with the knife to cut him.

He had her back against the rocks, and he had a hand on each of her wrists, pinning her as his hands slip up her arms towards her fist where she clenched the knife. A few inches more and he'd be able to close his hand around it and wrench kit away from her. She struggled underneath him, using her hips to try and buck him off her, but still, even in his emaciated state, he was much larger than she, and her wiggling around did little to upset his balance on top her.

She felt his hand on her wrist now, and she knew that any second now he'd have the knife. With a burst of energy she bent her arm and then thrust forward, hoping to stab downwards and plunge the knife into his back. Instead, as she plunged forward, her grip on the knife loosened and it flew out of her hand, bounced off the rock outcropping behind them and flipped onto the beach on the other side of the rocks. His hand found hers empty and it was then that he realized she'd dropped the knife. He spun around on top of her, looking down behind them, hoping to locate the knife and grab it.

She spun underneath him and then arched her back and bucked him off and she drew her legs up and kicked out and him catching him in the chest and knocking him backwards. He seemed not to notice though; his eyes were locked on the ground between them as he searched for the knife.

Amelia flipped over on her hands and knees and she scrambled around the edge of the rock-couch and she darted behind the rocks out of his sight. She sighted the knife instantly and she fell forward on it and she wrapped her hands around it. She scooted on her butt backwards to giver herself room in case he came charging at her from around the rocks, but he never materialized. He was obviously still searching for the knife. She got to her hands and knees and began crawling away as fast as she could to get a head start on him. He was bound to realize what had happened and come after her again. She needed to make it to the jungle. Distasteful as it was, the jungle gave her cover to avoid and evade him. She'd take her chances with the rats and crabs over the lunatic any day.

●●●

Noonan dug around in the sand for a few minutes and he finally realized what had happened. He crawled around the rocks and Amelia was gone. He looked at the crawl marks in the sand, following the trail until it met the jungle tree-line, just in time to see Amelia's heels as she crawled into the jungle. He knew she was scared if she was willing to take her chances with the rats and crabs in the jungle as opposed to making her way down the beach. She had a big head start on him, and he knew that she was hoping that he wouldn't follow her if she went into the jungle, but it was too late to give it up. He needed the knife; he needed her, as a food source now she was far more easily taken than the rats and the crabs. True they would be easier to catch and eat, but he no longer had the luxury of eating small meals like rats and the occasional big crab. He needed *her*. No, he needed the knife, at all costs. That knife might very well be the difference between life and death on rat island.

He attempted to get to his feet, and did so, using the rock to set up against. Once on his feet his head swam with dizziness. He stumbled forward across the beach to the tree-line of the jungle.

Night was coming on, and he wanted to get her and he'd have to drag the body back to his camp and he didn't want to do all that in the thick of the jungle.

•••

Amelia looked around. The light had been fading on the beach, but in the jungle it was already black as midnight. The rats were swarming all around her and rushing underneath her as she crawled, which was repulsive, but she no longer had the luxury of any alternate choice. She didn't even have time to brush them off her back as they ran across her as she crawled through the dense underbrush. When they managed to get underneath her shirt and run up and down her back she reached back to knock them out, but usually they would squeeze underneath her shirt collar and then run down her back and then out from underneath her shirttail, but occasionally one would try to tuck it's nose underneath the back hem of her pants and try to get under there and she would have to reach back and grip the edge of her jeans until it found its way out from underneath her clothes. The sensation of the sticky little rat feet set her teeth on edge, but she had no time to get comfortable, she was running for her life. She had the feeling that if Noonan caught her, he would kill her.

She scrambled along as fast as she could crawl, too fast for the crabs to be a bother, they simply couldn't keep up, and gritting her teeth against the sliminess, furriness and general repulsiveness of the rats. She aimed for the general direction of Noonan's camp, but it was slow going. She was simply too tired to expend any energy. She just didn't have much left in her.

She was no longer even sure if what she was seeing was real. She was so starved that this could all be a hallucination, a dream. Maybe she was already dead and in hell. Crawling on all fours through a jungle filled with rats and man-eating crabs; that sounded like a pretty good representation of what a hell could be like...

•••

Noonan was exhausted. He'd entered the jungle just as night had fallen over the beach, and the interior of the jungle was black. The moon was up, which allowed a small amount of light to filter down through the foliage, and by that dim light he followed Amelia's crawl-path through the jungle. It was easy enough to do. The crawl marks in the dirt, the trampled down leaves, to dead rats here and there. He couldn't hear her, so he knew she must be much further ahead, and it seemed as if she was headed to the general direction of his camp.

After a few minutes of crawling it occurred to him that that's exactly what she was doing. She was going to his camp! Realizing this, he headed back to the edge of the tree-line, thinking that if he was going back to his camp, he might as well take the easy way across the sand, rather than through the army of rats and crabs in the underbrush.

•••

For most of the night Amelia dragged herself through the jungle, and throughout the night she could hear Noonan following along behind her. She knew that if she stopped, he'd kill her, and it drove her forward. After several hours though, she was lost. She had no idea where she was anymore. The fatigue and lack of food had clouded her brain. Unable to pull herself to her feet and walk, she'd dragged her body along, using her hands, and unable to see where she was going, she'd gotten lost. There was no longer a trail, not even a tiny rat or crab trail to follow. She was reduced to crawling on her belly through the brush just like a snake. Hours into the journey into the interior she wrapped her arms around a coconut tree-trunk and slept. She tucked her cheek against the tree trunk and tucked her head down in between her should and the tree trunk, to keep her face hidden from the rats. As she drifted off into a fatigued sleep, she could feel the tiny feet of the hundreds of rats as they ran across her back. She was too tired to fight them or brush them off. Luckily, the crabs were not in the area, so she felt lucky that she wasn't feeling the razor cuts of their claws on her body.

●●●

Noonan heard Amelia stop. Either that or she'd outpaced him and was no longer within hearing distance. Not that it mattered, he was too tired to crawl another inch. He collapsed onto the dirt and dragged handful after handful of leaves over his body, hoping to camouflage himself from the rats. He fell asleep.

Two days later -

Amelia stopped and rested against a tree, panting like a dog. She was still on all fours, and she simply came to a stop and leaning to the right, allowing the tree trunk to hold her up. She knew better than to lay down because if she did she doubted she'd ever get up again. On the second day of crawling, she'd come across several dead rats on the jungle floor. Laying on her side, too tired to even sit up, she'd pulled the knife from her pocket and had slit the rat's belly open and gutted it. After the entrails were spilled out, she didn't even bother scraping the fur off the hide, she simply began chewing the inside flesh. The first mouthful had made her retch and gag, but there was nothing to throw up. After her stomach quieted, and stopped flipping over and over, she tried again. After eating the flesh from three of the rats, she continued on. The food, disgusting as it was, had flooded her body with energy, and she was able to get to her knees, and then finally, she stood on shaky legs. She attempted to walk, but still had no energy. Going back down to her hands and knees, she continued her crawl through the jungle, imagining all the while that Noonan was just a few feet behind her, snarling with murderous intent. It drove her incessantly forward.

She'd been crawling through the jungle for three days now. Noonan had been behind her the entire time. Neither had spoken a word. Speech was too tiring at this point.

She just wanted to rest a moment, and gather more energy. She was stopped before a clearing in the brush. The clearing was about thirty feet across and she could see something large blocking the middle of the area; a tree stump or something that she'd have to detour around.

Pushing on she began crawling past the object when it moved, startling her. She fell down with a cry and shoved back away from it, and finally in a flash of moonlight filtering down through the foliage, she saw it for what it was, an enormous crab. It was the biggest one she'd seen yet on the island. It was as tall as she was when she was on all fours, and it must be close to six feet across, maybe even seven or eight. For several minutes she simply stared at it, hoping it wasn't going to come towards her with those massive bolt-cutter claws. It never moved again, and Amelia finally realized that the thing was dying, or already dead. She had come up on it as it was in its final death throes. The rats and other crabs hadn't yet had a chance to feast on it. Amelia pulled the knife from her back pocket . . . he mouth was already watering.

CHAPTER 22

Noonan fell into the sand face-down, too exhausted to crawl one more inch. Within seconds he was asleep. When he awoke, he realized that he'd allowed her to get away. He had no idea how long he'd slept though, so he simply kept crawling onward. The sleep, however long it had been, had allowed him to build up a small reserve of energy, and he used it to propel himself forward on hands and knees.

He came to a spot where there were several rats that had been sliced open. He could see from the cuts that it had been Amelia with the knife. He could see from the chewed carcasses that she'd fed on them. Noonan picked up the leftovers and chewed on them. Luckily for him, the other rats hadn't found them. As for the crabs, he hadn't seen any since coming so deep into the interior of the jungle. He was lost too, he had no idea where he was. He knew that if he'd been walking upright the past two days, he wouldn't have gotten lost. Navigating down here on the jungle floor was a lot different from what one would see when walking. A few feet in height made a world of difference. He just hoped that Amelia wasn't leading them in a big circle.

Within the hour he picked up her trail again. He was obsessed with catching her now. He needed that knife. He'd get it too. And the first thing he'd do with it is use it on her. Then he'd feast. If she wasn't going to give him what he wanted, then she was of no use to him on the island. If she was no use to him alive, then he'd see to it that she served a purpose. Dead; she served a purpose, as his food.

●●●

Amelia stabbed through the outer shell and sat back, just in case the crab wasn't completely dead. She didn't want to be anywhere near those deadly claws if this thing had any more fight left in it. After watching it for a minute with the knife sticking in its back, and it still hadn't moved, Amelia knew it was truly dead and she grabbed the knife and began cutting away the shell and pulling out huge chunks of meat. She ate two handfuls, raw, and grabbed a couple of large leaves on the ground to wrap up some more meat to take with her. The influx of food gave her a burst of energy that flooded through her body. She stood for the first time in over twenty-four hours. Her knees creaked and groaned as she stood, but it was a relief to stand again. She began making her way towards Noonan's camp.

After an hour she was within twenty yards of his camp. They'd been crawling through the jungle for three days now.

She set her bundle of crab meat down and crept forward to the back edge of the clearing. She knew that Noonan always rested against a fallen tree trunk and looked out the jungle opening towards the sea, just as she did on her rock-couch. Sneaking up this way on his camp would be a way to remain unseen and come up behind him.

He wasn't there though, but she really hadn't expected him to be. There was no way he'd travelled that fast. She went back to the spot where she'd dropped the food-bundle and picked it up. She made her way back into his camp and looking around, she blew on the coals of his fire until she had it going again and she pulled out another piece of meat. The cooked meat would go down much easier and she was still hungry. She wondered if she would ever again, in her lifetime *not* be famished.

She ate a piece of cooked meat, and began wondering if maybe Noonan had died in the jungle. He was in pretty sorry shape, just as she was. At least now though, she had the strength to stand up again.

No sooner did she have the thought than she heard a sound behind her. Then the shout.

"Amelia?"

Scrambling as fast as she could, she stumbled across the clearing and started climbing the tree that protruded above the middle of the clearing. At the height of about eight feet off the ground about twenty feet up the trunk, she stopped and clung there, and waited for what seemed like an hour, by he still never materialized out of the jungle.

Arms and legs wrapped around the trunk, eight feet in the air, she lay there. It wasn't quite comfortable like a bed, more like a hard hammock, but she was sure that he'd never think to look up and see her laying there like a squirrel in a tree.

Whether it was due to the warm food in her stomach, the tremendous fatigue, or the fact that she was no longer moving, her body wound down and her eyes slowly closed and she drifted off to sleep.

•••

Noonan tried calling out for her, in hopes that she might have a change of heart and give up her location, but he got no response, so he clammed up again. Then he detected the unmistakable smell of cooking crab. His body immediately went on the alert. He perked up. The smell was coming from his camp, which was about twenty yards directly through the jungle from where he was. The short nap, and the rat meal had reinvigorated him and he was finally able to walk again.

He stumbled through the jungle until he came to the back edge of the camp. He peered through the bushes. The smell of the cooked crab made his empty stomach rumble and his mouth began watering.

The campsite was empty, but the fire was going. He saw a bundle of something on the ground next to the fire. It wasn't any of his belongings. He walked forward until he was in front of it. He looked around for Amelia but saw no sign of her. He found a stick that had recently been used to hold meat over the fire. This was obviously what she'd been doing when he'd first smelled the meat. She must have stumbled across a crab, or she had somehow killed one on her own, and cooked it. He stabbed the stick into the meat and shoved it into the flames. He cooked the meat until he couldn't stand to wait any longer and then began eating. He wondered why she would have abandoned the meat and the fire and left it here for him, but he didn't question it any further than that. He simply fed. He didn't stop until he'd finished every piece of meat she'd left behind.

•••

Noonan was sucking the juice, from the inside of one the claws when he glanced up over the flames of the fire and saw Amelia perched on the trunk about eight feet off the ground. She wasn't moving, and he realized that she was sleeping.

He walked to the tree, getting ready to climb up there and drag her down, but something shiny on the sand caught his eye. When he bent down to pick it up and saw what it was, he smiled.

In an instant he'd made his decision. It was plain to see that Amelia was never going to give herself over to him, and he had no strength left for the constant battle it would take to convince her. She was stubborn and prideful. Thus he made his decision. Rather than spending a lifetime fighting her for what was rightfully his, he'd take her by brute force; club her in the head, then lay her down and take her like a man. Then he'd take that knife of hers and gut her like a deer and feast. He wondered how long she'd last before the heat would spoil the meat, and how long he could hold the rats and crabs at bay while he grew stronger from her body. Survival. He was the fittest, she wasn't. It was nature's way.

•••

In her dream Amelia was sitting down to a sumptuous feast. The table was piled high with meat, mashed potatoes, peas, corn, gravy, bread, and wine. Her father was at the end of the table, making jokes about no longer being stuck on the island. She felt happy, yet hungry, and was wishing they could hurry up and start eating.

"So, Father, who do we have to thank for this wonderful meal?"

"Why Amelia, we can thank your co-pilot, Noonan."

Amelia looked around to see where Noonan was,

"Well father, why isn't Noonan here to join us? Can't we invite him to the table too?" she asked.

"We did. He's here," her father laughed and used a fork to point at the center platter full of meat.

Amelia frowned and looked at the meat which was rather undercooked and pale. She crawled under the table and wrapped her arms around the table leg, but her father began pulling at her leg, telling her, 'come on and eat dinner Meely!'

●●●

Amelia woke up and saw that Noonan was standing beneath the tree, looking up at her and laughing, "Rise and shine, Meely!"

"Get out of here. Get away from me, Noonan!"

"Hey!" he spread his arms wide, "I don't mean to ruffle your feathers Amelia, but you're here in my camp, spying on me, what gives you the right to tell *me* to leave?"

Amelia looked around, "Okay, Noonan, I'll leave, but you step back when I come down."

Noonan smiled and folded his arms across his chest.

"I'm not kidding, Noonan. You better *get away* from me."

"You're in *my* camp, if you wanted me to stay away from you, then why did you come here?"

Amelia was getting frustrated, "Never mind, Noonan, now step back while I come down."

Noonan made his intent clear by remaining in the same position. Amelia couldn't believe she'd left the cache of food down there for him to find, so she decided upon a lie,

"Noonan, I found a crab and wanted to eat, and I was going to share it with you, so I came here to fly the flag of truce, that's all, so let me down now, I'll leave."

"You're not going anywhere, this is my camp, remember? You're captured. Now come on down."

"Can't you just walk over there," she pointed at the opposite side of the camp, "while I climb down?"

Noonan swept his arm back, "Come on down, I give you free passage; on my word of honor."

"But, you're not going to move back?"

"No, Amelia, I'm not. In fact, I'm getting rather tired of seeing you up there, in *my* tree, and now I'm going to have to insist that you come on down, *immediately*."

Amelia gripped her legs around the tree trunk; this obviously wasn't going the way she'd hoped. If only she hadn't fallen asleep! She didn't want this to get out of hand, but Noonan was giving her no other way out.

"Noonan, you better think twice about messing with me again. I wasn't kidding when I said I'd cut you if you ever lay a hand on me again. *Especially* if you try that again," she spit the word out, "*rape*. If you think I won't cut you, you're going to be sorry."

Noonan laughed, "Oh, you'll cut me, will you now?"

"Yes, Noonan, I don't want to have to, but I will. You better believe it."

"I don't think so, Amelia. In fact, why don't you get down out of that tree, and when you do we're going to have a little fun, you and I, as only man and wife are allowed to have fun."

"No, *we are not* Noonan. I swear, you lay a hand on me, and you'll get cut-"

"Cut with what, Amelia?"

"What?"

"How, Amelia" he laughed, "How are you going to cut me, huh?"

Amelia reached to her back pocket for the knife and stopped. It wasn't there.

"Whoops-a-daisy! What's this? Is this what you're looking for, *Meely*?" he pulled something out of his back pocket and Amelia could see her knife in his hand.

"How did you?-"

"Found it on the ground, right there, Amelia." He kicked at the sand with his foot.

"Give it back, Noonan, its *mine*." Her voice went into a growl so much was her anger at his turning the tables on her.

"Come on down and *get* it, *Meely*."

"Stop calling me that, Noonan."

"But it's such a cute little childhood nickname, and there's no reason not to have pet names for each other, right?"

"No dice Noonan, I'm not coming down as long as you're standing there."

"I think you will, sooner or later, and when you do, we're going to have *relations*, as man and wife. It's high time that you fulfilled your wifely obligations."

"I'm *never* going to do that again, Noonan. Never."

"Yes Meely, you will. In fact, I'm going to insist upon it."

"No, Noonan. You can stand there for a week or a month, or for the rest of your life. I don't care, and I'm not coming down."

"Oh, I think you will, and rather quickly too." He answered, and then he turned and walked away.

Amelia started to scoot herself backwards down the tree trunk, then stopped. This was a trap. He wouldn't just walk away and let her come down and run off. He was hiding in the brush a few feet away probably, watching and waiting to spring upon her the moment her foot touched the ground. She reversed her direction and scooted higher up the tree trunk. She went as high up as the part where the trunk started growing straight up. This was as far as she could go without doing some serious climbing.

She cocked her head. She could hear him crashing around in the jungle now. What was he up to?

Her best bet was to wait until he slept. She could quietly crawl down, and then, if she saw the knife, she could reclaim it, and then run back to her camp, get her few meager possessions, and go to the other side of the island and stay completely away from him from now on. Not just avoid him, but actually hide from him.

She watched him as he came back into the camp with his arms full of wood. He dropped the wood, and then began emptying his pockets; *rocks*. Why had he filled his pockets with rocks?

"Last chance, Amelia . . . *Meely* . . . Come on down and *behave*, or suffer the consequences."

"Go to hell, Noonan."

"Okay, have it your way. We'll just have to get down to the nitty-gritty and I'll get you down by force," he said as he picked up a rock, reared back like a baseball pitcher and zinged it at her.

The rock whizzed by, and she felt the rock graze the side of her head, just missing her left eye by an inch.

"That almost took my eye out, Noonan!"

"Amelia, I've told you a hundred times, it's survival of the fittest out here, and now it's time to prove it to you. You go ahead and stand your ground though, I fancy a plucky woman."

"You're just a hateful bully Noonan. There's nothing in you that's made of man. You wouldn't be so condescending to anyone else, you're just jealous of me and the success I've had."

Noonan's face went grim at the insult and he picked up a second rock and tossed it hand to hand, "Well, one success I had was that I was a pretty fair pitcher in high school Amelia. And I won't miss again, not at this short distance, its death and taxes, sure as hell."

"Come on, Noonan." She pleaded, "Can't we make a deal?"

"A deal?" He chuckled and shook his head, "not good enough Amelia. Once again, you're late to the dance."

He reared back to throw again, and Amelia maneuvered her body around to the back side of the trunk. Her position was very precarious now, hanging on the back side of the trunk instead of the top side, and she felt as if was about to fall. She felt a sharp bite in her leg as Noonan's rock slammed into her thigh. She yelped in surprise, amazed that he would do this, and then hugging the trunk so she didn't fall off, she peeked over the curve of wood that she clung to.

She was just in time to see Noonan's next rock come sailing straight for her. She ducked, and the rock smashed into her hands on the other side of the trunk, and she almost let go of the tree. Her grip with her legs was the only thing that stopped her from falling.

She screamed, "Stop it right now, Noonan!"

"Sure, Amelia, I'll stop, as soon as you come down."

"I told you that I'm *not* coming down Noonan, not as long as you're in the area. Go to the beach and count to a thousand. I'll be gone when you get back. I'll never bother you again. We'll live on different sides of the island."

"That's the most namby-pamby thing I think I've ever heard."

"Ease off Noonan, I'm begging you, don't hurt me! Can't we just talk like adults?"

The only answer she got was a chunk of wood thrown at her feet. Obviously he could tell that her legs were strong enough to keep her pinned to the trunk for a long time, and that's where he was going to attack her.

When it connected on her ankle, it almost knocked her off of the tree trunk. She tried to scrunch her body up shorter; to present a smaller target, but Noonan had the advantage on her. He picked up another rock and walked under the tree trunk, and Amelia began shifting her body around on the opposite side of the trunk and turned her face with her other cheek against the wood. She clung there, holding onto the tree for dear life, trying to flatten herself out so that she could hold on with hands and legs, feet; she was even using her thighs to hold herself onto the tree.

Noonan winged another rock at her, and this one caught her in the side of her stomach and knocked the breath out of her lungs. Noonan was deceptively strong, and the rocks felt like baseballs coming at her at full speed. She knew that it wouldn't take long for him to knock her from the perch. She had to do something.

"That was my curveball, but my strong pitch is my fastball. I'm not hemming-and-hawing around here now. I'm going to get serious," he chuckled, "here, let me show you how it goes, Amelia."

He reared back and let it fly, the same way she'd once seen Dizzy Dean, the Cubs pitcher, throwing.

She ducked her face behind her bicep as the rock caught the top of her arm. If she hadn't ducked, the rock would have caught her right between her eyes.

"Noonan, you'll have to kill me before I'll allow you to do that to me again!" meaning of course, the *wifely duties* and the *man's prerogative* that he kept alluding to; *sexual relations in the biblical sense.*

Angered, Noonan began throwing a barrage of rocks and chunks of wood as fast as he could wing them at her. They began slamming into her legs, arms, and sides in every area that wasn't protected by the tree trunk. She yelled every time he connected, and he was connecting on almost every throw. Then he paused, she guessed that he'd run out of ammunition, and was re-gathering new missiles to throw at her.

She wiggled a little bit and raised her head up to peer over her bicep and past the trunk to see what he was doing. He wasn't re-gathering new objects to throw at her; he was pulling logs and branches from the fire, and positioning them under the tree trunk between her and the ground. The tree trunk began smoking almost immediately. He was going to burn the tree down!

"Stop Noonan, I'm begging you, *please*, Noonan. Don't do this!" she cried and wiggled herself further up the tree. She was at the part where the tree began growing straight up, perpendicular to the ground. Another few inches and she'd be able to stand on the horizontal portion of the trunk and hold on to the vertical portion of the trunk at the same time. The higher she went, the safer she was from Noonan. But, the higher she went, the more dangerous it was if he knocked her off the trunk. It was a fifteen or twenty foot drop and she had no desire to break her neck. She looked around, wishing there was another tree close by that she could jump to, but that would only move her predicament, not solve it.

The smoke was billowing up now from the tree trunk, and she could hear the fire crackling; the bark popping. She peered down to see what damage was being done, but it only appeared to be superficial damage. The tree was a foot or two in diameter and it would take a while to burn through enough to collapse. She hoped so anyway.

Noonan walked back to the opposite side of the clearing and sat down. His evil grin told Amelia that he knew that she was sure enough stuck now. She couldn't climb down now even if she wanted to. The fire was completely encircled around the trunk now, and was slowly working its way up to her.

She decided that she had to jump. She would scoot backwards down to just above the area where the flames were on the trunk, and she would jump. If she didn't break her ankle in the fall she'd start running and hope that she could outrun him and lose him in the jungle. She'd still come back when he was asleep and get her knife back, one way or another. That knife was the big key to her survival. The knife and Noonan's steel rod, and the bowl were the best tools on the island. The best way to win the survival of the fittest on this island, as Noonan was fond of saying, was to have the best tools.

The fire crackled, and the smoke drifting up around her head now, and she caught all the smells at once; the salty spray from the ocean, the clean smell of the sand, fire, the wood smoke, her sweat, the crab, and even the faint stink of Noonan's leftovers of roasted rat carcasses.

Amelia wished that Noonan would let down his guard just for one minute, just one moment of laying his head down, or gazing off into the jungle looking in the other direction for one tiny moment, all she needed was a break.

She should have come down while he was off in the jungle gathered wood and rocks to throw at her.

She knew that she had to fight him and, even though it was repulsive, being raped by him *was* preferable to death.

She'd never let him know that of course, and she hated to even admit it to herself, but it was true. The one thing that mattered in her universe was to survive. To win this race, to beat this situation, to survive was the only thing.

She would fight for her life, because deep down, she knew that someday rescue would come and she would get off this miserable island. It could be tomorrow, or next week, or next year, but she *would* get off this island. She would be back in civilization, and she would expend her last breath, if that's what it took, to see Noonan locked away in prison, or an asylum, forever.

Taking a deep breath she wrapped her arms more tightly around the tree trunk and swung her legs out into the air and hung there, legs swaying, her arms circled tight around the trunk. She was afraid to drop but knew she had to, and the moment she hit ground she would have to run for the jungle, the one place Noonan wouldn't follow. She hoped.

Her arms around the trunk, fingers clasped together on the top side, she hung there, waiting for the courage to drop.

She'd hesitated too long, and now Noonan was up and running towards her. She wondered if she had the strength to pull herself back up onto the tree trunk.

The issue was moot because she felt Noonan's hands slap her ankle. He was directly below her and jumping up to try and grab her foot and pull her loose.

She'd thought that she was higher up than that.

She began kicking her legs to stop him from grabbing, but every kick she made caused her hands to loosen their grip. She began to slip. Her fingers were aching now, and her shoulders hurt. She wasn't going to be able to hold out much longer.

She tried to stop swinging so she could tighten her grip with her hands and when her legs stop kicking, she felt a tug and then two hands were wrapped firmly around her ankles. Noonan had jumped up and grabbed her. Now she was holding her weight and his and her fingers began coming unclasped. Her body was taut, like a guitar string stretched between Noonan's hands and her arms and hands wrapped around the tree.

Noonan began wriggling; jerking and doing whatever he could do dislodge her with his weight. Amelia did her best to hold fast.

The tree was completely ablaze now, just a few feet down the trunk from her, and she could see and hear popping blasts of sparks erupting from the wood. Every now and then a huge plume of smoke would spew out from the blaze like smoke from a volcano.

Noonan was grunting, jerking using his weight to tug on her, and Amelia willed her hands fused to the trunk. She wasn't going to drop. She desperately began trying to think of a way to get away from him once they dropped, but it was going to happen soon and there was nothing she could do about it.

He was now trying to climb, hand over hand, up her legs and she began thrashing her legs to throw him off, but his grip was too tight. One hand was now firmly clenched in her belt, and she could feel his other hand touching her buttocks. Then his face was at her midsection and he was about to pull himself up face to face with her.

She heard a loud crack and out of the corner of her eye she saw and enormous whirl of fire sparks shooting out of the tree and she felt herself falling, but her hands had not come unclasped from around the tree trunk. The tree was coming down on top of them; Noonan's fire having done the job it was meant to do.

In a split-second she heard a whoof as Noonan hit the ground and she landed on top of him, and then she felt a crushing weight as the tree came down onto her shoulder and she passed out.

CHAPTER 23

Amelia opened her eyes to pain. Noonan was groaning beside her. The tree was on top of them, and still burning. She raised her head and looked to her right, across Noonan and down the length of the tree trunk. The flames were about six feet away from him, and he was using his foot to push against the tree trunk, his left leg pinned in between the tree and the sand.

"Help me, you stupid bitch, come on and push!"

Amelia tried to sit up to give herself more leverage for pushing, but when she moved, pain shot through her left shoulder and arm.

The tree had fallen on top of her left shoulder and she had fallen outwards, and now she was pinned by her lower legs, but her arm and shoulder were on fire with pain. She thought dully, my *arm is broken, and maybe my shoulder too*. This was a catastrophe. Her legs felt okay, but her other injuries would hobble her movements for quite a while. Still though, even at this juncture, all was not lost. She would fight to her last breath.

She lay back on the sand, while Noonan frantically kept pushing against the tree trunk on his leg but the tree wasn't moving one inch.

Amelia took a deep gulp of air, and waited to see what else was hurting. Her legs were trapped, and the right leg was throbbing in pain.

Pulling her left leg up towards her, she wriggled and wriggled until it came free, out from under the tree, and then she rolled to her left, and started pulling the right leg towards the depression in the sand under the tree where her left leg had been. Pain was shooting throughout her body in waves. A few minutes of struggling and she rolled free out from under the tree. She was drenched in sweat and out of breath. She struggled to keep from passing out from the pain. She leaned back against the tree trunk, taking deep breaths and watched Noonan struggle. He kept pushing with his left leg, hoping to push the tree off his right leg, but it was no use, the tree was simply too big and too heavy.

If the tree had fallen upon them when they'd been standing on hard ground, they'd be dead. But the loose sand allowed whatever was pushed against it to move a little, and for that reason, they weren't crushed, just banged and battered, and in her case, a broken arm or shoulder, and a fractured or broken hip. The pain was centered up next to her hip and she couldn't bend the leg at the knee. She tried not to think, right now, about how this made their situation almost hopeless. The main thing now, was to take stock of the situation and get things back to a relatively normal basis.

"Help me why don't you! Why are you just sitting there?"

Amelia leaned over, and with her free arm, her right, she began scooping sand out from beneath the tree, next to Noonan's leg. In a few moments he would be free.

"Great idea, keep scooping!" Noonan nodded at her.

Amelia realized that now was her chance. She stopped scooping and leaned back against the tree. She tried to ignore the pain coursing through her body.

"That fire is burning this tree up at a pretty good clip; wouldn't you say so, Noonan?"

"Hell yes it is, now stop talking and keep scooping. That fire is getting too close. I'm about to get burnt!"

He was leaning to his left, to avoid the flames as the fire worked its way up the tree trunk towards him.

"Let's make a deal Noonan, *right now*."

"Have you lost your marbles, woman? What the hell are you talking about, *a deal?*"

Amelia smiled at him, as if she hadn't a care in the world, although the pain from her shoulder and hip was so intense she felt as if she might pass out.

"You give me the knife, right now, and I'll help you out from under the tree. If not, you're going to be very uncomfortable in a few minutes."

"You crazy bitch!"

"Noonan, you were just minutes away from raping me, and *you* set this fire, so if it kills you, it's your own fault and I won't bat an eye or lift a finger to help."

"You can't do that, you sorry bitch!"

"Yes, I *can* do it Noonan, and I will. You're always going on and on about the 'survival of the fittest' and how it's nature's perfect plan, well, I'd say that right now, I am going to survive, and you won't. I suppose this makes me the fittest, wouldn't you agree?"

"Amelia, don't do this now, please!"

"Sorry, Noonan, but we don't seem to have a lot of time for an in-depth philosophical debate. Either make the deal, or you're going to have to paddle your own canoe from here on out. I want the knife, you want out, it's an even trade. So, do we have a deal or not? Tell me now or I'm walking away," she said, even though she knew she couldn't walk. If he called her bluff it would be over. Barring her risking her own safety, she would have to extricate him, no matter what.

Noonan looked her in the eyes, and then to his right at the flames as they crept up the tree trunk towards him. The fire was so close now that he was leaning over as far to his left as he could to avoid being singed. In less than a minute he was going to be on fire.

"Okay, I'll give you the knife, but, it's in my back pocket and can't get to it. Get me out of here and I'll hand it over."

"Lean over, Noonan, I'll get it. Let's not stand on ceremony, and if you try any hanky-panky I'll get up and leave you here to roast."

Noonan looked pained, and seemed to be trying to figure out a way to cheat her, but was startled when sparks burst out of the tree just a few feet from his right side.

"Okay, okay, get it! It's in my back pocket," he said as he leaned over to his left, his body twisted away from the flames, and offering access to his back. Amelia got to her knees and leaned over him, every move she made causing shooting pains throughout her right side. She lay on to him since she was unable to use her right arm or hand, and she used her left to reach in between their bodies and then under him and when her fingers wrapped about the hilt of the knife, she pulled it out of his pocket and for a moment she wondered if she should just plunge the knife into his heart and be done with it. She considered the implications of doing just that. It actually might even make sense too. She could feel the heat from the flames on the tree, just a few inches from her face. The fire would cook him for her, and she could live for . . . how long on his body? She shuddered at her own cold-bloodedness and wondered what was happening to her that she would think of such things. The thoughts of dining on him had repeated themselves several times now in the past few days and it bothered her that she would sink so low as to even consider such deplorable behavior.

Noonan didn't know that she was injured more seriously than he was and that she needed him more than ever for survival on the island. He didn't realize just how close he'd come to his own end.

"Come on, Amelia, hurry up, my back is almost on fire!" Noonan screamed. The odor of burning hair from his back made itself known and Amelia fought back a gag.

Amelia reached under the tree and began scooping sand out and away from his trapped leg. When she'd scooped out enough, she reached back and found the cuff-bottom edge of his pants, and she began pulling. The leg came free and she rolled over and struggling to her feet, which was difficult to do without using her right arm.

She sighed and then leaned back against the tree, exhausted and took a deep breath.

She rolled over on her left side and began scooting away from the tree, and once she made it to the other side of the clearing she used a tree trunk to slowly stand up, her eyes swimming from the pain. She leaned against the tree, and watched as Noonan slowly dug a heel into the ground, and used his foot and put his hands behind him to push and pull himself backwards and away from the burning tree.

It took Amelia a few moments before it dawned on her. *Noonan's leg was broken.* They were both severely crippled. Like it or not, they were in a pickle and now they would *have* to work together. There were no buts about it. They were at rock-bottom.

CHAPTER 24

The tree burned slowly and brightly with good flames for hours, while Amelia and Noonan just stared at each other from opposite trees, their feet almost touching. Amelia had always thought that a live tree wouldn't burn so well. She'd heard her father call it 'green wood' or something of this sort. Whatever it was, she must have misunderstood, because this one was blazing pretty well.

The tree had fallen across Noonan's fire pit so they were sitting where they normally would have sat if they'd been sharing a meal in Noonan's camp.

Noonan broke the silent spell, "My leg is broken."

"I can see that, Noonan."

"It hurts so bad I can't stand it."

"I hurt too, Noonan."

"Where are you hurt?"

Amelia was disgusted at Noonan's selfishness. The fact that he hadn't bothered to notice her injuries was typical. He was only interested in himself. Anything outside the realm of his self-pitying or self-important awareness was not worth noticing or thinking about. Anyone else would have seen her cradling her arm or the fact that she could barely move her legs and realized that she was injured. Not Noonan.

"My shoulder is broken, maybe my collarbone, and my hip. I can't walk."

Noonan stared at her, open-mouthed.

"What do we do? I mean, I'm in terrible pain here, Amelia."

"Noonan, there is nothing we *can* do for the pain, and for your information, I'm in a great deal of pain too."

"Well, this is your fault after all!"

"No, Noonan, it is not my fault, it's yours," she yelled at him, "If you hadn't been so hell bent upon . . . upon *raping* me, we wouldn't be in this mess."

"Again you're wrong, Amelia. Because if *you* had been willing to do what was *required* of you we wouldn't be in this situation."

"Noonan, talking to you is like talking to the dog, and I'm not going to argue with you, we have things to do, and we need to do them quickly darkness comes. We need to keep this fire going all night, unless you're willing to sleep with the rats tonight."

At the mention of night and rats, Noonan became visibly agitated. Amelia looked around her, hoping that there was enough wood in crawling distance to keep the fire stoked all night. She wasn't worried too much about the rats and crabs since it had been three days since they'd seen any of either of the creatures. She wondered if they'd just learned to avoid humans, or if they were hiding because of the time of year or something. She knew that rats and crabs didn't hibernate, but something was keeping them away, and whatever it was she was thankful for it. Her stomach was not in agreement with her though. Noonan's oft said, 'a hungry dog is an angry dog' and Amelia now knew the full import of the saying.

Tired of listening to Noonan muttering imprecations at her, she began crawling towards the tree nearest the beach, which just happened to be the one closest to Noonan. She lay down gently on her left side and began pushing with her good leg. Over and over she pushed, and using her outstretched good arm to help pull herself along, was able to make about eight inches per movement. There was sand all inside her shirt, and now the gritty sand was making its way down her pants. She tried to close her mind off to the multitude of indignities she'd suffered on this island, and realized that the list would undoubtedly be growing. Sand down her pants was the least of her problems. She wondered how long it would take for a broken hip and shoulder to heal, or would she ever regain her health? With the limited diet available to them, eating the same continual food over and over, with no vegetables, would their bodies take a month or two to heal, or would it be a year or longer?

For two hours, maybe longer, she scrubbed along in the sand, passing out from the pain on two occasions, and when she reached the tree trunk she propped her back up against it and breathed a sigh of relief, sweat rolling down her face and drenching her shirt.

Her hip was throbbing, and her shoulder and right arm was a constant searing pain. She'd have given everything she owned, back in the real world, for a mere handful of aspirin.

She looked over at Noonan. He was more mobile than she was, what with two good arms, but his leg was swollen, and there was no doubt it was broken.

She cocked her head and stared at him, something was wrong. Then she saw what it was; he was chewing on something! He had food?

"Noonan, what are you eating?"

He pulled his hand away from his mouth, "Nothing."

"Noonan, I could see you chewing. What is it? Where'd you get it? Can't you share? I did save your life after all."

"You did no such thing," he glared at her, and then deliberately brought his hand back up to his mouth, tilted his head back and opened his hand. He chewed with obvious motions designed to taunt her.

Amelia tried to figure out if he was just pretending to chew, and then her eyes spied the cloth bag next to his knee. Her cloth bag full of seeds! How had it gotten out of the jungle and all the way over here? That must be a distance of almost two miles. Could the crabs have dragged it here? He had the bag of seeds and he also had the bowl with water right next to him. The bowl of water was filled about halfway and was covered in the scummy-looking green bubbles. She wondered if he drank it with the foamy bubbles, or if he scooped them off the surface of the water before he drank. At this point she didn't care if there were dead rats floating in the water bowl, she wanted a drink. Amelia sighed, wishing that she had crawled over there to begin with. Now she was going to have to go through some more pain.

"That's right, Amelia, I followed you on your little seed and plant digging expedition."

"You stole my food bag?"

"No, I didn't. The crabs took it, and I found it in the jungle. So, by all rights, it's mine now."

"I don't believe the crabs took it, I think you did."

"Amelia, you should know that anything that's not tied down, or buried will be found and dragged off by the crabs, that's just the way they are. They're hoarders, like raccoons."

"I'm coming over there, Noonan, and you're going to share those seeds."

"I'm not sharing."

"Yes, Noonan, you will, I'll make you. I have the knife, remember?"

Noonan paled a bit, and then smiled, Come on over then, and we'll share."

Amelia repeated her earlier process of laying down on her left side and crawling, using only her left side, and after thirty minutes, she was a foot or two away from Noonan, the seeds and the water. She took a deep breath, which wracked her body with pain, and started crawling again. She heard a grunt, and looked over at Noonan, only to see him doing the same, crawling through the sand, but away from her.

"You stop that, Noonan! Stay where you are."

"Don't try and catch me, Amelia," he gave an insane giggle and scooted a foot further along in the sand, "I'm faster than you."

Amelia gave a grunt of her own and began double thrusting her leg, trying to move faster. When she looked up again, she realized that she was close and she reached out and grabbed with her hand and closed her fingers around his ankle. He yowled in pain.

"Stop it, Amelia, that hurts!"

"Stop moving then, stop trying to get away!"

"Okay, okay, okay, I'll stop," he yelled, "just release your grip, that hurts too much!"

Amelia tightened her grip and Noonan began thrashing violently. She squeezed with both hands as hard as she could and suddenly he went limp, passed out from pain.

Using his legs to pull her body forward, she drug her way up him until they were face to face, and then she rolled off him and immediately wished she hadn't as a wave of pain so fierce shot through her that she thought she might pass out as well.

She waited, heart hammering, until most of the pain had passed and she dragged herself backwards again and propped herself against a tree trunk. She reached down and took the cloth-sack out of Noonan's hands, and hid it under her good side, and then pulled him up until he was propped up beside her. She saw that the water bowl was just a few feet away on the other side of Noonan.

She lay herself down and dragged herself over to it and then set it as far ahead of her as she could and worked her way back to the tree next to Noonan. After moving the water bowl, and then following, she eventually made it back with the water bowl to the tree beside Noonan.

Now they were side by side, the fire in front of them, she had the knife, and the seeds, and their view was towards the opening of the clearing leading out to the beach. The campsite was a horseshoe-shaped area opening out to the beach, so they had the jungle on all three sides.

Not an ideal placement, but as long as they had the fire going, and the water and seeds, they would be okay for the night.

Tomorrow they'd need to crawl around and gather as much wood as possible for the night-time fire, and hopefully come across a crab that Noonan could kill for food. She knew now that she'd eat crab again. At this point she'd even consider rat.

She looked over at Noonan and wondered again, what flesh would taste like. What part would she eat first, his arm or his leg? She shuddered, but the thought stayed in her mind.

●●●

Noonan came to with a start.

"You bitch, you stole my food."

Amelia said nothing, but kept chewing the seeds and roots that she'd dug out of the bag.

"Amelia, my leg hurts awful badly, I can't stand this."

"There's nothing I can do about it, Noonan, I'm hurting too, you know."

"Well, *do* something, you're a woman."

"What's that supposed to mean, Noonan? That I can nurse you and make the pain stop, simply because I'm a woman?"

"I thought all women learned things in school, about you know, taking care of bumps and bruises and such things, for when you get married and have kids."

Amelia was about to tell him what a simp he was when something occurred to her. She pulled out the seed sack and rummaged through it until she found it. A handkerchief tied into a knot, with a lemon sized portion of the red seeds. The poisonous seeds! She remembered how they'd made her fingers and mouth numb.

She opened the handkerchief and looked at the seeds. They were a deep red, almost burgundy in color and each seed was about the size of a BB. Amelia had taken classes in first aid, not that anything she'd learned there would be of any help in this situation. One thing she had learned was that some pain-killer compounds were topical.

Her thinking was that if she could crush the seeds, mix the powder with water to form a paste, and then she could apply that to her hip, her shoulder, and Noonan's leg. If the compound numbed them enough that they could move around more freely, it would enable them to withstand the pain until they began healing. With the pain numbed sufficiently, she would be able to get organized for the night.

She looked around for something that she could use to hold the seeds as she crushed them.

"What are you doing, Amelia?"

"I need to crush these seeds to make a powder. . ." she explained what it was she wanted to do and he listened. Noonan had a doubtful look on his face.

"We'll try it out on your shoulder first though, right?" Noonan asked her.

"Sure." Amelia agreed. She thought it was odd that he volunteered her to be first. In normal circumstances, Noonan would have insisted upon being first to benefit from any sort of improvement or enhancement. She wasn't going to argue though, because her shoulder was sending out wave upon wave of pain.

She poured about a quarter cup of the seeds into her shoe, and then found a stick lying nearby and began crushing the seeds until she had a fine powder. It was difficult work, using only one hand, and Noonan seemed to have no interest whatsoever in helping her.

She poured in the water and mixed the powder into a paste. When the paste was ready, she simply smeared some across her collarbone and upper arm and waited for the results.

"You might as well get your pants off, Noonan, because as soon as I put the paste on my shoulder, we'll need to put some on your hip, I don't want the paste to dry before we have time to apply it.

•••

Noonan watched as Amelia worked on crushing the seeds. He'd been dubious at first, but then he realized what she was up to. She'd said that the seeds were poisonous, and now she was mixing this poison into a paste that she expected him to rub on his broken leg? How could paste help a broken bone?

No, he knew what she was up to all right. She wanted revenge. She wanted to castrate him. Rubbing poisonous paste on his *manhood* would certainly do the job. He figured that she didn't want to use the knife because the blood loss would kill him. Doing it her way would leave him alive, but castrated, and he'd live out the remainder of his days as her eunuch slave. He'd stop her when she got close enough, and while he was at it, he'd get his knife back too.

CHAPTER 25

"Okay, Noonan, the paste is ready," Amelia said as she slowly stirred the paste with a stick, "get your pants down while I apply the paste to my shoulder, we need to hurry."

She dipped her hand into the paste and reached inside her shirt and rubbed the cool paste across her shoulder, and her collar-bone. The heat from the mixture started seeping into her skin almost immediately. She sighed and felt like crying, the relief was so total and immediate.

She turned to Noonan. He had his pants unzipped, but wasn't working on pulling them down.

"Come on, Noonan, this stuff works fast. You get those pants down and you'll be feeling better in just a few minutes."

"I'll do it myself."

"What do you mean?"

"I mean that I don't want you reaching down into my pants, I'll do it myself, give me the paste," he held his hand out to her. Amelia handed him the paste.

Amelia frowned. Something was wrong here. How many times had he stripped and allowed her to see him fully nude, and in a state of arousal to boot, not to mention the times he'd tried, and succeeded, in raping her? Now, he was acting shy, as if he didn't want her to see him without his pants? It just didn't make any sense.

She watched as he reached his hand down into the heel area of her shoes, and then pulled his hand out with the blood-red paste.

"Go on, Noonan, I swear you'll feel better immediately, just rub it on your hip, or wherever the pain is, and it will deaden it."

Noonan pulled his hand up to his face, and bent his nose down towards his fingers to smell the paste.

"I'm not sure I believe you. This stuff is just some sort of nostrum."

"Noonan, I'm telling you, it works. It will take away some of that pain. But, I wouldn't get it in your mouth, or lips, or God-forbid your eyes if I was you, that stuff is highly acidic. I don't know what it is, but it's very powerful."

He moved his hand down and Amelia watched and waited,

"Go on Noonan, what are you waiting for? You need help with the pants?" she asked as she reached forward to pull the edge of the pants outward so that he could more easily slide his hand down inside, and he screamed, causing her to jerk back, and he lunged at her with both hands.

"Stop it, Noonan!" Amelia screamed and his hand found her face, her eyes, and she felt the burning as he began mashing the paste into her face, her mouth, and she screamed when his hand began rubbing the paste into her open eyes.

They struggled, and she bucked against him, trying to get away from his hands, and he grabbed the hair at the back of her head with his other hand, and kept rubbing and smearing the paste into her eyes with his other hand. She started using her hands to hit him as hard as she could and it was only when she began punching as hard as she could against his injured hip that he screamed in pain and rolled away from her.

Amelia began screaming from the pain in her eyes, and then everything went black. She was blind.

CHAPTER 26

Amelia came to feeling as if her face was on fire. She blinked several times, and realized with a panic that she was blind. She felt around on the ground beside her, trying to get her bearings. She scooted backwards until she felt a tree trunk and pulled herself up against it. She had full use of her arms, but her face was stinging something terrible and her head was pounding with a fierce headache.

"Noonan, are you there?"

"I'm here Amelia."

"You son-of-a-bitch, you've blinded me!"

"I was only saving myself, Amelia; I knew exactly what you were going to do."

Amelia whimpered as the pain pulsed in waves through her head. She leaned over and felt the cool sand on the side of her face. She was drooling, and tears were pouring out of her eyes.

"What are you talking about Noonan?"

"I know what you were planning, you had no intentions whatsoever of putting that poison on my hip."

"What do you think I was going to do, Noonan?"

"I know, Amelia, you wanted to put that stuff on my . . . my *manhood*, you were trying to castrate me!"

"Noonan, that's absurd, you, you *blinded* me because you thought I wanted to castrate you?"

"I *know* what you were up to, Amelia."

"Noonan, you're wrong. I was trying to help you, and now you've blinded me because you have some ridiculous obsession with your, your manhood. Noonan how could you have been so foolish?" Amelia said. She wondered if the blindness was permanent, or temporary.

"I am not foolish. I was protecting myself, Amelia; I know what you've wanted to do, ever since I made it clear that you were to fulfill your wifely obligations and duties."

Amelia moaned in pain, and began feeling around her for the water bowl. When her fingertips brushed against it, she leaned over it and began splashing the water into her eyes and rubbing.

Noonan kept prattling on and on about wifely duties, and how things would be different from now on.

After a few minutes of washing her eyes out, she could see a hint of light in her vision. It was no more than if she'd had her eyes closed tightly in the night and a flashlight was shone in her general direction, but it told her that the blindness would be gone in a few days, or even a few hours if she was lucky.

Meanwhile, it was getting dark, and their fire was still burning, but how long would it last?

She could feel the heat of the fire, and when she faced it full on, she could detect some light at the edges of her vision.

"Noonan, you better gather wood and branches for the fire tonight, otherwise, we may have problems later on."

"But, I can't walk, Amelia, my leg, it hurts too much."

Amelia was getting exasperated at his obliviousness,

"Noonan, *use* the paste on your hip. It will make all the difference in the world. Come on now, get a move on, we need to make sure the fire does not go out during the night."

"The paste is gone, Amelia."

"Gone? What do you mean, *gone?*"

"I threw it away, somewhere into the jungle," he swept an arm towards the jungle, and then realized that Amelia couldn't see what he was pointing at.

"Why would you do that, Noonan?"

"Because it was poison, Amelia, that's why. Look at what it did to you!"

"You blinded me, Noonan, the paste helped my arm, look at this," she moved her arm in a circle, "see that? That paste completely killed the pain. You need to find it."

"There's no way, Amelia, I'm not going into the jungle at night to try to find that stuff. We'll just make more."

"Fine, Noonan. Get the seeds and we'll make more."

She listened as he crawled around for a few minutes dragging his useless leg.

"Find anything Noonan?"

In a defeated voice, he answered her, "I found the rag, but the seeds are gone, scattered all over God knows where."

"Noonan, you brought this upon yourself, you need to go find that shoe with the paste in it."

"How Amelia, I wouldn't know which direction to start looking in. I tossed it while we were wrestling around. I wouldn't even know where to start," he paused, "I don't see it anywhere."

Amelia sighed and shook her head.

"Noonan, is it still dark?"

A pause, "Yes, but the tree is still burning. It should last until morning."

Amelia wanted nothing more than to get as far away from Noonan as she could get, forever, but she wanted to survive more than anything else, so she told him,

"Well, we should huddle together, that way I can wake you up if the fire runs low."

They positioned their bodies against the same wide tree trunk and waited. Amelia spent her time wondering what the next few days would be like. She made a list. As soon as she could see she would find more of the seeds. Even if they weren't healing their injuries, they at least acted as an efficient painkiller. If they weren't in pain, then they could move, and moving meant survival at this point. Moving to get water; the seeds, food, keeping the fire going, being able to move meant *everything*.

She needed to find the knife again, and as soon as she could see, and get the red seeds, she'd bargain with Noonan for the knife. If keeping the knife meant continued pain, Amelia was sure that Noonan would make the trade.

She could see the brightness at the edge of her vision, and knew from that light and from the heat, that it was the fire. She just needed to make sure that she kept Noonan awake through the night.

She cocked her head, maybe her hearing was more acute now that she couldn't see, and realized that she was hearing Noonan already snoring. Damn him, barely two hours or so into the night and he was doing the one thing that he shouldn't do. She was about to wake him when she decided to feel around first, to see if she could find the knife.

After a few minutes of crawling around, her hip still wasn't numb enough to stand, she found it. She was about tuck it into her back pocket when two hands grabbed her. They immediately began wrestling for control of the knife.

She was at too much of a disadvantage though, being blind, so she rolled over on the knife with it still in her hand, and just as she did, she felt him on top of her. They were both whimpering in pain. The paste was good, but any movement still pained her, and when he sat atop her, the pain was indescribable. She screamed for him to get off.

"Give me the knife, dammit!"

"No!" she yelled back in his face, and that was when he raised up a little and then dropped down hard on her pelvis and she screamed in pain again, and while screaming at the top of her lungs, she arched her back, reached under her and pulled out the knife, and then plunged it into Noonan's leg on her waist.

He screamed in pain and reached down and pulled her hand off the hilt, yanked the knife out of her leg and then brought it down into her shoulder and everything went black.

•••

"Help me, Noonan, please," Amelia mumbled when her eyes opened.

She felt stickiness on her shoulder, and she knew it was blood. Noonan had stabbed her, after she'd stabbed him in his leg, and now they were leaning against the tree trunk.

"You hurt me, Amelia."

"And you hurt me too, Noonan."

Amelia felt so weary that she only wanted to sleep, but she was driven to surviving, no matter what the obstacles, and now those included broken bones, blindness, and having been stabbed. Still though, she would go on. There was nothing else to do, but go on. The stab wound was minor simply because the blade was so small. It hurt and it was bleeding a little, but she knew it was her least significant injury at this point.

"The fire Noonan, is it dying down? I still can't see."

"Yes, Amelia, it's burning faster than we thought it would. Probably another hour or so until it goes out."

"But, it'll be daylight soon, right?"

"I think it's only about three a.m., so we have maybe two and a half or three hours."

"Build the fire up, Noonan. Come on, you can do it."

"I'm too tired Amelia, I hurt too much. I just need to sleep, and tomorrow things will be better."

Amelia was sure now that he was giving up. The man simply had no fight in him.

"Get up, Noonan, and stoke the fire, come on, you can do it."

"It's too late Amelia, it's going out now."

Amelia moaned in fear. This was not right. It was Noonan who was afraid of the dark, not her. He was afraid of the dark, the rats, and the jungle, yet here he was, ready to sleep as if nothing was happening.

She turned her head to see if the light appeared at the edges of her vision, so she could locate the fire. But none appeared. The fire had gone out, completely. She felt the warmth disappear from in from of her, signaling that the fire had indeed gone out. She could see a dull light at the edges of her vision when she turned her head so that the side of her face was nearest the fire. There was still a dull glow. She knew that dull glow was from the coals glowing in the fire pit. It meant that there was still a small amount of light from the fire, a glow that allowed vision about five or six feet in circumference from the fire. They were losing time just sitting here doing nothing.

"Noonan, get up, do something. Come on!"

Nothing. She used an elbow to jab into his side and he startled awake.

"Come on, Noonan, do something, get the fire roaring again."

"Too late Amelia, the fire's gone."

"Build it back up, Noonan. You can do it!" She knew he was lying because she could see a hazy orange light a few feet away from where she was sitting, and she could feel the heat from it. But it was ebbing slowly. She needed to convince him to stoke the fire, get it roaring again.

"Doesn't matter, Amelia, we don't need it anymore," his voice changed and took on a happier tone.

"What are you talking about Noonan?"

"The fire, we don't need it."

"Why not?"

"Because, Amelia, they're here."

"Who's here, rescuers?"

"I see them right there on the beach in front of us, see them? See the lights in their eyes?"

"Who are they Noonan? Is it the Navy, or a private ship, do you see G P anywhere? Is he with them?" Not that it mattered who was in the rescue party. It could be anyone and she'd be overjoyed.

"No, it's not the Navy, Amelia," Noonan said, his voice was now dreamlike, "it's the rats."

Amelia cocked her head, she could hear faint squeaking sounds, like the rats used to make when they came up a mass of them in the jungle, and now she could also hear the faint click-click-click noises of the crabs snapping their claws.

Oh my God, the rats, and the crabs together, and coming towards them?

"Noonan, what is it? Tell me, what do you see?"

"Eyes," he whimpered.

"Eyes, what do you mean, eyes?"

"All I can see is their eyes, Amelia, looking at us," he gasped, oh my God."

"What Noonan? What's happening?"

"They're coming for us. Oh God, please God, take us away from here!"

A shower of sparks burst out of the tree trunk in the outer edge of the fire and the flames shot up, and the fire was rekindled.

Noonan whimpered, "Oh, Jesus, I want a drink."

Amelia grabbed his arm in her hands and squeezed, pulling closer to him, "Noonan, what happened?

"The tree trunk started burning again; the flames are coming back stronger."

"We know the rats won't come too close now."

"I don't think they're scared by the fire anymore. They're all here Amelia, the rats and the crabs, the big ones."

"They're here, you mean right *here*?" she lowered her voice to a whisper, "*How* close, Noonan?"

Noonan said nothing but he whimpered in fear and pulled in closer to her.

Amelia squeezed his arms in her hands, "How *close* are they, Noonan?"

Noonan whispered, "They're right in front of us."

"In front of us?" she felt her heart start hammering in her chest, ". . . how *close*, Noonan?"

"Just an arm's length away."

As soon as he said it Amelia felt a rat-tail flick across her foot. She shrieked and jerked her legs up under her, ignoring the pain and leaning in closer against Noonan, trying to slide behind him, but he was pressed back against the tree trunk as hard as he could manage.

Noonan screamed and Amelia could feel him bringing his hands up to cover his face as the attack started. She felt the swarm as the furry bodies hit her. She brought her good arm up to cover her face and she felt the tiny wet paws all over her, and then the hundreds and thousands of tiny sharp bites began burrowing into her body. She screamed in fright but quickly closed her mouth as the thrashing, wriggling vermin swarmed her face and she knew that if she opened her mouth they'd be able to chew on her tongue. She squeezed her eyes shut too, and brought her injured arm up to swat them away, but there were too many to fight off. They were attacking in wave after wave.

She hunched down in the sand curling into a tight fetal position and tried bringing her knees up to her face. Still they swarmed her, biting into her side and back, crawling into her pants and then up her shirt. The terrible biting, gnashing and gnawing of the hundreds of teeth made her delirious and pain began coursing through her body and finally, mercifully, she passed out.

Noonan's screams ended soon after hers and the island quieted, save for the hissing and clicking sounds of the islands only inhabitants, and the sound of the surf rolling up the shore.

Coming to, Noonan used his arms to drag himself away from the burning tree and the dual hordes of rats and crabs as they swarmed over her body. He used his good leg to help propel his body along, heading away from the edge of the jungle and out onto the wide expanse of beach.

He could hear the savage hissing, the gnawing, the grinding of teeth, and the spooky clicking of the crab's claws as they fed upon and fought among themselves over Amelia's body. He wished he could go back and fight them for it, because he knew that he could feed on her for many days. It was all about survival.

It took all his strength to pull away from the fire, but he knew that something had changed. The rats were no longer scared of the fire. They seemed intent upon feeding upon the body that had invaded their territory. Noonan knew that it was a ridiculous thing to believe, but he wondered if the crabs were seeking revenge upon him for having killed their leader, Big Blue. The rats too, seemed as if they were driven to avenge their fallen comrades, the hundreds of rats that Noonan had feasted upon. It was absurd to think of these animals as having the capacity to seek revenge but Noonan still believed it to be true.

He knew that the crabs wouldn't get near the ocean waves; it would kill them, that much was certain. The fact that they were seeking revenge wouldn't keep them from physical harm though, that was sure, so Noonan pulled himself slowly across the beach towards the waves.

At one point he looked back towards the fire still burning, and he believed that he could still hear the rats feeding upon and fighting over Amelia's body. It was a gruesome sound.

Then he panicked at what he saw thirty or forty yards behind, following in his body's drag marks were three large crabs. Almost as big as Big Blue had been, and Noonan knew, even though it was dark and he couldn't see to be sure, but he knew these were three of the large 'blue' crabs. They were coming after him slowly and surely, and he knew what he must do.

He dragged himself into the incoming surf, just enough that the waves flowed around, but not over him. He felt the wet sand settling underneath him, and smelled the salty water, felt a clump of sea-weed against his neck. He stopped and turned himself around so that he was facing the beach. The crabs had some to a stop at the place where the incoming waves flowed up the sand and stopped, about eight feet away inland from him.

They were at a stand-off.

Noonan knew that he couldn't stay here. He looked back to see if he could see a place where the rock and coral jutted above the water, thinking maybe he could take refuge on a make-shift island, but he froze when he spotted the two fins of the ever-present sharks. He could see their ominous fins knifing along in figure eights just twenty feet out from him. The fins slid like shadows through the moonlight on the waves.

This time though, they were swimming in so close to shore that Noonan pulled his legs up closer, thinking the sharks might just get close enough to take his foot off.

He was trapped, halfway in the water, halfway out, with sharks behind him, and crabs ahead of him, with nowhere to go.

He waited.

The crabs crept forward to the very edge of the incoming tide, but they refused to come onto the wet sand where the waves washed in and receded. They never even scissor-clicked their claws, they just stared at him with their small bead eyes and wiry antennae.

•••

Amelia came to and screamed, flinging the rats and crabs off her body. They scattered away from her and she moaned. She took stock of where she was. The fire was still going, she could see the flames through what was left of her blurred vision and damaged eyes. She remembered seeing the water bowl, and she wondered if she could find it. She felt around her, and got her bearings, and believed that she knew approximately where she was positioned in the camp. She knew that the water bowl was probably ten feet away from her, but on the other side of the downed tree trunk. She hoped that the tree hadn't fallen on the bowl and caused the water to spill. If it hadn't spilled, she would drink some, and splash some on her face, which was still burning, stinging from the poisonous seeds. She took a deep breath and began crawling. She went over the tree trunk, and then aimed herself towards where she believed the water bowl to be. She crawled slowly, her arms sweeping the sand before her. After a few minutes her fingertips brushed the bowl. She nearly cried with relief as she pulled herself towards it, being careful not to bump it and spill the precious water.

When she was next to it, she leaned back against a tree trunk, she knew she was on the outer edge of the clearing, just before the clearing edges led out onto the beach. She wondered where Noonan was. The rats and crabs seemed to have gone away too.

She carefully lifted the bowl into her lap and then lifted it with both hands and lowered her face to the surface of the water. The cooling sensation of the water on her burned face was immediately calming. She felt strength coursing through her body again. She dipped her face into the water again and this time she also drank some. When she lifted her face this time, she blinked and realized that she could see more clearly. She was still partially blinded, but the act of rinsing her eyes out seemed to have been helpful. Maybe the effects of the seeds burns were only temporary. She looked towards the beach. She felt compelled to go out there. She drank more of the water, and washed her face some more. She cupped her hand into the water and then dripped the water over her shoulder where Noonan had stabbed her with the knife. The wound immediately felt less painful. She looked out again towards the beach area. Then she went to her stomach, and began dragging herself towards the beach. She didn't know why, but she knew she must get out there.

CHAPTER 27

When the light from the sun began creeping over the horizon the crabs turned and scuttled quickly away and Noonan drug himself out of the water and collapsed onto the warm sand of the beach.

Waking a few hours later, his mouth dry with thirst and nasty with the rancid aftertaste of his last meal of rat, he heard the droning of a plane far off in the distance. His eyes scanned the cloudless skies overhead; he never spotted the plane, but the sound of the plane spurred him to develop a plan.

Maybe Amelia had been right about rescue, and even if she wasn't, he had to do something to, as Amelia would say, better his plight. He began dragging himself along the beach with his arms and scooping the sand as he crawled. He ignored his pain and gave what he considered to be a herculean effort. By mid-afternoon he was finished with the letters. N O O N A N the letters read, spread out over more than a hundred feet in length and ten to twelve feet in height. He was exhausted.

Now, he needed to crawl into the jungle and gather leaves and branches to fill in the letters. That should make the letter dark enough to be seen from the search planes.

He crawled back to the incoming waves and drank his fill of water and then began the long crawl back to the edge of the jungle. Looking at the sun overhead, he realized that he needed to be finished by the time the sun set. He couldn't chance getting caught by the rats or crabs. He strongly detested the idea of spending the entire night in the water, but without fire, or a way to walk, or his killing tool, the steel rod, he had no other chance to survive the night.

Ignoring the pain in his hip as much as he could, he crawled towards the tree-line and wondered how he was going to drag branches while using his arms to drag his body. He solved the problem by grabbing handfuls of brush and piling them onto his back and dragging himself forward as a sled burdened with its freight.

Hours later, the sun was dipping towards the horizon and he was exhausted. He'd only been able to fill in the first two letters; he would have to wait until daylight again to finish his project.

His stomach was pinching and squeezing him to the point where he could only think of food. Drinking more salt water did nothing expect quench his thirst and leave a rotten salty taste in his mouth. He found a soggy clump of sea-weed lying on the beach, and he realized that it was edible. Laying on his side on the wet sand, his lower legs in the surf, he crammed a handful of the sea-weed into his mouth and began chewing. The taste was horrible, but his mouth began salivating and he realized that the sea-weed was a good idea. There were probably some good nutrients in it too. It was difficult to chew and swallow though, being soggy and wet and spongy. It swelled up in his mouth and throat when he chewed and swallowed. It wasn't until he choked down a few swallows of it that he became alarmed.

The insides of his mouth and throat began stinging and then his forehead became hot and he started sweating profusely. He dug out a clump of the seaweed from his mouth and threw it down and began spitting out the rest. There were translucent slime-strings inside the sea-weed. Jellyfish remnants. That was what was causing his mouth and throat to sting so badly.

He began hunching over and retching. His eyes began watering so fiercely that tears were pouring down his face.

He moaned in misery and lay down, his back to the incoming waves, his body just ahead of the rising tide. If he fell asleep he didn't want to drown, but he also wanted to be in the water far enough that the crabs wouldn't get him. Too far out into the surf too, and the sharks would be able to take a foot or leg, or drag him back into deeper water.

He moaned, and looked up at the stars which were now appearing overhead. It's as if his spot on this planet was gradually shrinking until he almost had no spot left on earth, not even a few square feet to stand on unmolested by God's creatures where he was safe. The planet was literally shoving him off of it, but being human, without wings, he had no place left to escape to.

No sooner had the thought come to mind, and he felt something bump him from behind. The sharks! He turned over quickly, pain wracking his body, and was rewarded with a huge piece of driftwood which was trying to wash ashore. He pulled his body up onto it. Just large enough for his torso and upper legs, his arms and feet dangled over the sides, but his body was heavy enough that he anchored it in the surf. It wasn't going to wash ashore any further, and it didn't seem to be getting pulled back out to sea. It was a respite of geography and chance.

He sighed and slept.

Awakening the next morning, he realized that he'd made it through another night, but he simply had to get out of the sun and water. His face, neck, and arms were blistered to the point where boils were starting to rise. He didn't know whether the boils were from the relentless sun he'd endured, or if they were due to his diet, or the jellyfish stings, or any of the dozen or so other indignities that he'd endured.

He dragged himself off the driftwood and made sure that he pulled it up the beach a ways so that it didn't get pulled back out to sea. He dreaded the idea of spending another night on it in the water, but he would do whatever it took to survive. This was survival of the fittest, and he was determined that he would not be beaten by stinking rats and crabs.

Dragging himself towards the jungle tree-line, he finally made it back to their original camp and he was surprised to see the tree still burning. He noticed one of Amelia's hands lying near a clump of bushes. The rats and crabs hand left it behind.

The remainder of Amelia's body was so badly disfigured that it was gross to look at and he averted his eyes. It appeared to have been getting dragged into the jungle by the crabs and rats, and they'd left it there while they went into hiding during the daylight hours.

Noonan backed himself up to a tree trunk a few feet away from the burning tree and looked around. He wanted to sleep and restore his body, gather some energy for the task of finishing the letters, and then waiting out the night in the water.

Overhead, some lightning flashed. It was such a foreign sight that it stunned Noonan. How long had it been since he'd seen lightning, heard thunder, felt that pleasant sensation of rain drops upon his skin. He knew that unless the rain began falling soon, it was a sensation that would be forever lost to him.

He knew that he shouldn't sleep too long though. He had a lot of work to do. His hip and leg was throbbing unmercifully and his insides seemed on fire with hunger, hurt and constant uneasiness. He knew that he had to eat or he would die soon.

He looked around thinking that there might be some rat carcasses. When they swarmed, they fought and bit each other and sometimes there were dead rats just lying about. Today though, there were none and no crabs either.

His scanned his eyes once again across the clearing hoping to see a rat carcass and then he stopped at seeing Amelia's hand by the clump of palm fronds. The steel rod was next to it. His mouth unconsciously salivated and he swallowed the small amount of spit he'd generated. Sighing, he crawled over to the steel rod and picked it up. Using the steel rod, he speared her hand and then leaned forward and dipped the hand into the flames and cooked his meal. When the hand was roasted and dripping, he was unable to contain his hunger any longer.

He ate.

Afterwards, he urinated and brought his hand it up to his mouth and drank the urine from his cupped palm.

After he swallowed the last of it, he leaned his head back against the tree trunk and closed his eyes. He tried not to sleep, because he knew he must crawl out onto the beach and complete the sign. Once he had it done, he would try to figure out a way to avoid spending the night in the water. He wouldn't live another week under these conditions. He had to do something for shelter and food.

He needed to be ready for the rescue. He needed to hold out, to survive until they arrived. Maybe Amelia had been right, and they wouldn't stop searching until they found them.

Becalmed at last, he managed a few hours of sleep. Upon waking he sat up and stared in disbelief at the beach. The crabs were back, hundreds of them, covering the beach, turtles too. The big ones.

It wasn't the thought of food though that caused him to scream, it was what the crabs and turtles were doing. They were crawling across the beach, across his sign.

He began dragging his body along the beach out towards them. They were scuffling across his sign, completely erasing his letters!

He yelled and screamed at them but they were already in the process of moving out of the area. The turtles scrabbling out towards the sea and the crabs down the beach to the north. They must have places they hid in during the day and they were migrating back there now. Noonan looked at his sign, it was ruined.

The sun was getting low on the horizon now, and Noonan heard the droning again. The rescue plane was back! It was flying over, and this time he could see it. He was lying prone practically next to his first letter, the N, and it was one that the turtles and crabs hadn't destroyed yet.

The plane came in over the island, flying south, at about a thousand feet. Noonan waved and screamed as it buzzed overhead. He was deliriously happy now. There was no doubt whatsoever that they'd see the letters. He was rescued!

•••

"Seagull one this is seagull two, come in. Are you reading?"

"Seagull two, reading you loud and clear."

"We are doing a flyover of this small island, in quadrant X-one. Repeat, we are doing a flyover in Quadrant X-one."

"Roger Seagull two."

The pilot turned to his co-pilot. "See that down there? What do you think?"

"Turn back and let's take another look."

The pilot banked and they took another pass over.

"What do you make of that?"

"Just a small island, maybe a couple of natives, if that; it couldn't possibly have more than a few people on it. Tiny, I'm surprised there's anyone on most of these islands."

"Yeah, but what do you make of that?" he pointed at the beach.

The co-pilot laughed, "Just two letters, 'N' and 'O'"

"Meaning what, do you suppose?"

"I bet one of the search ships already searched this island, and told the few natives . . . if there are any, I don't see anything down there now . . . told them to let us know there's nothing here. 'N' and 'O', meaning No sign of them."

"Either that, or they made it themselves before heading back to the ship. You know those Navy guys, one or two of them actually has a sense of humor."

"Yeah, well, whatever it is, it's obvious they're letting us know there's nothing there."

"I'll call it in."

"Okay, I'll turn back."

"Seagull one, this is Seagull two. Reporting in."

"This is Seagull One, go ahead Seagull two."

The co-pilot keyed the mic, "Finishing search of quadrant X-one. There's nothing here, we're turning back now, and we'll try the last quadrant tomorrow morning."

"What do you think anyway? Think we'll ever find anything?"

"Nah. They ditched in the drink a ten days ago. This whole thing is just G P's money being poured down the drain. It's useless."

"I agree. But hey, he keeps paying my salary, I'll fly around out here forever if that's what he wants."

"No, I talked with G P before we took off, and he said that tomorrow is the last day. We don't find them in this next quadrant, the search is over."

CHAPTER 28

Noonan waited until dark and made his way out to the beach in order to get back onto his driftwood. He was miserable. Why hadn't the plane seen him? He knew they hadn't because they hadn't flown back by and wagged their wings at him. S & R pilots would always do that, just to let you know that help was on the way.

He stopped walking. Between him and the water he could see the black mass of rats waiting for him, to their left was an army of huge crabs. He'd feasted on them, and now they were about to turn the tables. He swallowed nervously and looked to his left and right. He needed to get to the water, where he knew he was safe from the rats and crabs. The rats wouldn't get into the sea, they'd drown, and the sea-water would kill the crabs, for some crazy reason, who knew why?

Out in the surf he could see the same two ominous fins swimming back and forth. They'd been a constant reminder that he was a land-based creature. The island was ruled by the rodents and crabs, the sea ruled by the sharks. There wasn't room on this island for one man. Yet he intended to stay. He'd get to the surf, and deal with the sharks then.

He walked forward into the roiling mass of rodents and immediately felt the furry bodies wriggling all over him, their small sharp teeth making thousands of cuts. His knees buckled and he went down. The blackness covered him. Using an arm he flung outwards and saw daylight. He began crawling forward under the weight of the rodents and the crabs attacked his legs and he felt the razor sharp cuts beginning. He dragged himself forward, inch by inch. He cried out once, 'Amelia!' and the silence descended.

Hours later he awoke. He'd made it to the driftwood and he'd managed to keep it in the surf by hanging his body partially off it, in order to anchor it from being swept backwards into the deeper water where the sharks waited. Several times he'd felt their smooth skin brush against his leg or foot and he'd jerk spastically before they could latch on with their fearsome jaws. Using arms and legs to keep himself positioned in the water away from the rats and crabs, and far enough out of the deeper water, away from the sharks had depleted his last reserves of sanity. Death literally nipped at his heels and stared him in the face.

He knew he was in dire straits now. No food, no water, his body battered and broken. The sharks in the water behind him, and the rats and crabs awaiting him further up the shore. He was trapped and his strength was almost completely gone.

He could see that the fire in the campsite was almost burned out. When it died out this time, he knew that all his hope was lost forever. He was as good as dead.

He lay, with his head against the wet bark of the driftwood and watched as the last flames of the fire burned down. There was no moon tonight, and when the fire went out he would be in complete darkness.

The thought of the darkness scared him more than anything so he stared at the fire slowly burning down. As if the imprint of the firelight on the inside of his eyelids would preserve the actual light as long as the afterimage burned. It was just one more thing he'd never experience, man-made light at the night.

He sighed and watched the flames as they winked out slowly, and the silence and darkening sky descended all around.

Noonan looked up at the stars, and slipped off the driftwood and into the foamy edge of the waves.

Noonan saw thousands of red eyes as a light behind him swept the island and reflected in the rats and crab's eyes. He turned slowly and saw the searchlight sweeping. The ship was probably a mile or two offshore.

It would be a miracle if it saw him, and even in it did there would be a half hour or more before they made shore. The idea of rescue no longer concerned him. Survival was the only thing now. Noonan was that aware the outcome was already decided; maybe he'd surprise himself with his own strength and cunning, maybe not, but he'd be well fed, whether the rescue materialized or not. He'd simply tell them that Amelia had succumbed days earlier. If not, he'd live longer, perhaps even long enough to rule the island over its current inhabitants. He had no interest in rescue, back in society he'd be a man among many whereas here he would rule his own kingdom. Ocean storms would bring more like him in the future and he'd rule them too. He would become a mighty king over every living creature within sight, his rule extending from horizon to horizon.

Above the jungle tree-line ahead of him Noonan could see millions of twinkling stars; below the tree-line on the beach were millions of beady-red eyes; the rats and crabs, massed and angry, an army ready to face their only enemy.

A smudge of lightness on the horizon told him that it was morning; the sun would be up soon.

Turning his gaze back in towards the island, he could see that the horde of creatures awaiting him was enormous. They had retreated in the night, back to the tree-line of the jungle, so he had forty or fifty yards of beach between himself and the creatures. The crabs were the first wave he'd have to breach, then the rats. Beyond them lay his prize; Amelia and a feast of flesh. He crawled forward, his strength so low that he dragged himself on his belly, using his hands. Starvation and injuries had taken their toll, and last night he'd been as near his death as ever. Though the night spent in the surf had revitalized him somewhat his pace was still incremental. It was as if he had no clue as to how to walk upon two legs. He felt something in his back and legs and assumed it was just his wet clothes, but reaching back, he found that he was covered with slimy seaweed. He grabbed a fistful of the mossy wetness and slung it away from his body, and he heard the slap as it landed on the sand a few feet away from him. Squirming forward, his legs finally left the surf and the warmth of the water. Dragging himself up the beach he could hear the swarming horde of rats as they began hissing in anticipation of him, and the pinchers of the crabs began clicking in counterpoint creating an otherworldly symphony.

Crawling up the beach, the smear of wetness from his body created a drag mark from the ocean as he made progress across the white sand of the beach. Little by little he progressed towards the jungle tree-line. Twenty feet further and he brought himself up on his hands and knees and covered another twenty yards. The closer he came to the edge of the jungle the higher the noise-level from the agitated rats and crabs became.

He'd said it to Amelia just recently and it was still true; life was simply a matter of survival of the fittest.

He felt another surge of energy in anticipation of what lay before him. The light behind him swept from his left to his right across the beach again, this and in the flashing of light he saw what appeared to be millions of rats and crabs, their red eyes glowing hellishly in the darkness. He was unafraid, for he was man, freshly arisen from the sea, and as such, claimed dominion over all creatures.

On the far side of the swarming horde of rats and crabs, between them and the jungle line, Noonan saw a large dark figure crawling on the beach, moving slowly forward. Too large to be rats and crabs, but not upright, and yes, it was moving towards him. Noonan couldn't make out what it was, but it didn't matter. If he could get through the rats and crabs, he was deal with it. As if sensing his thoughts, the dark form rose up off the sand, and Noonan could see it clearly.

He felt another surge of energy, anticipation and will, and stood fully upright now, flinging off one last chunk of wet seaweed. To his right the sun was beginning to climb above the horizon, the clouds dark and red as blood.

He walked towards the massed vermin, ready to claim his dominion over the island.

– The End –

ABOUT THIS STORY

The story you've just read is obviously fiction, a figment of my overheated brain's imagination. I have never heard of Noonan portrayed as a misogynist of any sort, and have no idea as to whether or not Amelia Earhart knew how to swim, or had daddy issues. As I said this story is composed of equal parts fiction, fantasy, and what if? . . .

The truth is that no one knows what really happened to Amelia and Noonan on their flight, but scientific evidence points to the island known as **Nikumaroro**, or **Gardner Island**, which is part of the Phoenix Islands, in the western Pacific Ocean as having been their final resting place.

Interestingly enough, the most fantastical aspect of the story, the rats and the large fearsome crabs are quite real. The small uninhabited islands throughout the Pacific are well known for having uncommonly large rat populations. The coconut crabs described in the story are real too. The coconut crab can grow to very large sizes; just as described in the story and are strong enough to drag a body, and have claws which are strong enough to cut open a coconut shell. They have an acute sense of smell, and can live well past 50 years of age. Some scientists have in fact, theorized that if Amelia and Noonan had been stranded on Nikumaroro, that the rats and crabs could very well have killed them. In their fragile state of existence, fatigued, possibly injured, without food and water, they could very well have been overwhelmed by the island's native non-human inhabitants.

Search efforts were extensive, but were directed to south of Howland Island. A week after the disappearance, naval search aircraft flew over Gardner Island, which at that point had been uninhabited for over 40 years. Report on Gardner Island stated: ". . .signs of recent habitation were easily visible but repeated flyovers failed to elicit any notice or answering waves from possible inhabitants. It was finally assumed that none were there… At one end of the island a tramp steamer lay high and almost dry head onto the coral beach. The lagoon at Gardner looked deep enough and certainly large enough that a seaplane or even an airboat could have landed in any direction with very little difficulty. It is believed that Earhart could have landed her aircraft in this lagoon and swum or waded ashore. It was also found that Gardner Island's shape and size was recorded on charts inaccurately. Some Naval search efforts were directed north, west and southwest of Howland Island, on a presumption that the Electra could have ditched in the ocean just offshore.

The official search efforts lasted until July 19, 1937.

Theories regarding Earhart's disappearance

Crash and sink theory:

Most researchers believe the Electra ran out of fuel and Earhart and Noonan ditched at sea. Many researchers agree that the flight was doomed in part due to sloppy planning and failed execution.

It is generally accepted that the Electra went into the sea about 10 am, July 2, 1937 not far from Howland Island. It has also been theorized that Earhart's Electra was not fully fueled at Lae, which is where they left on their last leg of the journey. It is also thought that Noonan may have miscalculated their approach to make it to Howland. If so, this error could very have been a fatal miscalculation.

The main gist of the crash and sink theory is that they went into the water just off Howland Island. Earhart's stepson George Palmer Putnam Jr. has been quoted as saying he believes "the plane just ran out of gas." Susan Butler, author of the Earhart biography *East to the Dawn,* says she thinks the aircraft went into the ocean out of sight of Howland Island and rests on the seafloor at a depth of 17,000 feet (5 km). Tom D. Crouch, Senior Curator of the National Air and Space Museum, has said the

Earhart/Noonan Electra is "18,000 ft. down" and may even yield a range of artifacts that could rival the finds of the *Titanic*.

Gardner Island Hypothesis:

Just after Earhart and Noonan's disappearance, the United States Navy expressed belief the flight had ended somewhere in the Phoenix Islands some 350 miles southeast of Howland Island.

The International Group for Historic Aircraft Recovery (TIGHAR) in their quest to investigate and solve the Earhart/Noonan disappearance has sent six expeditions to the island. They suggested Earhart and Noonan may have flown without radio transmissions for two and a half hours along the line of position Earhart noted in the last transmission received at Howland. They then arrived at then-uninhabited Gardner Island (now Nikumaroro) in the Phoenix group, landed on an extensive reef flat and ultimately perished. This theory is what I believe is closest to the truth, and is what I based **Over the Horizon** upon.

From the Wikipedia entry detailing the numerous Earhart theories:

TIGHAR's research has produced a range of documented archaeological and anecdotal evidence supporting this hypothesis. For example, in 1940, Gerald Gallagher, a British colonial officer and licensed pilot, radioed his superiors to inform them that he had found a "skeleton... possibly that of a woman", along with an old-fashioned sextant box, under a tree on the island's southeast corner. He was ordered to send the remains to Fiji, where in 1941, British colonial authorities took detailed measurements of the bones and concluded they were from a male about 5 ft 5 in tall. The measurement data by forensic anthropologists indicated the skeleton had belonged to a "tall white female of northern European ancestry." The bones themselves were misplaced in Fiji long ago and have not been found.

Artifacts discovered by TIGHAR on Nikumaroro have included improvised tools, an aluminum panel (possibly from an Electra), an oddly cut piece of clear Plexiglas the same thickness and curvature of an Electra window and a size 9 Cat's Paw heel dating from the 1930s which resembles Earhart's footwear in world flight photos. The evidence remains circumstantial, but Earhart's surviving stepson, George Putnam Jr., has expressed support for TIGHAR's research.

In 2007, a TIGHAR expedition visited Nikumaroro searching for unambiguously identifiable aircraft artifacts and DNA. The group included engineers, technical experts and others. They found artifacts of uncertain origin on the weather-ravaged atoll, including bronze bearings which may have belonged to Earhart's aircraft and a zipper pull which might have come from her flight suit. In 2010, the research group said it had found bones that appeared to be part of a human finger. Subsequent DNA testing at the University of Oklahoma proved inconclusive as to whether the bone fragments were from a human or from a sea turtle.

Myths, legends and unsupported claims

The unresolved circumstances of Earhart's disappearance, along with her fame, attracted a great body of other claims relating to her last flight, all of which have been generally dismissed for lack of verifiable evidence. Several unsupported theories have become well known in popular culture.

Spies for FDR

A World War II-era movie called *Flight for Freedom* (1943) starring Rosalind Russell and Fred MacMurray furthered a myth that Earhart was spying on the Japanese in the Pacific at the request of the Franklin Roosevelt administration. By 1949, both the United Press and U.S. Army Intelligence had concluded this rumor was groundless. Jackie Cochran, another pioneering aviator and one of Earhart's friends, made a postwar search of numerous files in Japan and was convinced the Japanese were not involved in Earhart's disappearance.

Saipan claims

In 1966, CBS Correspondent Fred Goerner published a book claiming Earhart and Noonan were captured and executed when their aircraft crashed on the island of Saipan, part of the Mariana Islands archipelago, while it was under Japanese occupation. In 2009, an Earhart relative stated that the pair died in Japanese custody, citing unnamed witnesses including Japanese troops and Saipan natives. He said that the Japanese cut the valuable Lockheed aircraft into scrap and threw the pieces into the ocean.

Thomas E. Devine (who served in a postal Army unit) wrote *Eyewitness: The Amelia Earhart Incident* which includes a letter from the daughter of a Japanese police official who claimed her father was responsible for Earhart's execution.

Former U.S. Marine Robert Wallack claimed he and other Marines opened a safe on Saipan and found Earhart's briefcase. Former U.S. Marine Earskin J. Nabers claimed that while serving as a wireless operator on Saipan in 1944, he decoded a message from naval officials which said Earhart's aircraft had been found at the airfield in the village of As Lito, that he was later ordered to guard the aircraft, and then witnessed its destruction. In 1990, the NBC-TV series *Unsolved Mysteries* broadcast an interview with a Saipanese woman who claimed to have witnessed Earhart and Noonan's execution by Japanese soldiers. No independent confirmation or support has ever emerged for any of these claims. Purported photographs of Earhart during her captivity have been identified as either fraudulent or having been taken before her final flight.

Since the end of World War II, a location on Tinian, which is five miles (eight km) southwest of Saipan, had been rumored to be the grave of the two aviators. In 2004, a scientifically supported archaeological dig at the site failed to turn up any bones.

Tokyo Rose rumor

A rumor which claimed that Earhart had made propaganda radio broadcasts as one of the many women compelled to serve as Tokyo

Rose was investigated closely by George Putnam. According to several biographies of Earhart, Putnam investigated this rumor personally but after listening to many recordings of numerous Tokyo Roses, he did not recognize her voice among them.

The mystery is part of what keeps us history buff's world-wide interested. We see in her a heroine, an adventurer and free-spirit . . . who is mostly remembered as the world's favorite missing person.

The fact is; we will probably never really know just how their flight ended.

– Doyle Sinclair

ABOUT THE AUTHOR

Doyle Sinclair lives in Dallas TX. and works in sales when he's not writing at his favorite coffee shop. He currently has 6 more novels planned and draws his inspiration from his overactive imagination, and the people, places and events around him. He enjoys photography, music, psychology, philosophy and history.

Please visit Amazon.com to see his titles.

FROM THE AUTHOR

Thank You

I would like to thank you for investing your money in this book and for taking the time to read it. Taking a chance on a new author is a risk that is not always rewarded, especially when there are so many good books out there waiting to be read.

Speaking on behalf of independent authors, I would ask that you help increase our chances of finding success. Trying to break through as an author takes a lot of hard work, and most authors find very limited success.

If you feel that this story has been well-written, is entertaining, and worth the price of the book, please tell your friends about it. Mention it on Facebook, or find other ways to spread the word about it. Independent authors have miniscule advertising budgets and most only sell handfuls of books that may have taken that author years to write. We write out of love for the craft, for the chance to tell an interesting, entertaining story, and we welcome any and all feedback. Each and every sale is exciting for us, and we truly appreciate it.

I would also urge you to ***go online to Amazon, whether you purchased the book there or not, and add an Amazon review.*** The ratings help, the feedback is appreciated, and I will do my best to reply to each and every review, whether that review be negative or positive. Furthermore, anyone wishing to contact me to comment on, discuss or critique this story, or my writing in particular, may reach me at dwstxs1969@yahoo.com

Doyle Sinclair – Dec. 2012

Bonus Chapter: The following excerpt is a bonus for readers of Over the Horizon, the first chapter of **RED DOOR** by Doyle Sinclair.

Red Door

By – Doyle W. Sinclair

"I see a red door and I want to paint it black."

The Rolling Stones – Paint it Black

". . . thinking of a series of dreams,
Where the time and the tempo fly,
And there's no exit in any direction,
cept the one that you can't see with your eyes . . . "

Series of Dreams – Bob Dylan

"The final mystery is oneself"

– Oscar Wilde

"All we are is dust in the wind . . ."

Kansas

Chapter ONE

THE INCIDENT IN THE STREET

July 7, 1963 Dallas, TX.

Husker Virdden jerked upright at the steering wheel, as the cat darted across the street in front of him. The sudden movement caused him to sideswipe a parked Ford in a screeching crash of metal. The car ground to a halt. He didn't know what street this was; just that it was a residential area he'd never driven through at this time of day. Further up the street two kids were in their front yard, playing a game of catch. They looked up owl-eyed at the sound of the crash and then went back to tossing the ball back and forth. Husker leaned back and took a breath. His eyes swam. He knew to get a move on before the owner of the car came out to see what the noise was about. He looked down at his watch. Normally, at ten on Sunday mornings he would be at church with Tabitha.

His head still woozy from the liquor, Husker turned the wheel back towards the middle of the street and stepped on the gas. Metal screeched as the cars separated. The sooner he got home and slept himself sober, the better.

He drove fast and tried to keep the car centered in the middle of the street. He didn't want trouble with the owner of the car he'd sideswiped. The car lurched in fits and starts as Husker struggled to keep it in the center of the street, and tried to keep from passing out from the booze and exhaustion. Towards the end of the block, something in the street caused him to step down hard on the brakes, but nothing happened as the brake pedal went all the way to the floor, and a sickening thump-thump-thump of something passing underneath the car caused Husker to sit up straight. He'd felt whatever it was on the soles of his shoes on the floorboard as it had rumbled underneath the car. He stomped on the brake, and the brakes took hold and the car skidded to a stop in some loose gravel at the end of the street. The car rocked twice on its springs and settled. Husker shifted into park and, with the engine idling, he took a deep breath, and turned to look out the back window.

He saw a boy standing over something in the street. Husker wondered if he'd run over the someone's pet cat. There had been a cat. He stared at the boy, and the object in the street. It slowly dawned on Husker that there had been two boys in the yard.

Husker gasped at the thought, and tried to re-focus his eyes sharper. Now he made out a sneaker, blue jeans and a twisted arm, a leg askew, and the head. There was a dark red stain on the pavement between the boy's body the middle of the street. The sun slid behind a cloud and a shadow covered the scene.

The second boy stood over the lifeless body, and Husker could hear him crying.

"No! Oh my God!" Husker heard the anguished scream of a man running out from the house towards the child.

Husker turned around, too scared to watch. His heart pounded in his chest. His stomach heaved and he vomited onto his lap. He glanced up to the rear view mirror just in time to see the man bend down and scoop the child up into his arms.

"David!" He cried as he picked up the boy and held him to his chest and ran to the house. As he ran, he glanced back towards Husker, and yelled out, "You! Stop! Get back here!"

The other child stood in the street, one hand out, pointed towards Husker.

Husker sat for a moment, hands shaking, heart racing, not wanting to accept what he'd just done. He caught his reflection in the rear view mirror. The reflected image showed a man with blood-shot eyes, vomit on his chin, tears streaming down his face, a look of shock on his face. His mind reeled from the booze. This was an accident, wasn't it?

He should go back. He just killed a little boy. What should he do? His mind scrambled for an explanation. The cat! A cat had run out. It was the cat's fault! Husker knew better, no one would believe him, especially if they smelled the soured whiskey and vomit all over him.

Lip trembling, Husker realized he was a murderer. He'd killed a child. He realized that his life was over, just as surely as the child's was.

There must be a way though, to get past this. What should he do? What was the right thing to do?

Husker didn't want to spend the rest of his life behind bars. Everyone who knew him would look at him with disgust. Look at him; Husker, the child-killer! He simply couldn't go through life as a murderer. It wasn't fair, and it wasn't right. He and Tabitha had so many plans for the future. Nothing would bring back the little boy. Why should his life be ruined? Heart racing, he made a decision.

Looking left and right before pulling out, he drove away and prayed that no one had seen him.

July 7, 2005 - Dallas, TX

David sipped his coffee and gazed out the window of the coffee shop, where he could see his reflection in the plate glass window in front of him. He was on a two-week vacation and was relaxing, catching up on some reading. He had just picked up a book someone had left behind, and on opening it, saw that someone had written on the flyleaf page - *He who controls the past commands the future. He who commands the future conquers the past.* – the quote was circled in yellow highlighter.

David closed the book and gazed out at the street.

The Binge Lime Café was located at an upscale storefront area of small shops on Dallas' upper north side. Slightly larger in size than the average Starbucks, it drew a young hip clientele. There were tables set up on the sidewalk out front, and the cobblestoned street was a replica of a street in Paris. David never sat outside. The sweltering Dallas summer heat easily melted away any imaginings one was sitting in Paris.

The northern edge of Dallas area was filled with strip malls, apartments, and business warehouses. The west end of the street was bricked and narrow for the short section that housed the Binge Lime Café. The street was known as restaurant row because of the many pastry shops, coffee shops, juice bars, and specialty shops. The Binge Lime Café sat on a corner, its front and east sides were plate glass windows that looked out onto the street. Across a short driveway, separating the Binge Lime Café from the rest of the strip mall was a tanning salon.

A customer opened the door and a gray tabby cat walked in as if he owned the place. David watched, but no one bothered to shoo it out. The cat sat on its haunches in front of David, and focused on him. David thought it strange it had one blue eye and one green eye, but maybe it was just a trick of the light. It gazed at him as if it expected him to do something. David was about to give it a scratch behind the ear, but before he could, the cat reached forward with its paw and placed it on David's knee, and then gently withdrew.

David felt a tickle in the pit of his stomach. The cat continued to stare at him. A bell tinkled and it scampered away. After he glanced up, David jumped to his feet, almost knocking the table over.

He walked towards the door, keeping his eyes locked upon the man crossing the street. It just wasn't possible. He squinted and focused again. The lined face was full of character and world-weariness, and he had a peculiar gait. He'd once described it in his own self-effacing way as, 'a hitch in his get-along'. There was no doubt it was him.

The conversations of the customers, the clinking of coffee cups behind the counter, the rich smell of the roasting coffee, and the hiss of the latte machine all blended together, becoming a muted fog. David stood, his hand on the door handle, watching as the man bent down to pick up something.

The man held the object up to examine it, and David could see that it was a string of prayer beads.

He watched as the man dropped the beads into his pocket.

David stepped out of the Binge Lime and hurried across the street, hoping to get across before the man disappeared. He noticed a long line of black cars parked along the curb.

He made it to the sidewalk as the man reached to open the door leading into one of the storefront shops. The door was red, with a black number seven painted on it.

"Dad?" David said.

The man turned to face him and smiled.

"Hey David!"

David's heart skipped a beat. He was stunned. There was no doubt it was his father, a man who'd died of lung cancer sixteen years earlier.

●●●

An Amazon.com reader's 4 star review of: **BLUE-EYED SON** by **Doyle Sinclair.** Available now, on Amazon.com in both print and Kindle versions.

Blue-Eyed Son by Doyle W. Sinclair

4 stars review - **Not One Catchy Melody, But Many** - review by Walt Eddy author of *Making Expression Less Taxing, a Freelancer's Tax Handbook*

If you didn't experience Woodstock, the bohemian lifestyle, the nomadic make-peace-not-war routine, the openness, the protests of '60s and '70s like me--I was a Mormon missionary in Munich--but want some sense of the experience and culture, you've got to read this novel. It'll clue you in; big time. And if you did experience some or all of the '60s and '70s Zeitgeist, this novel will resurrect some of it for you. Not only that, but it has a mythic structure characteristic of all great storytellers. Now, take your thesaurus and look up synonyms for "favorite". You'll find "blue-eyed". Now look up "paradox." You should--but won't--find Doyle Sinclair's novel, BLUE-EYED SON listed. But, believe me, the novel is, in the best sense of the push-me-pull-you word, a paradox.

In the dog days of 1969, a self-absorbed, too-smart-for-his-own-good 17-year-old testosterone-driven blue-eyed son, David St. John, gets busted for smoking pot. Not by cops in the school parking lot but by his parents in his bedroom at home. His father takes a belt to him, while mother dear urges Papa on--"Don't you stop . . . He needs a damn good thrashing!"--and promises to trash David's hippie toys: posters, record players, vinyl albums, clothes. It's clear to them that David has immersed himself in decadence. No more allowance. They tell him he is grounded and can't do anything.

"Aufwiedersehen, Texas, David says. "Guten Tag, hippiedom." He decides to Peter Pan it. Well, not literally, but you get the drift. David begins his nomadic adventure that takes him through the '70s with a band of fellow hippies to travel with, a psychedelic bus to tour in: foul-mouthed, chain-smoking pot and cigarettes, shooting-up exotic drugs, open and free sex, defiance, endless booze, petty to major crimes, and then: eluding the Man. For years on end. Stuck. And aside from the free-love, genuine love interests: Maggie and Munchie the cat. Oh, and did I mention the creepiest of antagonists, named Aaron? Well, him too. It makes me squirm just thinking of him. Then, finally, in New Orleans in 1980, "For the first time in years, David felt comfortable enough to relax and stop worrying about running from the law." And then it takes at least twenty more years to have a breakthrough in recovery. And all of this is set to the music of the times. How? Well, Sinclair has sprinkled lyrics from hit rock and roll songs of the era throughout the narrative to hype the setting and enhance his characterizations. The tactic brought for me the melodies of yesteryear to life, almost as if a needle was coursing its way through the vinyl grooves of a record on a turntable.

Don't get me wrong. Reading Blue-Eyed Son wasn't perfect for me. But it was like finding an old 1969 Camaro convertible in grandpa's garage after he's died and learning he's left the old classic to me. It's a treasure, but it needs some work. It had a few implausibility and deus ex machine dents. There were some repetitions that seemed like scratches in the paint that needed to be buffed out and repainted. And it could use a tune-up by at least a copy editor.

Overall, though, the basic story is iconic, like Woodstock itself. David chooses to leave a comfortable home and ordinary surroundings to venture into a tough, new, transformative world. And believe me it has consequences more dire than the wicked witch or the big bad wolf. It is both an outward journey and an inward journey for David. He grows and changes. Weaknesses slowly become strengths--and at times it seemed excruciating. His despair gives way to hope. Foolishness yields to wisdom.

Love moves to revulsion but returns again. It hooked me and made the story worthwhile reading. It is not a book for the faint of heart or those too put off by strong language and alternative lifestyles. I can't convey the harshness of consequences on the blue-eyed son, but even more than that, on his one true love: Maggie. It is their saga. It is their song. You should listen to it. It's not just one catchy melody, but any.

A Barcentor Books Publication

www.ingramcontent.com/pod-product-compliance
Lightning Source LLC
LaVergne TN
LVHW020534100826
845148LV00010B/1458
9780615752082